BACK FROM THE FUTURE

Herrilmin's time machine was suddenly visible again, hovering above Midpassage for the few seconds it took to dump a glittering metal box from its bottom.

Instinctively, from her watching place in the sky, Kylene guessed what he had done. Tim Harper had described weapons that tore cities to shreds in a single ball of flame, and Fesch had joked before he died that Herrilmin had some of them. It was all too conceivable that the Agent had chosen to destroy Midpassage to get to his enemy, Harper.

But could she stop him?

Yes. She had a time machine. She made herself be calm.

By Mike Shupp
Published by Ballantine Books:

THE DESTINY MAKERS
Book One: *With Fate Conspire*
Book Two: *Morning of Creation*
Book Three: *Soldier of Another Fortune*
Book Four: *Death's Gray Land*
Book Five: *The Last Reckoning*

MIKE SHUPP

THE LAST RECKONING

Book Five of
THE DESTINY MAKERS

A Del Rey Book

BALLANTINE BOOKS ● NEW YORK

For
Roger and Karen Parks
. . . friends in deed

The First Compact

To end eternal war, it is agreed by the telepaths and normal men that never again shall telepaths establish a separate state and exercise their dominion over men.

This Compact shall be preserved by the thoughts and actions of both human races and witnessed by the tiMantha lu Duois.

The penalty for violation, in thought or action, shall be death.
—circa Anno Domini 30,000
(Long Count correspondence unestablished)

The Second Compact

To end the Second Eternal War, the Great Compact is reaffirmed by the Teeps and the Normals. It is also agreed by the Teeps and the Normals that never again shall Teeps employ their abilities in the service of national states and thus exercise their dominion over men.

This Compact shall be preserved by the thoughts and actions of both human races and witnessed by the spirit of the tiMantha lu Duois.

The penalty for violation, in thought or action, shall be death.
—41,000 to 43,000 on the Long Count
(chronologies vary)

Hemmendur's Solution

"We have observed that neither Compact prohibits the employment of the Teeps, in whole or in part, in any role whatsoever, by a single all-encompassing world state. I suggest to you that such a state must ultimately arise. By its nature, it will be everlasting and unopposable.

"I suggest as well that given that inevitability, we attempt ourselves to give birth to that state and shape its growth. If our intentions are worthy, our actions honorable, and our ambitions steadfast, we shall be successful, for we shall gain strong allies.

"Not the least of these will be the Teeps, who are entitled to a role in human affairs, and for whom I propose a most sacred responsibility—which is to ensure that men exercise no dominion over men . . ."

—Jablin Cherrid Hemmendur
47,350 L.C.–47,727 L.C.
(Algheran City Years 313–690)

Part One: Sums Due

CHAPTER ONE

*T*im Harper's fingers wadded up the torn pieces of paper into tiny balls, then made fists to hide them from the world, but that did not change the message they had borne.

The sounds men made as they died did not change, either, no matter how tightly he squeezed his eyes against the sight.

Soon the Algherans would launch another attack.

"I'm not a general," he said dully.

A musket snapped behind him. The sound was the gruff cough of Lopritian powder rather than the sharper bark of the faster burning and more powerful Algheran variety. Harper, a very tall and burly man, with auburn hair that made him a distinctive target and the scar of an old gunshot wound already high on his temple, did not duck for cover.

But I should have. Our own shitty gunpowder was enough to kill Cherrid ris Clendannan, even if it took a barrel of it.

Christ, Cherrid! Couldn't you be careful!

"What shall I tell the Hand?" the messenger asked, looking at him stolidly, and Harper, reading the gaze as accusation, wished that he could flee but felt too weary.

Another gun went off on the parapet atop a nearby ridge, and the messenger's horse shied, then pounded the ground with its front hooves. One of the small cannons, Harper judged. He could only hope it had been aimed at a worthy target and would be reloaded when the Algherans made their next charge.

"Tell the Hand of the Queen—" He stopped.

Tell the Hand of the Queen that without Cherrid ris Clendannan in charge the situation is hopeless. Tell him we've run as far as we can run and we've fought bravely but it wasn't enough. Tell him we're outnumbered three to one and Mlart tra'Nornst will crush us with his next assault and that he ought to because Loprit never should have fallen into this war.

He was sure the Hand knew all that.

Tell the Hand of the Lopritian Queen I am an American citizen and not his subject and that I am a sergeant in the United States Army and that this is not my conflict.

Tell the Hand of the Queen that I was defeated in Vietnam and in ninety thousand years I have never been on the winning side in any war I have known. Tell the Hand that I am a time traveler and a spy and that I do not love his land. Tell him my true loyalties lie with the Algheran Realm and that I fight for Loprit to serve causes he will never understand.

Tell him I've killed too many of his men already and I don't know how to be a general.

"Tell the Hand—" He stopped again and swallowed as the messenger stared at him.

A million million worlds and more, all seeming just the same, but just a little bit different even if by no more than the placement of a grain of dirt and on every one of them, I stand here being offered this commission. And whether I accept it or reject it, each choice will give rise to a million million different outcomes, a million million different histories.

Even my own feeling of free will is an illusion.

Probability rules history.

"I shall probably lose," he said quietly.

"He knows. But the alternative is surrender, Ironwearer."

And that would also be a defeat, Harper knew. The brigade's surrender would leave the south of Loprit undefended, and its capital vulnerable to attack. F'a Loprit would be besieged and it would fall.

And in four centuries, if he did not prevent that Algheran victory, there would come plagues to kill half the world; in six, nuclear war to kill civilization. And then endless millenia must pass before men recovered the skill and ambition to build cities.

That fate, too, awaited a million million worlds.

He kicked at the ground with his toe, sending dirt flying.

"Then tell the Hand of the Queen I shall do my duty."

"Yes, Ironwearer. Thank you, Ironwearer."

The messenger saluted and Harper tried to keep from swallowing again, because there was only dust in his mouth to swallow.

"Tell the artillery commander and his chiefs I'll want to talk to them. On the road, in a few minutes. And Gertynne ris Vandeign should be there."

"Yes, sir." The messenger remounted and rode off, his hand uselessly batting at drifting smoke.

Five years preparing to stop Mlart. I can't complain now because I was given the opportunity.

Harper turned and trudged on wooden legs through soldiers, going up the steep ridge to find Dalsyn lan Plenytk.

When the boy came back from across the river, Ryger ris Ellich was burying the innkeeper by the front stoop of his inn. Awkwardly burying, for with only one hand, the Lopritian cavalryman was hard put to thrust a shovel into the stony ground.

"Give a hand here, farmboy," he called out and Rallt obediently trotted through the apple orchard, past the lumberyard, to the edge of the walkway that led down to the river wharf and the mound of dirt beside the shallow hole. He took the shovel from the nobleman's hand.

The bandage wrapped around the young Lopritian's stump was stained with dirt, blood, and yellowish fluid, he noticed, and there was sweat on the man's forehead, despite the coolness of the evening air.

"You don't mind," ris Ellich said.

"No, Lord." He knew a falsehood was expected.

Mercifully, there was little to smell. Most of the blanket-wrapped parcels at the bottom of the pit were lightly covered with soil already, and the others did not reveal their content.

"I thought Sugally—" the boy started to say, and ris Ellich stopped him with a gesture.

"In cleaning the floor," he said. "He did the digging."

Rallt was quiet. He would have preferred to let the ugly little slave fill the grave as well, but from ris Ellich's expression that would not happen.

It was only work, after all. Dirty work—he pulled his shirt over his head and set it aside to stay clean.

"I couldn't stand looking at the stain any more," ris Ellich said, "and if we're going to have company—"

Which was a question.

"I found a lady patron, she say yes, she be coming," Rallt told him. "Not young, Lord. Married. Husband be in the army."

In Innings, Lopritian nobles were not famed for chastity.

Ris Ellich waited without comment, and the boy hurried on: "She be here shortly, say she. Mayhap she had a pig to feed I wasn't to know of. Heard one snorting, sound from the shed be on back her house. Not full grown yet."

Ris Ellich smiled wanly and rested himself on the railing at the side of the porch. "I shouldn't be polite and ask about it? My daddy'd tan my hind end if word came back I didn't talk livestock to the folks in our villages."

"Think not, Lord." Rallt paused with a full shovel over the grave site and let dirt fall into the pit while he considered the propriety of an answer. "Army took livestock off most people when it left town. Farmers here, now they got little enough left to eat or breed, be in hard place by spring."

His father would have said none of that, he knew. His father would not have spoken up to a nobleman without apology.

But his father had never shared a nobleman's table at meal time, nor helped an injured nobleman to a lavatory seat. Rallt had done both in these last few days.

Ris Ellich did not take offense. "Trust you to know such things, farmboy," he said. Though he continued to face toward Rallt, his eyes were closed.

"Rallt, Lord Ellich. Not be farmboy." There had been no land in his family for three generations.

"Rallt." It was said in the Lopritian style, without the trill that properly belonged to his name, but it was an apology, as completely as a man who had probably had whole fields for his childhood play could apologize to one as poor as he.

And that was another experience his father had never known.

The boy concentrated on moving dirt from the pile into the pit, until there was enough sweat on his forehead to justify wiping at it. It was excuse for regaining his full breath and resting his hands—other years at this time, late in what should be harvest season, field work had built up callouses on his palms and lower fingers, but because of the Lopriters' war, his only labor this season had been driving ambulances. Until now.

Inside the inn, Sugally had turned on the lights, and their bright glow spilled out the windows and open door onto the road just as it must have during peacetime. But now the inn was empty of travelers and conversations, and for all the invitation of the lights, they hissed like angry snakes. As he rested, Rallt moved his shoulders uncertainly.

"Gets at you, doesn't it?" asked the nobleman. "Worst of it's having to bury him without knowing his name. We can't defend these people, it adds another hurt on us."

He was thankful he could respond to that. "Sassen Rhokyll, Lord Ellich. I asked the patrons, they said he were Sassen Rhokyll. Mayhap he had family down to Barlaynnt's Tower, they thought but didn't be sure."

"The Tower lands, huh? Probably some kind of family plot, if he was like most southerners. Too many Algherans in the way right now—" Ris Ellich smiled faintly.

"After the war, we'll see to it that Sassen Rhokyll gets to his proper resting place."

Rallt turned away too slowly to hide his expression.

"We'll move his bones, boy. That's all that will be left by springtime and people don't expect to find bones stuck together. They'll know he was murdered, can't hide that, but there's not going to be any other tale to fret his kin."

Rallt worried his lower lip, thinking about that. A man killed by strangers, then bled and cut to pieces like a carcass going into a smokehouse . . .

"Most likely, it'll be around," he said finally. It was the sort of story people told around campfires during the winter period when no one had work and the nights were too long to fill with sleep. It was such a story as could be retold for centuries, even without the embellishments tradition would add.

"Who's to tell of it?" ris Ellich asked and swung a leg to one side to spit between his feet. Then he straightened up.

"Me, you, Sugally, your pa and his partner, the last officer—only half a dozen of us know what happened here, and the Teeps, and they'll not peddle a profitless tale to a market which won't repay them for it."

"There be still the killer," Rallt pointed out. He looked gloomily at the grave, reckoning how much of it was left to be filled, then picked up the shovel again. The evening air was stiffening his muscles and he wished to complete the work before it became too dark to tell apart rock and soil.

"I think we'll find the killers," the cavalryman said. "And I think we'll find them in Midpassage. Maybe the Teeps don't know just where, but . . . I've seen Teeps make mistakes. They're not that different from us normal people."

Rallt grunted. Conversation wasn't filling the pit.

It was already dark inside Tim Harper's quiescent time machine, for the small girl huddled in the pilot's seat was too frightened to turn on the interior lights.

She had been in the same position for hours, it seemed. Hours for her since she ran to the giant levcraft and hid herself behind its walls, days for the world beyond as the machine hovered over the deserted hillside behind Harper's house.

The levcraft waited for her commands. She had steel walls for strength, impregnable locks for privacy, the weapons of three Eras for defense, and she could not move.

"Get to the time machine. Wait for me. Don't let anyone else in," Kylene—the other Kylene, so angry and decisive, who had appeared so suddenly—had said, and she had obeyed, running to the study as men came to the door of the house, then slipping out the window and hiding as she was told. But after that, the other Kylene had never come.

The men had come instead, without the other Kylene, seeking her and a way into the levcraft. Algheran time travelers, like Tim Harper, but their words had shown them to be his enemies instead of friends. Her enemies.

She had heard them pounding on the sides of the levcraft, felt the vehicle rock as they tried to break the locks that barred them from entry. They were outside the levcraft, trying to break into it, determined to find her, to—

—to do to her what they had done to the other Kylene.

The metal walls kept her from seeing into their minds but devices in the levcraft let her hear their boasts and curses. She knew their manners. She knew their names.

Herrilmin, Gherst, Fesch, Lerlt.

They bullied each other, yet posed as friends. What had they done to the other Kylene?

Sensors in the walls of the levcraft reacted suddenly. Figures had appeared on the hillside. Outside the field cast by the time machine, they were blurred by the haste of their movements, but instruments brought their voices into high-pitched intelligibility.

"—gone completely insane. When Timt ha'Dicovys finds—"

"—won't find out. Have to kill . . . Herrilmin let him because . . . Say to Vrect . . . Lerlt on a mission again." The second voice faded in and out of audibility, as if the speaker was afraid to voice its thoughts.

"Just toss . . . Dead . . . Cimon-taken heavy." The first voice.

"Not yet." The second voice, and then there were only grunts from men breathing with too much difficulty to speak.

They stopped under the bow of the vehicle, where she could not see them. The first man said something she could not distinguish, but it sounded like a complaint.

"Cover it up," the second man said, followed by some remark about the spring, and she heard scuffling noises, which might have been feet, which covered their voices for a time.

Then one of the men left. The other stayed.

Nervously, she touched a control which turned one of the camera lenses, and shifted it minutely, afraid the man beneath the vehicle would notice the camera's movement or her own.

But he saw nothing. He was on his knees, leaning forward and sweeping up double handfuls of fallen leaves. He picked the leaves up and threw them down quickly, covering something before him as if he wished to hide from himself what he was doing.

Then he paused for breath and Kylene saw what he was trying to conceal.

"No!" she screamed.

The leaves were to cover another person. A female, nude, young, unmoving, with limbs stained by still flowing blood, with a head twisted at an unnatural angle. A corpse.

"No! No! Never!"

The other Kylene's corpse.

CHAPTER TWO

"**D**alsyn, there's been some trouble, you'll have to take the regiment for a while. One day or two, I expect. Cherrid's not feeling well."

"Sure."

Dalsyn lan Plenytk's hand was reassuringly solid, and as they clasped forearms, Harper was able to pick his words deliberately. "Tell the men things will be normal before long."

Dalsyn's jaw moved silently, even while an eyebrow registered disbelief. "Sure. Are we to stay in this spot?"

"Unlikely." Harper was not willing to be definite. "Do you know how to move the regiment out of here during a firefight?"

"I could start running. I think the men would follow me."

"No jokes, Dalsyn! Do it this way: Keep your battalion firing while Pitar's men evacuate the hill. They settle on your right and start firing, and you pull your men out and send them to Pitar's right. Then he moves again, to your right. Sidle along like that till you reach the road. If there's no fighting, do the same thing but without shooting and keep as quiet as possible. Do I need to repeat anything?"

"Have you ever seen that done? Successfully?" Dalsyn raised an eyebrow again.

"Unfortunately, I have, at too close a range. Most of my unit survived."

Harper paused, sorry he had made that unnecessary remark. "Don't move until you get an order. You'll have enough time to explain what I want to Pitar, and then make it clear to every one of your men. I don't want slipups!"

"Ris Daimgewln?"

"Don't mind him. He won't be in your way."

"Are we going to march at night?" Lan Plenytk snapped his fingers. "Just in case the men wonder."

"If we pull out tonight, we'll march." Harper shrugged. "We'll have a quarter moon."

"Do we have a real chance of stopping Mlart eventually?" Dalsyn might have been asking about the weather.

A million million worlds.

The redhead hesitated. "Nothing's certain."

Dalsyn spat to the side. "I've heard that."

"Well. We've got about as good a chance of stopping Mlart as we had with Cherrid. I'm nowhere close to being as good at strategy as he is, but I've had some experiences he hasn't."

Endurance matters as much as strategy.

Mlart and Cherrid, by accident, it seemed to Harper, had recreated a Napoleonic battle. Neither had shown any awareness of twentieth-century tactics.

You don't know what Bad is, Dalsyn.

Harper's thoughts were focusing on Passchendale.

"All right." The surveyor put his hand out, to shake a wrist-to-wrist goodbye. "I'll send Quillyn off to you. You take care of yourself, Timmial."

Harper tried to smile. "Take care of my men, Dalsyn, and they'll take care of us both."

"Lord Daimgewln?" Despite a handful of fires, it was already too dark to make out faces.

"Ironwearer?" That came with a salute more meticulous than courtesy to another regimental commander demanded. Evidently the message of his promotion had gotten through. Harper had feared that the elderly noble would resent being subordinated to a commoner, but ris Damgewln was reacting with courtesy.

He returned the salute and stepped forward to the edge of ris Daimgewln's position. Lost and then retaken, this narrow waist of the ridge had changed appearance considerably since he had last seen it. It was no longer smooth. Shell holes had turned the ground into a lunar landscape.

At the crest of the ridge, captured muskets had been jammed into the ground to provide posts. Stacked against them was a fence formed of bodies. Nearby, someone moaned. Even nearer, unconcerned soldiers were eating their evening rations.

Harper controlled his reactions. "It's very likely we'll evacuate this position tonight, Lord Daimgewln. We've been lucky twice, but I'm not eager to argue points of possession with Mlart tra'Nornst any longer."

The nobleman exhaled loudly but added nothing to the sound.

The Ironwearer continued. "Tell your men they've done well. Now, when you're notified, I want your leftmost battalion pulled out and sent to the road. They should be ready to march some tonight. After they are clear, pull out the middle battalion, and send it, and then your right side battalion. I don't want a rush and I don't want noise and I don't want congestion, so I'm relying on your judgment. Is that all clear?"

"Yes. Yes, sir." If there was hesitation in that answer, it was almost too slight to detect.

"How far could your men march tonight?"

"How far do you want them to march, Ironwearer?"

Harper was sure he was asking too much, but he had to give his best answer. "West Bend, if they can. There's no good stopping point between here and there, you see."

"Then it will have to be West Bend."

"Yes."

"We can make it to West Bend, lan Haarper."

The nobleman saluted again, then indicated the battlefield with a hand. "The men have had a bad day, Ironwearer, and frankly so have I. We're all willing to do what we're asked if someone will do the thinking for us."

"I see." Harper swallowed, hearing that soft moan again.

A fire flared up and he saw that in the midst of the wall of bodies, an arm hung down, brushing the blood-soaked ground. Rhythmically, slowly, the hand's fingers clinched and relaxed.

* * *

The artillerymen had also had a bad day, Harper discovered. Unlike ris Daimgewln, they seemed inclined to take it out on their new commander.

He had made the mistake of asking for numbers.

In the deepening darkness, his eyes fixed on torches moving across the plain. His ears heard voices and weakening cries.

"I apologize," he said at last. "You tell me you've got twelve man-weights of powder in your primary cache and twenty man-weights in secondary and fifteen in reserve, but part of reserve is secondary and—"

He was conscious of Gertynne behind his back. And beyond Gertynne, other men. Not gunners.

Aides. His now. Cherrid's staff, and maybe other men who had somehow attached themselves to him, more from curiosity he still felt than from any other motive.

The big Ironwearer shook his head sadly. "Gentlemen, can we fight a battle tomorrow? That's what I really want to know."

"No," one of them said at last.

Lan Halkmayne, he recognized. The Steadfast-to-Victory Regiment's chief gunner, and his subordinate when he commanded the militia. He could trust the answer from that source. But it was not the answer he wanted and he asked for an explanation. "In simple words, please."

Another gunner sighed. "We brought powder and shells sufficient for one major engagement and one small action. If we needed more, we were supposed to get it from the southern cities, and we didn't get through to them."

"No, we didn't," Harper agreed. "But the stuff we got from the Algherans—what about it?"

"They were also prepared for one major fight. This is—" the artilleryman clearly was groping for polite words. "—standard procedure, Ironwearer."

"Doctrine, what sins are committed in thy name!"

Gertynne guffawed.

"Ironwearer?"

"So we had supplies for one big fight," Harper said, already resigned to what he was about to be told. "I take it this was the big fight?"

"And your previous engagement was a small fight. Yes. We fired off our powder in our guns and the Algheran powder in their guns and it's all gone." The artilleryman snapped fingers on both hands. "You asked."

For a moment, the only sound was a gunner spitting.

"Where do we get more supplies?" Harper asked. "We're going to have to go north."

"Could be Northfaring, could be F'a Loprit," Ian Halkmayne volunteered. "Depends which one has them and which was asked, Timmial. And what the officials in those cities decide to do."

"Did we ask? When?"

"The old Ironwearer did that." The artillery commander re-entered the conversation. "Sent a man upcountry to ask for supplies, oh, four or five days ago. If he had Nicole's cloak over him, we might get something in . . . End of the tenday from Northfaring, more if he had to go to the capital. Haven't heard from him yet."

Someone in the background murmured agreement.

Three days to six to get supplies. Harper translated. This was not good news. What was the next question?

"Any way to speed that up?" Three to six days for ammunition to reach this location. But only one to three days for the same ammunition to reach Midpassage, he reminded himself.

Could he retreat as far as Midpassage?

"Tie a cannon ball on each passing duck, if we catch them migrating north," someone suggested, and someone else snickered.

Harper frowned. "Assuming we get stocks in time, will it be suitable for all the guns? Will the Algheran guns fire our shells, I mean? If they won't, I don't see holding on to them."

"They'd fire Algheran shells though, Timmial," Ian Halkmayne said. "You don't want to give them up."

Harper snorted. "I can tell you how to fix guns so they won't hold up to piss. Double shot, triple load of powder, and you bury the muzzle in the ground before you touch it off."

"Uough!" The gunner seemed sickened by the thought.

"Gun's a gun." The artillery commander scratched at his groin. "I think in a pinch . . . Jerrd, you remember that time two years ago we had to use staving?"

"I do. Guns won't take it forever," he was told. "We can get forty to fifty rounds through them, but it wrecks the barrels, and the aiming isn't any too wonderful from the start."

The commander turned back to Harper. "Well, Mr. Iron-wearer, what do you think? Forty to fifty rounds, thirty in the worst case. Course we wouldn't have those mighty big fireworks you were just talking about."

"Wouldn't want to make anyone unhappy, would we? I guess we take them all." The big man grimaced. "Which regiment's guns are furthest from the road? Okay, the other two move out now, but guns only, leave your powder and shells for Jerrd here. Make as little noise as possible. Stop when you get to Midpassage and deploy for a fight. Any questions?"

There were none.

"Start now, gentlemen. Gertynne, I don't know what's really required, but I trust you can write up the necessary orders and do whatever else you do. Tell Northfaring to send whatever supplies they can to Midpassage. Later tonight, you can explain proper staff procedures to me, okay?

"Aide, please? I want an update report on Cherrid's status."

Someone ran.

"Another aide? I want good estimates of Algheran casualties. Smallest possible, highest possible, most likely for killed and wounded. Talk to the company commanders—I can assure you, regimental officers had no idea of what was going on today.

"Someone else. We had some prisoners?"

"About a hundred, Ian Haarper." Gertynne.

"Thank you. Someone form up an adequate guard from wounded men who can still shoot. Let's get those prisoners out of here. March them up to West Bend and get them digging some trenches. Take some sergeant or corporal from the Steadfast-to-Victory along; he'll know what I want."

No movement. It sounded too much like work, he suspected. Well, he'd expected recalcitrance at some point.

"Don't trample yourself rushing, gentlemen. I want this done. I want to tell Cherrid good things about all of you. Show some initiative. No volunteers? Gertynne."

"Sir?" The executive officer moved closer.

"You know these men. Select the two best for the job."

Ris Vandeign, with an expression hidden to Harper, pointed. Men moved at last. The Ironwearer raised his eyes toward the torches on the plain.

"Are those looters or men bringing in casualties?"

"Some of both, I expect, sir."

So his new staff had one tactful liar. "I want that organized, gentlemen, and I want the looting stopped. If you can't find something useful to do in the next quarter watch, each of you go out with a squad of volunteers and bring back casualties to the surgeons. Bring the dead back too and stretch them out."

"The Algherans—" The inevitable objector.

"Bring back Algherans, too."

"I meant, sir—"

"I expect the Algherans are doing the same. Gentlemen, nothing but humanitarian efforts are apt to hold off another attack this evening. I hope you see that, and I am getting Cimon-taken tired of arguments. Is all that clear?"

Most of the throng dispersed.

Harper pointed. "You, give my compliments to Ironwearer Wolf-Twin, and I suggest that he attempt to collect all the Algheran weapons and ammunition he can find. His own people should be sufficient. Thank you.

"And you. Go check among the camp followers. I want you to find a woman named Wandisha lin Zolduhal. Blond, stocky, young. She's blind. Bring her back here yourself."

He turned again to Gertynne. "How's Merryn holding up?"

Something like duty required the question. Despite his affection for the older ris Vandeign, Harper was sorry that the man had come on the campaign. Merryn was not a soldier and not even pretending to be. *He should be off hiding in F'a Loprit, like his wife is.*

Oh, well. He was sorry his voice must sound so dull.

"He's all right," Gertynne said noncommittally. "The Hand has been very kind to him."

"Sure." Harper thought for a moment. "I've been thinking it would be nice to have a memorial service tomorrow or the day after. Someone needs to say that the men haven't died without purpose, that the Gods approve what they did. That kind of thing. Religious more than political. It might be good for *morale*. If Merryn could say a few words—ten or fifteen minutes would be about right—I'd appreciate it."

Gertynne did calculations of his own. "I'm sure he will."

"Good. And the Hand, after that, for about five minutes. If he would be so kind."

"I imagine ris Andervyll will want to say more."

Ris Andervyll had better things to do than make inane

speeches, Harper thought. He could walk around and let himself be seen. The men appreciated that he had not fled to the capital. They respected the taciturn Hand. "Merryn's a much better speaker," he said politely.

Two tactful liars.

"Ironwearer?" An aide had returned, awkwardly holding at arm's length a woman wearing a dingy skirt and a cloth jacket. "Is this the girl you want?"

His interview with the head surgeon was shorter.

There wasn't a thing that could be done for Ironwearer Cherrid ris Clendannan. He waved off the explanation.

"You'll be receiving additional patients, doctor. That's going to cost you your sleep, and I'm sorry. Feel free to grab any of the camp followers and put them to work—give us a count and we'll leave rations for them."

"Thank you." The surgeon was washing his hands in a bucket.

"Now the bad news. I don't want any more wounded men sent to the north unless they can recover and fight. Starting now."

A second passed while the surgeon stared at him.

"You can't be serious!"

"I certainly am, doctor. How many of your patients die on the trip north? About one in three?"

"I don't know, Ironwearer."

"I do. They can die here just as well, and I need the ambulances for other transportation."

The surgeon waved a hand. "How am I to move these men?"

"You can't. Don't try. You've been working on both Lopritians and Algherans, haven't you?"

"Basically." The surgeon bit his lip.

"Then I expect Mlart tra'Nornst will take care of both sides as well when he gets here. He's got a reputation for kindness—in Alghera."

"He's—the men may starve, Ian Haarper!"

Harper sighed. He was sure many of them would.

"That's my order, doctor. You're a lot closer here to the southern cities than you are to Northfaring or F'a Loprit. In my book, that makes them Mlart's responsibility. I'm sorry."

He wasn't.

* * *

A farmer's wife was not Lord Ellich's only guest for the day. That evening, when Rallt returned from escorting the woman home, he found a pair of horses hitched to a column in front of the inn. Inside, the thin officer and another soldier were busily *Ryger*ing and *Derry*ing each other at a corner table, acting like old friends, though Rallt noticed ris Ellich was pouring wine out of a much dirtier bottle for this visitor.

Rallt was almost into the kitchen, to see what supper Sugally was preparing, when the cavalryman called him.

"Sir?" Then, remembering the visitor, "My Lord?"

"Bring in the packages from the horse outside, will you, please, Rallt."

There were five packages, he discovered, in a sort of double sack one of the horses carried in place of a saddle. He brought the three long boxes in first, then the envelope and the heavy cubical box.

"I'll keep this." The visitor put the sealed envelope into a pocket inside his jacket. "Ris Mockstyn'd shoot me if I lost it."

"Got a—never mind." Ris Ellich used the table knife with which he had opened the wine to slice open the boxes. "A present for you, Rallt, unless you would rather go hunting with squirrels. Sugally!"

The box held a gun, a musket smaller than Rallt had noticed soldiers carrying. The barrel was polished metal, almost dark blue in color, the stock equally polished hardwood. It looked new. Was it a real present? Was he to express thanks for it?

The gun was broken open in the box, so he could see narrow grooves spiraling up the inside of the chamber. "This be cracked, Lord Ellich."

"Cracked?" The cavalry lifted up the gun and rested it over his stump so he could look into it comfortably. He made a disgusted sound and handed it right back. "That's rifling, you boob. You can buy people for less than what this gun cost the government. Sugally!"

Rallt couldn't imagine circumstances in which he bought either guns or people but ris Ellich didn't seem to expect an answer. He lowered his head apologetically and was just as pleased to have the nobleman's servant appear and save him from the trouble of responding.

"Master, you call Sugally."

"Uh-huh." Ris Ellich pushed another box forward. "You can shoot a gun decently, can't you, Sugally?"

The little man beamed at him. "Sugally shoot real good, not be here, still be in Necklace Lakes, Sugally still shooting Lopritians, you bet."

The visitor laughed and after a moment ris Ellich did the same, while Sugally continued to smile. Rallt looked down at his gun—and the twin in front of Sugally—and frowned nervously.

"Maybe you'll get a chance to shoot somebody yet." The tall man pointed his stump at the remaining box. "There should be ammo and patches in that. You want to load up the guns. Rallt—you pay attention. Rifle loading is a bit trickier than dropping nails into a musket."

"Yes, sir." It was pointless to admit he had never loaded a musket.

"Me find Lopritian, go practice bang bang plenty," Sugally said cheerfully.

Ris Ellich pointed to the kitchen. "Bang down supper first."

"Supper be fatally good, yes, master." Sugally tugged Rallt's sleeve. "You come kill potato, chop small pieces, right?"

Rallt left his gun willingly and went to kill potatoes.

"Well, I shall be off," the visitor said finally. "Any message of courage and cheer you'd like me to pass on to ris Clendannan?"

"Good Lord, no!" Ellich exclaimed. "If you value your career, Derry, you didn't visit me, you didn't see me, you never heard my name. If you know anything at all of me, it's a rumor that I have committed suicide—in some painful fashion—leaving behind a firm promise to never do it again."

"What have you done, Ryger? Seduced Lady Clendannan?"

"Much worse, I think. Not that there is a Lady Clendannan, by the way, hasn't been one for must be ninety years; why I know, she was a second cousin of my mother's half-brother. Beautiful, I'm told.

"Anyhow, I got some sort of aide of his—of ris Clendannan, I mean, not the half-brother—a bit dead in a cavalry action, the same one that took my hand, and it was made very clear to me that the wrong people had suffered the wrong injuries and I should reflect on my sins while I was convalescing."

"They going to take your commission?"

"No chance of that, it turns out. The fellow was a captain, after all, even if it was just in the Requisitionary Corps, and you can't really be blamed if someone who outranks you attaches himself to your unit and gets himself shot out of the saddle. But it's definitely a blot on the old escutcheon and a rude remark in my personnel record and unless hoof-and-mouth disease does dire things to senior cavalry officers in the next few decades, my prospects look pretty bleak. I may have to become a gunner or something to support Sugally and my mistresses and—"

"I don't think gunners have mistresses." The visitor frowned. "Something in gunpowder ruins them for that."

"You're not serious?"

"Ryger, you've known me for years. Would I invent such a story? Well, I must ride. Have fun with your new toys."

The visitor was gone before the cavalryman was willing to rise from the table. He walked into the kitchen, where Rallt was slicing vegetables to Sugally's specifications, and pointed at both men. "You two," he said solemnly. "Get lots of practice. I may want you to do all the shooting."

Buzzing. Creaking. And nearby, harsher rasping tones.

In darkness, he hovered above the sounds, among them, floating. Then swimming—he sensed he was laboring in some fashion.

Suddenly the buzzing became voices, near but low, almost whispers, almost familiar. The rasping sound was his own breath, the exertion a strain felt throughout his chest. He was lying on his back, swaying gently, and much too warm. His throat was sore and dry. He was thirsty.

He coughed feebly, almost silently. "Water!"

There was no sound.

His eyes refused to open. His arms did not move.

Panicking, he tried to free himself. His left foot—bare, he noticed in that instant—struck against wood, making a hollow, reverberating *thud*. His right leg was immobile.

The buzzing alien voices stopped.

That heightened other sounds: horses hooves, the footsteps of marching men, wagons creaking on squeaking axles.

"He's awake," someone—Wolf-Twin? Grahan?—said. It seemed almost a warning. Footsteps came toward him. Boots shuffling over boards, he sensed at once. *An ambulance.* Then he wondered for an instant how he could be sure of so much with his eyes closed.

"Cherrid?"

Timmial lan Haarper. He croaked softly, to show recognition.

"This is Harper. If you understand me, nod your head twice."

He had freedom for that. He nodded.

"You've been hurt. An explosion. Remember?"

Pain. Noise. Surprise.

No. He had no recollection. The words stirred up images, but they were not memories. His lips moved, trying to explain.

"Here." Hands touched him, lifting, then twisting, till he was half sitting up, half leaning away from whatever supported him and bending into space. An arm was wrapped about his chest, another draped over his back.

"You've got a bruised leg, some burns, a lump on your head, a concussion, and badly congested lungs. Does that mean anything to you?"

Timmial's arms, he deduced—hard-muscled and broad. He tried to speak again, without success.

"We're going to get you to a hospital. You're a lucky old goat, Cherrid, but a lamb could knock you off right now. Don't pull at that bandage; your eyes need some rest. Okay, I want you to cough. Not your wheeze, but like this: huh, huh, huh, *huh*!"

Little panting coughs. He obeyed, forcing air and phlegm upward till he seemed close to suffocation, then let a last paroxysm fill his mouth with salty liquid.

For an instant he was close to panic, but lan Haarper's words calmed him.

"Just some fluid. Spit it out, Cherrid. Get rid of it. It's not blood."

He coughed, then grimaced, wishing he could rinse his mouth out, but lan Haarper did not give him the opportunity to ask. "Do it again," the young man ordered. "Feel better?"

Surprisingly, he did, though the effort had tired him. His face felt damp, and he tried to move an arm to wipe at it.

"Lie back," lan Haarper said, replacing him on his litter. Now that he knew it was a litter, it felt like one to Cherrid, instead of the bed he had first thought it was.

"Here." Lan Haarper wedged padding behind him so he was

only half reclining. "Whenever you want to cough something up, go ahead and do it. There's a pan under you, but don't worry too much about where it falls; we can always clean it up. Cough up a *lot*, Cherrid. You're close to drowning from the stuff in your lungs. Are you thirsty?"

A funny request of a drowning man. He coughed a laugh.

"Here." Lan Haarper held a glass to his lips. "Drink a lot of water. It's good for you."

The water was flat and tepid. He guessed it had been boiled to suit lan Haarper's preferences, but his mouth wanted moisture. He sipped till he was content, then stopped, and waited till the young Ironwearer removed the glass.

"Where?" It was more breath than whisper, but Timmial understood.

"You're in an ambulance about a half day's march south of West Bend. It's night. The battle ended about two watches ago."

"The brigade?" That was only a hiss.

He felt himself sinking.

"We survived. I'm waiting on reports myself."

He was too weary to listen. The words were only muffled echoes, without meaning. But he wanted to say something. "Tell—Terrault—tell—him—"

What did he want to tell Terrault?

Tell Terrault I'm ready to—

He slept.

Harper pulled the blanket to the old man's neck. "Grahan? Wandisha?"

They slipped through the front curtain and took handholds. It should have left room, but to Harper the space in the ambulance seemed uncomfortably small. And smelly, with the reek of both new and ancient wounds.

"His mind is all right. He's sleeping again; he'll do that a lot during the next few days. Let him, it's good for him. The biggest problem is his lungs. He's got to cough up every bit that he can. Have him lean over the side of the bed twenty minutes every morning, that'll help. Lots of water, also—boil it like I showed you. And some fresh air now and then."

"How bad is he?" Grahan asked.

Wandisha stared intently at the sick man, and Harper wondered what the blind girl saw.

"He's nine tenths dead," he said bluntly. "And he's going to get a lot closer before he recovers, if he recovers."

Grahan inhaled noisily, like a boy holding in tears.

"Yeah." Harper used a knife to pry open seams on his belt, then twisted it to release a tiny handful of pills. "Give him one of these each watch, with a glass of water."

"What are they?" Grahan looked down as if the pills would explode in his palm.

"Those are the last oxy-tetracycline capsules in existence in the world, and that makes them more valuable than a wagonload of gold. It's medicine."

Grahan put them in his shirt's back pocket as delicately as if they were and Harper smiled grimly. "I don't know if there are enough of them, to be honest," he said, "or if they'll kill the right bugs, but if I have anything that gets Cherrid past a lung infection, it'll be those."

"Will it help his eyes?" Wandisha, with the question Harper could see Grahan wished to ask.

But it made sense that she asked it.

"Don't tell him about his eyes as long as you can put it off," Harper suggested. With an effort, he added, "Wandisha, you know if I had anything that worked on eyes, I would have tried it on you back in Midpassage."

"I didn't mean—" she started to say.

"I know." He sighed. "Probably you should tell him rather than Grahan. I trust you'll find the best time for it."

"There's—"

She stopped short and Harper pretended he had not heard. "I might as well go. Remember, he needs sleep, lots of bed rest, water, clean air, and one pill each watch. And he's to cough up that crap whenever he can. Have a good trip north, and I'll look for you after the war."

"Ironwearer?" Grahan stopped him halfway through the flap. "What is the condition of the brigade? He'll want to know."

"One thousand seven hundred seventy-one effective men and officers. Four hundred twelve walking wounded."

Harper nodded as Grahan shrank back.

"Eight hundred seventy-eight dead, captive, or disabled. About thirty percent. We got off very lightly, Grahan. When you get to F'a Loprit, tell Cherrid he did good."

"How's the old general?" a soldier called as he dropped from the wagon and began unhitching his horse.

"Pretty good," Harper called back when he stopped dancing. "He asked how you men were doing."

"Doing all right," someone else muttered.

Harper laughed and led his horse as he walked beside the men. "Don't say that; you'll make me out a liar. I was telling him you all had sore feet and were bitching at his replacement."

"We're doing that, too," the second voice told him.

"You've got a right," Harper said seriously. "On the other hand, you people must have got Mlart mad today. He isn't used to seeing people stand up to the Swordtroop and just walk off, like we're doing. Wouldn't you like to move off a bit and let him calm down some before you meet him again?"

"I'll go to F'a Loprit, Ironwearer," someone volunteered.

"Not that far," Harper said.

Just sternly enough to get amused snorts. That was enough. He waited for the next set of talkative soldiers.

Clouds had obscured the moon by that time.

South of the fleeing brigade, men in blue and green uniforms lay side by side in rows beside the hospital tents. The bravest and the weakest of the maimed slept; others awaited dawn and the return of the Algheran bombardment.

Before the watch was over, and long before the brigade reached West Bend, it began to snow. Under their blankets, as the snow deepened, slumbering men shivered, grew still, then sank forever into motionless rest.

"Fesch! Fesch! Don't be afraid, Fesch! Come back, Fesch!"

Lerlt stood on the hillside behind Timt ha'Dicovys's house in Midpassage, wiping snowflakes and tears from his eyes.

Only wind whistling through branches answered his pleas.

CHAPTER THREE

He must be on an island, Fesch ha'Hujsuon thought when he woke. An ocean island, deserted, unspoiled, idyllic—he had heard of such places.

In a fog. The sky seemed completely white, satin-textured, until his eyes came to a yellow-white sun, so painfully bright he had to look away.

The tropics. He was warm even in this fog.

He could hear breakers roaring in the distance. When he lifted his head, he caught glimpses of brown sand beyond the edge of some trees, the cloudlike sky, majestically rolling white-topped waves. A paradise, he thought languidly, and the lack of concern seemed part of paradise.

But for some reason a spotlight had been focused on him. The grass beneath him was daytime green, littered with fallen ordinary-looking leaves. Nearby tree trunks showed smooth gray and red bark. Only the trees beyond those were dark behind the gauze-like mist.

Morning or afternoon? His body gave him no indication of time. The air was laden with spicy scents he did not recognize, and dust motes floated before him in the sunlight. His nose tingled until, beyond endurance worth bearing, he sneezed.

Only his head moved.

Thin white ropes were bound around his wrists and ankles and waist. They were smooth, made of some plastic material, and were fastened to stakes firmly wedged in the ground. He struggled briefly, experimentally, and could not free himself. The cords would not move; his tugging only made them tighter and painful. He stopped, troubled by illusions that the cords would squeeze so tightly they could amputate his limbs.

His arms and legs were bare. When he looked the length of his body, he saw that he was nude.

Bark and leaves scratched at his back and pillowed his head. He lay in a kind of bower, he realized at last, made of debris from the forest floor. Carefully, not tightening the cords further, he raised his head and looked about, noticing the bare places which had been swept to create his cradle.

Where it was exposed, the earth was red-tinted, with streaks of yellow clay beneath. Tiny black forms, mercilessly exposed to daylight, wandered aimlessly over the dirt—beetles, weevils. Scavengers and agents of decay, scuttling at insect pace in quests for targets of destruction.

Listening, he heard sounds in all directions. His own heart and breath, tree limbs rustling, birds screeching, waves rippling softly, insects chittering . . . The soft leaves and bark beneath him seemed glassy hard, sharp-edged, and cold. His heart raced. What other things were touching him?

Only imagination, he forced himself to think, hoping it was true. It must be only grass and air which tickled the hairs along his spine, only his inability to move which magnified the minute scratchiness beneath him and made each tiny scrape into growing wounds. He had not been harmed.

Slowly, his breath grew less ragged. His heart calmed. He felt himself saner, less fearful and more patient.

Lassitude filled him. Idly, he wondered if that was of his own willing or the effect of a drug, but the question could not be answered and was not important. Could he remember what had brought him here?

He was Fericshin ha'Hujsuon, Algheran, born in City Year 868, student, time traveler, Agent . . . *I once made love to a woman in a blue dress on the grounds of the Institute, late at*

*night . . . My father had brown hair, my mother blond . . .
They were so tall and I looked up at them from the playroom
floor . . . I didn't want to share my toys . . . Arguing with old
Sict tra'Ruijac about a test grade . . . The war . . . Conscription looming . . . "We're losing, son. Get an education now
because afterward—" "Yes, Father." . . .*

*Afterward, he wept, ashamed that he had been talked out of
enlisting . . . Then all the refugees sleeping in the hallways of
the Hujsuons' lodge, spilling into the courtyards of Patient Holdfast like maggots around a log . . . F'a Alghera in flames and
women screaming and men shouting angrily in the basements at
the Institute, trying to fit too many people into fragile floating
boxes that were time machines . . .*

*The sterile scent of the empty corridors of the Station . . .
Lectures and training and demonstrations in underground
classrooms for students learning to think of themselves as
soldiers . . . Uniforms, weapons, uncertain men holding bewilderment under tight faces till it seemed tension would
pull their bodies asunder, no children in sight, no laughter,
no hope . . .*

All the data was present, without meaning. He waited, unable
to think.

Herrilmin shook him awake.

"Huh?" Lerlt asked groggily. "What's wrong. Is Fesch
back?" Dimly, he recognized that it was still night and that he
was on the couch in Timt ha'Dicovys's house. Had he heard a
noise? His hand reached to straighten the blanket that had slipped
from his feet.

"No, Fesch isn't back." Herrilmin shoved at him. "Get up.
There's been some trouble. We're getting out of here."

"Huh?" Lerlt closed his eyes again. It was hard enough to
find sleep, what business did Herrilmin have to steal it from
him? "Go 'morrow."

"Now, Lerlt!" Herrilmin bent and suddenly yanked at him
with both hands, dumping Lerlt on the floor. "Now you have
to get up, you bastard!" He seemed pleased with himself.

Lerlt stood and glared at him. Then, in the doorway, he saw
Gherst, dressed in pants and a checkered shirt taken from Timt
ha'Dicovys's closet. That was a sight unusual enough to still
anger, and he had to snort to hold back laughter.

"It's still snowing," Gherst said, as if to excuse himself. His face was sullen. Lerlt noticed bags in his hands.

"Where are we going?" he asked Herrilmin. "Is the time machine back?"

"No!"

"Why are we going anywhere, then? Cimon, Herrilmin, I thought you wanted to wait here for Timt ha'Dicovys."

"I don't now. It's too risky."

"Risky?" Lerlt asked. "Why? What'd Fesch—"

"Lerlt, if Fesch took the time machine he ought to have come back by now. He isn't here. *So who took it?*"

Why was Herrilmin so unreasonable? "Fesch. Who else could it be? Who do you think it was?"

Herrilmin swore. "Get dressed, Lerlt. Shut the fuck up and just do as you're told."

Lerlt looked around sadly. The house, for all its defects, was warm. The outside, Gherst's attire suggested, was cold, and it seemed insane to trek halfway across the continent to F'a Alghera during a snowstorm. But Herrilmin was obviously being unreasonable again.

He revenged himself as much as possible by dressing slowly and covering up his uniform, as Gherst had, with Timt ha'Dicovys's pants and shirt. It took a *long* time to make those elephant's clothes fit on him, and he smiled to himself every time Herrilmin shouted.

When they left, Gherst took the lead. Herrilmin went second, after gracelessly shoving a bag of food into Lerlt's hands. Gherst did not take the road down the hillside; he went across the intersection and down through the spaces between houses, following some trail only he or children could see.

Lerlt's breath steamed in the air. He lost track of the streets they crossed and houses they passed. When they neared the bottom, he felt as if half the tree limbs in Loprit had snapped at his face, all casting over him the snow that had not noticed Gherst and Herrilmin.

Gherst stopped behind a low building. "This one's empty."

Lerlt had never seen anything bleaker than this gray-walled building with its long row of blackened windows, but he was ready for a halt. Enough light had come up for him to see the footsteps he had made coming down the hill, and it seemed that

every snowflake he had kicked had taken residence in his shoes
and the folds of Timt ha'Dicovys's clothing.

The building faced the great road; he noticed part of the inn
on the other side.

"We'll have to break in." Herrilmin bent to pick up a dis-
carded brick.

"There's a side door," Gherst said quickly.

"All right." The blond man dropped his brick reluctantly.

There was a side door, and a front door as well, Lerlt noticed
when they entered. There were two long rows of beds, each
with a pillow and a pair of brightly colored blankets. But there
was no heat, and after Gherst had shoved the door shut the
winter cold still seemed to pour through the windows.

Outside his shoes had made *schrunch*ing sounds in the snow;
inside they *skwootch*ed on wood planks. The improvement
seemed negligible. "I've seen more livable sewage channels,"
he pointed out. "Aren't there lights?"

Gherst gestured laconically at hoop-and-saucer arrangements
beside the doors. "Torch holders. That'd be the light."

Lerlt grimaced. He had thought they were decorations.

"No decorations here." Gherst said gruffly. "This is a barracks for workers. It isn't supposed to be fancy."

"Is there a toilet?"

"Go outside. There's a shed."

He calculated distances and contrasted comforts. "I can go
back to Timt ha'Dicovys's place."

"No, go here if you really have to go. Use a corner or something."

He'd only wanted the concession. Lerlt smiled.

Herrilmin, crouching, moved back and forth in a corner. "I
can't see the bridge from here," he grumbled.

"You couldn't see it from Timt's house, either," Gherst said.

"That was different."

Gherst sighed.

Lerlt tossed his bag of groceries on one bed and sat down on
another to shake out snow. "How long are we going to be here?"

"As long as necessary. Gherst, didn't you find any guns?"

"No."

Lerlt pulled his shoes off.

"I can't believe Timt ha'Dicovys would go off anywhere
without guns."

"He must have them with him then. He sure didn't leave any."

"There must be some!"

"You go back and look, Herrilmin. I'm through."

"Well." Herrilmin hit at a wall. "Someplace else then. We've got to keep looking. That big farmhouse on the hill. Somewhere—"

Lerlt didn't hear an end of the argument. He pulled blankets over himself and fell asleep again.

Time had passed. Several minutes or several watches, Fesch could not be sure. The satiny fog surrounding him was unchanged, and he could not remember a day passing, but his bowels had moved and he did not remember that, either.

His muscles were weary, some numbed from inactivity. He wiggled his fingers and toes and shifted about as best he could till tingles told him all his body had returned to life.

He was starting to feel quite hungry, and it seemed to him that he was thinner now, lighter, more wiry.

And weaker. The plastic cords which tied him down seemed stronger than before, even less capable of being stretched. He only hurt himself just as much trying to pull free.

Ruefully, he waited, wriggling his buttocks from time to time in a futile effort to shift his excrement to one side. At last he abandoned even that effort, realizing he had smeared more of a mess onto himself and could not make it better.

A breeze from the sea passed over him. Over time, the sound of waves had become monotonous and had blended into the background until he no longer paid attention, but he turned his head that way once more.

Seconds passed before he realized he was seeing a vehicle land on the beach—a great silvery axe-head shape, visible more as a set of sun glints and reflected images than as a complete entity. Close to the ground, it became more substantial, and through gaps between the tree trunks, he watched it flutter gently back and forth as it drifted down like a leaf onto the sands. Memory suggested to him he had had troubles learning to fly a levcraft, and he guessed that the pilot of this vehicle was also inexperienced.

From descriptions, he recognized it immediately as Timt ha'Dicovys's time machine.

Dimly, sensing the identity of his captor, he felt alarm, but the sensation did not rise to full panic. Apprehension remained with him, but the tall redhead had never seemed the type to take a lengthy revenge. Fesch remembered without detail that he had committed misdeeds, but only in the company of others, and never crimes but only the things soldiers could be expected to do in response to danger. He let himself hope this period of bondage was the punishment the Ironwearer had decided fit for his acts.

An opening appeared in the side of the levcraft. The vehicle remained in the air, about waist height above the beach, but steps extended downward and after a moment a woman came out of the vehicle.

Fesch regained perspective, and with it the landscape changed. He was near the bank of a river. The dark sand was actually gravel—if he squinted he could make out individual pebbles. And the woman was very close.

Packages were in her arms. He could not see her face, but he sensed she should be familiar to him. She moved directly toward him, and he guessed from her footprints that she was barefoot, though he could not imagine why this seemed important. She was dark-haired and thin. Her dress was dark.

Yes, he knew who she was.

He sighed and let his head fall back, and listened to her climb the bank with his eyes closed. He wondered if Timt ha'Dicovys was watching him.

Footsteps were behind him at last. They pattered toward him quickly, then stopped, and he felt something cold against his neck. For an instant he felt incredible pain as every muscle in his body twitched and froze in place, but the sensation died almost at once. He was still conscious and could still look upward but he could move nothing now, nor feel anything.

From his training, he could guess he had been shot by a neuroshocker at low power. When feeling returned, in perhaps a quarter of a watch, unless treated with more drugs, he would know torture. He wanted to whimper at that thought, he wanted to ask if she had more of the drugs which had kept him passive and uncaring, but it took great effort simply to continue breathing; he could not ask and that was torment also.

Minute pressures told him she was checking his bonds. Her breath was loud, though surely not from effort, and he guessed she felt strong emotion. It was not to be wondered at; he imagined how he would feel with an enemy bound and defenseless at his feet. He hoped he would feel pity in such a situation and that it was not too late to feel pity.

"So you've peed on yourself already." Her voice was clear, single-toned, not quite high-pitched, not loud but surprisingly *present*, as if she had shouted. How long had it been since he had heard a woman's voice at normal volume?

Distaste, triumph, anger, fear—he tried to assign emotion to what she had said, but nothing matched. This was not a voice he remembered.

"Crapped, too." His voice was only a whisper, husky, unintelligible, all he could manage without gasping for breath, but it was necessary to speak. She had to be shown she had captured him—if it was she who had captured him—but not conquered. He was not humiliated by what had been done to him. His will and determination remained.

In response, her footsteps went away. He heard rustling sounds. The footsteps went further, then returned within a minute. Leaves rustled beneath him. She snorted softly. He heard water flowing and felt pressure on his abdomen and guessed that he had been cleaned and washed. Some sodden mass *plosh*ed on the nearby ground.

"We want you nice and comfy," she said and he wondered if he heard bitterness or a small child's satisfaction in her voice. Or both. He realized suddenly he had prepared himself for an angry captor, not an insane one.

"Where—are—we?"

"Stoptime," she told him. "Where your little friends can't find us."

She was inventing that, he knew. Herrilmin still had his locator. This place was close to Midpassage. He would be found.

She laughed until his confidence fell again.

"Have you recognized me yet?" Her face leaned over him, at a distance, and he realized she was standing astride him, just below his armpits. Her dress was dark blue, of velvetlike material, close-fitting and taut across her knees. *Why blue?* he wondered briefly, then moved his attention upward.

Dark hair, a narrow face, skin pale and dotted thickly with freckles, light-colored eyes with an alien almond shape above high cheekbones, a thin body with underdeveloped breasts . . . In a way, he did not recognize her, yet he knew who it must be.

In full truth, he had paid no attention to the details of her body, he had to admit. Once it was clear there would be no aftermath, the woman had been unimportant to any of them. It had mattered only that she had the normal features of a woman's body, and none of them had spent that much time with her. *Except for Lerlt—Cimon have mercy, what would she do to Lerlt?*

"You're—dead—the dead—Teep," he whispered, each word needing a separate breath. "Gherst—Gherst—said—Lerlt'd—finished—you.—Supposed—to—"

So Gherst had failed also. Gherst and Lerlt, in different ways. And even Herrilmin, for not realizing Gherst could fail. And—and he had been no brighter. *We were so proud of ourselves. We were the best. We kept saying that. And we thought it was true.* He would weep when he was free again.

"Think of her as my little sister," the Teep said coldly. "You hurt my little sister. Now it's my turn, with you. And no one comes to save you, Fesch ha'Hujsuon, do you know that? I've seen everything with my time machine and no one saves you. You are going to stay alive only as long as I let you and only as long as you do what I say. Is that clear? Yes, I see it is."

She smiled, and came closer to the ground. "You can never fool me, Fesch. You can never lie to me, and now you can never surprise me. We're going to have fun, Fesch, won't we? Because you want to stay alive, and I'll always know just how much you'll do to stay alive. Isn't that wonderful, Fesch? There are bad things about being a Teep, like meeting people like you, but now and then seeing into someone's mind gives me all sorts of power.

"You like power, don't you, Fesch. I heard you tell your friend about it—about being able to break things. Like people. You were choking my sister then, remember? Now it's time for you to choke."

Her smile increased. "What are the worst things that could happen to you, Fesch? Show me. Think of them."

Her face was very close now. Her breath sounded in his ear. He could count her teeth and knew she would kill him.

"Oh, Fesch! You haven't even guessed!" She smiled happily. "You can rape and murder, but you're still very innocent. I know I'm going to have fun teaching new things to you. I think I'll like you the best of all."

She kissed him suddenly, open-mouthed so her teeth clicked against his and her breath mixed with his, then sat up just as abruptly. "And while I'm with you, I'll be all yours. Not Tim

Harper's girlfriend, not anyone else's, so you'll never have to share a woman again with anyone. I'll even be faithful to you. For the rest of your life. Isn't that nice?''

She patted his face. "Thank me, Fesch. I'm giving you just what you want from a girlfriend, after all.''

He was silent. None of his muscles moved yet.

If anything, that made the woman seem happier. From a pocket somewhere on her dress, she took a short wide-bladed knife and held it over his face. "I don't want to hurt you much today, Fesch, but I will cut out an eye. Just say, 'Thanks.' A little courtesy never hurts, does it?''

He did not know whether to believe her but the blade was coming closer, so he said the meaningless word.

She seemed disappointed. "Why are you thanking me, Fesch, dear? Tell me why, and call me your dearest.

"Oh, my! You never learned my—little sister's—name, did you?'' She shook her head with mock vexation. "After all you did to her? I'm your dearest Kylene, then. Call me that.''

The blade dropped closer to his eye until only the tip was visible, with her hand just a pinkish background. "Dear—est,'' he rasped out, then paused to cough shallowly and to pant till his breath was back. "Dearest—Kylene—thank—you—for—being—all—mine!''

Then he closed his eyes, feeling sick inside.

"We'll start now,'' her voice said from a distance. "Do you like my dress, Fesch dear? I wore blue just for you.''

Something pointed touched his eyelid. "You like my dress, don't you. A girl likes to hear compliments, dear.''

"I—like—your—blue—dress,—dearest—Kylene.'' Somehow, it was easier to say the words when his eyes were closed.

"I'm very pretty in it, aren't I, dear? And I'm still your dearest.''

"You're—very—pretty,'' he whispered. "You're—very—beautiful—in—that—blue—dress—my—dearest—Kylene.''

She exhaled loudly. "Oh, Lerlt! I mean, Fesch! You learn so well, so quickly. I am so proud of you! Oh, I'll just love you to pieces!''

She hugged and kissed him again, and Fesch wondered if Timt ha'Dicovys had ever felt such fear. "Why—must—I—call—you—'dearest'?''

"Because sex is part of love, and we're lovers,'' she said

plaintively. "In a sense, anyhow, we've had sex. I'm just repeating what's in your mind, Fesch dear. The nice things you said to the girl in the blue dress at the Institute, for example." She kissed him again. "Don't you wish you were me, now? Tell me you love me. Over and over."

"I—love—you,—dearest—I—love—you,—dearest—Kylene—I—love—you,—dearest." He stopped suddenly and sniffed, for that was as close to crying as he could get.

"Please—Kylene—I'm—sorry—for—what—we—did.—Please—don't—do—this—to—me.—Let—me—go."

"Ask my sister for mercy, not me," Kylene told him. "But she's not here, and I am. And, Fesch, *dear*, we've gone too far now to stop and pretend this isn't happening. I see you recognize what I'm talking about.

"So. I'm your 'dearest Kylene' and I'm all the woman you'll want for the rest of your life, and we're going to do the things you've shown me you like to do, and we'll have fun, won't we?"

"We'll—have—fun. Dearest." The knife had poked his eyelid again.

She kissed him once more, then bit his lip gently. "And you know what's funniest? You don't have to guess, dear. I am getting sort of fond of you, Fesch. I really will be your girlfriend, in many ways. No one wants you to stay alive longer than me, for example. No one will ever be more concerned about your health. And you're going to share things with me that you never would with anyone else. No one will ever miss you more than me."

"Why—didn't—ha'—Dicovys—kill—you?"

She laughed softly. "Oh, Fesch! Such pillow talk!"

"Timt doesn't really know about me," she whispered in his ear. "He's only met—little sister. Other people made my sister and me what we are, Fesch dear. A Teep you never met, a Lopritian nobleman—far more elevated than an Algheran Septling, I assure you! A whore I used to watch. A whole Algheran army. And for me, my little sister, some—she was a dumb little bitch, or she wouldn't have—and I know she wanted me dead, which makes it funnier. Then you and Lerlt and Gherst and Herrilmin . . . No one ever had as many parents as I do!

"Will that excite you, Fesch? If it helps, you can call me your little girl, as well as your dearest Kylene. You don't have to, but I'll let you."

She licked her lips and leaned over him again, and Fesch tried to tell himself he had not seen what he read in her eyes. "I want you to stay motivated, after all. What's good for you will be good for me, won't it? But it's going to be very good for me, regardless. Are you hungry yet? Do you want to eat? Ask your little girl to feed you."

Her knees were over his shoulders suddenly, while she supported herself with a hand. Seams opened in the dress. Velvet folds fell on either side of Fesch's head; the light lasted just long enough for him to see she wore no underwear, then flesh pushed against his lips. He tasted salt and hair. He struggled for breath.

"Enough foreplay," she said brutally. "Enough talk. You use your tongue on me and maybe I'll feed you something else later. I'll let you breathe if you're good at it. And, Fesch, my dearest dear—"

She laughed hysterically as, desperate for breath, he began muzzling her. "Eating me is just the beginning!"

While the effect of the neuroshocker wore off, he shook very badly. She went to bathe in the river, while he bounced on the bark-and-leaf bier and felt the thin cords tearing into his wrists and ankles. The pain was just as severe as he had feared, and between bouts of agony he prayed that he might die. He prayed that she would drown and not come back. He prayed that she would return quickly and inject him with something to stop the pain.

She was a Teep. She came back only when the pain was bearable.

There was no bath for him, though he had wet himself again. She let him drink from a canvas bucket till she thought he had had enough, then squatted over his face a second time, not troubling to support her weight, and gave precise directions to him, telling him to be more inventive in the future.

He was hungry and afraid of being shocked again. He obeyed.

The sun—if this was stoptime, and if that was the sun—was still high in the sky when she let him stop. She rolled to his side as Timt ha'Dicovys's time machine reflected light at him and lay curled up against him with her head on his outstretched arm and her own arm across his belly.

"That really was good," she said finally, in a small voice. "I wish . . . I know I'll never get Tim to do that. Not like that."

"Let me go," Fesch said, half whispering himself. "Stay with me. I'll do that for you every day if you want."

It was almost a sincere promise. Kylene laughed nervously in recognition, and brought her hand down to fondle his genitals. Fesch stiffened almost despite himself, and she smiled wanly as her hand moved over his shaft. "This is all you ever wanted," she told him, "and the rest was playacting."

"No." He could barely breathe from the tension.

She turned further and bent over him, replacing her fingers with her lips. Her tongue moved as she sucked at him and fingers thrust into his anus. Fesch shook violently with his own orgasm.

She swallowed as his erection dwindled, then released him from her mouth. "That was your *freebie*, Fesch. Dear."

She turned again, lying on him at full length. "Kiss me and taste it."

Awkwardly, not liking the taste on her lips and tongue, he obeyed. "You didn't have to do that."

She looked beyond him. "I have things to learn, too. Besides, that was very tame. I know of a man who liked to bite at such moments and hit and—" She laughed nervously again. "Some women let him. Sometimes they liked it."

Fesch swallowed, feeling her weight against him, and wishing he were free to wrap his arms about her. "I haven't been the only villain in your life, Kylene. I'm sorry. I'm being punished. Let me go and I'll make amends."

Her breath came in snorts. "You mean you'll give me money to be quiet. You'll let me sneak into your room for sex. That's your amends!"

He sighed hopelessly. "That's how it's done in the major Septs when there's some . . . kind of involvement. It is amends. I'll protect your interests. I'll give you help when I can. I'll be your friend."

She breathed heavily and her weight seemed very great though she was not a big woman. "I don't need friends," she said, and he heard truth in her voice. "All I ever wanted was to be the one woman in the world to a man who was the only man in the world for me. And I found him."

She was close to tears, Fesch realized, and she was speaking of Timt ha'Dicovys. Was this what it was like being a Teep? Seeing deeper than words where there were no words? He wondered if such power was ultimately good or evil.

"Maybe I could help?" he offered, his words tentative, his mind not sure what help he could give or even offer in honesty.

"You can't help," she said. "All I can do is be patient and wait. And live as if life makes sense even without him, and hope that that's really true and I'll have someone else someday and won't mind, like old folks say."

It struck him finally how young she was. "We all have to learn that, Kylene. It's part of growing up, and it's true. One love goes away and it hurts but another comes and everything is bright again."

He nodded his head as well as he could and smiled ruefully then, realizing how ludicrous his position was. But the words had been honest and spoken without hope of reward, and his offer of amends had been truthful as well. There was good in him, he realized clearly for the first time in his life, and the sins he had committed had not completely wiped out that good.

He wondered to himself if that thought were another part of the wisdom that came with age, another truth Kylene would someday learn. He felt something close to affection for her now. He wished her well, and he regretted that in his ignorance of her, he had harmed her younger image.

Kylene pulled herself together and stood. "You'll never understand, will you, Fesch?"

"About you and Timt ha'Dicovys?" He said it lightly, not sure what she referred to. Would she let him go now? "Really, no. He's a very odd man."

"He's an Ironwearer," she said. "He'd never think rape was all right, as long as he limited it to strangers. Dear." The last word was clearly an afterthought.

Fesch exhaled, realizing he would not be freed today. "Will you give me something to eat before you go? Kylene, my dearest. My own little girl."

She frowned at his bravado. "Not today. You aren't hungry enough, and you aren't in love with me enough."

"When will I be?" He tried to smile as she raised the neuroshocker.

"Soon, I promise. And I keep my promises." She pulled the trigger.

He felt agony only long enough to recognize it.

CHAPTER FOUR

Harper's night had ended on the floor of a peasant's parlor in West Bend. His morning also began with a shaking, and when he was alert enough to react he threatened the shaker with a court-martial.

Quillyn ignored the threat. "I'll get your breakfast?"

"Uh-hhh." It was consent. Harper sat up, yawning, and wasted a few seconds on his normal morning conundrum: *I know who wakes up me, but who wakes up Quillyn?*

As he stretched, he noticed at last he had an audience. Several members of his staff were standing around him, looking apprehensive. "Just a joke," he said quickly and concentrated on pulling on his pants. As he tied shoelaces, he saw a man and wife staring at him from across a small table in the kitchen. Beside them, a small boy picked at peeling wallpaper. None looked happy.

"Good morning, everyone. Sleep well?"

That produced a chorus of agreement, except in one corner of the parlor where behind a table an aide was discreetly kicking a still snoring officer.

Harper approved. When the general was up, the troops should be up.

"What's the weather like out there?" The parlor had no windows and the one in the kitchen was frosted over.

An aide stepped forward. "Snow has stopped, sir. It's about a handbreadth deep. Light clouds are moving toward the southeast. Still freezing outside, but by third watch it should be warm enough to melt some snow."

"Excellent." Harper wondered if the aide had really checked outside or was simply guessing, then decided that Cherrid would also have wondered about the weather each morning. "Any idea of how long till the next snow?"

"Ten days or thirty days, sir. Not tomorrow anyhow."

"No risk of your Ironwearer getting rust on him today?"

"Very little, sir." The aide smiled. Harper wondered how often he had smiled at Cherrid's bum morning jokes.

A door opened, admitting chill and Quillyn. The orderly's hands were filled with a steaming mug of stew and a spoon. He closed the door most of the way with a foot; an aide sprang to finish the job. "It's breakfast, sir?"

"I'm never sure, either. Aide? Someone dig up the cavalry chief, please. I want to know what Mlart was doing last night. Aide. I want Pitar lan Styllin, of the Midpassage battalion, here at his convenience. Aide. I want the prisoners fed and on the road within a day tenth; someone see to it. Aide. I want Ironwearer Wolf-Twin to distribute Algheran muskets and ammunition today to anyone needing a better weapon; go help him set that up. Ship the extras to Midpassage."

Men scattered.

As good as Cherrid did it, Harper told himself and sipped his stew contentedly, feeling welcome warmth enter his gullet. The house was cold, he had noticed, even with the penned-in body heat from a dozen people. Was this normal for peasant life?

Quillyn sneered toward the kitchen, and suddenly much was clearer.

"Okay, I'm out of bright ideas. The rest of you gentlemen, have you had breakfast yet? No. Well, go out and get some, all of you."

He ducked through the doorway into the unheated kitchen, smiling sardonically as he looked at the bare table and the sullen woman behind it. "You can light your stove now. We wanted a place to sleep, not your food."

"Yessir." Still doubting, perhaps, the woman did not rise.

Harper patted the boy on the head, smiling again as the youngster angrily pulled his head away. What horror stories had he heard about soldiers?

More to the point, which horror stories were true? With two thousand troops crammed into a town of several hundred, trouble of some kind was inevitable, he suspected.

Something else unpleasant to check on.

"You've a fine-looking son," he told the man, lying with worthy purpose.

"Hers, not mine," the man said morosely. The woman flushed.

Quillyn guffawed, then stopped as the Ironwearer glared at him.

"I'd like the people in town to meet in the big barn in a quarter watch," Harper said. "Everyone should be there. If you would tell your neighbors, and have them pass it on, I'd much appreciate it."

Glumly, the man snapped his fingers.

"Good, good." Harper nodded at the happy family. "Have a nice day."

The morning conference was in the house the Hand and his staff had taken, at the end of the lane near the river. Ris Andervyll had been lucky enough to get a real bed, Harper noticed from his position by the central table. A woman's leg stuck out from blankets in the next room, and he wondered idly if toe tickling was a royal prerogative.

The house was crowded. Gertynne ris Vandeign was the last to arrive, and some of his staff had to move into the bedroom to make space. Harper was amused to see the woman's foot pulled back under the blanket. Evidently leg watching was a privilege for the higher ranks in this army.

Some incentive for promotion. He cleared his throat.

"Good morning, Lord Andervyll, Lord Daimgewln, Lord Salynnt, gentlemen. I'll try to make this short.

"Just two major items of business. The first is that, according to our cavalry, as of fifth watch, Mlart was still in his camp.

Assuming he moved at daybreak, he could reach us in two watches in good weather. Three is more like it now.

"You'll remember the cavalry lagged behind during the march last night. They chopped down some trees across the road, and I'm told they poured water across it whenever they could. If the Lady's cloak is where it ought to be, there's ice on that road, and it won't help Mlart's wagons at all.

"So I suspect we have another day before we get Mlart's attention, and I'd like to spend it resting here. The men could use some rest. Does that have your agreement?"

It did, mostly. Harper had made sure of that in conversations last night, as the troops settled into the town.

"Just in case, I want a blocking force out there tonight. There's a stand of trees about three hundred man-heights south of here which can be cut down to make lean-tos, and I'd like to keep a company there to sound the alarm if necessary. Of course, we'll have cavalry further out. Lord Daimgewln?"

"Ironwearer?" The lean man nodded gravely.

"If you'll put a company there fourth watch? I think that's the time of maximum danger. Ris Salynnt, I'd like a Guards company there fifth watch."

Dalsyn raised his head. "I'll cover for the third and in the morning as long as necessary."

Harper nodded. "I think that's settled then."

He waited for head shakes, then hesitated a bit longer. "The next item is a suggestion, rather than a definite order, but I think we need to reorganize a bit. We've lost officers during this campaign and some of the companies are getting very small. Ris Salynnt, you have about nine hundred men in the Guards now?"

"Very slightly more." Perrid looked at papers before him. "About eight hundred if I don't count men with slight injuries."

"And you have three battalions, one of which is officially still yours."

It was not a question. Ris Salynnt agreed silently.

"I suggest that temporarily you make it two battalions. Consolidate the companies under your best captains, and give platoons to the others. We can restore officers to their normal commands when we get replacements."

If we get replacements. He tried to keep that thought off his face.

"It can be done, sir." Perrid's expression suggested he was already planning his purge.

"Ris Daimgewln, you're in the same position, I believe?"

"Six hundred thirty-two effectives. One hundred ninety who may be back before too long. Yes, I can eliminate a battalion."

Harper nodded thankfully. "I repeat, it's just suggestion. I don't intend to meddle in how you gentlemen run your regiments."

He did, though. "Lan Plenytk!"

"Sir."

"You've got the problem child. What's the state of the Steadfast?"

"Three hundred and forty, and about a hundred wounded." The North Valley man shook his head slowly. "That's about enough for one battalion."

"Yeah." Harper paused, regretting what he must say. "Let's go on calling the Steadfast a regiment—I think it will be one again after the war."

"Absolutely," ris Andervyll interjected.

"Thank you, sir." Harper nodded respectfully and gratefully. The Steadfast-to-Victory Regiment had been disbanded thirty years before, after some discreditable episode not yet explained to him, and it had been re-created as a militia force for this war only as a political gesture toward Merryn ris Vandeign. The Hand's word meant that it had regained its honor. When peace came, there would be a regular army unit which bore its name with pride.

Not bad doing for us peasants. He turned back to Dalsyn.

"I'd like to see one battalion under you, run by whomever you want, and I think it should have just two companies, one from the North Valley and one from Midpassage."

"Hmmm." Dalsyn considered that. "Demote lan Styllin?"

"No. I have another job for him. I talked to him this morning, and he was agreeable, so that's not a problem. I suggest ris Fryddich would make the best captain for the Midpassage men. He's regular army and he's already there, so—"

"Uh-hh, sir!" Dalsyn leaned forward. "Ris Fryddich's dead."

Harper stopped, embarrassed by his gaffe. "I hadn't heard."

"He didn't come back to the hill after—" The surveyor waved

a hand about. "They found him at the foot of it. He'd been shot in the head."

"I'm sorry," Harper said. He swallowed. He was sorry.

"Well, yes." Dalsyn nodded glumly. "So I thought—"

"Whomever you prefer." Harper waved the comment aside.

Dalsyn was not through. "Sir? I had a young man talk to me last night, after you'd left. He's a captain already in another unit, but he's interested in transferring if I had a vacancy. I did, even though I hadn't heard about ris Fryddich then, but I thought I should check first with you. Sorry, I haven't had a chance. Anyhow, he's got army experience also, and I think a company slot would be a good post for him now. I sounded out some of the Midpassage men, and they were willing to have him as an officer. So I'd like him for the job."

"I'd have settled for the name, Dalsyn," Harper said dryly.

"Yes, sir." Dalsyn turned toward the Hand. "Dighton ris Maanhaldur."

A-ha! The oratory was suddenly explained. "If you want—"

"I need him!" Rahmmend Wolf-Twin snapped. "He's my top officer now."

Harper turned to the swarthy Ironwearer, glad of an excuse to avoid seeing ris Andervyll's reaction. "Rahm, your Requisitionary Corps has had one casualty so far—"

"Two. Some idiot got his foot run over yester—"

"Two casualties," Harper agreed. "You're mostly intact, and the rest of the brigade has been cut in half, so you can't have that much more work."

"That's why we do have more work!"

"Sorry, Rahm. I'm going to overrule you. You can afford to lose ris Maanhaldur, and if Dalsyn wants him, I'm agreeable."

Harper turned back to the Hand. "I'll leave it up to you, sir. This is your brigade, and transferring an officer from one unit to another is something you should approve."

"The men will accept him?" Ris Andervyll did not look happy. He was moving a sheaf of papers minutely up and down as he looked at Dalsyn.

"Be pleased to, sir. We've seen a fair amount of him."

The Hand sighed. "Do you think he has enough experience?"

"Yes, sir." Dalsyn nodded respectfully. "It's an experienced company, and that's the best kind for a young officer to have. It's not very strong on manners, I admit—''

"I hadn't heard," the Hand said gravely, and several young officers were brave enough to smile. "And I'm sure it wouldn't be a consideration for—ahh—ris Maanhaldur. You don't see any problems?''

"No, sir. We'll take good care of him, Lord Andervyll.''

"Don't do any special favors, Ian Plenytk. You aren't to hide him from danger. Treat him like an ordinary officer.''

"Yes, sir.''

"You can have him." The Hand sighed again.

Rahmmend Wolf-Twin sighed.

Harper tapped the table to regain attention. "I think that settles everything. Regiment leaders, be sure and provide Gertynne with your revised TOs, and I'll want the usual strength reports this evening. Other matters, we've already covered last night. Does anyone have something to add?''

Gertynne ris Vandeign stood. "We had a messenger from ris Mockstyn this morning. He'd like to send us reinforcements from Northeastern Corps, but he's maneuvering against the tra'Ruijac's army in Sun's-Glorious-Bounty Forest and expects a fight soon.''

Harper stopped for thought. "Tell him we'd like to say thanks.''

Gertynne grimaced.

"Be diplomatic. Now, do I have a volunteer to take my place fighting off the peasants? I didn't think so. Wish me luck then. Good day, gentlemen.''

"Today, we start hunting," ris Ellich said confidently. He bit into stew-soaked toast and looked out the kitchen window with every emblem of contentment on his face. "Yes, today.''

Rallt, looking out the same window, saw nothing but the unpainted wall of the lumber warehouse. It was cold out there, he knew. At dawn, dressing in the small room he shared now with Sugally, he had seen smoke sliding horizontally from the chimneys of houses in the town, kept from rising by winds sweeping down from the north. It was a day for farm workers to stay inside and rejoice that weather had finally made the patron's fields metal-hard and unworkable.

"Ready to go hunting?''

It dawned on the boy that the nobleman wanted some sort of response, and Sugally was resolutely ignoring his master as he cleaned the sinks.

"Thee knows," Rallt said hesitantly, "the lockers still hold food." He had a nightmarish vision of dragging a rabbit's carcass, heavy and bullet-torn, through the snow with Sugally. "Be nothing we need more of."

"Man hunting." Ris Ellich sprang his trap.

Rallt glared at him.

"We don't have a choice. The officer before me sent a message to the Northfaring garrison; that's why the dispatch rider stopped here last night, and the commander there wants this killing looked into. Believe me, I won't disappoint him. Now, according to the Teeps in Northfaring, no one in the city knows anything about it, so they're going to send someone to Coward's Landing in case our killer went there, but if he doesn't find anything there, and no one thinks he will, he'll be here next. Until then, I've got orders to scour this town. So we do. And if our killer's here, we'll find him."

The cavalryman pushed his plate away. "Let's saddle up, troops."

"Fighting peasants" wasn't the joke it was supposed to be.

Once there had been generals, Harper could not help remembering as he walked into the big communal barn, who were paid to wear glittering uniforms and to travel across the country, giving speeches to people and TV reporters.

He estimated that the barn held well over a hundred adults this morning, and perhaps ten children, perched on parental shoulders, all already glowering at him. *Lucky bastards, actually. This town is so small, none of the men had to go as soldiers. Or so small, F'a Loprit doesn't know of it, and so none of the men—*

"Careful, sir," an aide said.

"I see." Harper stepped carefully from wooden planks to the dirt. There were scorch marks and broken glass on the concrete runnels at the sides of the barn. "What happened here?"

"Prisoners, sir. Those Algherans who were here? It seems they burned up the floor one night. Just barbarians, sir!"

"Sure," Harper agreed soberly. His eye focused on a ladder

leading to a small loft, and he steered his party in that direction.
Soldiers held the townsfolk back.

The generals he recalled had come to distribute largess, he
remembered. "We will build an air-force base," they would
say, and demonstrators would protest and congressmen would
deplore the unwanted intrusions. Or they would say, "We will
dismantle a nuclear waste dump," and demonstrators would
protest and angry taxpayers would complain and congressmen
would point with alarm at lost jobs. "Film at eleven," the news-
casters had always said, smiling happily in either case.

A simpler, happier, kinder world it had been, a better world,
with the protesting peasants properly trapped on the far side of
television screens.

He climbed the ladder and waited for troops to occupy the
corners of the barn as he hung from the top rung. His novelty
value, if nothing else, eventually quieted most of the mob.

"You're probably wondering—" He stopped, feeling foolish.
Oh, go ahead, chum. Be trite.
Speak in general terms.

"My name is Timmithial lan Haarper. I'm an Ironwearer,"
he told them. "I think you've heard who I am, and you're wondering why I called you here.

"It's to give you bad news. I'm sure you've heard we—this
brigade—fought Mlart tra'Nornst yesterday, and . . . We did not
win." He let a minute pass while the townsfolk pretended this
was a great discovery, then cleared his throat till he had their
attention again.

"Mlart will reach West Bend tomorrow, and we are not strong
enough to keep him out. Winter's about here. He will need your
houses to put his men in; he will need your grain and your
animals to feed his men. He will push you out when he gets
here and you will starve. And there's nothing we can do about
it."

Another rhetorical pause. Harper looked for his troops, establishing eye contact when he could. It made him feel no less
awkward to realize he was telling unvarnished truth.

A veneer-able spokesman said today . . . "People. People!
People! You have to evacuate the town. Today. Take your animals and your seed grain and your tools and your blankets and
your favorite possessions. Everything. Go to Midpassage.
There's space for you there."

"For how long?" someone shouted. And—a woman's voice—
"There's no room for us in Midpassage!"

"There's space," Harper called back.

He waited for silence again. "There's space because more
than two hundred men from Midpassage have already been killed
in this war. There's space because that's more people than this
whole town has. There's space, there's houses, and there's going
to be work."

"But our houses here—" someone started.

"Go to Midpassage," Harper said again. "Go today. It's not
going to be perfect, but it's better than nothing, and that's all
you'll have here. Go to Midpassage, and don't come back. There
won't be anything to come back to. Take what you can. We have
some wagons you can use. We'll give what help we can. I'm
sorry. I wish I could tell you something else, but I can't."

And there will be a nonexistent question-and-answer period.
He sighed.

"I'm not going!" someone shouted. "I'm not, either!"
someone else called out. Predictably.

Harper nodded at soldiers and pointed with a finger. The
soldiers moved into the crowd and several small flurries ended
with two of them holding each of the men who had shouted.

The crowd looked up at Harper, aghast.

Damned fools. Harper stared back glumly. "Anyone else who
doesn't want to go to Midpassage? Let me explain that I was not
making a suggestion. I'm in charge, and I'm giving you until
the fourth watch tonight to pack your possessions and leave.
Anyone who remains after the fourth watch is going to be tied
and dragged to Midpassage. Man, woman, or child. Don't make
me do it."

He dropped from the ladder, dusted his hands, and left with
his escort.

The rest of the day he spent in places where he did not have
to look at the townsfolk.

Behind the barn was an unused pasture. On the left, behind
a clover field, Rallt saw a triangular coppice reaching like a
tongue from the lip of a gully. To the right was a graveled path
which ran to the house on the back of the hill.

By the end of the first watch the thin trees had shaken off
much of the snow that had fallen upon them and the sun's heat

had done the same for the gravel. Rallt, heavy in the dark coat he had found in the inn and which must have belonged to the dead man, was able to shake snow off his pants legs and know it would not return.

Fortunately it was a short walk to the patron's house ris Ellich had selected to inspect first.

A very wealthy patron, Rallt soon realized. The house was large and made of cream-colored brick, which reminded him of buildings he had seen on his one trip to F'a Innings.

"We wait maybe, someone come home?" Sugally shook his head cheerfully at the latch that fastened the tall door.

"We not wait." Ris Ellich shifted his gun to the crook of his arm and pulled the peg free. "Someone could have come through a window. Everyone got your rifle cocked?" He pushed the door open and entered. Sugally followed immediately, but Rallt held back, unsure how he would explain his presence if the patron should appear, and half-certain an unexplainable presence would soon produce a patron.

"Come on, boy. Work to do." Ris Ellich grabbed Rallt's elbow with his remaining hand and pulled him inside.

Given no alternative and a noble to make excuses, Rallt was willing to indulge curiosity. He was in a room unlike any he had seen in other patrons' houses: a narrow hallway stretching the length of the building. It held three tall arched entryways with dark wooden doors; between the doors small tables covered by hanging cloths held candelabra. Thick mats of colored cloth lay over the floor.

Sugally had already opened the middle door.

"A bit old-fashioned, I see." Ris Ellich went into the next room and looked about as curiously as Rallt did. This room held long tables below windows reaching to the high ceiling, a pair of couches on carved wooden legs, and stiff, high-backed chairs with satin-cloaked padding. A little light came through the shutters of the windows on the longest wall. The cavalryman seated himself on a couch with his rifle leaning against his knee and brushed his hand over fabric.

"Haven't been any guests welcome here for a while."

His eyes had pointed to a large fireplace, lined with tiles. Rallt, on wandering up to it, got the impression it had been washed or never used at all. The tiles were cold, and after touching them he put his hands back in the pockets of his coat.

There were open doorways in the room but no other rooms, Rallt had noticed. Only hallways, it seemed. "What will thee have me do?"

The cavalryman smiled. "Well, stick to Sugally. Go through the house. Look in every room and every closet to see if anyone has been here. If you find someone here, you bring him back to me. Use your gun or threaten to, you shouldn't get an argument."

"I think, Lord Ellich, this house be empty," he said, indicating the fireplace with his head to make the point politely.

"Then it shouldn't take you long. Good, we've more to do today. Every room, remember, including the servants' quarters and the root cellar."

"Come, we go look." Sugally touched Rallt's forearm gently with the muzzle of his rifle.

Cherrid woke in darkness in the rumbling, complaining wagon and listened to muffled voices and dull, chopping hoof-beats. He coughed and leaned over the litter to spit-spew what he had coughed into the pan beneath. He wiped his mouth out with his tongue and spat some more.

Then he slept and woke again. Coughed and spat again.

And tried to stand.

He swallowed, feeling stabbed in the side by his ribs.

Just sore muscles, isn't it? He sidled past the litter, half crouching, breathing quickly between steps.

"Oh, no, you mustn't do that." The woman had entered. It was her voice that he had heard beyond the flap, low-pitched, sometimes calm, sometimes laughing, unmusical but pleasant to listen to. He could hear her coming toward him, with the peculiar slippety-slappety sound of bare feet on wood that already—for some reason—seemed familiar to him. "Lie down, please, or sit down, Ironwearer."

What was she seeing? he wondered, thinking of himself as he must be then. An old man, disheveled, weary and tired despite sleep, face tight with pain from injuries no more serious than a complaining shin and sore muscles confined too tightly by cloth and tape. Or a ghost, only outlined in the darkness of the ambulance, whose shape proclaimed its haggardness. Not the Ironwearer now, he thought. Bandage-wearer, perhaps.

Damage-bearer. Grahan might appreciate the humor.

"Please, sit down, Lord Clendannan." She crept closer.

"I need to—" He gestured toward the back of the ambulance. "I am going to piss." An old man should not be forced into euphemism.

It was unexpectedly pleasant to have a speaking voice again.

"There's a jar around here." He sensed her arm moving around him, heard her fingers fumble for a moment. "Here. Piss in this, Lord Clendannan, and I'll dump it out for you."

Awkwardly, wanting to argue but not sure how, he sank back on the litter and untied his pants strings, waiting for her to depart. But she stepped closer—holding the jar before her like an offering, he was sure—until her foot clanged against his spitting pan.

Clumsy, he thought automatically. She should have opened the flap and let some light in.

"I'm blind."

He winced. Temporary lack of sight was unpleasant enough. *I'd go insane if I could never see again.*

"I got used to it." Her voice was matter-of-fact, as if she had decided to answer his unspoken thought.

She added, "I'm a Teep."

"Oh." He blinked behind his head bandages. Then, since he could not hide the thought: "What a very unusual combination."

"Please, unfasten yourself." The jar pushed gently against his crotch. He felt her fingers wrapped around it.

Embarrassed, unsure if he should be pleased because she could not watch him now or troubled because even in darkness she knew his movements, he took it from her, urinated, then refastened his trousers as she groped her way to the back of the ambulance. Canvas flapped, and he thought for an instant he heard a splash from the road behind them.

He felt better, he admitted.

The air was fresher. He felt a great deal colder also. *Like winter out there.* Mechanically, he pulled the blanket over his shoulders like a shawl.

And wondered about her. A camp follower from her sex, and barefoot. Poor as the rest of them, certainly. Did she have proper clothing?

She replaced the jar. He could smell urine faintly at the side of the litter, and her own close odor of sweat and dirt and femininity. A pleasant odor, actually. There was something satisfying about having her so near.

"It's been snowing," she told him. "The first storm of the year, about as deep as your index finger. The air is cold and it feels like a wind is coming but hasn't reached you yet, and the snow has collected in long triangles on tree branches and corners and canvas where we haven't shaken it out, and there are a few blue and brown birds sitting on branches pretending worms will come out if they're just patient enough."

What does it sound like when you march in it? Cherrid wondered. *Does it scrunch or hiss? Does it fall back in your boot-steps or lie about the holes when you step on? Does it pack well; does it leave a white star when you hit a tree with a snowball?*

"I apologize. How do you know all that?"

He was tired again, he recognized.

"It's in Grahan's eyes. I can look through them when I—you know. Should I ask him to make a snowball for you?"

He chuckled. "Grahan has not made a snowball in three hundred years."

"I can show him how." Despite his bandages, he was sure she smiled, sure she moved her hands in snowball-shaping curves.

"It would be bad for Grahan's dignity," Cherrid confided. "Otherwise I could just have ordered him to make one for me. I could do that, you know—"

"You're a general!"

"—and an old friend, so I won't. I know I can, and that is enough, isn't it?"

"No. Make him do it! It would be good for him!"

"Maybe someday." Cherrid smiled. "Someday, because I think you may be right. But we can keep it secret from him that I might do that, can't we?"

"Yes, sir." She chuckled. "I'm saluting, Ironwearer ris Clendannan."

"And I am sure it is a very bad salute," he told her, certain it was and certain also it was not meant to be and certain she would not mind what he told her. "Now. I am an old tired man and the excitement is too much for me. Let me get back to sleep."

"Yes, sir." He heard her opening the flap at the front, and felt the cold creeping into the wagon. "I think you're nice."

Nice? What a horrid thing to say to an old man half-seriously thinking of ordering another old man—a nice old man, too—to make a snowball!

Nice? His wife had called him nice, and he had only accepted it to please her and because he knew years at court had ruined her judgment of men.

And perhaps because he had been—something like "nice"— when he was with her. Nice. Well, it was nice that a nice young lady—he was sure she was young—had called him nice. Foolish but nice.

He smiled as he settled into his blankets.

Fesch's paralysis wore off in his sleep. When he woke, he was stiff and sore, and there was a raw red feeling in his eyes which made him want to rub them, but he felt none of the pain he had known when Kylene first shot him. He was grateful for that.

His head ached.

His fingers and toes were very numb, though, and that was worrisome. He had heard once of a disease which attacked numbed extremities. It had sounded very gruesome. If, of course, the Teep-told story was true.

The sky was still white, filled with diamond glints of light drifting downward at an almost imperceptible pace. The ground outside the bubble had a thin white cover.

Like snow, he thought, though the ground beneath him was dark and summer-warm. The sun was lemon-bright. He could not tell if it had moved. Kylene was not in sight, though the blue dress she had worn was resting on a nearby tree stump. He took it as a promise that she would return. Leaves had been dropped over him, in lieu of a blanket. He did not need more in this warmth and it seemed a good omen that she had taken that much care of him.

He was ravenously hungry and hoped she would appear soon to feed him. He would even tell her he loved her if that sped things up.

"I love you, Kylene," he said aloud, enjoying the ridiculous sound of the words. "Dearest Kylene. I love you. I love you, my little girl."

Cimon! Thinking about the last phrase really did have an effect on him, as the little witch had half predicted. It was just as well she was not here yet, he reflected, though she would probably see it in his mind when she arrived.

Well, it was her own choice of words. She had put the thought in his mind. It was only a thought, and if it troubled her, it was her own fault. And she wasn't apt to tell anyone, was she? Teeps kept thoughts like that to themselves as long as they were only thoughts. It was just politicians and Ironwearers who had to bare their motives to the one world.

He was safe, he was sure. Kylene might keep him a prisoner, but he would not be humiliated.

He had made another mess again, but that was not important. Kylene would just have to clean him up again. That was part of her role in keeping him a prisoner, and the sooner she tired of it, the better, because the sooner she would free him.

On the whole, his second—or was it third?—day of captivity had started well, he decided. His body was holding up and, just as important, his mind. He was definitely not in love with dearest Kylene and would not be, and she had a surprise coming if she thought yesterday's understanding and warmth of heart would become anything else.

In the warm lazy light of a new day, with time to think, he saw she was merely an adolescent adrift on an emotional sea whose squalls were of her own making. He felt sympathy, of course, remembering his own adolescence, but that was really no more than pity.

I'm all the woman you'll want or have for the rest of your life . . . How silly that pretentious little threat sounded now. How pathetic, and how foolishly romantic she was to think of punishing rape with unrequited love. She really was an idiot, and she and Timt ha'Dicovys would make a proper pair.

Once he was trained, of course. How had the rest of the threat gone? *We're going to do the things you've shown me you like to do, and we'll have fun, won't we?* He knew what she meant by "fun" now, and it was her own admission that Timt did not. Fesch smiled grimly, yesterday's taste still present in his mouth, since undiluted by food, and reflected that he had gained one well-earned superiority over the big redhead.

After she released him he would see more of Kylene, he was sure. Experience would teach her that love and sex were different appetites, both requiring attention, and she would come to him for the things ha'Dicovys would not give. She would *crawl.*

He might oblige her, if she paid properly, orgasm for orgasm as she had shown she could do.

Eyes closed, he concocted fantasies in which a properly docile Kylene gave him orgasm after orgasm in return for modest outlays of his own effort. She'd be trapped, after all, fearing exposure of the affair if she really did become ha'Dicovys's hearthsharer. She'd do what she was told. She'd make Fesch's friends happy also. There could be parties: Fesch and Herrilmin and Gherst and even Lerlt—and Kylene.

His eyes continued to itch, so he closed them, to enjoy scenes of a future which would never exist. Gradually, he drifted back into sleep.

Below the bank of the river, Kylene watched his dreams from her chair in Timt ha'Dicovys's time machine. She smiled grimly. "Soon," she promised the sleeping man, and blew a kiss in his direction. "Soon."

CHAPTER FIVE

"The guns will probably be on the ground floor so we'll look there first," Herrilmin commented as the Agents drew near the house, and Lerlt shook his head in agreement. Gherst, lagging behind, only grunted.

Lerlt turned to smile at him. Gherst didn't agree with anyone anymore, Lerlt had noticed. He obeyed Herrilmin's orders. He kept his mouth shut. He did as little else as possible. Even Fesch had been braver, in retrospect.

We can't all be heroes. Given time, Gherst might regain his manhood. Lerlt hoped so in a disinterested fashion.

He kicked at gravel, pleased with the way it exploded under his heel and flew out from the path to shower the snows that still lingered on the grass. The day had become bright and sunlit, the air cold only for those—like Gherst—who insisted on feeling the cold, and everything seemed possible.

As Herrilmin had explained, Timt ha'Dicovys's failure to do anything to them showed that the Hujsuon Agents were certain to destroy him. A little work, a little more time, and everything would be settled. If guns weren't in this empty house, then another. There were no problems which could not be solved with sufficient willpower.

"How do we get in?" Gherst asked, his voice a grumble.

Except for Gherst's loss of confidence. Lerlt smirked.

"Break the door down," he suggested, and reached to pull the doorbell. "Now you do something, Gherst."

"Don't play games, Lerlt," Herrilmin growled. "You know no one's here or there'd be fires. Just open the stupid door."

Lerlt did, revealing nothing of interest. It was amusing, though, to notice how Gherst crowded Herrilmin and him when they entered the house, seeking protection in the company of his Septlings.

Tables. Candles. Doors. There were no guns in the antechamber, and Lerlt led the way through the open interior door into a room that seemed equally bare. Herrilmin turned about, as if seeking closets, and found none. He stepped toward the fireplace. "There ought to be a dining area this way and the kitchen. Look for the steps."

"Not yet." A man came through the door by the fireplace. He had a gun in his hands. "Get your arms up."

The man! Lerlt had one shocked moment to see the scene clearly—the man in the doorway, tall, almost as tall as Herrilmin but gaunt in his thinness, dressed in blue, his musket swinging up in the crook of one arm—Herrilmin, closest to him, slightly bent forward, his hands rising—Gherst, at Herrilmin's right, his mouth open in surprise—then himself, just left of a table, two man-heights behind Gherst.

Without thought, he dived instantly beneath the table.

The gun followed. To Lerlt, the room was suddenly filled with the white knuckles of the hand holding it, the skeletal fingers jerking suddenly—

"Wait!" Rallt stuck up a hand, trying to listen, his head bent to avoid the sloping ceiling in the small room under the eaves. "I heard something."

"Hear wind." But Sugally stopped obediently, and brought back into view the rifle he had been poking at dust with beneath a narrow bed.

"Were a bell, I think." Rallt held his breath, concentrating on sounds other than the hissing light behind his head. The doorbell was three stories below. Could it be heard up here? He wanted to look outside, suddenly, and cursed the room's lack of windows.

Blam! The house seemed to shift beneath him.

"That be a gun," he said quickly.

"Mistake maybe," Sugally said. "We not done, last floor to search."

"No!" Rallt heard scuffling sounds, confused shouts. "He needs us, Sugally." He ran into the hall, toward the distant stairwell. His rifle was suddenly light in his hands.

Lerlt saw the gun go off. Flame and smoke erupted from its mouth with an ear-shattering roar. Fire lanced at him.

Herrilmin struck. First with his right at the gunman's belly, then with his left at the man's head, then with both hands fisted together as he fell-knelt onto the gunman in the doorway and smashed over and over at his neck and shoulder.

Abruptly, the slow motion images ended. He was alive. Lerlt winced with pain from the wrist that had struck the table's edge and the arm that had caught and overthrown the chair before the table. He raised his cheek from a spindly chair leg and rested his fingers delicately against the ache.

He came to his knees slowly, barely noticing the bent-over Gherst, as his eyes focused on Herrilmin, cursing and screaming as he squatted over the thin man. The Lopritian had been pulled all the way into the room now. Herrilmin had one hand fisted in the lank dark hair, one at the neck as he slammed the thin man's head against the floor again and again.

Blood was already spraying onto the wood. The man could not resist. As Herrilmin shook him, Lerlt saw the musket bouncing up and down beside him. A stump-ended arm rocked beside it independently.

Help Herrilmin, he told himself coolly, amazed at his presence of mind. *A club, a stick—find—make a club!* He seized the chair and smashed it down to break it.

"Get the gun!" Herrilmin screamed at him as he rose. "Get the gun! Get Gherst out of here!"

If those were words. If he heard those as words. Herrilmin's mouth moved, the lips pale in a reddened face, but it was motion Lerlt understood.

Carefully, deliberately, he stepped around the thin man's flailing legs and picked up the musket. The man was already dying, he sensed instantly. His face was shattered. The angles of the bones beneath were wrong. There were jagged lines etched in blood along his forehead and left cheek. The staring blood-rimmed eyes belonged to nothing human. This was only a mask for something insectlike, for something new and strange Herrilmin was shaking into the world.

Blood was spurting from the end of the bandaged arm.

Glorious! It was what he had done with the woman, Lerlt knew, only more violently, more quickly, and improvised. How Herrilmin must enjoy himself!

Breathing hard, he stepped on the thin man's truncated arm to better watch—to share—Herrilmin's performance, and as the head thudded on the floor again, gray and red fluids splattered upon him. He shifted position, trying to keep his feet where they were and still reach over Herrilmin, to smash at the thin man's body with the musket.

"Gherst!" Herrilmin screamed, throwing out an arm suddenly to trip Lerlt and send him crashing against the doorway. "Get Gherst out!"

Lerlt got back to his knees, his feelings hurt more than his body. He was about to argue, when he noticed the brown-haired Agent.

Gherst was on one knee, his fingers scrabbling at the tile on the outside on the fireplace. His mouth was open wide, his eyes staring desperately at Lerlt. There was a burned splotch—black, tattered—on the checkered shirt he had taken from Timt ha'Dicovys's cupboard. Lerlt could see his green uniform beneath, dark-stained by fluid. Heaving flesh, red-tinted.

Gherst was wounded.

He looked to Herrilmin for direction but the man was not noticing him.

Gherst! Yes, of course! He put the gun down carefully. He would rescue Gherst, pull him to safety, bandage his wounds, save his life. He would fire the shot with the musket he had captured that slew Timt ha'Dicovys, slow-toppling, surprised, weeping abjectly at Lerlt's feet, foolishly scratching at cold earth as his lifeblood trickled from the wound Lerlt had inflicted, horror-filled as Lerlt whispered into his dying ears what had happened to his companion . . . He would open up Timt ha'Dicovys's sealed time machine, pilot it back to the Station, to anxious Agents filling the hangar, shouting their acclaim

thunderously as he and Herrilmin emerged from the captured
leviathan, carrying Gherst in just the nick of time to angry, tight-
lipped surgeons, then the council meeting where Herrilmin
briskly outlined the details of Timt ha'Dicovys's treachery while
Lerlt listened modestly, righteously, head erect and did not notice the envious admiring stares of other Agents. Vrect smiled
at him approvingly . . . Yes!

Herrilmin moved past suddenly. He thrust a soggy mass of
cloth into Lerlt's hands, then bent toward the ashen Gherst.

"Run, Lerlt!" he shouted. "Run. Someone's coming! *No,
you idiot! Take the gun, too!*"

Run where? Lerlt stopped himself in midmotion to wonder
about that, absentmindedly picking up the musket as Herrilmin
pulled the shrunken Gherst over his shoulder. Outside? To the
barn? Back to Timt ha'Dicovys's house? There were too many
possibilities.

Herrilmin was too excited, he understood, listening to the
blond man's panting as he stood before him, too confused. Too
unsettled to make his meaning clear. A steady mind was necessary now to prevent disaster, and he at least was ready for the
moment of crisis.

The footsteps on the stairway were coming closer, he sensed.
Anguish. Loss. Terror. He could feel the emotions of the men
racing down the steps as certainly as any Teep. Their steps—
Herrilmin's steps as he moved to the antechamber—rattled the
house.

Plenty of time. He moved to the door behind Herrilmin, musket ready, and started to struggle his way into the jacket the
blond man had handed him.

"You run," he called over his shoulder. Steadily, determinedly, even nobly, he admitted privately. He breathed evenly
and deeply, filling his body with strength. "I can hold them
off."

"Just run," Herrilmin snarled. "Get your ass to the barn."

He smelled powder smoke at the foot of stairs. His eyes began
to sting with it. Rallt, his heart beating frantically, raced through
the hallway past the dining room to the reception room.

The body he had already expected to see was on the floor.

"Sugally," he called, "go get—"

No. It was too late to get aid, even if he had known where to send the little man. The cavalryman was dead.

He was on his belly, his arms flung wide, unconnected it seemed to bone and muscle like the limbs of a rag doll tossed by a child. His head was turned sideways. His shirt was undone, his blue army coat removed to show narrow shoulder blades rising from his back like embryonic wings.

Rallt, despite himself, could only think of a stepped-on bug. Nothing human would have survived with that smashed skull, puffy-sided with fluid above, paper-flat against the floor. Blood, brighter than the soiled scarlet on his pants legs, had spilled from the dead man's mouth. The bitten tongue had a grainy, corned-beef look.

Bloody footprints covered the wound-reduced arm.

Dead. The spirit that had animated his flesh was gone, to what mysterious place it had come from, perhaps—as some men claimed—even to the cloud-top realms where Lord Cimon and Lady Nicole held judgment for the dead. And this very moment, Ryger ris Ellich might be kneeling before Cimon while spirits loaded the great scales with his sins and good deeds and Nicole pleaded for his fate to her dread sovereign and husband.

Did the dead remember the living? Was the young nobleman watching as he and Sugally stared down now at his body?

"Where's his gun?" Sugally asked hoarsely.

Rallt stared at him. The gun was gone. And the coat—the ammunition the cavalryman had carried in its pockets was gone with it.

Ris Ellich's killer—*the killer*—now had a rifle.

They had reached the barn safely. They had outdistanced their pursuers and climbed into the loft and escaped and—Lerlt leaned against the wall at the end of the platform and caught his breath. Had he really seen pursuers? He waited, listening for outside sounds, then stepped back cautiously to the rear wall. Straw dust floated about him as he bent to look through a slotted ventilation window.

No pursuers. Nothing showed itself except the prison-barred landscape and the now tranquil snowcapped house. Had there been anyone else? Had there been anyone at all?

He heard cloth tearing behind him. Feet moving through straw. His hands squeezed the butt and barrel of the musket.

Yes. His eyes looked down dully at the blue jacket beside his feet and the bronze-tipped bullets half-spilled from a pocket. Yes. There had been a man in the house. A soldier.

He bent to pick up cartridges. A Lopritian soldier.

And muffled excited voices. Trampling feet on stairs.

It could have been an illusion, he thought now. No danger at all, but some sound from outside the house, freakishly distorted to seem as if it came from inside. It might have been the soldier's thrashing about on the floor after Herrilmin released him. Dying men made strange sounds. Maybe it had been Gherst's instinctive moans and motions.

He turned, hoping for reassurance.

Herrilmin was bent over Gherst's body, a knife lying at his side. The brown-haired man's belly was exposed, pale beside the straw, and Herrilmin was wrapping a ribbon torn from his outer shirt around his stomach. Under the ribbon was a pad made from the same garment. Blood was seeping through the folds of checkered cloth.

Lerlt swallowed. "Can I help?"

"Stop waving that Cimon-taken gun," Herrilmin growled. He barely looked up. "And why don't you try loading it?"

When Sugally returned, his appearance had changed. Rallt stared at him, open-mouthed. "We can't do anything for him," Sugally had said. His mouth had twitched. "Wait. I'll be back."

Now he was back. His hair had been trimmed along his temples. Under the coat he had worn into the house, red and blue garments Rallt had noticed in one of the upstairs bedrooms rested comfortably on his body. Braid torn from his white livery peeked out of one pocket.

"Thee's been in the boy's room," Rallt said, only half-conscious of the body at his feet. "Thee's taken—"

"Clothing a slave wouldn't wear? Yes." Sugally stared bleakly at Rallt until the boy's eyes dropped. "Not as fine as he gave me—" The little man looked down dispassionately at ris Ellich's body. "—but they'll do. If you're wondering, these were at the back of a closet and smaller than the other clothes. No one's apt to miss them until spring and maybe not then."

His eyes moved carefully up and down Rallt's form. "You'd be back in Innings then, wouldn't you? You might want to look around some yourself, you could use a better-fitting coat."

Rallt ignored the provocation. "Thee'll be found out. Take them back, Sugally. The patron—they anger quickly."

"I can pass well enough now as a Lopritian, I think. For long enough, anyhow, unless I meet a Teep." Sugally lifted his rifle, his face impassive. "Don't you think so?"

Rallt nodded his head unhappily. "If thee wishes to play, be it thy pleasure. But we must bury Lord Ellich before we—"

He swallowed and stared down at the broken body, making himself notice the blood that had splattered onto the fireplace tiles, the gouges in the floorboards, and the damage to chairs and the upturned table. For the first time, he was conscious of the work necessary to make the patron's house clean again. "Other things," he said weakly.

"You can bury him," Sugally said coldly, "and do those other things, if you think it so important. But I don't recommend it, boy. The ground's frozen, so it won't be easy work, and I imagine his family will want his body sent north. I know what these Lopritians are like—if you're the one who buried him, they'll decide you're the one to dig him up."

Rallt stared. "Would thee leave thy master on the floor?"

"That's where he is, isn't he?" Sugally snorted. "Don't you understand? I don't have a master now, boy, and no one knows it but you. I'm free. If no one stops me, I'll be back to the Necklace Lakes before the next snowfall, and the Gods have pity for any Lopritian I see again. I'm going home."

Rallt suddenly noticed how easily Sugally's gun could be pointed at him. He swallowed nervously.

Sugally snorted again. "Don't be more frightened than you need to be. I'm not a fool, boy. They'll look for—" He used a word Rallt had never heard. "—before they look for an escaped slave. Tell the authorities whatever you want and unless you do it immediately, it won't matter."

Rallt had nothing to say.

"No snake's tongue in you? Well, say what you will when it comes back. Good-bye, Rallt."

Sugally turned and left the room. The front door closed behind him.

To Rallt, it seemed he had the stride of a taller man.

Dighton ris Maanhaldur found Harper near nightfall. He seemed eager to speak. Merryn ris Vandeign's "short" me-

morial service, as Harper had half expected, had run on and on
and the redhead was eager for only supper now, but behind his
back a pair of elderly women were stacking bedding and jars of
preserves in a supply wagon; under civilian eyes, he preferred
to look as if occupied by military duties.

"You've got the Midpassage crew, I hear. My sympathy."

Wasn't the young fool supposed to be with his company on
duty at the south-of-town checkpoint right now?

"Yes, and I wanted to thank you before I got to bed. Dalsyn
said to sleep earlier tonight because he'll want me tomorrow
to—"

Harper put a hand up. "By 'Dalsyn' you mean your superior
officer?"

"Yes, sir. Force Leader Ian Plenytk, that is. Oh!" It dawned
suddenly on the young man that he had made an error of eti-
quette. "Anyhow, Force Leader Ian Plenytk said you had recommended me, and I've realized since the start of this campaign
that I wanted to be a professional soldier, like you and Ironwearer ris Clendannan, so I appreciate—"

Harper wasn't willing to take compliments prisoner.

"Dighton," he said finally, after he had scraped mud from
his boot soles long enough to form a response. "You've gone
up a grade in rank, haven't you?"

"Have I, Ironwearer?" The tall man seemed puzzled by the
thought.

"You're an A-level captain now, since the Midpassage company is back to full size, aren't you. Do you know how much
that increases your pay?"

"No, sir." Dighton was still puzzled.

"One and a quarter mina per day. Not quite enough for a
glass of beer in a good tavern. Now, Dighton, listen carefully."

"Sir!"

"Someday that extra five hundred mina a year will seem like
a big sum."

"Yes, sir? I have an estate, sir. I earn . . . enough."

Harper held up a hand. "Someday, Dighton. When it does—
and only then—you will be a professional soldier."

That earned the redhead a thoroughly aristocratic frown.
"Ironwearer?" Dighton asked in a small voice. "Did you think
about pay, when you—uhh?"

He hadn't thought about it, Harper admitted. When he *uhh*ed or at any other time. Come to think of it, did a mercenary's contract cover pay raises? He couldn't remember relevant clauses in the one he had signed.

He probably had not gotten a pay raise for replacing Cherrid ris Clendannan. Hadn't Dieytl lan Callares always accused him of carelessness with money? Had the Teep gone to his grave, being right again in his mind-reading guesses? Probably, he realized again.

A grievous fault, and grievously has Harper answered it.

But he was not willing to lose the moral high ground. "You forget the important difference between us, Dighton. Mercenaries aren't paid until the end of a war."

"You mean?" Calculations went on behind the young man's eyes. "Sir?"

"Yep. I can afford to be a little cavalier about being paid. Something beats all hell out of nothing, doesn't it? Go to bed, Dighton."

Fesch woke, shivering uncontrollably, for only handfuls of leaves covered his body. Dew or rain had fallen; he licked as much as he could from his face, but it did no more than coat his tongue. It did not slake his thirst.

His stomach pains had lessened, perhaps because the rest of him felt so miserable, perhaps because he was now accustomed to hunger. His head continued to ache, but the worst of the hurt had collected behind one eye, which he learned to keep closed. There was nothing new to see after all.

His arms and legs were very numb and there was no feeling at all in his fingers until he had patiently wriggled them for what seemed an entire watch.

The snow beyond his bubble was deeper. The firefly specks of snowflakes had gone from the air, and the minute forest sounds soon lost interest. He thought of the women he had known but they all seemed shallow to him, simple and easily manipulated, and somehow indistinguishable. Their faces eluded him. The other memories of his past life were without interest.

He fantasized about Kylene, imagining she had returned and relented. He was magnanimous as she wept and asked his forgiveness. They swam in peaceful oceans and made tranquil love on the beaches. Kylene performed fellatio on him again and promised to return to him regularly after she was wed to Timt ha'Dicovys. Returned from his mission, back at the Station, he made discreet arrangements and met her often. He met other women, more suited to an aristocrat's life than she, but they were jealous and not understanding, and only his involvement with Kylene continued through the years. On his deathbed he realized he had never loved another woman.

The pictures were so convincing and detailed that he grew an erection. He twisted himself about on the bier for greater stimulation, telling himself the leaf touches were Kylene's fingers and lips, until he had ejaculated, but the orgasm lasted only a few throbs. It was not as intense or lengthy as those he imagined.

He was striving to repeat the experience when Kylene returned. The light showed she wore pants made of blue canvas and a white blouse.

Her hands were empty. His stomach twisted unhappily; he began to hiccup.

"Aren't you glad to see me, dear?" she asked before he could speak. She took her clothing off before him, slowly and sensuously, and struck poses before him in the nude before again donning the blue dress she had left near him. Fesch's eyes kept returning to the lacy undergarments she had left on top of the folded pants.

She put her hands on her hips. "You haven't said you missed me yet."

"I missed you," he husked. "I love you, Kylene . . . Dearest, can I have a drink and some food?"

"Men!" she said rhetorically, but she filled the folding bucket from the nearby stream and held it to his lips again. With the rest of the water and a second bucket, she washed him off again, though this time she did not bother to dry his body.

"Time to eat!" she said then, and squatted over his face again. "Show me what you've learned, Fesch dear."

He touched her labia with his tongue, then hesitated. "My eye hurts."

"Keep them closed then," she ordered. "You don't need eyes for this."

"I'm afraid something's wrong with it," he whispered, and hiccupped again. "It hurts a lot. I think something's in it, dearest."

She sat full on his face to answer him and wriggled her behind

so his lips were pushed back and her hair was between his teeth.
"Don't complain about yourself, Fesch. Think of my little sister
and think of me. You have to keep me happy before you can be
happy. Is that clear?"

"Yes, dear." He couldn't say the words aloud; he had to think
them before she relented. Her genitals had a strong odor today
and he could guess she had not bathed before returning to him,
but he had no choice. He tried to make her happy.

He did lose his hiccups.

After half a watch she rolled off. "You aren't very good today," she grumbled. "I think I'll go now. I won't come back
till you love me."

The idea terrified him. "I do love you, Kylene," he said
earnestly. "Please don't leave me. I love you. Want you happy,
really. It's just—I'm thirsty again, that's all. And can you look
at my eye?"

Wordlessly, she refilled the bucket and let him have another
drink. "I'll look at your eye, later," she said, her voice still
showing complaint.

This time she lay down on his belly, with her legs extending
past his head. Her thighs clamped against his ears, so he heard
them roaring at him. Her fingers toyed with his genitals, but not
persistently. No erection came.

She rested her head on his stomach. "Now do me!" she
demanded.

He was better this time, he was sure. Her body shook against
his regularly; her legs threatened to pull his head off and he
could feel the cords cutting at his ankles and wrists as her movements pulled him about.

But he was not happy. He thought once of biting her to show
his annoyance. Not seriously, of course. Just a nip to show his
independence—he'd say it was involuntary and a response to
hunger. She pulled away from him abruptly, while he searched
for the right moment. She grabbed his limp penis with one hand
and poked the opening in the glans with the tip of her knife.
"I'll hurt you much more than you can ever imagine if you hurt
me," she told him coldly.

"It was a thought, that's all." Fesch tried to grin. "It wouldn't
have been a real bite. A love bite, dearest."

The knife poked again at his genitals. "Never lie to a Teep."

He swallowed. "It wasn't a lie. See my mind, Kylene. See? I've thought nice things about you."

"I see parties in your mind. Four rapists and me." She turned her head and spat.

"Just imagination. To kill time. I'd never really do anything like that, Kylene, you know. You mean more than that. See?" Almost desperately, he tried to re-create his morning fantasies for her, strangely eager that she should see and appreciate his imagined loyalty.

But her face turned curiously blank. Immobile. Frozen.

"I'd like to hold you," he said quickly. "I want to feel my arms about you. I want you beside me in bed, making love the regular way. I do want you with me, Kylene, all the time, dearest. Sweet dearest? My little girl?"

"You don't love me enough." It was a statement, not a complaint.

"Yes, I do!" He breathed heavily. "I just can't show it, because you've got me all tied up."

"I can let one arm be free," she said slowly. "But I have to know you won't try to hurt me."

"I promise, I won't," he said, and she nodded unhappily.

"I need more of an assurance. I'll have to think about it. I'll have to be sure that you love me. Maybe tomorrow. Maybe I'll feed you tomorrow, if you're ready."

Fesch wanted to scream.

"Maybe you won't want to eat," she said, as if explaining matters to a small child. "There won't be much, after all. The food has to last. Maybe you'll never want to eat again, or you'll want your meals far apart."

His good eye blinked to show his incomprehension. "Dearest, I could eat a whole rotten hippopotamus!" He could think of no more ludicrous example to make his point. He snickered at his own remark, and even Kylene smiled wanly.

"I cut your eye out," she said when he was silent.

He smiled at her, letting her make her joke.

"I cut your eye out," she said again. "I pushed my knife into it, till it burst like a grape, and I let the fluid drain out, till I could hold it with my fingers and I twisted it and cut it off at the base. There's a little sort of stalk there, at the back of the eye, with stringy things in it."

He stared at her, his eyes—eye?—wide.

"It's really very complicated," she said calmly. "The eye has different layers of things about it, and there's little muscles to hold it, and they all had to be cut. And blood comes out from different places—I put ice in it—where the eyeball used to be, I mean—so it would clot."

He could still only stare at her. It must be a joke.

"I can show you, darling. I threw it somewhere around here. Do you want to look for it? Better yet—"

She had carried a small mirror in her clothing. She showed him.

She had cut his eye out! Fesch started to cry and pulled at his bonds simultaneously. But the plastic cords were too strong.

Filled with pain, he lowered his head and sobbed all the louder.

Kylene was unmoved. "Teeps don't make jokes. I thought you knew. I told you the other day I would take one of your eyes out. I told you I would keep my promises to you."

He did not hear, and she went away, not to return until he had wept himself past feeling emotion.

"Do you still love me?" was her first question.

"I hate you. I want you to die."

She nodded gravely. "That's honest. I won't punish you for it."

"How could you do such a thing?" He stared at her, both eyelids raised so she could see both the good eye and the brown crusted pit beside it. "Was it an accident? Is that it? Did you make a mistake?"

She met the awful gaze without blinking. "I told you, I did it deliberately. I said I would take it out and so—I had to take it out. That was it. You have to know I keep my promises. I had no other reason."

"I don't love you," he said, trying to hurt her.

"I never wanted your love. Neither did my little sister, and what do you think she is seeing with now?"

Fesch swallowed. Kylene pushed her dress aside and squatted over his face again.

"I won't," he said, trembling. "You can kill me but I won't touch you."

She laughed. A clear, bell-like tone filled the air and bounced from tree to tree. He thought the laugh and the echoes would never end.

"I can cut your other eye out," she said finally, smiling happily at him. "I can cut your testicles in half, and your penis, right down the middle. I can get pliers and yank off every one of your toenails and fingernails—I've heard it hurts tremendously and they take a long time to grow back. I won't kill you today, Fesch, but I can make you wish I did.

"Or you can keep doing what you've been doing. Maybe you'll escape."

She laughed again, insanely. He trembled beneath her and she shook and he realized sickly she had managed to reach orgasm without him.

Maybe he could escape. If he stayed alive long enough. Reluctantly, hating himself, he stuck out his tongue and began licking at Kylene.

Where are we now? he wondered, and the woman sitting on the opposite bunk said, "Midpassage. Almost. We're coming up to the bridge into town."

The ambulance creaked. Cherrid listened again to its complaints and decided once more the right rear wheel axle wanted grease. A whip snapped, sharp sounding and loud against the constant drumming of hoofbeats.

"The regular driver," Wandisha lin Zolduhal said. "He's taken the reins back from Grahan."

Answers even to questions his mind had not formed. He wondered what it would be like to be a Teep.

His heart fluttered weakly.

The woman was silent.

Midpassage. He pushed his blanket down, then coughed fluid up. Spat it out. Stayed on his elbow, remembering how the town looked.

Ignored the aching chest and side muscles.

"It's darker now," she said. "Only a few of the houses are lit. Lord Vandeign's house and his barns and factory buildings are dark. The inn is dark . . . There's just one light on, on the bottom floor."

A deserted town, he thought, hearing that description, and the woman did not argue. Midpassage's men had gone to war and the town's lights had gone off. It would be a long time before all the lights came back.

*After this war, if I still have influence, I've got to persuade
Molminda to do something to help the south.*

In death and occupation, the Shield Valley towns had paid
more than their share already and the war had gone on for less
than one year tenth. It seemed impossible that a major conflict
had unfolded this way this quickly.

"Crossing the bridge," Wandisha said.

Like the war, he thought gloomily, trying to construct an
analogy between its movement and the progress of the ambulance, in which passage over spanned waters and solid earth
seemed the same to passengers.

"To me," Wandisha said slowly, "it seems people's minds
are like fires. If I'm not concentrating, it would be like standing
in a field and seeing bonfires and torches on all sides, where the
people are. Some of the fires are big and some are small and
they have different colors. Some are tall and steady; some are
flickering little campfires. I can move back and forth and if I get
very close to a fire I can see things I wouldn't see at a distance,
but I have to ignore the other fires."

"And that's mind reading." She was trying to divert him, he
recognized. But the words had provoked his curiosity.

"No." He sensed she was smiling. "What you did is mind
reading, in a sense—your belief that you know what I'm thinking. What I was describing is how minds look from the outside.
To me. And to me, being inside someone's mind is like being
in my own mind; everything seems perfectly normal."

"Except you can think people's thoughts for them—make
them think what you want them to think." He was testing her.

"No, I can't do that." She hesitated. "Some Teeps do, but
not many. You know slaves are sometimes made 'loyal' by treatment of that sort? Most of us don't approve of that any more
than you do."

He shifted position awkwardly. He hadn't heard what he had
expected.

"We don't," she said intensely. "We just don't. You can walk
down a street, can't you, and swing a sword at all the people
you meet? But you don't, even though you have the ability. Well,
we don't."

He coughed. "I'm a little old for impromptu sword fighting."

The wagon jerked beneath him. Braked wheels slid across the
pavement.

"What?"

Wandisha was beside him to keep him in place as the wagon skidded to a halt. Her hand gripped his arm painfully. "Cherrid. Lord Clendannan. Please listen to this boy!"

"Huh?" He was still adjusting to the sudden standstill.

"Kylene is missing. Lan Haarper's wife—I can't find her."

"Cherrid?" Grahan had pushed his head through the front curtain. "We'll be on the way shortly. Some fool boy just pulled the horses to a stop."

Rallt sniffed, keeping back tears. He hadn't realized the horses were so large until he was suddenly among them in the darkness, trying to hold them back, and understanding too late that the driver had not seen him or was willing to run him down without stopping. It seemed a miracle now that they had.

He swallowed, close to choking, cold all the way through as the snow that still lingered on the ground.

He hadn't had a choice. None of the ambulances that had come through town that day had stopped, and without Sugally, he knew neither the innkeeper's nor ris Ellich's death would be avenged. He couldn't let that happen.

"Come here, boy." The man sitting beside the driver beckoned, and Rallt sidled past the horses to meet him.

"Get your breath back." An old man, slim, in army uniform.

Rallt did, trying to smile, while the driver glared at him and spat at the road. The nearest horse pushed its muzzle at his chest to satisfy its curiosity. He stepped away quickly.

"I thank thee, sir. I wished to know—"

"Don't thank me." The soldier pushed the entrance flap aside. "It's Ironwearer ris Clendannan decided he had to speak to you."

In the time machine, after she left Fesch, Kylene stared at her reflection in a full-length mirror. She was nude. She had bathed repeatedly. Her skin was pink from scrubbing; blood oozed from scrapes created by the coarse Lopritian soap.

Dry-eyed, she went from locker to locker in Tim's room and the front cabin until she found a bottle of whiskey. The taste was sharp and musty, stomach-turning, but she did not notice. Still nude, she sat in her chair in the darkened cabin, control panel snug against her waist, staring at the pink and crimson brightness of stoptime as she sipped from tiny glasses of liquor.

After a while she twisted to one side and vomited onto the floor.

Tears were in her eyes. She wiped them away on her forearm, then wiped her mouth as well, and continued to drink.

Once she touched the steering ball at her side and moved to change the controls, but the motion was not completed. Her hand dropped back to her glass.

She drank a third of the whiskey, then slumped forward, to sleep on her arms. The uncapped bottle fell. Liquor gurgled onto the floor as she slept.

CHAPTER SIX

"**G**un went off," the man on the litter croaked. It was an old man's voice, raspy, discordant as the fire crackling behind him, precarious as the tables that supported the ends of the litter. He waved a hand feebly, then made a sound which if louder would have been a cough.

The woman sitting beside him pushed a basin closer with a foot. Her blond hair swayed with the movement.

Lord Clendannan. Ironwearer ris Clendannan. He had forgotten the woman's name.

Wind tossed a restless shutter upstairs. How strange that no one wished to sleep now. Awkwardly, he put his hand on the mug of beer the old man's soldier-companion had given him, moved it over the tabletop.

"I want you to think about the room," the woman said. The old man's withered right hand was intertwined with hers. The other she used to brush aside hair that had descended to the bandage that covered his eyes. "You're standing in it, Rallt, looking at Lord Ellich's body. You're turning around, looking to see what damage was done to the room."

Her face, broad and serene, and her eyes, opaque and unblinking, swung up to him. Rallt stared back, almost hypnotized by the scar in the center of her forehead. Half-remembered threats from his childhood terrorized him. His eyes dropped to her knees, where green trouser legs met a white dress. He let himself wonder where she had found her shiny boots.

Behind the woman, the old man's left leg stirred. His blankets and the woman's green jacket, dropped over his feet, shivered together.

Near the kitchen door, the old soldier from the ambulance was on his knees, silent, no longer arguing with the man on the litter. He was examining the spot where the innkeeper had died. Rallt watched as he scraped at the floor with his fingernails.

Rallt turned back to the woman.

"You are all alone," the blond woman who was a Teep said carefully, stressing the last word. "You see mud and grit on the floor. There's a broken chair, upturned, with one leg lying beside the body. A table is on its side. You see a scratch where it has scraped the floor."

"Yes." Rallt swallowed, trying to see the room again as it was.

As it had been with Sugally standing beside him. Somehow he sensed she would not mention Sugally until he did. He sipped his beer cautiously.

"Did you see a bullet mark? Was plaster on the floor at the back of the room, for example? Was a tile cracked on the fireplace?"

He tried to think. Tried to remember without noticing the old man's knuckles whitening as the Teep woman squeezed his hand, without noticing the smudged marks on her frock. Was she his daughter? His wife? Did Normals have Teep children?

In his mind, he saw holes in the wall. In the floor. Damage in the hallway behind the reception room. Tried to see them.

"I be very sorry. I really remember not anything," he said.

The woman turned her chair underneath her, clumsily, scraping the floor, so she was facing the man on the litter more directly. "I don't think he did see any," she said.

The old man coughed in response. Over and over, weakly. Rallt thought he was trying to laugh, until he twisted sideways. Then the boy could see the effort it cost in the set of the old man's mouth and the cords of his neck. Slowly, the old man

brought himself up on one elbow. Veins and tendons stood out
on his wrist.

Rallt thought of a derrick he had once seen, overweighted by
a load of bricks, hoisting its burden skyward in fits and starts,
with the ropes creaking under strain, turning slowly as the platform that held the bricks, so slowly that as he watched it seemed
the load was fixed in place and the world instead revolved beneath his feet, as other men stood silently, waiting . . .

The woman moved to support the old man by his shoulders.
His head drooped below her breasts, and he coughed again.
Dollops of yellow sputum dropped into the basin, sticking to-
gether like fragments of jelly.

The old man breathed deeply while the woman lowered him
again on the litter. His head moved slightly, and she pushed the
blanket that had slipped over his chest further down, to his waist,
so Rallt could see the grime and dirty lace on his sleeves and
the front of his blue uniform.

For a moment there was no sound but the old man's breath
and an echoing hiss from the fire. Then the first soldier stood
and went into the kitchen.

"We'll have to check," the woman told the man on the litter.
"When it's daytime again. With Grahan?"

To Rallt, it sounded like agreement. She turned back to him.

"Your friend may have wounded someone. That would mean
he had at least two attackers."

He swallowed. "I thought—he said—" His head pointed to
the blackened flooring where the innkeeper's body had lain.
"Only one been killing."

"Trust me, boy," the old man rasped, and Rallt thought he
saw a smile on the pale lips. "Man with a bullet—wouldn't do—"
He coughed, filling his sunken cheeks with puffs. "Has to be
one more. Ris Ellich—" He exhaled gently. "Poor—never more
smarts—than the horses he rode. Someone will have to tell his
father."

"He needs more than this," Herrilmin whispered, and Lerlt,
trying with no success to sleep in the straw of the hayloft,
wrapped his blankets tighter about him and wished the blond
man would stop talking to himself.

Gherst, after all, had finally shut up.

In fact, after he revived in the afternoon, the wounded man

had kept his voice low when speaking, a relief to everyone since he had nothing more interesting to say between moans than "It hurts, it hurts," or "I want to go home," and he had said that over and over.

Gherst was not measuring up, Lerlt told himself. Even with only his Septlings present, a man should endure minor injuries with more fortitude.

His censure was lessened when Gherst passed up supper, allowing Lerlt and Herrilmin larger portions. Not that Gherst had any reason to be hungry, of course; he had done no work for longer than Lerlt could remember.

"Ought to go get help for him," Herrilmin whispered. Lerlt heard his knuckles striking the floor of the loft.

Herrilmin would need help to get help, he thought sourly. It was Herrilmin who had decided to fix the meal that evening, after dumping on Lerlt the more difficult task of carrying provisions from the workers' dormitory.

To any sensible observer, that division of labor was misguided. Gherst could have been carried to the dormitory in one trip; it had taken Lerlt three tedious round-trip journeys to bring back blankets and several sacks of food. And Herrilmin had waited unnecessarily until evening before giving his orders; in the darkness, Lerlt had fallen painfully in the snow in the orchard on one of those ill-considered trips; he had had to grope on the floor of the unlighted dormitory to find where Gherst had hidden the Agents' possessions.

And when Lerlt had done all that, he had to wait on Herrilmin's cooking, and the big man served up slices of cooked meat and potatoes on bread, without even a pretense of a sauce. Fesch had prepared better meals in less time.

And where was Fesch now? Enjoying himself, Lerlt was sure. Hiding from responsibility in some private paradise, sating himself with every indulgence the rich could buy in the impoverished world.

Hiding from deserved resentment and punishment, as well. He wondered if the annoying little coward would ever dare return to the Project.

To Lerlt, miserably wrapped in a blanket in the drafty loft, trying to keep straw out of this pauper's meal he was forced to eat with his fingers, and barely able to find his plate in the nighttime darkness, it seemed hardly possible that less than half a day had passed since leaving Timt ha'Dicovys's house. With all its failings, its running water, plumbing, solid walls, and plush furniture now seemed as desirable and as hard to attain as the realms of heaven Cimon reserved for his paladins.

"Don't know what went wrong," Herrilmin mumbled, feeling sorry for himself, as he did so often. To Lerlt's disgust, he sniffed loudly, not trying to hold in decently the sniveling sound or to conceal it under his bedding.

Herrilmin had gone wrong, Lerlt saw now.

There was other blame to assign. Fesch had sinned first, of course, by stealing the time machine and abandoning his companions, but Lerlt had never expected anything praiseworthy from Fesch. Gherst had not been able to find the guns the Agents needed to defend themselves from Timt ha'Dicovys. Ironically, he had found the scruffy hovel Herrilmin had first selected as a refuge and now refused to take him to.

Fleeing Timt ha'Dicovys's home in panic, however, was Herrilmin's idea. Seeking weapons in a house filled with soldiers was Herrilmin's fault. It was Herrilmin's untimely leap at the soldier which had got Gherst wounded, Herrilmin's stubbornness which left them all cowering in a barn loft.

"Couple days at most. Go now . . . then go back to the Station . . . What route to take? Horse? How get around?"

Unending drivel. Lerlt thought of the groans that abandoned buildings make, their age-rotted timbers querulously fearing the demands of weather and human footsteps. Herrilmin had once seemed solid, strong, and capable!

Where was Fesch, anyhow?

When Fesch woke next, he felt quite different. His temperature seemed elevated, his body clammy and heavy. Though he was freshly awake, he felt weak and exhausted, as if from great labor. It was difficult to concentrate.

The ground was damp. A puddle was nearby.

There was not a mess beneath him, for once. The ache in his missing eye had faded, but there was a new soreness in his right shoulder and arm.

Another thin white rope had been fastened over him, across his chest from armpit to armpit. He caught glimpses of it when he raised his head. He twisted and tossed; painfully, the cord was tugged a finger's width lower, leaving a shallow groove with a reddish bottom in his chest.

Unthinking reflex brought his hand up to touch it—and his arm moved.

It felt stiff and sore and the sensation of movement was subtly different from the way he remembered it, but he felt it move. The cord that tied it down was gone; it was only habit that had made him imagine it this morning.

Kylene had freed his arm, as she had promised. He wanted to kiss her. He wept with gratitude and joy.

Reality intruded soon. His tears stopped and he stared determinedly into the depths of the surrounding mist. He could free himself now; he could overpower Kylene, and escape in her time machine.

He must make plans. He must be prepared when she arrived. He repeated those thoughts endlessly, but could go no further.

Reason rather than energy finally made him move. Listlessly, almost reluctantly, he brought his arm up to push at the new bonds.

But though his arm moved, his hand touched nothing.

He looked down his chest, then to the side. Slowly, he brought the limb closer to his good eye.

He flexed his fingers. He *felt* them move. He made a fist. He felt the comfortable tension as the fingertips pressed into his palm. He felt the firm muscles rippling down the length of his arm as he raised and lowered it.

What he saw was the stub of an arm. It ended at the elbow in a blood-soaked bandage.

He made a fist again. His elbow remained in front of him. The skin adjacent to the bandage had been scrubbed clean and white; the rest of the arm was dark and, when he brought it near his nose, rank.

How long had he lain here? He put the question aside and slapped at his chest. He continued to feel sensation in the hand, but the palm did not register the shock of contact. His chest felt untouched.

He did it again. Again. Harder. Again.

There was nothing but the palsied shaking of his truncated limb in the leaves beside his body.

Feverishly, he beat at himself, then screamed as the still tender elbow hit an unyielding piece of bark.

He recognized the truth then. He wept without reserve. His useless, shortened arm jerked spasmodically at his side, as if in helpless sympathy.

When his crying ended, Kylene was watching. She had donned the blue dress. She looked down at him dispassionately, silently.

She was beautiful, Fesch realized, and therefore terrible. Nothing on her body or face showed what she had done to him—what she had become.

"Why?" he whispered finally.

"I said I would." Her voice was strained. "I told you I would let one arm go free, if I could still be safe from you. I kept my promise."

He raised the useless arm, staring at it rather than her, and could not move his eye from the bandaged elbow to her face. He could not speak; his thoughts showed yesterday's bondage was preferable to this freedom.

"It wasn't yesterday. It was two days ago, by your time. You had a fever. You lost a lot of blood." She swallowed. "I gave you a lot of treatment while you were unconscious. I'd never amputated a limb before. I made mistakes. I'd seen Tim operate on people and thought it just took being quick and determined, but he's so—*organized*."

The last word was foreign. She translated it for him, her voice mechanical, but he was not listening and never understood it except as a cruel but unemotional directness.

His mind went back to her first words. "You cut off my arm because you made me a promise?"

She smiled. "That's right. I cut off part to let the rest be free. Now you can hold me while you love me." She began removing her clothes.

"I don't love you." She ignored him. He said it again, louder.

"We'll have sex then before I feed you. It's the same thing, isn't it?"

"You'll never feed me," he said, without thinking, and she pointed to a container that lay beside her garments.

"That's for you, if you can love me."

His arm instantly became much less important. Kylene

laughed curtly, then went to fetch water from the river while he stared at the container.

"What did you bring?" he asked eagerly, when she had slaked his thirst.

"A surprise." Her eyes were bright and expectant. He sensed she harbored great excitement, which she was trying to conceal from him. "You have to love me first."

"Can't I eat—" His eye feasted on the container. "Please, dearest?"

"No. Me first and then you. It will always be that way." She lay down on him before he could answer, nude, with her legs over his head, already shaking inside herself as she wrapped her arms around his waist. "Really show me you love me now. That's it—stroke me with your arm. Like you wanted."

He was eager. Saliva already brimmed in his mouth and his tongue had never been so long and supple. She reached her first orgasm in minutes, screaming joyfully as she found release, then went to another and another.

Mercifully, she let him stop before a half of a day tenth had passed. Her eyes seemed glazed as she looked at him. She smiled fatuously.

"Can I eat, dearest?" He broke the mood deliberately. "I'll do even better for you after I eat."

"No you won't." She swallowed. "Yes, I'll feed you."

On hands and knees, she scrambled after the container of food. Fesch, watching and enjoying the sight of her, thought briefly of Timt ha'Dicovys and felt he had won an enormous triumph.

"I'll have to help you." Kylene took the lid off the container, and sat with his head on her leg. She raised a wooden spoon to his lips, showing him a mixture of cooked vegetables and slivers of meat. "Eat what you can."

It was not Algheran cooking. There was no broth, though a more fastidious eater would have detected a slight glaze on the food. The meat was firm but not stringy and still juicy; it was light-colored. He was pleased that she had cut it in small pieces which were easy to chew. Some of the vegetables were still crunchy and spices he did not recognize puckered his tongue. Despite that, he ate eagerly, swallowing the food almost as quickly as she brought the spoon to his mouth, until she told him to chew properly and waited with the spoon until he obeyed.

"This, too." Kylene broke the last piece of potato with her fingers, then mopped up white beads of congealed fat from the sides of the bowl and put them in his mouth. "All gone." She held the container for him to inspect.

"I'm still hungry." Feeling stronger than he had for days, he pushed against the ground with his shortened arm, wishing he could sit up.

"You had enough. Just lie there. Trust me."

Time passed. Fesch felt he could detect his stomach working on the food as he lay there, then that the food was swelling within him. He felt faint touches of nausea, which suddenly could not be denied.

"Deep breaths," Kylene told him. "You won't throw up. It was just a little food, your body takes time to get used to it, but you'll be all right."

With her help, he kept the food down, that time and in the brief attacks of nausea that followed. He had never imagined she could be so patient and so gentle, and he regretted the times he had been cruel to her.

Remembering his earlier promise, he offered to give her pleasure again. She refused, laughing at his term, but not the offer itself.

"Never go swimming or make love on a full stomach," she advised him. "I don't want you getting sick at the wrong moment."

"I won't."

"No." She stood and gathered the bowl and the spoon. "I'm going to leave now. Did you enjoy your meal?"

"Both meals, dearest." He managed a grin. "Can I have two more tomorrow, bigger ones?"

"I'll think about it. I only have so much meat. It has to last."

"I can live on vegetables and you, love." He grinned again, hoping.

"Any meal you get will have meat," she promised. "I'll think about it."

She did feed him the next "day" and the next, though the portions continued to be small. Both times, she explained that she did not have much meat to give him.

The sex always came first, to make Fesch understand his meals had to be earned. It lasted longer on both days, and she climaxed frequently, but the orgiastic response she had experienced on the day when she first fed him was missing. Sometimes he sensed she came to him from duty or from obligations he could not understand rather than from desire.

Was it his fault? Fesch wondered.

It wasn't, she told him. She sat beside him and hugged her legs with her head resting sideways on her knees, and despite the failure of the sex, Fesch felt accepted and comfortable at that moment.

"I can't pretend you're Tim," she told him simply. "Not all the time, that's all. Or Dieytl—I think about him, too. That was my biggest mistake, I think now. I should have let Dieytl seduce me—he did try so hard. Dieytl was very good at sex. I used to lie in bed and watch him through a woman's mind while he was with her and pretend it was Tim and me, or my father and me when I knew it didn't matter. Sometimes he'd know I was there and pretend the woman was me and let me see that . . . I laughed once and he started laughing and it took him forever to convince the woman it was all right."

His head shook with incomprehension, but she was not through.

"My father— He married again before he got sick the last time, and there was a new woman in the house for him to pay attention to and all the housework I'd done for him was just forgotten. I was jealous, I just didn't know, I went away to punish him, that was one reason. When I get lonely I think about the way it was when just the two of us were together and what I could have done just to keep us that way . . ."

She laughed brittlely. "Tim told me I was like that, once, that I was obsessed by my father, as if it were something dirty I was supposed to get over. I thought he was making it up, just to hurt my feelings, because I didn't understand anything about people then. I was so mad, I wanted to steal his time machine and go back and save my father from that woman and live forever on a desert island with him!"

She inhaled loudly, sniffing, and Fesch became afraid she would cry, but she hiccupped, then stopped. "He'd be just a man if I went back, wouldn't he? He'd be just like you, and I'd have to see everything petty and cruel in his mind, and I'd know when he looked at other women or was tired of me. It wouldn't be like I imagined at all . . . So you see, he was right, wasn't he. Tim. And I outgrew my father obsession just like he said I would.''

She sighed loudly. "So now I have you, and I know more about people than Tim does and I am going to use it.''

"What are you going to tell Timt about what you've done?'' He asked the question quickly, knowing it was his only device for bargaining with her.

"What would *you* tell him?'' she countered. "About what you did, not me.''

He had to remain silent.

"Tim won't hear about you,'' she said firmly. She rose and went to her clothing and got dressed to leave, while he watched. When she was done, she said, "There are doctors—Teep doctors—who can make you forget things. Maybe I'll go to one of them someday, and I'll forget you and ris Jynnich and anything else I don't want to think about.''

When sleep finally came, he was still wondering if that was possible.

CHAPTER SEVEN

"Let's get the show on the road. Move this thing!" Harper cried, slapping at a bay horse hitched to one of the supply wagons which was testing the snow on the roadbed with a dainty hoof. "A touch of whip, driver, or you'll wind up in the infantry!"

Down the line, he heard echoing bellows from Rahm Wolf-Twin and his crew of quartermasters, applying equal diligence but less effective threats to the same task. Farther on, in the pasture beyond the barn, artillerymen were repacking caissons and pouring lubricants on carriage wheels; an officer was checking an elevation crank.

Morning had come. An unenthusiastic sun had climbed onto the eastern hills and was gathering strength for a further rise. Its reddened face suggested this would not be a day for great exertion on its part.

In the streets before the houses, soldiers slurped their breakfasts. Campfires showed to the south as well, where Dighton ris Maanhaldur and his company had taken over the checkpoint by the trees.

No cavalrymen were visible. Harper interpreted that as a good omen.

An enterprising camp follower had liberated a bathtub and some stove coal from one of the vacant houses. Now she was washing clothing just outside of the bedroom the Hand of the Queen occupied. Half-dressed soldiers crowded around like acolytes at a sacrifice. Soap bubbles, steam, and smoke from her fire rose like a pillar of burning fat straight into the pale sky; the unheavenly odor remained closer to observers on the ground.

It wasn't that much different from boiling stew, Harper had noticed.

"Eh, governor," the teamster protested. "I'm doing my bit. It's the driver what's three carts back, he isn't here, no point going without him, you see. He's what's holding us all up."

"Jesus, Joseph, and Mary!" There was more than one driverless wagon and Harper was unwilling to be reasonable. "You move. We'll get someone for that!" He stuck fingers in his mouth, whistled.

One of Wolf-Twin's men trotted up the ramp to the roadbed. "Sir?"

"Tell the Ironwearer, for the driverless wagons to find camp followers who want to move up in the world as teamsters. I think he can get volunteers today. And immediate discharge for any driver not in his spot."

"Oh, governor!" the driver protested. "Take away a man's cart and livelihood, as he's packed himself!"

Harper turned back. "What difference in hell does that make?"

"And besides, we're all what you'd call intimate with these animals."

"Nonsense, they're geldings," Harper said firmly. "Now you get your wagon rolling before I finish what I'm saying, or you'll be down in the traces yourself, driver, and I'll have a whip on you while you're doing a duet with your favorite that—by the Gods, man, I'll see you going where no man has—"

The wagon moved.

"—gone before!" Harper finished. He pointed to the next wagon in the line. "Roll 'em, buster!"

But when the first three wagons were dispatched, the absent driver had not returned and his wagon still blocked the ramp. Harper swore, uselessly.

"They want to go through the buildings one more time," the quartermaster said apologetically, as if the explanation was needed. His eyes lingered regretfully on men stacking firewood inside the houses on the street below. "Seems if things are going to be wasted . . . It's only natural, Ironwearer."

Harper raised an eyebrow in response, then limited himself to a more useful rebuke. "You're here. Drive that cart up onto the road and park it. Do the same for any others that need drivers. And don't block the road."

"Ironwearer Wolf-Twin will be wanting me back, sir." The quartermaster looked enviously himself at the town's empty buildings.

"Ironwearer Wolf-Twin wants you to make me intimately happy. Do it!"

"Teeps can conceal their minds from each other," Wandisha said thoughtfully, "but not for this long."

Cherrid grunted mechanically, clued by her voice, but his thoughts were elsewhere. Even without his own dispatches, Samstyl ris Ellich, the garrison commander in Northfaring, should have heard from Teeps about the Shield Valley battles. The wounded from Timmial's fight should have passed through the city seven or eight days before this, and the officers taken captive should reach it tomorrow or the day after.

And soon, the wounded from his own battle. His hand brushed awkwardly at the blankets at his breast.

Northfaring had to know his needs. Reinforcements and stocks of ammunition from the armories *must* be headed south by now. Would they be enough for another battle? Would they come in time?

"There are—I have heard of, I mean—Normals who can hide their minds from Teeps," Wandisha said. "If they killed Lord Ellich—"

"Have you met one?" He tried to remember what she was talking about.

She hesitated. "I don't think so."

"Then why mention it?" He stopped to cough as Timmial had taught him, then resurrected his train of thought. *Mlart.*

Mlart should be . . . He struggled to make the calculation, then abandoned it. Detail was unimportant. Near West Bend the Strength-through-Loyalty Brigade had been closer to Northfaring than the Swordtroop was to the cities Mlart had captured.

That was the important thing. He had a defensible position and his reinforcements had been closer.

A race to pull the Algherans ahead of their supplies . . . One battle to bleed the Swordtroop and run down its ammunition . . . A second battle, with additional men and supplies, to wound Mlart's force more seriously and force his retreat . . . Constant attack while the Algherans fell back southward . . . To ris Cornoval and the remnants of his corps still waiting at Barlynnt's Tower . . . Relief of ris Clendannan, and another battle, if necessary . . .

Yes, it should work. The first part was done. The rest of the plan should still work, even with another man commanding the brigade.

Timmial. Timmial lan Haarper was in charge of the brigade now, he remembered. How amazing. How—

No, it was not pleasant to be replaced.

Temporarily, Grahan had stressed. He stressed that young lan Haarper himself stressed his tenure would be short-lived. He had tried to make it seem unimportant early that morning as he stowed unresisting pieces of Cherrid's anatomy into clothing. He had speculated about division commanders from ris Mockstyn's force as replacements for Timmial. He had assured Cherrid he would be well enough recovered to direct the final battles of the war.

Cherrid had too much sense to believe any of it. His fist tightened on the blankets.

Gods help us all if Timmial doesn't realize everything depends on him.

"Rallt," Wandisha said stolidly. "There's a problem, Lord Clendannan."

The farmboy who stopped the ambulance. What about him? Cherrid wondered.

"He's unhappy."

He smiled weakly. Surely, Wandisha had not interrupted him to recount Rallt's complaints.

"He wants to find the killers of the innkeeper and Lord Ellich. He's bothered that we haven't done more. It's why he stopped us, remember?"

Cherrid sighed. If the killers were gone, what could be done?

"Let him take his gun," the Teep suggested. "So he'll feel

prepared in case they meet someone. And . . . Lord Clendannan? Grahan wants him to bury—''

He snorted weakly, letting his thought provide volume his lungs could not. ''In this ground?'' It would take a cannon to dig a burial plot.

And ris Ellich's people wound want the body taken to Northfaring, he was sure. They had a family plot there. Burial would only make a mess of his yard and annoy Merryn ris Vandeign.

He smiled at the thought. It must have occurred to Grahan. ''No.''

''Should I tell them before they go?''

He sighed to show agreement and listened as Wandisha groped her way to the door and down the stairs. What depths he had fallen to, he reflected. Two days in the past, he had given orders to a brigade. Now, he had an army of one soldier, one driver, one camp follower, and one farmboy. And the farmboy's complaints were a calamity!

And another man had his brigade.

Cherrid seldom prayed. It was not proper to ask the Gods to do what men could perform. But judgment could be requested. Understanding. Wisdom.

That morning he prayed for Timmial lan Haarper.

It took half a day tenth to get the last of the supply wagons onto the road and moving toward Midpassage. The Guards Regiment marched next, followed by ris Daimgewln's Defiance-to-Insurrection Regiment, and then the dozen artillery guns that Harper had kept with the brigade. The militia regiment was assigned to the last place, and camp followers fitted into the column wherever they chose.

Harper had 1,836 able-bodied men when he left West Bend, 324 sick and wounded who might return to duty in the future.

He was not as sanguine as he pretended to be that morning. He had a small force to oppose a large force, and delay might serve his purposes as well as defeating Mlart's army. To him, it was a situation which screamed for guerrilla warfare.

Unfortunately, he did not have a guerrilla force. He did not have a convenient large force of regulars to smash the Algherans after guerrillas softened them up. And he had the wrong environment for irregular war.

Harper had never been convinced that guerrillas ''swim in

the sea of the people,'' as Mao Tse-tung had stated, but he did believe guerrillas needed a sea of some sort—a broad area of operations, inadequately policed, in which small groups of men could easily hide—and Loprit was not such a sea. Loprit, as Cherrid had several times lectured him, was a road.

Part of him yearned to hold the brigade aside until the Algherans passed and then strike their communications. It would be exciting. It would add something new to Fifth Era history.

The rest of him knew that would lose the war.

Behind him as he rode north, the road was strewn with paper, children's toys, and other mementos taken from West Bend and dumped as their weight outgrew their value by their original owners or soldiers.

The town burned.

"Up you go!" Grahan stood behind, as if to push.

Rallt, standing on the edge of the sidewalk with a live horse before him, was less eager. "I can walk, sir. I'd not be far behind thee."

"Not for long." Grahan stepped forward, to hold a stirrup with one hand and the back of Rallt's shirt with the other. "Come on, boy, you were brave enough saddling her. Put your foot in and step up."

He didn't want to ride any of Lord Clendannan's horses in any manner at all, but Rallt had problems establishing that. "What if—if a bad thing behaps, sir? My father—" He swallowed, unhappy with the admission. "Thee must know, be none in my family wealthy enough to—"

"You're not going to wind up in a hospital falling off a horse," Grahan said briskly. "It's part of learning. Happens all the time. If you fall, just get up and get back on. The horse will wait. Usually."

Rallt quailed inwardly. He hadn't thought about falling. Only his father would have found a counterargument. Rallt wound up on the horse, facing forward. He flexed his knees uncomfortably. The horse moved its rear feet to the side. He swallowed. It stepped toward the hitching post, then backed off. He clutched the reins till it seemed blood would pop from his fingers. It whinnied. He jerked convulsively. It lowered its head and kicked thoughtfully at a patch of snow. He braced himself against the saddle.

"Born rider," Grahan commented. He slipped Rallt's rifle into a leather holster at the side of the saddle where it was sure to bounce painfully on his knee. "All your basic comforts. You want to be a for-real cavalryman, son, they teach you how to shit while you're galloping. Well—" He swung onto his own mount. "Let's go off and look at ris Vandeign's place."

Lerlt's morning had begun badly and was getting worse with each moment.

Herrilmin had wakened him at what seemed first light, to say he was leaving. He would return with his time machine to take Gherst away.

"Only Gherst?" His eyes had moved involuntarily to the spot where the wounded Agent, gray and featureless in the morning sun, lay like a dead man in the gray straw.

Herrilmin demonstrated what he thought was patience. "Be reasonable. There's only space for one passenger. I'll come back for you, Lerlt. You won't think a minute has gone by." He smiled unconvincingly.

Lerlt kept his temper reined, seeing Gherst's eyes focused on him. The brown-haired Agent was lying without motion where he had been all night. He hadn't even known the man was awake. "How long?"

"Not very. Five minutes, or a day tenth. Something like that. Just be patient." Herrilmin kicked straw aside to reach a ventilation window. Lerlt watched without comprehension as he picked up something shapeless and fitted it onto his back. "Sun's up, Lerlt. I'll need all the daylight I can get."

He had taken all the food, Lerlt found when it was too late to protest, and the warmest of Timt ha'Dicovys's shirts.

By midmorning, Gherst was restless and thirsty. He breathed shallowly. When Lerlt brought him water from the office at the other side of the barn, he hiccupped before he was able to drink. After that, Lerlt would have thought him asleep but for his eyes, which followed him as he moved about the loft.

Herrilmin did not return.

An error, Lerlt finally decided. Herrilmin had mistaken the date. He would be late, a little late, but he would return. He just had to wait.

He waited. And waited.

Hunger restored his attention to practical matters. There must be food in the big house. Gherst must want something to eat as much as he did. He nestled the wounded man firmly in the straw and went to see.

He had reached the kitchen when he heard the front door open.

The gun, he suddenly remembered, was in the barn loft, useless, next to equally useless Gherst. He cursed silently and tiptoed to the closest door.

A stairwell waited. He sat there glumly, his back to the door and his ear to the crack, until he heard the intruders leave.

He missed the morning sun's warmth on his blankets, Cherrid admitted. He missed walking and riding—

"Rallt wouldn't miss riding." Wandisha, sitting beside him on the bed, to face the window she could not see. "He's feeling sore already."

He coughed. "That gentle old mare?"

"She doesn't know Rallt, I suspect, so she doesn't have the automatic reactions she does to you. No, I can't read a horse's mind, Lord Clendannan—"

"Cherrid." No one could empty a chamber pot and still think of a bedridden patient as Lord Anything.

"I can't see the horse's thoughts, but I can see what Grahan saw and how he took it. They're in the house now. In the room."

She clinched his fist tightly, and he could guess what she was seeing, and he shifted back on his pillows to raise himself and patted her back with his free hand. She slid over to shield herself against his body. He could sense that she was half crouching on the edge of the bed.

"He is not feeling anything now," he whispered. Even to him, his voice was barely audible. "It may have been very quick, Wandisha. Better than he would meet in battle." He hoped there were memories in his mind and Grahan's that she was not examining.

She swallowed. "I've—seen accidents before. And Rallt—"

"Our innkeeper." He was touched by a trace of guilt. Ris Ellich's death seemed the greater matter now, probably because his body was still available for view. The innkeeper was buried—somewhere, he'd have to ask Rallt—and it took an effort to remember that the cavalryman had been concerned with finding his killer.

The innkeeper. He remembered the theory Wandisha had extracted from the boy's mind. Ris Ellich's notion that four men had killed or witnessed the killing of the innkeeper, and one had returned to the body.

Over and over. And over and over again. He sighed.

What brought out this madness from time to time in men? Were the Teeps correct, with their accounts of demons greater than stupidity and stubbornness which laired in every person's mind?

Wandisha shifted her weight beside him. She let his hand go but still seemed restless.

"Dying happens to all of us," he said. "I tell myself, in five hundred years, no one will ever care how it happened."

In one year, actually. We do forget that quickly.

His stomach churned. For a moment, he remembered his wife's final illness, her rasping breath and shallow coughs, her gray-faced stillness on her bed, the flutters of heart and throat that showed she still clung to life . . .

In appearance, I must not be far distant from the same point.

Or was that only in appearance? Deliberately, he forced his mind back to his youth, when he was newly wedded. An outdoor reception, he and she in the sunlight, wearing the now quaint fashionable attire of the day; himself unbent and tall, conscious of his dignity as a commander of a regiment; his wife, chatting like a maiden to her friends whom she had left at marriage, no more than girls at that age but already learning to think of themselves as ladies of the Court in Loprit's brand-new kingdom . . .

Dalsyn ris Vandeign had been at that occasion, he remembered, red-faced and stout, dourly stumping the pavilion floor with his dark cane, sneering at the peacock finery and recently acquired manners of the aristocracy. The king and queen had certainly been present as well, but they were absent now from Cherrid's memory.

"I'm sorry." He realized suddenly he was not with his wife. His right forearm was on the lap of another woman and his left was massaging her back. Her hip was pressed against his stomach.

He brought his hands away immediately. His life had been better than that of most people, he understood, and he had no wish to remind others that they had received smaller portions of joy.

"Don't be. You were happy then." Wandisha's voice was small. "I didn't mind seeing it."

He smiled, unable to prevent the image of Wandisha as she

might have been at that long-ago reception, a waif in her simple dress, barefoot probably, blond hair stringy and uncut, staring wide-eyed at the richly dressed nobles and their food-laden tables. Would he have noticed her then, with his wife at his side?

In the vision, her sight was clear. It troubled him.

"I could see when I was small."

"Yes, I know." She had mentioned it to him. He was still troubled.

"I'm used to it." She put her hands on his again. "I have happy times of my own, Cherrid. Gentle times. And others. I make people happy and I share it with them. Is that so bad?"

He sighed, not wishing to argue, though his thoughts did.

"I stay alive and I try to be happy, Cherrid. That's all the purpose most people find in life."

"You'll never be an Ironwearer, Wandisha." His voice was grave.

"I wouldn't want to be." She squeezed his hand softly.

"Might as well get out of here," Grahan said. "Nothing more we can do, Rallt. Wishing won't bring him back." He looked around the reception room once more, shaking his head when it pointed at ris Ellich's corpse.

The boy gestured futilely. Walking away did not bring the dead back to life, either. *If Sugally and I had stayed with him . . .*

No one would have attacked a man with three guns to defend him, he was sure. But Lord Ellich had been alone, and almost defenseless.

And where was his gun now? On his horse's saddle, he realized uncomfortably. He and Grahan were waiting prey as much as ris Ellich had been. Yes, they should leave. He pivoted and stared blindly at the overturned table.

"Do we bury him?" he muttered.

"No." Grahan paused as if about to say more. "Maybe we'll want to come back and look at some other details."

Rallt touched the rim of the table, concentrating on the feel, wondering what force had tipped it over. It would be right to bury the cavalryman, he knew, and Sugally had warned him against the gesture. *These Lopritians . . . if you're the one who buried him, they'll decide you're the one to dig him up.*

A slave's practicality, but nonetheless sensible.

* * *

Grahan, to Rallt's surprise, did not return immediately to the inn. There was another house to visit, he explained.

Ten minutes later they were riding on a tree-lined street near the crest of a hill. Grahan turned aside at the front gate of a low wooden building with no resemblance to anything else Rallt had seen in Midpassage. No one had stopped them, no one had spoken to them.

"Anyone home?" Grahan called. It was the first thing he had said since passing the patron's barn. Without waiting for an answer, he dismounted and fastened his reins to a bush near the front door.

Rallt noticed suddenly that children watched from a nearby house; he guessed that women waited indoors, fearful of being noticed in a town abandoned by men.

Grahan paused on the doorstep with a knife in his hand, then pushed the door open with a foot. A bell tinkled tinnily.

Was it a house? The building was dark inside, the antechamber empty. Awkwardly, Rallt dismounted and hitched his horse beside Grahan's.

He joined the man in a large unfinished living room. Curtains had been pulled to one side along the interior walls, displaying the central garden beyond tall panes of glass. There were ashes in the fireplace but no flame. Paint-daubed canvas had been fastened here and there to the wooden walls. Dust showed on the few pieces of furniture. Through an open window, Rallt saw bushes, a neglected yard, a narrow blue-painted house, trees.

Grahan stared blindly at the wall decorations, unmoving as Rallt walked behind him.

"What be we looking for?"

"A woman that lives here." Grahan shook his head abruptly. "Wandisha says she's gone and shouldn't be. Look around sharp, Rallt."

The kitchen was empty. Scraps in the honey bucket gave off a rancid taint when he opened the lid to the refuse chute. Withered fruit and age-darkened meat were on racks in the wall cupboard. The grating beneath was dry, the ice that had sat there melted into water in the unemptied pan below.

Snow was scattered on the walkway in the central garden. He couldn't tell when someone had last tended to the plants or sat at the concrete table.

He moved on to a bedroom, finding the bed unmade, the wardrobe empty. Dust was on the floors. He did not know if that showed neglect or bad housecleaning. Had there been dust in the house where ris Ellich died?

Another bedroom, empty, the bed much rumpled.

The next room held machinery of some kind: racks with weights on chains and pulleys. It was also empty of people.

A room by the kitchen had windows on two sides and its own skylight. Shelves held trays and balances over Rallt's head and powder-filled jars and small containers below. Upside down, a wooden frame held canvas on a sloping workbench; knife slashes had torn the paint-daubed cloth to tatters. Other canvases of different sizes were propped against a wall or on the floor; they had been kicked into tangled scrap. When he tried to straighten them, the images meant nothing to him.

"Who lived here?" he called out.

"An *Ironwearer*," Grahan called back.

A curtain swung, attracting Rallt's eye, and he went to the window. It was ajar, slipped a handbreadth to the right. Snow had entered at some point; there were purplish stains on the wall where the red brocade had been dampened. The curtain was dry now. He closed the window and, after staring at the now gloomy world outside, let the curtain swing back into place.

Beyond the room were two more doors. One was for a storage area, and held steps leading into the basement. The other, ripped from its hinges, opened onto a bedroom.

Grahan was there, rummaging through a wardrobe. After touring the small cellar, Rallt joined him.

A bed was in the center of the room. There were long brown stains on the mattress and on the floor on the opposite side of the bed. A window had been broken from the outside and he saw bloodstains on the shattered glass.

"Maybe she got away."

Grahan's voice. Rallt did not know he had been watching him as he stared at the window. There was a wide belt in the old man's hands. Rhythmically, he clenched his fingers in a fist about the buckle and released them.

Rallt almost wept. "I'm sorry," he said thickly.

"Maybe she got away." The man sounded doubtful, as if trying to convince himself. "We haven't found her body, so maybe she got away."

"Grahan? Thee does not believe that."

The old man swallowed. "Rallt, the man who lived here was Ironwearer Ian Haarper, who took over the brigade from Ironwearer ris Clendannan. It's his wife that's missing. If she's dead, like your innkeeper, what kind of job do you think he'll do? And am I to tell Cherrid, in his state, what may have happened to his friend's wife?"

Rallt shook his head. "We must look outside first and then thee can believe what thee wishes."

Wordlessly, the Lopritian followed him.

Outside, Rallt walked around the left of the house, Grahan to the right. Lights were on in some of the neighboring houses. Rallt had an uneasy feeling that he was being watched, but he saw no one when he turned about.

The broken window was at arm's reach when he reached the corner of the building. Grahan had turned on a light and he could see the top of a wardrobe, and part of the open doorframe. Improbably, it seemed very normal, and he half expected to see a girl come through the door and make herself ready for bed.

An aristocrat's wife. He had no idea of what she had looked like, and imagination created a slimmer, more elegant version of Wandisha lin Zolduhal.

"Footprints," Grahan said when he reached the spot. "Before the snow, but they still show." He wiggled a finger at shallow depressions below the window. Rallt shook his head as seemed expected.

"Don't think we'll see anything on the grass." Despite his words, Grahan moved across the yard. Rallt trailed after.

It was not a big yard. It ended at the side of the hill, in a steep drop. Trees and unkempt brush were beyond the edge. Rallt saw many rocks and a narrow trail animals might have left, then another steep hillside.

"Would thee have me look down there?" he asked.

"No, the canyon only goes out of town. There's no reason to go down there." Grahan nodded unhappily. "I looked in the shed and she's not there. She's dead, boy. Let's get back and tell Wandisha."

CHAPTER EIGHT

About noon, Pitar lan Styllin arrived at Midpassage. It felt to him that the air had a pre-storm quality to it though clouds were few in the sky. South of the town, as he crossed over the bridge, women stood in the doorway of a yellow barn. Behind him, his spare horse breathed heavily, as if feeling relief, though it had moved no faster than the artillery caissons. Turbid water churned under the bridge; friezes of ice had extended the riverbanks, and waterwheels turned sluggishly in the distance.

At the gate on the town side of the bridge, he dismounted to raise the pole that blocked the road. It would be a very long time before travelers paid a crossing toll again, and something other than peasant thriftiness made him enjoy the thought.

A line of cannons and artillery wagons was already crossing the river. He pulled his horses aside and waited for an officer to appear.

In seconds, the first gun had reached him and was rolling past, slowing rather than stopping.

"Where to, sir?" the driver asked, and Pitar suddenly recognized his difficulties. Where should the guns be placed?

He wasn't a gunner. Was he supposed to have opinions about such things?

He had to run to stay even with the carriage. "Go past the orchard, stop at the turnoff on the right. You'll get more orders later."

There was an officer on horseback when he got back to the gate, a long-faced brunette with a thin nose and doleful expression. Pitar saluted uncertainly, unable to read the man's rank badges under a winter coat.

"Well, the old burg looks all right," the officer said, dismounting. Stiffly, he moved behind Pitar's horses and stepped to the side of the road.

Pitar watched against a backdrop of moving wagons. "I thought at times I'd never see it again."

"We all felt that." The artillery officer kicked at dirt, and knelt to touch the long grass on the roadside. "Nice enough town." His eyes rose to the tall hill on the north side of Midpassage, then turned to the ridge that bounded Merryn ris Vandeign's farm. "Good-sized."

"Bigger than I remembered," Pitar said, moving his eyes across the landscape, seeing houses and fields spread from Shieldboss Mountain to the hills on his right. Everything seemed strangely alien, as if he were only visiting a town he had once known. All the land he saw was in use, but there was a disquieting abandoned look to it, which was due to more than snow. The town had a shabby aspect he had never noticed until now and knew he would never forget.

He had a wife and a baby daughter and a grandfather here. They would never consent to leaving Midpassage.

He got on his horse slowly, sore, his legs weak after the long ride. "Not much I'd like to see changed," he said.

"Plenty I'd change," the other man said, his face blank as he stared at the town, and Pitar felt troubled again. He drew a finger through the air, pointing at pastures on hills to the south. "There's a good road between those fields, isn't there?"

"It's dirt," Pitar said. He had worked those fields as a boy, before coming to the foundry. His own son would work in them someday, for some descendent of Merryn ris Vandeign. "Wide enough for two wagons in spots. There's turnabouts, I mean."

"We can put some gravel in," the artillery officer said. His head turned further. "The roads dead-end, I suppose. Any other paths up there?"

"For what?" He tried to smile. Lan Haarper's orders had been for him to answer any questions the artillerymen had. His thoughts had been of sleeping places and meals and fodder for the horses.

"The cannon. The elevation gives us range for the big guns, and we can move the small ones behind the troops into the lower pasture for support. Then . . ." The artillery officer's voice trailed off.

"You won't fight here, will you?" Pitar swallowed sickly. During the ride to Midpassage, the artillery column had stopped at none of the level places that Pitar would have identified as possible battle sites. He had allowed himself to think that none would be found, that there would be no battle, no return to the Strength-through-Loyalty Brigade.

"We've got roads. A foundry. A town. Hills and river to restrict movement." The officer nodded slowly, then shook his head. "Valuable territory, young man. And time to get ready. I'm sure the Ironwearer had all this in mind. There's no finer place to make a stand this side of Northfaring."

"But it's home for many of us." He said it woodenly.

"Too valuable to give up without a fight." The artillery man sighed. "It'll be a right awful mess, you know. Maybe you can get the women and kids out of town."

Was that what lan Haarper expected of him? Pitar swallowed, feeling sadness wash over him even as he evaluated the task. "I suppose."

Swarms of men had collided on the great road. From the south had come what seemed a regiment, with more guns than Lerlt had seen in one place before this. From the north, a smaller group of men accompanying a double line of low, enclosed wagons. The groups mixed at the edge of the orchard. Soldiers wandered in all directions. Lerlt heard officers screaming.

On this road, just a short distance away, were two more men. Lerlt pushed himself into the ground behind the shrubbery by the signpost as they rode past, and strained to hear their words. There had been hoofprints, and more easily detected droppings, in the snow outside the door of the big farmhouse when he left. Were these the same horses, the same intruders?

They had left a trail across the yard and past the barn where Gherst lay, then over a small field to the street which held Timt ha'Dicovys's house.

Had they gone there? What had they been looking for? What had they looked at in the farmhouse? What else were they seeking?

More soldiers. Like the man Herrilmin had killed. The muskets on their saddles were all too plain.

What were all these soldiers doing here? When would they leave?

When would Herrilmin return? How much longer were he and Gherst to hide?

"So that's the situation," Grahan said after the supper dishes had been taken away. "It's a queer town we've leaving to you, lan Styllin. The innkeeper was killed four days ago, ris Ellich yesterday. We don't know of any others, yet."

"Kylene," Wandisha said tonelessly.

Grahan nodded slightly and turned back to the fourth person at the table, a young man in what Rallt could now identify as a militia uniform. "Lan Haarper's wife is not in his house, Pitar."

"Not anywhere where I can reach." Wandisha tapped her bent fingers on the tabletop and looked intently at both lan Styllin and the old soldier. "And that's important. She may be dead also, Pitar."

Three killings, Rallt thought. One seemed hard enough to believe, even for people like his companions who had seen much more of life than he. He touched his upper arm and chest gently. Grahan had taken him behind the inn to teach him to shoot his rifle; he had inflicted great and lasting damage on three wooden boxes and—it seemed now—his right shoulder.

Grahan had been able to hit hand-size targets at the end of the dock, shooting from the right and the left. Rallt, firing at the same targets, had managed only to hit the dock. It colored all his reactions to the older man.

"She could have gone to F'a Loprit, like ris Vandeign's wife." Grahan had said that before.

Wandisha tapped the table again. "I'd know if she had. Someone in town would remember. Her husband would know it."

"Wouldn't be the first man to—" Grahan chuckled weakly.

Lan Styllin frowned. Grahan looked back sheepishly.

"Don't be foolish, Grahan," Wandisha said sharply. "Lord Clendannan expects more from you than bad jokes. Besides, she was here a few days ago."

"I didn't say it! Look, Wandisha, this is off the point. It's Cherrid we're concerned about, not these dead people we can't do anything for. Pitar says there's apt to be a battle here in another day. I say we move Cherrid while we can. Pitar knows now about these two—maybe three, if you want—violent deaths, and he can tend to them."

"What is 'tending'?" lan Styllin asked. "I was sent here to give advice to the artillery chief. Lan Haarper said nothing about killings."

Grahan snapped his fingers. "The killers aren't here now. Don't worry about it; bury the bodies and the Teeps can straighten things out after the war."

"You're sure of that?" The militiaman looked at the Teep.

"I'm not sure of that," Wandisha told him, her face troubled. "I've said no one in town whose mind I can read knows who did the killings. It's a different thing."

"It's close enough for me." Grahan stood. "I'll see you people in the morning. Rallt, dig that driver out of the cellars and tell him to plan for an early start."

He left. Rallt found himself staring at Wandisha and the militiaman.

"Can thee perform an injury and not remember?" he asked the Teep. He was reluctant to leave.

"That happens." Wandisha nodded thoughtfully and he had the impression she was seeking remarks to agree with.

She smiled at him quickly. "Most commonly, someone will not remain aware of something he or she did; that's forgetting in a way, but it's still remembered somewhere in his mind and a Teep can reach that spot."

"Or an accident can erase memories, I've heard." Lan Styllin turned his eyes to the room where ris Clendannan lay sleeping. "Can you look for hidden remembrances like that? How long would it take, for an entire town?"

"I already did it." Wandisha looked the same way. "Several times. It takes—if you know what you are looking for . . . if all the people in this town stood in front of you, Pitar, how long would it take you to pick out people with bright green hair?"

Grahan interrupted from the balcony. "I'd just count the dead soldiers. Good night, everyone." The door to his room closed behind him.

Lan Styllin tried to smile. "It'd be like that, that obvious? If you haven't caught anyone then, it doesn't seem a serious worry, Wandisha."

"There's a machine." Wandisha bit her lip. "It must be something in the Plates. It lets a Normal keep his mind from being seen."

She turned to Rallt and gestured with her hands. "It looks like metal mesh, like a wide sieve, which fits over your hair."

"Leather band around it, goes just over the ears." Lan Styllin also turned toward the boy and showed him a measurement with thumb and forefinger. "Rallt, ever see anything like it in Innings?"

"No. Thee knows—" He stopped, embarrassed.

"He thought Teeps were a myth," Wandisha confided.

"Things would be simpler," Pitar said. "Well, Wandisha, so that's what it was for. He told me it was custom in his homeland, to bring luck."

Rallt stared back and forth. What was going on?

"Does it really work?" Pitar asked next.

"He could be standing by you and I wouldn't notice him," the woman said. "And I didn't tell Grahan and—" She looked up again at the room where Ironwearer ris Clendannan slept. "It didn't seem right, somehow. It's supposed to be secret."

"Maybe Kylene has one on, and that's why you can't find her."

"No." Wandisha flashed a smile at him.

"Demon-loving foreigners," lan Styllin muttered. "Sorry, Rallt!"

"It be all right, I know foreigners be strange," the boy said carefully.

Lan Styllin started.

Wandisha put her hand on Rallt's forearm. "Timmial lan Haarper, the Ironwearer who commands the Strength-through-Loyalty Brigade now, wears one of these 'Teepblinds.' Pitar noticed it once when it was raining and his hair was matted down."

"No," lan Styllin said quickly, seeing the direction of the

boy's thoughts from his expression. "He's an Ironwearer, I'd swear to that, and he couldn't have done these killings."

Rallt blinked.

"Foreigner, though," Ian Styllin said again. "He could have enemies. He used to travel a lot and he wasn't an Ironwearer until—"

"He found a reason to be an Ironwearer one night," Wandisha explained. "Or an excuse—I never thought to find out. That was just before the war started, Rallt."

She turned away from the boy. "But he was an Ironwearer before that, Pitar. He had the insignia with him all along."

"I've heard." Lan Styllin scratched his head. "Well, what do I do? I don't know where to start on this, Wandisha. Rallt, what was your officer trying to do?"

"Look in houses. He'd been sure—" Rallt looked forlornly at Wandisha. "He said—a Teep would come to help us look."

"And three of you looked for four men?" Lan Styllin shook his head unhappily. "I'd want a dozen soldiers and a Teep, at least, to be sure of making a capture. Wandisha, do you think the killers are here?"

"I do. They aren't in Northfaring and—"

"That's enough. Rallt?"

"They be here." He had never doubted it.

Lan Styllin sighed. "I think I can shake loose men to look for them, but I still need a Teep. Wandisha, it will have to be you."

"I know." She seemed angry.

"You'll have to stay here."

"*I know!* I'll do it somehow. Don't badger me, Pitar. Just—" She stared blindly at both men. "Go away now. Leave me alone!"

It was dusk before soldiers ceased to wander about the hillside, and it was cold. Only then did Lerlt feel safe to return to the barn, and each step of the way he feared a shout would arise from one of the sentries. When he reached the loft, he felt close to collapse.

Gherst was whimpering in the gloom. The wounded man had lifted an arm as Lerlt came to the top of the ladder and waved it feebly. Hungry, Lerlt supposed, ignoring the gesture. He was hungry, too. Back recesses of the barn held bins of unappetizing meal, but he had passed that up for the fare he expected to find in the big farmhouse, and then the cellar of the farmhouse had held only a few moldy potatoes. He had eaten a fist-size portion of one raw while waiting for the Lopritian intruders to leave, but nothing else.

He, at least, had the sense not to complain.

And it was Gherst who had told the others not to eat the grain at the barn in the last town. Why should he have any of what Lerlt had found here?

It stank in the barn. It smelled like an overturned outhouse. Lerlt had noticed a taint in the air from the moment he entered, and in the loft the rancid odor of diarrhea was plain, a reek which the cold somehow made worse. It was Gherst's dirtiness—the man was lying in the same spot, in much the same position he had had in the morning, so it was clear he had done nothing to help himself. Herrilmin had left a pan for sanitary matters at the edge of the loft and only sheer laziness would have kept Gherst from moving to it.

Lerlt wanted to kick him, but Gherst was crying already.

"Keep quiet," he muttered. He looked to make sure the musket and its ammunition were still where he had left them, and went to look through the ventilation windows. The smallness of the tiny loft was less oppressive with his back to it. The smell was less there.

Someone needed to stay alert. Deep in the enemy's country, with his soldiers close to the barn, surprises were possible at any moment. Nothing would be more frustrating than to be recaptured by the Lopritians, this close to success.

He saw no one, but it was almost dark enough to hide figures. He heard no one, which was more reassuring—in Lerlt's experience, soldiers talked incessantly. No lights were on in the big farmhouse, but there were torches farther away, on the ridge that ran parallel to the great road. What was happening in the town, however, could not be seen from this side of the barn. It was characteristic of Herrilmin, he had noticed, to pick a refuge where threats could be overlooked.

As was his greed. Herrilmin was probably getting himself fat dining right now on the food the Agents had taken together from Timt ha'Dicovys's house. Stupid unthinking bastard!

He and Gherst were *suffering*. And it was Herrilmin's fault, for not returning as quickly as he had promised. It was infuriating to starve while surrounded by food. It seemed impossible, but Lerlt knew they were in the midst of hundreds of Lopritian soldiers laughing around their campfires at this very moment, and that on all sides the people of this town were eating themselves fat at their supper tables.

Gherst groaned.

"Quiet!" Lerlt snapped. This was as much Gherst's fault as Herrilmin's, after all. If Gherst were healthy, the barn would not stink. They would not be hungry. They would not be cold. They would not be hiding from the Lopritians and picking straw from their hair.

If Gherst were healthy, Herrilmin would not have gone away.

Why was he taking so long to return? Did Herrilmin have a reason for not coming back yet?

The brigade marched until darkness, then rested on low hills about eight thousand man-heights south of Midpassage. The position, like much else in warfare, was a compromise. The men were capable, in Harper's view, of continuing another watch, which would have brought them into the town that night. That could have given them more rest on the next day; that could have put more of them into decent shelter.

All that was desirable; but the confusion attendant on a night-time deployment was more likely to keep everyone up until dawn. In addition, he was sure the brigade's position would be reported to Mlart, and it was likely the Algherans' advance would conform to his own; the longer he took to reach the town, the better.

He went to bed that night uneasily, three-quarters certain gun-fire would waken him before dawn.

Herrilmin ha'Hujsuon was impeded by the snow and the need to stay out of sight from the great road, but he managed to travel about twenty thousand man-heights that day. He steered by the sun and the first stars and rested for the night only when the moon was high.

The dying flames of West Bend showed upon the southern horizon as he wrapped a blanket about himself. They were campfires in his imagination; they warned him to stay away from the road for another day.

He was weary but the fatigue would evaporate in sleep, he

knew. In the past, training for competition, he had run ten thousand man-heights a day in mud holding a sword before him. This was only more of the same, preparation for a greater fight.

In his sleep, his fingers moved restlessly across the scar that reached across his abdomen.

When Cherrid woke, Wandisha was there to wash his face and tend to him. Grimacing at the taste, he set a bitter pill at the back of his tongue and washed it down with water and leftover stew.

The room was cool. After she moved the tray to the side of the room, the woman helped him tug a blanket to his chin, and checked the fit of the window. Downstairs, in the tavern room, he heard a man pacing irregularly. The ambulance driver, restless with inactivity, Cherrid thought, or one of the refugees who had come into the town. He felt pity for a man whose mind could not supply his own occupation.

Overhead a child cried. Its mother tried to quiet it.

"Where are Grahan and Rallt now?" he asked.

"Sleeping." Wandisha laughed uncertainly. "It's almost fifth watch, Lord Clendannan. Nighttime."

"Oh." Wryly, he wondered how he would fill the hours ahead.

"Let me get . . ." Wandisha withdrew her hand, "There's a messenger from Lord Mockstyn downstairs. Let me bring him up."

Going to the brigade, he recognized. To young Ian Haarper. Not to an old man too tired to leave a bed and too awake to sleep in it.

But he was silent as Wandisha left the room. He heard her feet on the stairwell, then slower, fainter sounds as she crossed the tavern floor. His hand stretched toward the wall, not finding it or the window that had framed the sun during the morning. How he longed to see again, to look through the window, to watch Wandisha and Grahan and the faceless Rallt.

And he longed to know what was in that dispatch. It should have gone straight on to the brigade, but Wandisha had done what he wanted in holding back the messenger, he admitted.

Surely curiosity in an old man was a minor sin, a sin becoming even less significant as age and curiosity mounted. In an infinitely old man . . .

Did that explain the interest the immortal Gods took in human affairs? Boundless curiosity, with infinite power to indulge that inquisitiveness? The Gods never seemed happier than when muddling human affairs, it seemed. Was it really the encouragement of human virtue which motivated them? Or simple curiosity—boredom, actually?

He smiled. That was a notion he would enjoy spreading out for Merryn ris Vandeign to view. Or Terrault ris Andervyll, in more peaceful times, when the Hand was able to relax and laugh again.

Good laughers, most of the Andervylls. It kept them sane, he supposed. It took a sense of the ridiculous to govern men. One of the ris Vandeign weaknesses—he could not imagine either Gertynne or Merryn enjoying a laugh. Or Ironwearer Wolf-Twin.

Young Timmial seemed to have some capacity for humor, which Cherrid hoped would increase. *My dying bequest for the worthy young Ironwearer Timmial lan Haarper . . . A dependable guffaw, a box full of chortles, a score of chuckles suitable for all occasions, and a selection of smiles . . .*

Footsteps entered his room.

"Ironwearer?" A voice at once young, deep, concerned. A good voice for a messenger and a good messenger if sound reflected quality. Ris Mockstyn would not use fools to carry dispatches.

From breaths and minute creakings of the floor, he could place the messenger, halfway between his bed and the doorway, with Wandisha behind and to his left as Cherrid viewed the room. As he would view the room with his bandages removed. He felt impatience.

"I would like to read your dispatches."

"Uhhh." It was not protest. The sound demonstrated uncertainty and awe for an Ironwearer's rank. Some other characteristic, like but not exactly volume, showed Cherrid the messenger had turned his head toward Wandisha.

Strange how hearing, touch, some knowledge of humanity came to substitute for missing sight, which had once seemed all important, as if experience were a flood to pour into awareness from one large conduit or many smaller ones while still maintaining the same volume and intensity.

So this was how Wandisha—blind people, generally—kept

sane while imprisoned for eternity in blindness's dark cells. Was it for eternity? Or did the Gods, in their mercy or curiosity, give back sight to the blinded in the afterlife? Sight and the skill to interpret what was seen?

He snapped his fingers casually. "It is my name on the dispatch envelope, so I think I am entitled to read them, although you must carry them next to Ironwearer Ian Haarper."

"It's dark, sir," the messenger said.

Foolish of him not to guess that. "Fix the lights," he said gruffly.

A moment passed before the messenger realized the instruction was for him, a longer time before Cherrid heard the faint hissing which showed the electric arc was established. He moved back on his elbows to make his insignia visible.

Diffident fingers put an oilskin pouch in his hands. He traced the seals with a fingertip, then handed it back, unable to figure the parcel's top from its bottom.

"You read it to me," he ordered. "Ris Mockstyn's summary, not his department reports and not the personal mail." He was conscious of Wandisha moving close to him. He moved to make space for her on the bed, but she remained standing.

"Sir?" He was certain he heard the messenger swallow. "I can't read."

Cherrid coughed to show annoyance. "Wandisha, you can see it while he looks at it? You read it. Or—"

"Slowly." It was an answer for him, not the puzzled messenger.

I'll listen as if you read like a scholar, he assured her, amused in part by the blind woman's vanity, in part by his own willingness to facilitate the mild deception.

Papers rustled as Wandisha put herself beside the messenger. Cherrid kept his face impassive as he waited.

"Well?" It seemed almost a minute had passed.

"Lord Clendannan?" Wandisha's voice was strained. "I can't do it. There aren't ideographs on the paper. It just looks like scribbles to him."

Demons! He hit the mattress with his fist. "Is it scribbling?"

She hesitated and he listened blindly to the messenger's feet scraping at the floor. "I don't think so. But without training, it's what he sees. I think any Teep would see this the way I do. I'm sorry."

And doubtless there was some explanation a Teep could make. "Grahan." He wasn't sure himself what he was suggesting.

"If Grahan read it, I could read it. I'm sure. I've done it before."

He put a hand up to stop her. "Grahan is sleeping."

"I could wake him up." She seemed eager.

"Grahan is an old man. Let him sleep. Here."

Intention came almost with the action, and Wandisha was not able to stop him. She gasped as he slipped his thumbs under his eye bandages and flipped them up briskly, leaving the bandage balanced across his eyebrows.

He blinked, expecting glare, expecting blurriness. "Give it to me."

Nothing happened. The room was still dark even with the bandage off.

Was he blinking? He caught himself with his hands upraised, remembering all Grahan's warnings against rubbing his eyes. "Wandisha—"

It was troubling that she made him ask this aloud. "Are my eyelids stuck shut, by gum or anything . . . Is there trouble with my eyelids?"

"They're raised, Cherrid."

"Grahan?" He felt lost and betrayed.

Why? Grahan! He could only croak.

"We didn't know, Cherrid. The doctors said . . . In the explosion . . . Had to give time . . . We all hoped . . ."

Hope. He wanted to scream. He wanted to stand and shake the window frame until it let in light again.

"Leave now," Wandisha was saying briskly. "Don't wake anyone up. Take your messages to Ironwearer Ian Haarper, you'll meet him by daylight."

She hesitated. "Don't tell him about this."

Behind her, by the door, a man was stammering. He had forgotten the messenger. Cherrid, gasping for tears which did not come, heard the voices from far away, from behind a barrier of darkness.

"Cherrid?" Wandisha's hands fell to his wrists. They were rough. He hated himself for noticing that, knowing she was trying to comfort him.

The bed creaked as she rested her knees on it. He sensed her body hovering over his, protecting him.

"In five hundred years, no one will care." He was bitter as he said it.

This is not five hundred years. Wandisha gave him time to think that.

"I know what you're feeling," she said gently.

"You're a Teep." He tried to smile, suddenly jealous of her gifts.

Beyond Wandisha's breath was the louder hiss of the useless light. He made a fist. She pried it open with a thumb.

"Being a Teep doesn't always help." She was crouched over him.

"But you can go from blindness to seeing." He swallowed, awkward in this confinement by blankets and woman. "Instantaneously."

Her weight shifted till she was lying down beside him, still holding his wrists. Her hands tightened for a moment. "You saw how well that worked."

Even in his near-panic, he smiled at her slip.

She shifted again and he felt her body, on the other side of the blankets, slipping along his. Pleasantly. Comfortably. Something touched his chin. Again. Then his cheek, below the bandage.

Lips. Her breath was warm. Her tongue licked at his own lips and he tried to move his hands but she would not release them.

She kissed his neck. Then his ear. Her hair brushed against his mouth. "The first half day tenth is the worst."

It sounded as if she were telling him a secret. Her voice was low and controlled. It was her hands that trembled, even when he stopped resisting. "Let me help, Cherrid. We can forget it that long, can't we?"

Asking permission, he realized, even when his mind must be open to her. He tried to temporize. "I am old."

"Not that old." He heard a murmur of cloth and felt her weight settle onto him. Laces were besides his fingers. Solid flesh. The scent of her body. Below his blanket, without sight to distract him, he sensed the truth of her words. The woman wriggled atop him and he responded.

"I want to do this, Cherrid. I want to be with you. Make me happy," she whispered.

He tried to sound like a brave man. "Get the lights out, please. There are things I do better in the dark."

* * *

Fesch thought carefully about what he would do, between the dawn-gloomy hour of his wakening in the white mist and the time of Kylene's arrival. He greeted her with the words of affection she wanted, steadying himself for the moment all the while as she raised him to drink and during the period when she opened her blue dress and lay across his face.

He was thorough and methodical with her today. He thrust his tongue into her as deeply as possible and sucked and chewed at her until his lungs groaned for air and his chin was wet with her secretions.

He felt elation as he registered each of her orgasms. He wanted her very pleased today.

At last she let him stop. She lay beside him then, her breasts still shuddering as they rested against his side. She seemed preoccupied. Her fingers still moved, stroking her groin and clitoris, and Fesch felt a vague sense of disappointment and regret.

But he began, anyhow, as he had resolved: "I was born in late summer in City Year 868, dearest. Hujsuon has three settlements just beyond the hills south of F'a Alghera; two are farms and one deals in light manufacturing. Mostly in support of other Hujsuon settlements, though we made hand tools for general sale. My father's name was . . ."

Kylene continued to play with herself, while his voice droned on.

He faltered while describing his earliest memory—his sadness when he heard his mother explain she would never bear a brother or sister to keep him company. His own voice sounded monotonous to him; his memories now seemed trite, the events themselves undeserving of the emotion they had once evoked.

Kylene's fingers reached to his face. Her thumb, sticky and scented, pressed lightly against his lips as she turned his head. Tenderly, he brought the stub of his arm against her back and stroked at her, while he tried to read her expression.

She spat in his face.

She pulled away from him abruptly and stood, then shook off the dress and reached for her other clothing. Dumbfounded, he realized her face showed contempt. He could feel her spittle slipping along his cheek.

"You can babble your baby stories to the birds," she said

coldly. "They'll like it as much as I do. Maybe they can feed you, too."

He swallowed as the threat sank in. "Kylene, dearest. Don't go, please. I promise. I won't—bore you—dear. Any more."

She pulled up her skirt and fastened her blouse in silence, while Fesch listened to his breath and heart. She took up the bowl and turned away.

"I love you. I'd do anything for you." His voice was small and frightened as she walked back to her time machine. "Please come back, Kylene!"

She did not turn.

The silvery levcraft rose into the air and vanished. Fesch was alone with his shortened arm and unimportant memories.

He tried, finally, to touch his genitals and convince himself there was still reason to exist, but his bandaged elbow would not reach that far. The memories and invented stories which might have built an erection for him did not come.

Empty, he listened to the unthinking forest and the unending night.

"Cherrid, Grahan wants to leave later in the morning," Wandisha said, tonelessly, sometime later, lying at his side.

"Oh?" She held his hand in hers. Her hair brushed his ear. It was still nighttime, he was sure. It was easier to bear darkness in the night.

"Lan Haarper is coming back to Midpassage for his next battle."

He held his breath, dismayed. That was not his plan.

"He has his reasons, Cherrid."

"I want to know them." Letters, an appeal to the Hand, a quick trip to give advice to the boy . . . Which would be best?

She waited till he was through planning his protest.

"Grahan says you're leaving in the morning. Between the killings and the battle, it's too risky for you to stay."

"I'll decide what I do!"

She seemed not to hear him. "Pitar lan Styllin is here now. Lan Haarper put him in charge of the town. He's willing to take over the hunt for the killers, if someone can tell him what to do first."

"What is he thinking of doing?" It was a grumble.

"Go from house to house, searching for people, I suppose. Until he catches someone. That was ris Ellich's idea."

"Someone a Teep cannot detect." He coughed. "Not possible."

She waited for him to spit. "Perhaps. Rallt is going to stay."

"Young idiot." What would it take to search for someone invisible?

Almost invisible. It was a solvable problem. Very simple really.

"You are going to stay also." He knew suddenly.

"I owe a debt to the Haarpers." Her body was stiff beside him.

A farmboy, a young woman, an ill-tempered young man. Searching for something which might not even exist in a town engulfed by war.

"Very Lopritian." He coughed but could not work up material for a satisfying spit.

A minute passed.

He stared at darkness and all the years of darkness to come.

"I assume you told Grahan—" He coughed again. "—it is easier to drive livestock from town to town than old soldiers."

"I—" She turned beside him.

"Maybe he forgot. He is an old man, you know. Old men forget. Be a little gentle with him."

CHAPTER NINE

By direction, the morning command conference was sparsely attended.

Harper anticipated arguments.

"What's the latest news, Gertynne?" he asked, when everyone had settled on boxes on the wagon. His eyes moved past the executive officer to Quillyn, who had taken over as driver for the duration of the meeting. Harper trusted the little man to be discreet but his eyes watched Quillyn's hands and the rears of the horses carefully, to make sure other disasters did not occur.

Handling a team of horses was not simple, he had discovered. He had wrecked several wagons himself in his early days in Midpassage before developing the knack. The tuition had been expensive, and in retrospect what he had learned best, next to remounting broken wheels, were the reasons for Henry Ford's success.

"Ris Mockstyn and the tra'Ruijac have clashed," Gertynne ris Vandeign said, reading from a dispatch. "Lightly—the Algherans pulled back before the situation developed seriously." He put the paper back into its pouch and looked at the faces before him. "No mention of reinforcements for us."

Terrens ris Daimgewln grimaced. "Are we ever going to get anything from that quarter?"

"I begin to doubt it." Gertynne took another sheet from the pouch. "We are getting supplies for the artillery now, and that's building up in Midpassage. I don't have numbers here, but we ought to be able to fire a sovereign's salute by evening time."

Harper couldn't resist. "For Molminda or Mlart?"

Gertynne smiled politely. "It all depends on the aim of the guns, Ironwearer. Lord Ellich used some initiative up there, I gather. We're getting stocks from Northfaring; Northfaring will draw down from F'a Loprit to refill its arsenals."

He held up a paper for general view. "This is the next matter, gentlemen. I've been asked to show this to you. I ask you to not discuss it with anyone, because it's unofficial, and it may not lead to anything."

Rahmmend Wolf-Twin saw the paper first. He blinked and handed it to Dalsyn lan Plenytk. His lips began to move in and out silently. His fingers tapped between his knees at the crate he rode.

"When did you send this?" Dalsyn asked. He turned and handed the paper to ris Daimgewln.

"Two days ago," Harper said. "After that last message from ris Mockstyn. It was the Hand's idea, to be honest. That's why it's his letter. I never heard of the Bedrock-of-Valor Regiment before that."

"No reason you should have." Ris Daimgewln passed the message to Perrid ris Salynnt. "The Bedrock is little more than a military joke, Ironwearer. It has four battalions, two of local people, two made up of foreigners—they have to serve if they live in Northfaring, it's sort of a tax on them—and it sees two days of duty a year. There's an annual parade through the city—that's where Terrault remembers them from, I suspect. They spend one day relearning how to march and one day on the parade, and that's about it."

"That seems to be what's left," Harper said. "Guards regiments don't grow on trees, Terrens."

Ris Daimgewln frowned. "This regiment, Ironwearer, is just what I first imagined your Steadfast-to-Victory to be. Badly trained militia."

"Hmmm," Harper said. "Still better than nothing. Perrid?"

"If we get them—"

"If's definitely the word. The Hand requested them, you'll notice, but apparently he doesn't have the power to order the garrison commander to release them."

"There's nothing left to defend Northfaring if the Bedrock-of-Valor goes," ris Salynnt explained. "I don't know if Iron-wearer ris Clendannan discussed war strategy much with you, Ironwearer, but almost every soldier Loprit could spare was sent to the North East Army."

"Can't be strong everywhere," Harper agreed. "But you were about to say something else?"

"It was a question. If we get the Bedrock-of-Valor in time to use it, will you use it as a unit, or break it up as reinforcements?"

"I'll take a vote," Harper said. "Assuming they get here in time to use, which of you wants reinforcements?"

Four hands went up. Five, counting Gertynne, who wouldn't receive any.

"That was quick," Harper commented, unsurprised to see the decision he had already made ratified so easily. "Well, if Mlart gives us time, we'll break up the Bedrock and spread the gravel around. A battalion for each of you, and one more for reserve, I suppose. Depending on where we meet up next with Mlart. That all right?"

He nodded at a chorus of yeses. "I'll make an exception for any parts of the Bedrock good enough to stand alone. Are there any?"

"Artillery, maybe," ris Daimgewln said. "They get a bit more practice. They show off when the queen comes to North-faring and some holidays."

This all had a familiar ring. "Fancy uniforms?" Harper asked.

Gertynne looked at him quizzically. "Yes, as a matter of fact."

The redhead smiled. "We'll see if they shoot just as pretty in khaki."

That brought the additional smiles he had looked for. "Gentlemen, I'd like to continue this, but I promised the surgeons and the cavalry some time this morning. Let's resume again this afternoon. Okay? Thank you."

* * *

It took Grahan and Rallt a quarter of a watch to check the houses on one street. Pitar lan Styllin had gone through the veterinary quarters and the sheds around Merryn ris Vandeign's house and was on the way to the equipment shelter in the outlying fields. They had found no one but legitimate residents of the town; there was no sign of the killers.

"It takes time," Cherrid said. He could sense frustration in Wandisha's voice as she repeated the information to him. "Two or three days to clear a town of this size. Longer if they actually find anything."

A cannon boomed. *The artillery would be firing at intervals the rest of the afternoon, he had been told. Range and registration.* Timmial lan Haarper had issued written requirements; Cherrid had never heard of a general who had dared give such elaborate pre-battle orders to his gunners.

"I thought they would find something obvious." He heard her pacing.

"Sit down." He patted the bed. "Sit down, Wandisha. Be patient." He coughed for a moment. "Believe me. These are better quarters to run a search from than you usually get. Usually—" He coughed again.

Usually, the officers in charge of a manhunt established a command post by kicking some family out of its squalid hut, and soldiers tore down buildings during the search. Done properly, it made peasants eager to volunteer information.

She would see that without words. He spat into a pan beside the bed and settled back, then sighed. *Why soldiers don't take wives on campaigns.* "Most of the time, nothing happens."

A normal search of a town this size would take two companies of infantry and last one to two watches. Cherrid had twenty-two people, counting himself and Wandisha. But a normal search was done without telepaths.

He coughed again and held up a hand. A soldier snapped to attention in the doorway—he could tell what that sound was without eyes.

"Sir?"

"A glass—two glasses of water. No, make that beer, please."

"Sir." Footsteps receded.

He let himself down on his pillows again, satisfied with himself.

Feeling possessive. Predatory.

"Sit down, Wandisha. I'll scratch your back."

"Well—" She stopped pacing and sat beside him. Air currents, minute sounds, and other senses told him she faced the window and that her hands were clasped. "How do you pass the time doing this normally?"

"Drink a lot. Gossip about other officers." He coughed. "Other talk." *Talk about women.*

She chuckled. "That would be interesting."

He grimaced wryly. "Better if I keep my mouth shut."

"You've got that beer to drink."

"I mean—" He sighed. *I would have thought it impossible for telepaths to develop a sense of humor.*

"Normals can be very funny, Cherrid. It doesn't hurt anyone, you know, when a poor man laughs at the rich. Let us enjoy our laughter, dear."

I would not stop anyone from laughing, would I? He sighed and patted her back awkwardly.

She stretched for his hand. "Grahan and Rallt are on the next street. What should I look for?"

He hadn't really expected to shake Dalsyn. The militia officer found Harper a short time later, riding companionably at the rear of the column beside the cavalry commander.

"Morning." Dalsyn nodded politely at the cavalryman, who echoed the greeting but seemed puzzled by it. That was more conversation than he had had with Harper.

The Ironwearer nodded in return. "Problem, Ian Plenytk?"

"Not as big as yours," Dalsyn said bluntly. "You ended that meeting kind of quick, didn't you, Timmial? I think we were expecting some discussion of your future plans."

I don't want to discuss my plans. No one would like them. Harper smiled wryly. "Why aren't you all talking about the good news I gave you?"

"Two thousand untrained replacements? Maybe? In ten days? We don't have ten days! What is bad news to you, Timmial?"

Harper snorted. "Getting beat." *You don't know what Bad is, Dalsyn.* "I'm not going to get beat."

"Well, you can get beat, and if you don't tell your regiment commanders what you expect, you can count on it. Are we going to fight in Midpassage?"

Harper hesitated, then reflected that the guns on the hillside would answer that question shortly enough. "We will," he admitted. He leaned forward to pat his horse's neck. "Good old boy! It depended on getting that ammunition, but it sounds as if we can go another round with the Algies. I'll be sending orders out on deployment before we get to Midpassage."

Dalsyn raised an eyebrow. "Without the Bedrock-of-Valor?"

The redhead shrugged. "I think getting them is a longshot."

Dalsyn stared a long moment. "That's not the impression you gave."

"I'm sorry if you feel I misled you, Dalsyn." That was very true, if carefully worded. Not for the first time, Harper wished he could explain his intent to his officers, or at least to Dalsyn lan Plenytk. Not for the first time, he decided he could not. "Very sorry."

Dalsyn was still staring. "You said we'd get those reinforcements before we fought again."

Harper sighed. "No, I didn't, Dalsyn. I asked what I should do if those reinforcements came in time. I didn't promise anything."

"But—" The surveyor shook his head sadly. "Do you really think you're going to fight Mlart at Midpassage? You can't defend the town with a force this size, Timmial. I thought you and ris Clendannan showed that before the campaign started."

We showed Cherrid couldn't defend the town. Harper exhaled slowly, then forced a grin. "Let's hope Mlart hasn't heard about it."

"What was wrong with where we were? We had a good position, Timmial. It wasn't great, but we stopped Mlart there."

"Mlart stopped Mlart, not us." Harper spat and watched it splash. "That place was a death trap, Dalsyn. We lost a thousand men on that ridge."

"Mlart got hurt, too."

"Not three thousand men's worth, and that's all that would have justified staying there. *Jesus Christ*, Dalsyn, those Algherans walked all over us! They attacked twice, and both times they went into us like a knife through milk. Oh, we pushed them back, but that was luck. *We never really held that ridge.* If we had stuck around there, Mlart would have had our asses for breakfast and you know it."

The surveyor grunted. "The Algies didn't get through the Steadfast."

I didn't notice them trying. "You did a good job with it, Dalsyn."

"I'll give the credit to your trenches."

Harper shrugged. "Not a new idea. How did your men do on the looting, Dalsyn? Everybody feel they stole their fair share from the West Bend folk?"

Dalsyn stared at the ground. "Uhhh. I didn't look, lan Haarper. I didn't do it myself, if that's what you're wondering."

"That's not what I asked."

Lan Plenytk hesitated again. "I'm surprised you allowed it, frankly. I don't think the old Ironwearer would have told the men they could do that."

Harper nodded curtly. "I'm sure he wouldn't have. And the men would have looted anyhow. Any other complaints?"

"Yeah," the surveyor said. "I don't think he would have burned that town. I've heard you say the Algies would have kept it for themselves otherwise, but it was too small for any real garrison. I'm sorry, Timmial, but since you took over the brigade, I think the only people you've really harmed were Lopritians."

Harper was also sure Cherrid wouldn't have burned West Bend, but his face was impassive. "We'll never know, will we?"

"We can ask him if we meet him again. Is he still alive?"

"I hope so." Harper looked at lan Plenytk until the surveyor's eyes dropped. "I'm not Ironwearer ris Clendannan, Dalsyn. I never claimed I'd do things just as he did and I don't claim to be better. But I'll tell you, everything I've done is something I thought was necessary."

"Maybe," Dalsyn admitted.

Harper grimaced. "Just curious, Dalsyn. You think the men in your regiment know what to expect now if we have to retreat to Northfaring?"

Lan Plenytk rode away without speaking.

A day passed for Fesch without Kylene, and part of another. When she came this time, she fed him, quietly, almost sullenly. She rebuffed his conversational sallies.

Her demands for lovemaking were perfunctory. She no longer put on the blue dress when she squatted over him or lay across his body. She was nude when she appeared and nude when she left.

Several days passed this way.

She seemed unhappy, he finally remarked.

"I don't know what I'm going to do," she said, then sighed.
"No, I know what to do, but I don't know what it will do to me."

Another day passed.

"I should just leave you," she said.

"Walk off and leave me to starve?" He smiled, trying to tease
her.

"Yes."

She stirred herself finally and rested on top of him, her hands
clinching at his knees. "Give me your best, big boy."

It sounded as if she were trying to cheer herself and failing.

He was not surprised when he woke the next time to find she
had removed his remaining forearm.

Lerlt saw the soldiers.

More soldiers, as if the town were not already aswarm with
them, like fleas on the coat of a dead dog.

The arriving column made a diagonal line across the venti
lation window, stretching from the bridge into town on the right
to some point in the far south on the left. No matter where Lerlt
stood, he could see no end to it.

He cursed and stepped over Gherst on his way to the ladder,
and stared at what could be seen from beside the doorway of
the barn.

Soldiers. And guns. Soldiers with sticks, prying cannons into
position, shooting them, moving them again. Soldiers beside
horses, drawing planks from the lumberyard across the ground
to the riverbanks. Soldiers sitting on fences dripping oil into the
jaws of their muskets. Soldiers on wagons, practically on the
scrapestone of the barn, ferrying pointed shells to the guns.

And civilians, bright in going-to-town finery, cheerful and
laughing, ahead of the soldiers on the great road and mixed with
them in the orchard and milling around the entrances of the
buildings that faced the road.

It was enough to drive a lesser man insane.

The potato he had eaten the day before was heavy in his gut.
He thought he could feel his stomach churning from hunger,
and he grimaced, knowing he could not search for food with
that mob of observers.

Nighttime. It would only be safe to move about at nighttime.

Pensively, he climbed back up to the loft and settled himself
in a corner where he could ignore Gherst's little squeaks and

moans. He did not mind the wait, he realized. It gave him time for thought.

What must he do to make Herrilmin come back? Where was Fesch?

The house search continued into the afternoon, but Rallt was not part of it. Instead, after lunch a preoccupied Wandisha came down from the old Ironwearer's room and sent him and Grahan to the bridge on the edge of town.

Soldiers were already crossing over it. Rallt could not evaluate their condition, but they seemed in good spirits, although rather tired. Their clothing was dirty and ragged. Most of them seemed hungry and they were only walking, without any attempt to maintain parade-ground order. Women and old men and a few children were perched on boxes in some of the wagons.

It took a few minutes for him to realize these were the same soldiers he had seen days before in bright uniforms far to the south. It seemed like an army from another country.

Grahan kept a grip on his forearm as if expecting Rallt to rush into the middle of the traffic, but he had no inclination to do so. Curiosity made him stare at the soldiers and their weapons; few soldiers seemed to notice him.

Grahan nudged him once. "Salute, boy," he muttered and Rallt awkwardly copied him by placing a hand over his heart as a wagon carrying a weary-looking older man and two women rolled by.

"We're looking for a big man with red hair," Grahan said next. Wandisha had said that also. To Rallt, most of the soldiers qualified as big men, and many of them had red or sandy hair, but none that he noticed satisfied the old man until the tail of the column had reached the ramshackle fence at the end of the bridge. "That's our boy," Grahan said.

By then, soldiers and camp followers filled the road from the bridge to the inn. Everyone still seemed to be in motion, but he noticed finally the column was not moving further. Soldiers already in the town were leaving their work to mix with the newcomers. He saw a child leaping from one of the wagons into the arms of a man wearing a smith's apron.

The wagon containing the man Grahan had pointed to came to a stop nearby and Rallt got his first look at Ironwearer Timmial lan Haarper. Lan Haarper was a big man, as he had been told, thick-shouldered and thick-chested. He wore a tan uniform

and a leather jacket; Rallt saw dirt-crusted boots at the ends of
his legs. His face was broad but seemed gaunt. His lips were
tightly pressed together when he was not speaking. When he
moved, his motions were abrupt and hard-looking, as if every
gesture were part of a fight. His voice was low-pitched, flat, and
loud, but unemotional.

A gun boomed and the Ironwearer looked around, then nodded to himself.

"Take this to ris Daimgewln," he ordered, holding out a
sheet of paper. One of the men riding beside the wagon reached
for it and galloped forward without a word. "Find me the artillery chief," he called out, and another man rode away. "Tell
Ironwearer Wolf-Twin I'm due a report—he knows which one."

Rallt wondered if he had done anything but give commands
in that fashion all his life.

An ugly little man in the back of the wagon leaned forward
and touched the redhead's arm. Rallt could not hear what was
said but the big man laughed briefly; for the first time he saw
the Ironwearer smile.

Then Ian Haarper noticed Grahan. Rallt saw surprise pass
over his face; then he jumped down from the wagon and came
over. Grahan saluted again, but Rallt did not. He had taken a
dislike to the big man.

The Ironwearer crooked his arm and half slapped at his chest
in response to Grahan. "What the devil are you doing here?"
he asked. "I thought you'd be in Northfaring by now, Grahan."

"Bad news," the old soldier said.

"Cherrid?" The Ironwearer frowned, and Rallt noticed he had
a face that had been creased by many frowns. Looking upward,
he saw sprinkles of gray in the Ironwearer's red-brown hair and
eyebrows. There were wrinkles at the corners of his eyes. A jagged
scar was in front of one ear; it crossed over the hairline. His hands
were large and raw-knuckled; the palms were callused.

He was a full head taller than Grahan, taller even than ris
Ellich had been, and his expression was cold. Rallt, without
thought, stepped backward to put himself behind the old soldier.

"Cherrid's as right as can be expected," Grahan said. "Wandisha's been good for him." He colored faintly. "Various ways.
But his eyes haven't improved and he's holed up in the inn and
refuses to go on."

"That is bad news," the Ironwearer said. "This is no place for a sick man. He can travel, I take it."

"Yes."

"Then go back and tell him I've ordered you to leave. Mlart tra'Nornst is apt to be here by morning, Grahan, so don't waste time."

Grahan nodded slowly. "He won't go. He's a nobleman of Loprit, lan Haarper, and the only person he has to take orders from against his will is the queen. Cherrid can be very stubborn. There have been some killings here that need to be looked into, and he's determined to do it."

"Killings, eh?" The Ironwearer raised a thick eyebrow. "Not brawls. Hmm. Stubborn. Hmm." He looked at Rallt and blinked. "So you found this young miscreant? Cherrid sent him to me for judgment?"

Rallt took another sideways step behind his human shield. The big man chuckled. "Teasing you, kid. You wouldn't have that rifle on your back if anyone had worries about you."

His head had risen as he laughed. The gesture lifted his Ironwearer insignia above his jacket collar and Rallt, seeing the tiny crossed swords, felt reassured.

"I seen the bodies, sir," he explained.

"Bodies, huh?" The Ironwearer looked at him quizzically. "You call Ironwearer ris Clendannan 'sir,' young man. I'll settle for 'Tim' or 'you there.' So what's the story, Grahan?"

"We have two dead bodies," Grahan said carefully. "All within the last several days. One is the innkeeper, one is a young cavalry officer. Your wife is missing."

The Ironwearer stared blankly at him.

"Wandisha thinks that's significant, Timmial. She thinks lin Haarper may be another victim."

"Kylene?" the Ironwearer said in a small voice. "Who? How? Who would hurt Kylene?" He seemed to have trouble breathing. For the first time, Rallt managed to feel sorry for him.

"We don't know, Timmial. Wandisha told me to tell you that the Teeps swear they've found no one from West Bend to F'a Loprit who knows anything about any of the killings. She said that would make sense to you."

"Partially," the big man said after a moment. He blinked slowly, not moving, and Rallt feared he would faint. "I need to take a look. Will you tell Wandisha I'll talk to her later?"

"Yes, but I have to talk to Merryn ris Vandeign first. One of the bodies is in his house." Grahan indicated Rallt with a shoulder. "The boy here knows as much about all this as anyone else. Why don't you take him to answer questions."

"All right." The Ironwearer suddenly seemed awake again. "Aides! I have an errand! Bring my horse over!"

The Ironwearer's horse, like the Ironwearer, was oversize and red-colored, but more docile-seeming than its owner, possibly because carrying the weight of two flattened its spirits.

Rallt would have been content to walk, but the Ironwearer insisted on his riding behind him, on the skirt of a lan Haarper-size saddle. Rallt had to hold to the hard leather seat with both hands to avoid damage, and all the way to lan Haarper's house a part of his mind wondered if the horse would actually permit him to dismount without a kick.

Lan Haarper asked for his account of the killings, then listened without comment as they rode. Rallt, at his back, could not tell if he showed any reaction at all to the recital. When he was done, they had reached the Ironwearer's strangely flat house.

The redhead grunted, then held out his arm. "Grab that while you slide off," he ordered. Rallt, obeying, wondered if he too had expected the horse to kick. He waited while the Ironwearer swung himself off the animal and tied the reins to a nearby bush.

What the Ironwearer said when they entered had no meaning to Rallt, but he could guess it was a curse despite its lack of emotional tone. Cursing seemed justified. He had forgotten just how devastated the building's interior had been.

He left Rallt to go to the front room. A minute passed and Rallt heard scraping sounds. Then the Ironwearer returned, after carrying the dismounted door to a corner. He had a rifle of his own over his shoulder then, a long gun with a short tube mounted over the rear of the blue-tinted barrel.

"Were the other places torn up like this?" he asked Rallt. "Or did I get special treatment?"

The boy hesitated, remembering the topsy-turvy furniture in the patron's house, then decided that was damage caused by surprise or accident.

"Thee's not been treated as the others," he agreed.

"Interesting," lan Haarper said tonelessly. He left the living room through a doorway that led into the central court and went beyond that to a bedroom. Small pages with bright colors on them lay on the floor. The Ironwearer touched them with a foot and cursed again, briefly.

In the room that held the blood-soaked mattress, he was even quieter. What he said at last was only, "Someone will be sorry for this." Rallt had heard his father discuss the weather with more animation.

"We don't know who." He spread his hands uselessly, to show he wanted to assist but was helpless.

"Yes." The Ironwearer sighed, and knelt to pick something off the floor. It was the broad belt with the ornate buckle that Grahan had played with the day before, Rallt noticed. He wondered if it were some kind of omen.

"I want you to stay here, Rallt. Just for a few minutes. I'll be back." The Ironwearer left, taking the belt with him.

True to his word, he returned in just a few minutes, but the belt was no longer with him. He seemed preoccupied.

"Did thee find her?" Rallt asked. He could not decipher the man's mood.

"No." Timmial lan Haarper hesitated for a moment. "She may have gotten away, or been taken away."

"Grahan said that, too."

"Oh?" The man seemed startled.

"He thought she might go to F'a Loprit and that would mean Wandisha couldn't find her."

"Not F'a Loprit, I'm afraid." He smiled wispily, without hiding his concern. "A much further place than that, if she's really gone."

"What's thee to do?" He tried to imagine how his father would search for him if he were lost.

"I'll get her back."

Rallt remembered how his father had told him to stay in Mid-passage. Those words had had the same certainty.

"Can you make it back to Cherrid and Wandisha by yourself? I'd like to think for a while."

"Yes." It was the only thing he could give the man.

At the front, lan Haarper turned and reentered his house without looking back. As Rallt walked away and for a long time after, he remembered the sound of the closing door.

CHAPTER TEN

P itar lan Styllin was arguing with his wife.

"Pack what's important," he told her again, "the things Ronnida needs and clothes and—"

"But the dishes? The furniture? We can't lose all that, Pitar!" She was a dark-haired woman, dark-complexioned, buxom. Carrying the baby had left her with extra weight, most of which remained, comforting to Pitar, who felt instinctively that mothers should be stout.

"We've got to," he said stolidly. "Put what you can in boxes outside the house, Zitta, and maybe some of it will survive."

Was he to hear the same questions and make the same responses at every home on this side of the river?

"You're lucky, really, dear. You've got Gramps to help. Most places, the women'll have to do it all alone."

"You won't help?" Her face was stricken. And accusing, through the expression of woe. Years had taught him to read her moods.

"I can't, dear. I have to stay with the soldiers." He raised a hand, as if to acknowledge the sketchiness of the excuse. "We're going to take the implements from the barns and move livestock to Lord Vandeign's place.''

''And burn them.'' It was as though he had admitted impiety.

''There's no choice, dear. We can't give them up to the Algherans.''

I have orders to obey. He could not use that alibi. Ironwearer Ian Haarper had explained his reasoning and Pitar had agreed with him.

''You can—'' She sniffed, holding back tears, and sank into a chair at the table, her elbows resting on it, her hands cupped over her eyes. About to weep, or thinking. She used the same posture for both.

''You can put soldiers in the houses. The Algherans wouldn't suspect, and you could shoot them in the back. Did you think of that?''

She raised her face triumphantly, and he smiled gently, remembering the girl he had wooed so many years ago. ''Wouldn't work, love. They will search houses, just as routine.''

At West Bend, he remembered, Lopritian soldiers had wrecked the interiors of many homes, even before they knew they would be set afire, from thoughtlessness or simple malice. How could the Algherans, with even less cause to respect property, be any different?

Zitta had never seen an occupied town. To her, he suspected, soldiers seemed no more than unwanted guests.

That was the difference between them, he understood suddenly. He had seen a battle and she had not. Two battles. It seemed impossible that he had ever been foolish young Pitar Styllin, a foreman in Merryn ris Vandeign's foundry, proud in the authority he held over a dozen men, with no more ambition than to add one or two others to his crew.

It was embarrassing to watch the man he had been in his memory. Had he ever seemed more respectable than a drink-befuddled peasant to Lord Vandeign?

It did not matter. He knew, suddenly, he would not return to the foundry when the war was over. He could not be that man again.

The regular army would take officers from the militia, Dalsyn Ian Plenytk had mentioned once. Particularly after a war, with vacancies opened by casualties. Dalsyn was older than Pitar; he had seen it happen before, after other wars, and was not interested.

Was he? Pitar was not ready to answer that question—his wife, he was sure, would not be willing yet to hear it posed.

There would be something, he decided, without knowing what. Some way to support his family and maintain his dignity at the same time. He grimaced, thinking of Wandisha, with her made-up "lin Zolduhal." His little Ronnida's last name would be genuine. Somehow.

Was this the difference between peasant and gentry? he wondered. Not the giving of commands and knowing they would be obeyed, as peasants thought, but the exact opposite, a knowledge of uncertainty with surrendering to it?

And was the distinction between gentry and nobility even more of the same, with greater doubt and fear to face and hide simultaneously from the lower classes?

An image of Cherrid ris Clendannan rose in his mind, wounded, bandaged. How many battles had the old Ironwearer gone through, earning his titles?

And Ironwearer lan Haarper, who might become ris Haarper. His house was ruined on the inside, Pitar had heard. His wife was missing. Dead, according to Wandisha.

Involuntarily, Pitar's eyes turned to the portrait on the mantel, showing a wide-armed infant in a baby's smock, bowlegged with a red ball under one foot. That was Kylene lin Haarper's work, a gift, at a time when Pitar had known her husband only as a name and a face. She had sought them out, he remembered, had insisted that Zitta and the baby come driving up that hill road just like gentry to visit her . . . The portrait had been painted in lan Haarper's house. The background showed his indoor garden.

Dead. What payments to fortune lan Haarper had made!

"I understand you want to destroy our house," Zitta said. "The house our child was born in. The house I was born in."

"I don't want to destroy the house, dear. We're doing this to keep the Algherans from using it." He controlled himself. He wanted to shout.

Civilians must make sacrifices in war, he wanted to tell her. Soldiers died in battle and a house, in comparison, was a very small sacrifice. Houses could always be replaced.

"We've an example to set, dear," he said heavily. "Find

someone to live with across the river and move over tonight. Believe me, nothing really matters now except you and the baby.''

''But our home, Pitar!''

He remembered Kylene laughing as his daughter danced with toddler's steps before her. He remembered Timmial Ian Haarper at the end of the afternoon command conference, staring blankly at the river, the corner of his mouth twitching over and over.

''Nothing else matters,'' he repeated.

When it was dark, Lerlt felt it was safe to go in search of food.

Lights were on in the buildings below the barn and behind it in the big farmhouse. A party was going on there, he was sure, light-headed, almost intoxicated, with hunger. He would go in with his gun, dance with the hostess, trade jests with the wittiest of the guests, shoot someone for a finale . . .

He would enjoy himself, while stodgy Gherst lay in his own smelly wastes, croaking to himself, his guts gurgling like faulty pipes as he rolled back and forth on the vomit- and urine-tainted straw.

But in the final consideration, he craved food more than social gaiety. He went away from the farmhouse, across the field of clover, humming snatches of songs, his musket bouncing on his shoulder.

Toward Timt ha'Dicovys's house.

Herrilmin would meet him there, he was certain. Nothing made greater sense. Herrilmin had been unwilling to land his time machine near the barn with all the soldiers around, and was surely waiting at this alternate spot to take him back to the Project.

The long wait had simply been a misunderstanding. He and Herrilmin would laugh about it together.

But Herrilmin's time machine was not at Timt ha'Dicovys's house. When Lerlt crept across the yard and peeked through the windows, it was not Herrilmin he saw in the light of the living-room fire.

Harper had gone to an afternoon conference in the orchard with his officers, listened without hearing to their comments, given orders, and left at dusk with instructions that he was not to be disturbed.

When Lerlt saw him, he was staring blindly at one of Kylene's paintings. He had his knees crossed and the bullet struck the top of his left thigh a few inches above the kneecap. The impact knocked him sideways.

He had enough wit to continue the turn, half falling, half pulling himself over the arm of the couch so that he ended up on the floor, mostly out of sight of the window.

Mostly. His head and arms reached beyond the cover of the couch. Few times in his life had ever been as unpleasant as those long moments sprawled on the floor, pretending to be dead, as blood pumped from his leg and he waited for the unseen gunman to shoot at him again.

The hurt was surprisingly little. His leg felt as if a baseball player had clobbered it with a bat, but the blow had registered as impact rather than pain. There was a noticeable ache, but not the consciousness-shredding agony he would have expected. That would change at some point, he was sure. He had to act while it was still possible to move without suffering.

He had known it was a gunshot wound the moment he was hit.

He peeked finally, seeing only a broken window before the nighttime sky. The gunman had gone.

He must act as if the gunman had gone, he knew. The alternative was to bleed to death. His vision was already edged with black. Blood had already darkened his trousers from the hip to below the knee.

Gritting his teeth from the effort required, he pulled a knife from his shirt and cut at the couch fabric to get a strip of cloth, which he wrapped above the wound, then tightened by using the knife as a twisting stick. He was sweating when he was done with that. He was too weak to sit up.

He panted like a dog, counting to fifty. With his arms and his one good leg, he pulled and pushed himself across the floor to the door. He groped for the handle, missed it, groped again and got it open, then pulled himself to where he could reach his horse's reins.

The horse was patient. It was tolerant. Harper breathed a sigh that was a prayer of thanks, then crawled under it to the right side.

For a horse, the wrong side.

He counted to fifty again, putting weight on a stirrup.

The hardest part was mounting the horse. Awkwardly, he pulled himself up on pieces of the saddle till one hand grasped the pommel and the other the back of the seat. Then, already grimacing with anticipation, he brought up his right foot and put it in the stirrup and pushed down with all his might before his left leg collapsed.

For a moment, he saw nothing but sparks and stars. He felt broken bone stabbing at the muscle of his thigh, making the damage worse.

Then he was rising. Tears filled his eyes. Blinded, he pitched down upon the saddle, started to overbalance, caught himself by stretching out his stirruped foot. He shook the tears from his eyes, paused for breath again.

Then he lifted his wounded leg with both hands and brought it over the saddle horn. It was not possible to do it quickly. Ugly little sounds crept through his clinched teeth despite his will. Finally, his eyes brimming with tears again, he admitted he would not criticize any of his soldiers who showed pain in similar circumstances.

He smiled, or thought he smiled, at the realization. It was the smile, rather than the little noises that shaped his mouth as his ankle slipped over the horse's mane.

It seemed a mistake for long seconds. Then he was able to wedge his left foot into its stirrup. By arching the foot, he was able to keep weight from hanging on the wounded thigh.

Absentmindedly, he tried to prod the horse with his left knee, winced, then did the job with his right knee and a tug on the reins. "Get me home, Old Paint," he muttered.

The horse did its job, helped by its natural tendency to stick to a road. Once Harper turned it at the gate, hedges and trees kept it moving in the right direction. He needed to turn it only one more time, where the dirt road came down to the paved Fourth Era highway. More by instinct than thought, barely understanding why the animal halted at the intersection, he turned it to the left again and rode the short distance to the hospital tents.

He kept his eyes closed. He never knew how long it took.

One of the tents had a lantern lit before it. He got the horse to stop by riding it up to the lantern. "I need help," he croaked.

No one came out. His voice was not loud enough.

He slumped forward and pulled his feet back from the stirrups. He tried to dismount, lost his balance, and fell headfirst into the ground.

The horse, distressed by a sudden obstacle under its feet, whinnied. That brought out a pair of surgeons.

What they shouted, he did not hear.

Orderlies accidentally twisted his leg as they moved him onto the plank table they had set up beside the tents. The pain brought him awake. His eyes opened enough to see cloudy forms maneuvering above his head.

"What's going on?" he tried to ask. It came out slurred.

Something was wrong. Something more than weakness. He was dimly conscious of people moving around him, of people lying in tents. Bad smells. Pitch bubbling over a flame. Dizziness. His throat was raw.

His mouth tasted of alcohol. His coordination was awry.

Drunk. They had force-fed him liquor.

His pants had been removed.

For an operation. He could guess which. He struggled to sit up.

"No," he mumbled. "No no no." He waved his arms to push the surgeons and their axes away. "No no. Pull it out."

He tried to make the words distinct, to seem too sober to operate.

Who would command the brigade if an amputation disabled him?

What could Kylene return to if another commander lost the town?

"Pull it out, please." To demonstrate, he plucked at the bandage that had been fitted to his wound. "Pull out bullet, not cut."

One of the blurs moved closer. "Hold him down."

"No!" he shouted. "You can't. I forbid it!"

The blur dropped down, and became a face. He forced his eyes to open wide, tried to stop them from blinking. "Can't be evacuated," he tried to explain. "I have to command."

God only knew how clearly that came out. He blinked again and shook his head angrily. "Take out the bullet. Let it drain."

The surgeon's voice came through as a blur also. "Broken

. . . tell where bullet embedded . . . bone chips and lacera . . . through the leg, Ironwearer. Not worthy . . . stew meat . . . Operate.''

"Pull me up," he argued, and threw his hands out.

Mercifully, they were caught. He was pulled upright, farther away from the operation the surgeon wanted. He closed his eyes for a moment, concentrating on the sensation, controlling his dizziness, feeling relieved now that he was erect again, not knowing how badly he was weaving backward and forward on the operating table.

Orderlies moved to his sides, ready to catch him when he fell. He caught the table's edges with his hands to brace himself.

"Pull out the chips," he ordered. "Get out the bullet. Pull the leg straight. Splint it. Don't cut it off."

Whispers. He said it again, nodding with each phrase.

The Project's surgeons could fix his leg properly at some point, as long as he kept the leg, he remembered. It was another reason to argue.

He was getting more sober, he realized. He heard more of the surgeon's words this time. The ones that mattered were "pain" and "time."

"Do it!" Tears came to him again in his intensity. "You've got the time tonight, Doctor. A couple of you can do it. Don't cut my leg off!"

He closed his eyes and felt himself spinning.

Time passed. He listened to his own breath. To the surgeon's breath.

He gripped the table more tightly, lessening the nausea. "Be sure and tell my orderly. I've got to be ready in the morning."

"All right," the doctor said. Then, over his head, "Bring another tot of that brandy."

He smiled weakly, relieved, determined to show his good sense. "That's terrible booze, you know."

"It doesn't need to be good."

"Bad as the pain it blocks." He was still trying to seem amused.

"Alcohol never stops the hurt," the surgeon said coldly. "Its purpose is to muddle your memory."

He put a glass in Harper's hand and closed his fingers about it. "Drink deeply, Ironwearer. Don't hate us when you're sober."

* * *

To Lerlt, it seemed the gun went off automatically. The flare from the muzzle dazzled him, and he blinked; then the man he had shot was on the floor.

Bleeding. Dying. He watched the fallen man's fingers twitch.

Aimlessly, not sure what he should do next, Lerlt moved away from the window. Only because he happened to face in that direction, he went deeper into the yard, over the crest of the hill, and down to the hollow where Timt ha'Dicovys had kept his time machine.

Perhaps Herrilmin was waiting there.

But Herrilmin was not there. Fesch was not there. The time machine was not there. The body of the dead woman was not there, no matter how long he stumbled through the darkness kicking the leaves and brush.

Why had Fesch taken the body with him?

Fesch. Gherst. Timt ha'Dicovys, dead now as Herrilmin wished, and yet Herrilmin had not returned.

Hunger. He had done something wonderful, he sensed, but hunger took all pleasure out of the recollection. Hunger and uncertainty.

Alone, unhappy, he wandered up the canyon at the edge of the hillside, mumbling his thoughts to himself as the night went on.

What else must he do to please Herrilmin?

In the moonlight, the great road glistened wetly. Most of the snow on the ground had melted during the day, but what was left was ice-crusted in the nighttime cold, matted at the bottom of the waist-high grass.

The crust would not bear his weight. Each step brought his feet ankle-deep in powdery, creaking snow which poured into his shoes and melted under his heel and toes. More snow caked on his pants legs. Winds blew cold burning sparks at his face.

Patiently, Herrilmin trudged across the ground, steering for the gap between a small hill and a long ridge. Birds croaked as he moved toward them, then fluttered sluggishly from a row of short stakes.

Additional hills were before him. He caught his breath, leaning on one of the stakes, and considered that traffic was not moving on the road. Surely he could move along pavement safely in the night, and he turned his path in the direction of the gap that held the road, grateful for the long swatches he could see where wind or water had brought down the tall grass.

He stumbled against something dark and unyielding.

Awkwardly, mindful of spilling his possessions from the improvised pack on his back, he bent and brushed away snow with numbed fingers.

Teeth. A face, blackened and hideous in the moonlight.

Birds had pecked away the eyes.

Wandisha wakened, nude, feeling her foot cramp in the darkness. An ankle had trapped it under the bedclothes. A knee was under hers. The smell of lovemaking was thick in the night.

And sweat. Stale food and beer and wastes which would have to be carried to the first-floor toilet in the morning.

She disentangled herself gently, careful not to wake the sleeping man. She rose, traced fingers close to the wall to find the window, and reached further to pull it sideways and admit fresh air.

Cherrid. Rallt. Grahan. Refugees sleeping three or four to a room elsewhere in the inn and Merryn ris Vandeign's barracks. Soldiers along the riverbanks. Townsfolk. Soldiers with alien dreams not far away.

Fires burning in the night in her mind, each unique and recognizable as her consciousness flitted between them, each with something new to notice and appreciate every time her mind approached. In her body, so limited and unimportant, even as she felt every bit of its being, she smiled at the slumbering flames. She felt herself dancing effortlessly across the world's dark landscape that was inside her.

Here and there she came to the brighter glow of conscious minds.

A surgeon coughed over raw brandy in the orchard, thinking of his distant wife and daughter in the darkness of his tent, fingers aching from instruments too tightly gripped a watch before, dreading the fatigue the coming day would bring.

A restless, irritable man, who still thought of himself as Mlarttra'Nornst and feared his aging, sat stooped over a trestle table in a lighted tent, only half-conscious of maps resting before him, brooding over vagaries of Algheran politics which no amount of probing could make intelligible to her. Sentries paced unheard behind him; he felt confidence and something akin to curiosity as he waited for dawn.

Rahmmend Wolf-Twin, lying in blankets, listening to his men's snores, daydreamed of professional fame and a return to his homeland, purposely avoiding thought of other futures.

When that paled, there were more minds and more, without end, as far as she could reach and beyond, of friends and acquaintances and strangers, each somehow familiar and somehow dear to her as she observed them.

But she found no Kylene chi'Edgart Waterfall of the distant Clan Otter—no black-flecked crimson coals waiting to soar, orange and scarlet, translucent and demanding as prairie fire when given fuel. And there was Dieytl lan Callares. No, never again would she come near yellow-sparkling, green-laughing, aquamarine-self-aware Dieytl lan Callares, and to Wandisha it seemed there would always remain a blackened spot on the hillsides of her imagination where no flames would ever burn again.

No Timmial lan Haarper.

No killers. No sputtering, oil-smoked secrets.

They were out there, she was sure. Minds hooded against all illumination, moving unseen across the landscape of her mind.

Intruders. Unlike lan Haarper, trespassers.

A blindness inside blindness which she could never penetrate.

The thought was defiling. And terrifying.

She pushed the window shut quickly and moved back under the covers, where Cherrid ris Clendannan's body waited for her, loglike, ash-wrapped now, but still aflame in its core, whitesteadiness and purple-impatience flickering alternately where only she could see. She kissed him gently, and settled against him, awaiting sleep patiently, soaking into herself the warmth he radiated, content to enjoy his presence while it lasted.

She waited also, fearful but undemanding, for morning to come.

CHAPTER ELEVEN

*D*awn came, *groping bloody-fingered over the scaffolding of* the horizon, *then full morning, crisp under pale blue skies.* Wind blew to the south.

Wandisha had learned of Timmial lan Haarper's wound. Before he had breakfast, she sent Rallt to ask him questions.

It took time for him to find the Ironwearer, even knowing he was near the bridge over the river, longer yet to reach him behind his circle of aides.

The river was chocolate dark with sediment, sluggish, stain-topped. On the opposite side, soldiers were digging into the bank, creating narrow ledges and a footpath. As they slung the dirt from their shovels, it splashed into the river, throwing up spouts which seemed more mud than water. Almost walking on their heads, it seemed, other soldiers moved along the top of the bank, hammering stakes with colored rags into the dirt as gunners on the town side of the river shouted at them.

In between, almost level with the river surface, sets of planks ran from one bank to another, supported on rowboats in the center.

Rallt watched till he was sure the scene would never end, then stared at men digging into the ramp that rose to meet the road beyond the river. Farther away, halfway to the horizon, other soldiers heaped dirt onto the road.

At last the circle of men around the Ironwearer thinned.

Lan Haarper came to morning in a wagon bed, Rallt discovered. Not an ambulance, as Lord Clendannan had ridden in, but an ordinary supply wagon, pulled by four horses. He sat on a blanket in the back with another blanket around his shoulders and his leg resting on a plank and a box. Smaller boards and straps held the leg stiff. He was in pain to Rallt's eyes, his skin pale and his eyes strangely sunk in his face, and the boy guessed the little man fussing behind his shoulder did little to bring him the comforts Wandisha did for her patient.

As if reading those thoughts, the little man glared at him malevolently. Rallt reminded himself quickly that Wandisha was the only nearby telepath.

"Your turn," the Ironwearer said, when Rallt could not be ignored longer. "Have you found Kylene?" His lips pursed stiffly.

"No, sir. Which way did thy attacker go?" He had learned from Wandisha some conversations could begin without pleasantry.

"He didn't stop for an interview." The redhead winced and ran a hand down his bandaged leg. "Are you sure it wasn't one of my soldiers?"

The words were mumbled. Rallt bent closer to hear them repeated.

"Paying the respects I've earned," the Ironwearer added. Not surprisingly, his mood was surly, something for which days of exposure to other wounded men had prepared Rallt. As adage in Innings held a peasant should, the boy kept the tempers of two men in check.

"A mindless man," he assured the Ironwearer. "Wandisha swears it."

"Doesn't rule out much," lan Haarper grumbled, and his ugly little man shook his head in agreement. "Dumb shits. Must have been an accident, you know. Couldn't be anything else. Why're you people still in town?"

"We've to keep looking. Grahan and more soldiers—" He waved a hand backward at the inn, where the searchers waited for instructions.

"Wasted effort. Better to have the men in line," the Ironwearer said sourly. He rubbed his leg again and drank from a brownish bottle, lips pulled back from his teeth, then shook his head. "Look, this is just a scratch—"

"Wandisha said I've to ask, would thee remove thy—" He pointed with a finger, unsure what to say with the orderly staring at him. "Thy cap."

The Ironwearer glowered. "No. You tell her curiosity killed the cat, and if she knows what's good for her little pussy— Forget that! Tell her all you people should get out of town."

The boy nodded politely. It would not happen. Grahan had asked that already of the old Ironwearer, and ris Clendannan's response had carried over the noise of the refugees from his room to the kitchen.

"Is anyone leaving the town?" It seemed a complaint.

"We went around, we asked," Rallt said. He snapped his fingers. "Doesn't be many, I think."

"Cimon-taken idiots," lan Haarper muttered. He raised a hand and snapped fingers till an aide appeared. "You! See if you can get ropes fitted to those bridges to help pull them up. Give orders and report back."

"Yes, sir." The aide sketched a salute.

Lan Haarper scowled again at Rallt. "We will have time for that, won't we? What can Wandisha tell me about what Mlart is up to?"

The Algheran general, Rallt recalled. Wandisha had asked him to pass some things along. "He slept poorly," he began.

"So did I." Lan Haarper coughed like the old Ironwearer, then smiled feebly. "Must be an occupational hazard."

"He will attack across the bridge and from the houses across the river."

"Planned for." Lan Haarper yawned and rubbed a hand against the back of his neck. "One big rush again? Where's this fellow's great subtlety?"

Rallt opened his hands wide, not sure what the question meant.

"Oh, never mind. When's the attack?"

He swallowed, looking toward the horizon. "Wandisha says, cavalry be already fighting cavalry."

Fighting had already begun, Lerlt realized. The sound was too insignificant as yet to reach the ventilation windows in the loft, but on the hillsides south of town, tiny men on horseback rode through the long grass. Slowly from this vantage—on the ground, it might be faster.

As he watched, the single shapes became formations. On this side, an irregular line, falling back toward the bridge that crossed to the village; on the other, a similar line of riders moving on a diagonal for the hills to his left, then a column of horsemen galloping in pursuit up the great road.

It puzzled him to notice none of the soldiers he saw near the river were interested in the chase, and then he realized his greater height had increased the power of his sight. The barn was atop a hill; he was near the top of the barn. For the moment, this scene was his own possession, the backward rush of the Lopritians his own victory.

Those were Lopritians retreating, he was sure. Those were his Algherans advancing, as certainly as if he led them himself, galloping fiercely on his favorite n   over the grasslands, hooves thundering on the earth below, sweat streaming unnoticed down his firmly muscled side as he hurled his lance at the fleeing foes, fear shiny on their faces as they hunched over their straining mounts, screaming in terror as Lerlt raced after them across the plains, driving his heavy thick spear too great for any other man to lift deep in the back of a fallen screaming enemy, swinging his crimson-dripping broadsword into and through the arm of a hulking enemy warrior, dealing death with every blow in the melee, fighting alone in the press of the foe, never surrendering, ever defiant, laughing fiercely as enemy after enemy toppled before him onto the blood-soaked loam . . .

A gun boomed before him. The Algheran horsemen on the road slowed as they came up to a pile of earth, then carefully turned their mounts off the pavement, down the steep banks. As they moved, dirt blew up in their midst. An invisible child's hand swept over men and horses.

In the confusion, some of the Lopritian cavalry reached the bridge and crossed into the town. Others came to the riverbank and rode along it, evidently seeking safe places to descend. Soldiers came from across the river to observe; Lerlt noticed them sticking their heads above the bank. A few even came up to the level ground as if to protect the retreating cavalrymen, then crouched low, regretting the impulse; Lerlt wondered how a man cowering behind grass could even hope to see an approaching horseman.

Other guns sounded.

The moment went on and on. When it made sense again, most of the Lopritians had crossed the bridge. Lerlt saw them cantering along the road and passing beyond his sight as they came to the orchard. Behind them, soldiers thronged near the rickety fence at the end of the bridge; as they swung the flimsy gate doors across the road, Lerlt saw guns uncovered, their muzzles pointing through holes cut in the wooden fence.

The Algheran cavalrymen were still across the river without a target for another attack. To Lerlt, they seemed amazed to find the town still standing; they sat on their horses staring about them, then drifted backward, one by one, without pursuit by the guns.

When they were distant, Lopritians pulling sledges went out into the grass and returned with the bodies of men and horses.

The sound of the guns could be heard in Cherrid ris Clendannan's room, and to Rallt it seemed that instead of being surprised, the old Ironwearer waited expectantly for each shot and relaxed more and more as the cannon booms passed over the town. He seemed impatient when they stopped.

The Ironwearer was on his feet today, fully dressed for the first time that Rallt could recall. When the windows rattled in response to the guns, he touched them casually, stopping the glassy echoes, then walked the few paces to the end of the room, and paused for breath, leaning against a dresser.

As if he could see, he turned to Rallt suddenly, his eyes fixed toward him in spite of their covering bandage. "Those are our guns. Have the Algherans moved up yet?"

He didn't know. "Yes," he would have said once, but Wandisha's patient questionings had taught him some of the difference between sight and speculation, and he would have been embarrassed to have his tale amended when she returned.

The truth he had to relate was that Ironwearer Ian Haarper had sent him away before there was anything to notice at the riverside. What Rallt had seen, coming back to Wandisha and Ironwearer ris Clendannan, were only Lopritian soldiers waiting in the orchard, then more soldiers riding along the road. As he had come into the inn, he had had a glimpse of the guns stationed behind the lumberyard, but the soldiers there had been idle. It was just the few cannon shots that told him the battle had begun.

If it was a battle, he wondered. "Could the noise be the whole of it?"

"You seem disappointed, boy." The Ironwearer smiled grimly, then pushed himself away from the dresser. Slowly, on bare feet, he padded back across the room, turned again at the head of the bed, came back to the window, and leaned against - it with his hands against the frame. His shoulders moved with coughing; then his head moved. He spat.

"Not disappointed," Rallt said carefully. "I were wondering, is all—"

"Was wondering," the old Ironwearer said. His head turned in the window; his blind eyes peered up the road to the bridge.

"Was wondering," Rallt said, correcting himself. "I never seen—sorry, Lord Clendannan—saw. Saw a battle."

Ris Clendannan turned away from the window. "No one sees all of a battle," the Ironwearer said calmly. "Not even generals. I don't know how much sense it would make if someone tried to understand all the details. They can begin with something like this, if that's what you wonder."

He hesitated, not sure what he wondered. It seemed incredible that on the outskirts of the town two groups of men were intent on killing one another. Had any died already?

It was troubling to see that ris Clendannan took that situation in stride so easily. There was something frightening about the old Ironwearer, Rallt discovered, something lizardlike about his countenance, something vaguely repellent.

Wandisha entered and smiled at him. He caught the smell of soap in her blond hair and something more of her scent as she moved past. She put her hand on ris Clendannan's wrist and steered him toward the bed, and the Ironwearer smiled at her, obeying. She was an attractive woman, Rallt noticed for the first time, and was troubled by seeing her and the Ironwearer on such familiar terms.

"How are my two young men?" she asked brightly. "Rallt, could you go up to the roof and look around for a while? So Cherrid will have a picture?"

He stepped back. "The killer—there be more streets to look through. I thought—with Grahan, and Pitar and—"

"There's only Grahan now," Wandisha said.

He stared at her. Saw the blind Ironwearer looking at him.

"The soldiers have had to go to the line, Rallt. They're needed there." She swallowed. "We'll have to search differently."

How? Searching for the killer had become part of life.

"It won't stop," she promised. "We just have to wait for a while. Until things are clearer, that's all."

He mumbled something.

"Just a minute, dear." She patted ris Clendannan's hand and left to hold Rallt's sleeve.

"It's not important," ris Clendannan muttered. "If he wants—"

"No! It's unsafe for two men. Not until—" She shook her head angrily.

"Come with me, please." She led Rallt out of the room and down the landing to where their voices would not carry. "Go up to the roof, Rallt, and take time to look around, please."

He wanted to refuse.

He saw that she sensed it. She traced her fingers up and down the front of his shirt. "Please? We'll keep the search going somehow, Cherrid won't let it stop, but do this first, will you? It means a lot to him, Rallt."

She swallowed. "He doesn't have a wife, Rallt. He doesn't have a family or heir and not even many friends. Is it too much to let him know what happens to his brigade?"

The roof was flat, and pitch-covered. A century of weather had dumped dust and leaves on it and rarely cleaned it off. Rallt saw scuff marks in the dirt as he climbed through the opening from the landing beneath; he remembered seeing twigs and leaves on the ground around the inn that morning and knew now where they had come from.

The roof held three men in blue uniforms—a sergeant and two corporals, though Rallt, unfamiliar with their rank insignia, thought they were officers. The corporals had sticks in their hands, one with a blue pennant, one that had been pushed through the sleeves of a red dress. They held these above their heads and turned slowly near a corner of the roof; there was no balustrade to keep them safe but the sergeant held them by their belts. Their muskets and a muddle of other improvised flags lay nearby.

He had never been this high in a building. For the first few moments after he was on the roof, Rallt crouched near the opening, convinced that moving in any direction would cause him to trip and fall from the heights. Fortunately, there was no breeze, and the structure seemed solid enough to deserve his partial trust. He dared to stand and when no disaster struck, he was able to step sideways several paces.

The men saw him then. They let their flags drop and came toward him.

"Don't even think of coming out here," the sergeant said, and from the way he said it, Rallt understood, as if Wandisha had told him that the man had a fear of heights. "You get back where you come from, boy."

"Ironwearer ris Clendannan sent me," he explained. "I've to look around for him and—"

He stopped to wonder why Wandisha had asked him to yield what his eyes told his mind to her, when three others were here.

"So you want to see Algies. Can't be patient?" The sergeant took him by the shoulder and moved him till he overlooked the great road. "Take your look. There they are."

He saw nothing. "Where?"

"That way." The sergeant stretched out an arm. "Look all the way to the horizon and bring your eyes down, just a bit. See that patch on the road that looks furry? That's them."

He still saw nothing. The road itself was not wide enough to be seen at the distance of the horizon.

He stepped back angrily. "You been funning with me?"

"Wouldn't do that, boy. You got to realize those Algies are still five, six thousand man-heights off. You can't figure they're going to look that big, but that's them all right."

Mollified, he raised his eyes again. Maybe there was some point below the horizon where the dark line of the road became indistinct.

"Ironwearer ris Clendannan, you said?"

"Downstairs." He covered his eyes with a palm, then tried to decide if that made the scene clearer.

"Ahh, the old gentleman!" the sergeant said cheerfully. "So he's here. Hadn't heard that. Thought he'd be in Northfaring by now."

"Things keep him," Rallt said, not wishing to be obscure, but convinced that telling these soldiers about the killer would take too long.

He stepped forward again, much nearer to the edge of the roof, not yet prepared to look directly down, but curious about what could be seen at closer range.

The roof of the lumber warehouse; a section of the river, with a soldier drinking from his hands beside the stream; the bridge—tiny from that height—and soldiers like ants against the bare earth . . .

It was the town that really attracted his eyes. He could see the steep roof of the house where ris Ellich had died, barns, the buildings he and Sugally had searched. Under tree branches, horses hauled wagons and guns up the winding hillside road and along the streets Grahan and he had been on. Only position and colorings made it clear which homes he had entered; the perspective was unfamiliar.

Not a fool, Timmial, Cherrid admitted as Wandisha related to him what Rallt saw. Putting sentries in high places was not new, but teaching them signals certainly was. A man with a message was expected to run to his horse and ride as if demons pursued him.

How did we miss this? The question was rhetorical. He knew the answer before he asked it of himself. Signalers with flags were not mentioned in the Plates. Radios were described and, for some later time, picture-sending machines, but the technology needed to build those devices would not be developed for centuries. Soldiers had discussed their uses, but without urgency.

Timmial—Timmial's generation—had changed war again.

"You can't have all the ideas," Wandisha said. He heard her smile.

"Why not?" It was not a real grumble. He slipped a hand onto her breast and moved closer.

She slapped it gently. "Just because. Greedy old man!"

He chuckled again. "Where are the Algherans?"

"Far away. It'll be another day tenth."

Long enough. His fingers moved over her body. "I'd be ashamed if my men marched as slowly as Mlart's."

"Hmmmm." She twisted to expose more of herself to him. "I can feel how upset you are."

"How long is that boy going to be gone?"

"Long enough." Her fingers danced over his.

"Likely to be one here. Somewhere."

"Hanging from a wall if it is."

Alien voices. In Lopritian.

Lerlt, crouched at the back of the loft, swallowed and froze in place.

Intruders in the barn. Two of them. The musket was far away and held only one bullet.

Defenseless. Herrilmin had left him without proper protection. He stared at the useless musket.

Steps sounded on the floor below. Going away. Loud in the empty space.

"Nothing here. You want to check the loft?"

He almost gasped, but stopped before making the sound, leaving his head thrown back and his mouth open.

Two of them. The gun would have to do for the first, he realized. Then his knife for the second, leaning over the ladder to the loft, striking the neck of the unsuspecting—

"No one's going to leave a scythe in a loft." The second voice, followed by the sound of a kick on a post. Lerlt found he could exhale again.

"I'll check the storage rooms and you can look at the back wall." The second voice again, characterless as all foreigners were in their language.

"All right," the first voice said.

Footsteps sounded again, while Lerlt lowered himself to hands and knees and crept across the straw to the musket.

The gun was loaded. It could go off. It could harm. He held it carefully, stroking it from the mouth of the muzzle down to the butt plate, staring at the trigger as the footsteps passed beneath.

A scraping sound was the back door of the barn. Lerlt noticed that the straw before his face was lighter colored, the shadows underneath sharper.

A scythe. Why was anyone looking for a scythe?

The Lopritians have no ammunition so they are going to fight with farm tools. It was unlikely but the thought generated images so funny he had to muzzle his mouth with his arm to keep from chuckling.

The results would be the same, though. The Lopritians might as well be fighting bullets with scythes and pitchforks. They were terrible soldiers. The Algherans always won wars with them.

Underneath him somewhere, a door squeaked.

"Want to go home," Gherst mumbled.

Lerlt swallowed, wanting to scream. Had Gherst been heard? He waited, feeling sick, for an answer.

Nothing happened. He listened to the sounds of movement under the loft.

Gherst mumbled again. His fingers scratched at the floor. Horror struck, Lerlt realized he was trying to sit up. Gherst wanted to be noticed!

"I'll kill you," he mouthed. He pointed the gun at Gherst.

Blindly, the brown-haired man increased his efforts. He grunted to himself. Lerlt saw fluid spurting from his belly as he moved.

There was no time to waste, Lerlt realized. He had to hush Gherst.

The simplest, quickest way. He crawled to Gherst. He took his knife from his belt. He pulled. He sliced.

Blood trickled over his knuckles. He stared down at what he had done.

"You made me do it," he whispered as Gherst sank back.

"Nothing. Let's go," one of the Lopritians shouted below.

"Probably in a toolshed. Check there next," the other Lopritian said.

UnSepted bastards! Lerlt screamed at them in his mind. *Look what you made me do!* He wanted to hurl his knife and the little pink thing at them.

The little pink thing. He smiled.

The little pink thing Gherst had given up to him. His tongue.

Gherst was certain to be silent now, he knew, feeling relief for the first time since Herrilmin had gone away. There would be no more complaints about hunger. No more babbling about wanting to go home or about how much his wound hurt.

"Hey, Gherstie boy, you're improved," he whispered, keeping his voice low so he could hear the pleasant sound of the Lopritians leaving the barn. "You still want to go home now? You want to have a big talk with your wife?"

He held the scrap of flesh over Gherst's face, laughing to himself as the sick man stared at him, gurgling on the blood sliding down his throat and the froth of his red-stained teeth.

"What'll you give me for this, Gherstie? Money? That's not good enough, Gherst. Your wife, Gherst. That's what, Gherst. I'll do to your wife, Gherst, what I did to that Teep bitch. You'll help me. It's your fault, Gherst!"

He brought the knife down on Gherst's chest. "It's your fault!"

He stuck the knife into a leg. Pulled. "It's your fault!"

He hit Gherst's face with a fist. "Herillmin'd be here if it weren't for you!"

He stuck the knife into Gherst's mouth and shoved it down with a palm. "If you'd helped me with the Teep, I wouldn't need to do this to you."

Gherst's jaw closed weakly. Lerlt pushed the lips back with one hand and wrenched the knife free and shoved it in the man's belly, making slimy textured fluid splash all about him.

"Pretending to be better'n us!" Lerlt snarled. He yanked the knife in one direction, then another, then another. "Pretending you was afraid of Timt ha'Dicovys! You were going to tell him everything, weren't you! He was waiting for you, wasn't he!"

He stabbed at Gherst's genitals. "That was it! Going to betray us! This is what you get!"

He shoved the knife into Gherst's face beside the nose. "Teach you! Teach you! Teach you!" He twisted and prodded with it until cartilage popped free from the torn flesh.

He pushed the knife into Gherst's belly again and again. "You go home to your wife now! You have fun with your wife now! You stop someone doing what they have to do now! See how you like it!"

Finally he was done. He waited on his knees, breathing deeply until his strength returned and the sweat on him had cooled. He got to his feet mechanically, not caring now if anyone saw or heard him.

He kicked the broken thing before him. Gherst had troubled him and Gherst had learned what happened to those who troubled him. He was only sorry the lesson had not lasted longer.

He dropped the scrap of tongue on the bloody straw and sighed. His mind turned to practical matters.

Herrilmin could come back now. He simply had to be notified it was safe to return, and Lerlt had already decided on the proper signal.

This was only business. A bore, really, now that his enthusiasm was spent. He should have done it already. Lerlt grunted to himself, then bent to push Gherst's dead chin back as he brought his knife down.

It would be more interesting with a scythe. He had to smile.

"Help me down from this horse," Harper ordered, and men moved to obey. Half walking, half carried, he was brought from the mare to a wagon sitting beside the Hand's carriage. They propped him up on cushions, where he could stare upward at an ominously rotten apple on a bare branch. Quillyn put a glass of water and brandy in his hand.

Across the river, a handful of soldiers moved methodically across the ground with scythes and sickles, striking down the tall grass.

Should have done that yesterday, Harper thought to himself. *I should have thought of that yesterday.*

Damn it! I'm no general! I'm no good for this.

He wanted to run away and hide, he admitted.

But that wasn't possible. He took a swallow of drink, then smiled fleetingly at ris Andervyll, pretending to be calm. "That's the prelude of our drama, I guess. Now we wait for the curtain to go up on the first act. *Exeunt cavalry all, enter Algherans, stage front.*"

"Ironwearer?" The Hand seemed worried by the incomprehensible words and there was no one near to console him.

Terrault ris Andervyll was an old man, Harper realized, almost as old as Cherrid ris Clendannan, and all alone today. Merryn ris Vandeign had retreated to his house for a bath and a genuine bed; the Hand's two women had gone to enjoy the same pleasures; his entourage of young nobles had been sent to Perrid ris Salynnt to replace fallen officers.

Must feel like being defeated already to him. He let himself feel pity.

"Nothing important, sir. Just a little joke." Harper winced and rubbed at his wounded leg, trying to push pain back into the flesh. "Ughh. Quillyn, bring me another hot pad!"

He closed his eyes and listened to movements,

Damned wound. Damned lousy shot. Why hadn't the Agent who tried to kill him shot at his chest? Which one had it been?

Which goddamned *partner*? Which smiling *friend* of his?

Bastards. God damn all Algherans!

Some fanatic. His thinking could not go beyond that point.

It seemed unfair. Being shot at by enemy soldiers was part of the job, as he looked at it. Being shot by another time traveler, by someone feeling actual animosity, was almost too bizarre to believe.

Almost. He did have a pain and a hole in his thigh. He did have fractured bone and bloody bandages to prove an enemy's existence.

And Kylene was missing.

He wanted to puke. He wanted to scream.

You don't know what Bad is, Dalsyn. He cursed his glibness.

"Everything is all right?" the Hand wondered.

"Sure," Harper lied. "I'm feeling fine. The men are in position. We've got ammunition and more is coming. We've got food in the town. All we really want are more men, and if we can put up with Mlart's siege for a few days, we'll have them."

Damned fool. He didn't really want the truth, Harper had decided.

"Is there anything I can do?" the Hand asked.

"Nothing much, my lord," Harper told him. "We just wait, now. I take it the ris Andervyll line doesn't include many soldiers?"

"Why do you say that?" The Hand stared at him.

Harper smiled, intending a pleasantry. "If you had more patience in you, you'd have settled for being generals instead of royalty."

"Perhaps." The Hand turned away.

"Nothing new from the south," an aide reported, and Harper turned from contemplation of his faux pas to look through branches at the top of the inn.

If I'd known we had this much time, I'd have cooked up better signals.

No, I wouldn't. It was hard enough teaching these to this lot.

Goddamned Plates. Why didn't they have something like Morse code?

He was tired of waiting, he admitted. Surely, the Algherans couldn't be that far away. He lifted a finger to catch attention. "Aide! Get across the river. Tell Major Ian Styllin he might as well start now."

CHAPTER TWELVE

"*G*rahan's coming back," Wandisha said, and her head moved on his shoulder. "I should get clothes on."

He must know, doesn't he? Cherrid stirred, half seriously inclined to pull her back against him. "Does it matter?"

"It matters." She was already sitting up. Bed motions told him she was putting on shoes. "There's no need to rub his hair in it, Cherrid."

He smiled, contemplating an image of himself and Wandisha struggling with an incoherent Grahan, rubbing something into the old man's hair.

A jealous Grahan. He couldn't believe that. He pictured the other's face, as it might be red with jealousy and suppressed rage. Was it dark hair? Sandy? Long and straight? Tangled?

How strange. He could not remember. Imperceptibly, Grahan had become a set of footsteps and a sound of voice. A chuckle and a hand waking him in the night. Even in memories, his face was unclear now.

My old friend. When did it happen?

He stared at the darkness, trying to make sense of it all.

Beside him, Wandisha dressed. Garments slithered into place,

151

tight on her skin, the unfamiliar sound somehow one he had heard a thousand times. He forced his mind back to her. He smiled.

"Always thought it would make sense for men to wear skirts. Faster than putting on pants and less of that buttons-and-drawstrings nonsense."

"You wouldn't like it, Lord Clendannan." He heard a rustle which was her hand smoothing down hair. "A skirt is an indoor garment. It tells people you have someone to keep you inside a house—that you're owned by someone who wears pants."

He paused, trying to remember the occasions when his wife had worn trousers. Never at Court. While riding in the fields and on visits to the village below his house, certainly. After marriage and decades together. Country living was casual—why should she have dressed formally with no one to impress but his tenants?

The housemaids all wore skirts, he recalled. Brindylla had been insistent upon it. Short skirts, all the same color—that was a maid's uniform, and he had never thought about it further. Was Wandisha right?

He sat up, stiffly, wondering how much guilt he should feel.

"Useful in my work," Wandisha said calmly. "Short dresses to suggest that you're pliant, I mean. Some men don't have the nerve to come to me without that kind of help."

He flushed.

"Not you, Lord Clendannan. Very healthy, you are."

It was not what he meant. He nodded grimly.

"I'm a whore, Ironwearer ris Clendannan. Don't pretend otherwise since you've known it right along. I've got as much right to talk about my living as you have to talk about yours."

"I'll talk less about mine." He wished he could see her face.

"Don't. I like to hear you talk. You're interesting."

"I—" He was unwilling to argue, afraid of what argument might lead to.

"Very practical," she said coolly. "But you needn't worry. The sex doesn't stop, Lord Clendannan. As long as you're feeding me, I'm paid for."

He gritted his teeth. "Just be a nurse. That is all I need, and I am sure that is all the service Timmial asked you to do."

"The more fool, him. He might have guessed how I'd do it."

"You have been a good nurse," he said, emphasizing each word.

"I'm a good whore, that's because. I'm used to doing for men."

He sighed, unable to find a response.

He wanted to spank her into silence. He wanted his illusions back.

She chuckled. "Don't be so emotional, Lord Clendannan. Whoring must be what I'm made for. I'm blind. I can't work in the fields. I can't work in a factory or a shop. I couldn't even be one of your housemaids, could I? I can't read a book or watch a sunset with my own eyes. I can't judge lawsuits. I can't give advice to queens. I can't sit on a veranda dictating my life story to a secretary and waiting on servants to keep my glass filled."

He grimaced. "Something. You do not have to— There is nursing. There is medicine. You might be a doctor."

She snorted. "I'm poor. I have sex with men and women for money. It's what people do when they're poor and hungry and can't do anything else, Lord Clendannan, and I never learned anything else. I'm a Teep, so I'm good at it and I don't starve and someday I'll have better clothes than these—they're rags even if you and I can't see them—and I'll have money and a house of my own and investments and land and the gentry will be polite to me and—and—"

She laughed suddenly, shockingly. "And then I'll be old and wrinkly and crabby and I'll have to pay big sums to have boys have sex with me!"

He was appalled.

"So that's grotesque and impossible, both?" He sensed that she was smiling at him. "I'm poor, Lord Clendannan. I have poor folks' daydreams and what's the harm of it?"

"No harm," he said hoarsely, feeling his mouth lined with something rancid and cottony he wanted to spit out. "It is ambition, I guess."

"No, it's not. It's nothing you'd approve of. You have ambition. Poor people want things different, that's all. They don't want to be poor but they don't know how to change from it. I suppose, most of them, you could give them lots of money and they'd still be poor."

He exhaled softly, sure she was correct. "Talk to Grahan, Wandisha. He is not as certain about such matters as I may be."

"You want Grahan to tell me his foolishness to make me happy?" She seemed amused. Cynical.

"Little poor peasant whore bottom-of-the-ladder you. Yes." He tried to make a joke of it. "Let me sweep you away and make you happy."

She wouldn't let that happen. "Make Wandisha happy and she'll stop saying awful things and life will be comfortable again?"

This was not fair, he realized. He did want her to be happy. In a totally disinterested sense, he would be pleased if everyone in the world were happy. Even Mlart tra'Nornst, though preferably Mlart should enjoy his happiness back in Alghera after losing his war. Even young Timmial lan Haarper—privately, he had found that he wished Timmial would be successful in his place but not easily successful.

"I'm poor," she snapped. "I don't have to be fair."

She was a woman, he told himself. She didn't have to be logical.

There must be something to say to mollify her.

Demon-seized Teeps! What sort of indirect approach—lies, to be honest—would work on her?

None. He was left with direct assault.

"Wandisha? I am sick. I am wounded. I am like a prisoner in this room. Of course I want life to be comfortable. That is only norm—natural, isn't it? Wanting a comfortable life? While I recover."

"Do you want comfort or *fucking*?" Her last word must have carried to the roof. He was sure it would bring that young boy from Innings storming down the stairs and into the room.

And he listened to her with his mouth open. She was correct. He wanted both comfort and sex, he realized, and he was horrified by the discovery. Two days of lapsed celibacy and he was already—

"Oh, be dependent, Cherrid," Wandisha scolded. "There's no harm of it, except in your imagination. You eat and breathe without moaning about it. So you have another need and you can use me for it. Or one of your housemaids—if you'd ever tried, you probably would have found they wouldn't mind, really, not from the master of the house. They'll probably be honored by it, coming from someone like you. Poor people know they're on Earth to do things for the nobility, so people like you give orders and people like me follow them. It's all right most of the time."

Cherrid grimaced. Other men faltered in uncertainty, but he had the talent to analyze circumstances and issue orders which retrieved stability from confusion. It was the justification for his rank, after all.

Until now, he had taken innocent pride in that skill.

He remembered that he had been broken from sergeant to private once, long ago, for doing something new-recruit stupid on a patrol he really had not had any business supervising. It had felt this way, standing in the ranks again, pretending the fit of his buckler was more important to him than the feel of other men staring at him.

Some people do have to be privates, some generals, he reminded himself. An army could not function without hierarchy. Without orders and obedience.

How could the rest of life be different?

"Just be a nurse, Wandisha. There won't be any more— fucking."

It felt good to give that order. It had a well-understood purpose. His voice had been even, with a hint of rasp to show seriousness. His words had carried the conviction that they would be obeyed.

She laughed at him. "Don't be silly. You're my patient. You have to do what I order, Cherrid. Lord Clendannan. Ironwearer. Take your medicine when you can and enjoy it."

Demons seize the woman! "You are not—"

She put a finger on his lips. "I like being your medicine, Cherrid. Don't you understand? You're very nice to me and when sex makes you feel good, I feel good. I wish—I wish—"

He listened to her swallow. "I like being your whore. Let me be that."

He tried to start over. "I do not—I have not—"

This has to stop. I have a reputation to uphold. Honor. Decency.

She answered his words rather than his thoughts. "Since you married. I know. But your wife is dead, Cherrid. Being faithful won't bring her back."

Her fingers fitted into his. Tightly.

"I—I—" It was intolerable that Wandisha should feel pity for him.

Then Grahan's steps sounded on the stairs below. He forced himself back to steadiness.

Before he cried.

Something new was happening, Lerlt noticed. The soldiers cropping the grass had retreated to their ledges on the riverbank, and that—whatever it was—was done, but now the edge of a gray-black cloud was visible at his window view. A storm cloud?

An omen. He craned to see more of it but failed. He noticed soldiers looking in the same direction.

Officers shouted at them. The soldiers turned back to staring at shadows or whatever else they were doing before.

He recognized trouble, though. "Something's wrong," he called to Gherst.

Gherst was silent, of course. Gherst was not speaking now, he reminded himself. Gherst had felt bad about something and he had made Gherst happier and now there was no more need for Gherst to say anything.

Good Gherst. His friend Gherst. He smiled happily, then put a hand to his knife, and retreated from the window to the ladder. Gherst would be curious and someone had to be practical.

On the floor of the barn, he remembered he was thirsty and pumped water into his hands for a drink, then went to the door.

Flame showed along the horizon. Trees and distance obscured the extent of the fire, but a wall of smoke was rising from across the river.

From the roof of the inn, the flames could be seen more clearly. The crackling and hissing carried across the river and some of the heat, though it seemed to Rallt a cool breeze had built up behind his back.

He watched, hollow inside, ears tingling as he waited for screams.

The sounds he feared did not come. They would never come, he realized finally. The fire was too big, its sound too loud, for human voices to overcome. It had come up too fast for anyone to escape.

There had been nothing to see. And then, in the space of a minute, he had seen smoke billowing through the sides of a wooden barn, then flames dancing under the gray-black cloud.

Then the house next to the barn had caught. Then an outhouse. Utility sheds. A pine tree.

Then, as he gaped uselessly, smoke rose over another farm. And another. And another, until it seemed everything built by man had joined the inferno. He had never heard of a fire which spread so quickly.

The taller of the two corporals came near him and then past to the edge of the building.

"Makes you sick, doesn't it? All that waste." His mouth churned, then he spat in the direction of the dock, and turned away. "Glad it's not my town they're doing this to."

"What do you mean?" he asked sickly. It was horrible to see a man so callous. He would have hated the corporal if he had the strength.

"They torched it," the corporal said. "Lord High-what's-his-face and our new Ironwearer gave the orders, and those people did the work."

His finger pointed. Rallt, staring beyond it, noticed distant men clambering down the riverbank.

"Just like we did in West Bend," the corporal commented. "Get everybody out and pack in some powder and throw in a torch and—*woosh!* This new Ironwearer we got, he isn't like ris Clendannan, I'll tell you. Real polite when he talks to you, clever, too, but he's hell on burning things. My captain said he was talking to him yesterday while we was marching and the Ironwearer just cursed and cursed because there was too much snow for him to burn the fields. I guess his hair's red, he wants everything red."

Rallt blinked. "Have you met him?" he asked when he recovered.

"Oh, yeah. Me and those two fellows. He asked around for people with sharp eyes when he was in West Bend and picked us for this job. He had a batch of signals already made up for us to learn and we had to come see him every watch to show how much we'd learned. Like I say, he's clever—he gave us some new ones when we'd learned the first batch, but he never changed any of them. I've had officers—well, Cimon's judged 'em so I've said all that rests in my belly."

The corporal smiled like a man with a full stomach. "I guess I seen as much of Ironwearer ris Haarper as anyone in his regiment."

Rallt shook his head and turned away, wanting to be far away. Despite his criticism, the soldier was clearly pleased by his new commander.

That was sad loyalty to show toward defenseless Lord Clendannan.

"You aren't being loyal, Grahan," Wandisha said. She patted Cherrid's hand on the bed beside her. Her smile took the sting from the remark.

The old soldier leaned back in his chair and raised an eyebrow. "Am I supposed to be loyal now or honest? There's nothing in the Ironwearer's house to show who is after Ian Haarper and the sooner Cherrid believes that fact the better."

Cherrid, for want of a better response, merely growled.

"He understands," Wandisha said soothingly. "He thought it was worth an inspection, just in case. It was an off chance but—"

"It was no chance. He doesn't like doing nothing and he didn't have the soldiers to send out to continue the other house checks, so he did what he normally does when he's out of ideas and sent me on a fool's errand." Grahan looked as if he could growl also.

"He has more confidence in you than anyone else, Grahan," Wandisha said. Then she blinked guiltily. "Than *in* anyone else."

"No dumb jokes, please," Cherrid muttered.

"Accident," Wandisha said with transparent insincerity. "Sorry, Grahan."

The old soldier snapped his fingers. "Look, Cherrid. It's foolish to wonder if someone has reason to want to kill Ian Haarper. You know there is. There's ten thousand Algheran soldiers on our doorstep who want to do that."

"Not the same thing," Wandisha said, repeating the Ironwearer's thought.

Grahan looked toward the window, pointedly ignoring the woman as she stroked the sick man's hand.

"Close enough if you're the one being shot at. Now, there is a body in Merryn ris Vandeign's house. Isn't it just as likely that someone wants to kill him? Or is that your next just-in-case? Am I supposed to go search his place next?"

"Who'd waste a bullet—" Cherrid said before Wandisha interrupted.

"Lord Vandeign's house is already occupied," she said quickly. "It doesn't need additional searchers."

"Did they move the body?" Grahan wondered. His eyes came back to her.

"It's on the back porch." Wandisha hesitated diplomatically.

"I already know the ris Vandeigns don't like the ris Ellichs," Grahan said. "It would be screamingly funny if Ryger did it on purpose."

"Well. Don't mention it to Rallt." She gestured weakly. "Lord Clendannan would like to hear your conclusions about lan Haarper's house."

Grahan sighed. "There isn't much to say. I can't tell how long that house was occupied. Maybe one night, maybe longer. All the beds were used, so there were two or three men, at least. The food in the larder is all gone, for whatever that is worth."

"Toilet," Cherrid said, his eyes closed.

Wandisha amplified. "Did they use lan Haarper's indoor plumbing? It's not something common in this town."

"One didn't. Took a dump in the front room, but I read that more as insult than stupidity. Anyway, people in town know about that bathing room."

"They do," Wandisha confirmed. She shifted position to look at Cherrid. "Lan Haarper's housekeeper gave tours when he wasn't around. She wanted people to know how silly her employer was."

Cherrid coughed. "I have people like that." He disentangled his hand from Wandisha's grip to pat her hip, then returned it, while Grahan's eyes moved upward.

"That plumbing isn't that uncommon, Wandisha," Grahan commented when the ceiling lost its fascination. "Cherrid's house is fixed up that way. You'll see you have all those rich folks' luxuries when you get there."

He paused for an interruption but none came.

"Well, even here, Merryn ris Vandeign could have done the same if he'd wanted. So I don't think the toilet gives us any sort of clue. Maybe it rules out some local peasants, but I never thought it was a peasant anyhow."

He scratched his neck. "Lot of books in his place. Old ones. They don't all look that old, I mean, but the writing in them is old. Primitive, some language I didn't recognize. Looks like some syllabary system instead of ideographs. Know anyone still using those, Cherrid?''

"Plates," Cherrid suggested.

"Not the Plates. I've seen them, but something like. They have equations in them, some of them, meaning only demons know what. No reason for him to keep a set of Plates, Cherrid; ris Vandeign has a set. Some other books, Lopritian and Al-gheran, about history and politics. He's interested in past eras, I'd say. No military books. That surprised me, unless—"

He rubbed his palm over his cheek slowly. "There was a big fire in his fireplace. Lot of wood, lot of paper, and the ashes haven't been taken out. There's still some warm coals in it. Lan Haarper could have burnt some books before he was shot yesterday. I won't say he did, just that he could."

"I don't see it in his memories," Wandisha said carefully.

"Okay. I found some payment warrants, his to others, lan Callares's to him, which I suppose are worthless now and maybe he was burning them. No letters. No diary. Some notes about training, which must have been written when he was just running the Midpassage Battalion. Some maps which I suppose he used for prospecting. Nothing that means anything that I could see."

Cherrid mumbled, then sighed, and Grahan turned an eye on Wandisha.

"Summarizing," she said, "there is nothing left belonging to Kylene which suggests she had any enemies—except the paintings that were destroyed and the damage in her room."

The Teep paused for breath. "I know neither of you knows what Kylene was like, but she loved to hate people. She could carry a feud on for decades. I don't think she could even be happy without enemies. I don't mean she always showed it or that people realized she didn't like them—she hid it well—that was part of the fun for her. She would smile at you and be polite and tell you how happy she was to see you and all the while she was thinking about the fun she could have draining your blood to put ants into your veins while you were still alive."

Several seconds of silence passed.

"Just summary, please." Ris Clendannan's voice was flat.

"Well, I know you never noticed, Cherrid," Wandisha said. "You're a man. She didn't mind you. You weren't any threat to her hold on Timmial. But Kylene was not a sweet little child. I want you to understand that she would fight ruthlessly as any man to defend Timmial. She has killed people. If I wanted to kill him, I'd kill her first.''

"Lady Ironwearer?'' Grahan asked pleasantly.

Wandisha smiled grimly. "She's a thief and a liar and a blood-sucking savage, and I wouldn't kill her myself but if she has really croaked, I'll give half a year's earnings to some temple to celebrate, and I promise I'll work hard that year.''

Grahan looked at Cherrid. "It always astonishes me, the warmth of the affection women have for each other.''

The old men smiled at each other, excluding Wandisha until she was able to laugh at herself.

And then the guns began to boom.

Everything happened slowly, Rallt noticed, as events did in certain dreams or seemed to do in fevers. Across the river, the fire was dying down. It had not reached the trees along the bank, and behind them a few blackened posts and beams still stood like sentries over charred earth.

On the road, the smudge or "furry spot" of Algherans moved nearer imperceptibly until it seemed that individual shapes in the crowd were just barely visible, then changed in some hard-to-define fashion. He had an impression that it had grown wider and diffuse.

"A rest stop,'' the sergeant commented when he asked. "They'll want to get a good breath of air before they get their last one. Probably break for a meal, too.'' He clicked his tongue inside his cheek and called out to the corporals. "Signal—column south—long cannon range—slow slow slow.''

He turned back to Rallt. "Likely we won't see anything, but you can't tell what the Ironwearer will do. See those shiny things behind the Algies? That's their guns.''

Rallt nodded politely, though he had already made the observation. At least the sergeant was not calling him "boy" any longer. It was pleasant to be treated as an adult. The sergeant had praised his talent for soldiering and attempted to recruit him; the corporals had added their own encouragements. But it had been more game than serious attempt; he had fended them off with no more than smiles and the reminder that he must serve

Lord Clendannan first. He had wondered for a while what length that service would have and where it might lead.

Grahan had been with the old Ironwearer a long time, it was clear. Centuries, he had said, and at times, speaking to Rallt or to ris Clendannan himself, he seemed more companion than servant.

Wandisha's arrival was more recent, he knew. Rallt had a memory of seeing her early in the campaign as one of the throng of hangers-on that moved about in the wake of any group of soldiers, and her own remarks had not disturbed that conviction. But her attachment now was not a temporary one from the way she acted—at breakfast that morning, Grahan had spoken of Lord Clendannan's estates and named the more important of his tenants and retainers, describing each with the careful patience of a teacher; Wandisha had listened gratefully, it seemed to Rallt, while pretending not to, absorbing Grahan's words like a child nervous about the impression it might make.

What impression had he made, or should he make? The rewards of a farm laborer's life were small and infrequent. If offered employment of some other sort with ris Clendannan, should he accept? His father would understand.

Ris Clendannan did not seem so fearful after the company of soldiers. Even the destruction across the river, now that he knew it had taken no lives, seemed acceptable, an inevitability in a soldier's life as much as a farmer's plowing or winter lambing.

Perhaps he would become a soldier himself.

No. He swallowed stealthily, remembering the almost-alive bodies he and his father had transported and more mangled remains he had seen buried while the injured men were placed in the ambulances. No, he would not be a soldier.

"Having fun, aren't they?" the sergeant said. He clicked his tongue again. "Isn't . . . going . . ."

Boom! BOOM!

"See what I mean?"

He didn't. The noise—where were those cannons?—sounded again.

"Oh, that's hitting 'em!" the sergeant cackled. "Ha-ha! Ha-hah!"

What was happening? The sound came from the left.

"Make 'em take it! Isn't that beautiful?" He laughed again. Wisps of smoke rose from distant fields, but he could not see what effect they had. Rallt could only shake his head at the sergeant's glee.

The man finally noticed his lack of comprehension. "That's shell, not shrapnel, boy. That's why you aren't seeing dust. But we're making hits. Take a look at the Algies' guns—watch 'em bounce."

Pitar lan Styllin, busy chivvying troops along the riverbank toward a section of the Lopritian guns, had a closer view of what the guns were doing to the Algherans and was not so cheerful as Rallt's sergeant.

He was worried, with cause.

Timmial lan Haarper had selected his southernmost guns for the attack, since those were closest to the Algheran column, but it had been an impromptu decision, made after receiving one of the signals from the top of the inn. Those guns were in the lane that ran between Merryn ris Vandeign's farthest fields; the site was far from the river and shielded from attack only by the far left end of ris Daimgewln's regiment.

Lan Haarper's original intent had been to wait for Mlart's attack before opening fire with that section, with the hope that the Algherans would not notice the guns until too late. After he changed his mind, precious minutes had passed before he had realized that the guns needed additional infantry supports and given the task of guiding them to Pitar.

On horseback now, incongruously riding past the spot where he had learned to swim as a youngster, Pitar saw enough of the Swordtroop's movement to realize it was recovering from surprise and was deploying for an advance; he could not tell which direction it was moving, nor if he would get to his assigned location in time to block an attack.

Unfortunately, in his opinion, lan Haarper had erred by limiting the gunfire to solid shot. Shrapnel would have killed or disabled far more of Mlart's infantry, and the effect of shrapnel was not critically dependent on a gunner's aim. Had the southern guns faced the front of the Algherans, each shot would have gone through the length of their column. Since they actually pointed at the flanks, only a narrow cross section of the column was in danger from each shot and even then it took luck to strike a target on the top of the road—neither cannon shot nor powder bags were weighted to precise specifications, and gun barrels deteriorated under use; no gunner's hand on an elevating screw, however well trained, could adjust for those imponderables.

Lan Haarper, however, had seen an opportunity to strike at enemy guns, and the young Ironwearer was obsessed by cannon. "Artillery kills, so let's kill artillery," he had told his morning staff conference, and that had ended the meeting. Pitar did not believe he had spent one minute considering the contrary opinions that he had pretended to listen to so politely.

He wondered if the Ironwearer was happy now with the results of his decisions. He saw some guns knocked from their carriages and there were dead horses in some sets of traces, so the Algheran artillery had taken damage, but Pitar doubted if it was serious. Mlart had many guns. The Lopritians firing at them had followed orders from lan Haarper to aim carefully rather than shoot indiscriminately. It seemed to Pitar this had produced a slow rate of fire with no gain in accuracy—a situation which provided the worst of both worlds, to use a slogan that had also originated with lan Haarper.

And yet, all those dissatisfactions were minor ones.

The symptom of Pitar's greatest concern was that the company he was escorting had originally been Dalsyn lan Plenytk's North Valley Battalion. He had no qualms about its quality, but in less than thirty days he had watched its numbers fall from almost four hundred to one hundred fifty men; the unit—and many another units in the Strength-through-Loyalty Brigade—simply could not survive much more fighting.

It was those reduced numbers which had forced the brigade to fight this battle defensively, and Pitar was acutely aware that in each of the three battles he had witnessed in his short military life, the attackers had won. It was all very well for Timmial lan Haarper to say that "the defensive is the strongest part of war." By Timmial's own admission, the definition came from a general who had never faced the Swordtroop. Pitar's gut feeling coincided with statistics.

Timmial was also fond of saying, "In war, the moral is to the physical as three to one." That was the catch phrase of another obscure dead general. It struck Pitar that if lan Haarper wished to quote from generals, with all that implied about taking advice, it would be reassuring to have him cite live ones or at least famous ones with sufficient good taste to die of old age.

Most importantly, Pitar was upset by Timmial lan Haarper himself.

He was not alone in that feeling.

Timmial was not a trained general, it was clear. His orders bred confusion. They were terse, vague, and incomplete. They were usually given orally, often by no more than a shout, and the man placed great reliance on something that he called "initiative" but which looked to most of his subordinates like mind reading. Proper written instructions were dictated to Gertynne ris Vandeign only when the Ironwearer found it convenient; they often came to their recipients long after the fact, and sometimes conflicted with additional orders given by Timmial and which Gertynne never heard.

Paradoxically, he took some tasks into his own hands which would better have been delegated to sergeants, and he had the habit of slipping into the ranks during marches to chat with soldiers. Ris Daimgewln had complained to Pitar that his privates knew lan Haarper's strategy better than he did; Pitar suspected that might be more truth than hyperbole.

Lan Haarper showed the characteristics of a good sergeant rather than a general, he had decided. Not a highly visible sergeant—a jovial platoon sergeant, say, on good terms with all his men. But this sergeant had a platoon of two thousand men.

Was that the real man? Pitar had never met lan Haarper until he began to train the Midpassage soldiers, but friends had known him when he was a prospector; they had called him taciturn and remote, even surly at times.

Which was the man and which the image? Did it matter to the brigade?

What were the thoughts he kept hidden from Wandisha?

Surely it mattered that the man's life was in danger and yet Pitar could not see that he was making any attempt to protect himself, or to let others protect him. He had already received a serious wound, which would have caused any other soldier in the brigade to be evacuated to a hospital. The injury must be painful; it could be infected and even cost his life. It was obvious that it hurt his concentration, and the brandy and water Quillyn kept pouring out for him was neither proper medication nor an aid to purposeful thought.

Kylene lin Haarper was missing in gruesome circumstances. Only missing, the Ironwearer kept repeating, but it was obvious from his behavior that Kylene's absence caused him more distress than the physical wound. It was enough by itself to disqualify him for command of the brigade, in Pitar's opinion, and Dalsyn lan Plenytk and Perrid lan Styllin had agreed, but none had been brave enough to bring the matter to the Hand.

And so the brigade was left with Timmial lan Haarper as its commander. Commanding a regiment, lan Haarper had taken great risks—far greater than his subordinates had understood at the time—and the Gods had blessed his gambles. Experience had taught Pitar that the Gods grow weary of those who rely on them. Timmial had not sought praise for himself; he was prompt to credit his men for his successes, but it was troubling that he had never once acknowledged that much depended on fortune.

Perhaps the Ironwearer actually believed the courage and determination of his men were strong enough to triumph at any odds. But he was now gambling Midpassage and what was left of the Strength-through-Loyalty Brigade against Mlart tra'Nornst with the Kingdom of Loprit itself as the stakes.

What would happen to them all when lan Haarper's luck turned sour?

Part Two: Settlements

CHAPTER THIRTEEN

*M*lart tra'Nornst *had expected to find Midpassage defended* by Lopritian troops but the shelling his forces met south of the town came as an unpleasant surprise. When he recovered from that, he saw that smoke clouds gave away the position of the Lopritian guns—they were on a hillside on his flank, about a thousand man-heights due east, separated by fields of furze and tall grass and by the small river that bordered the town. Presumably the guns were defended by infantry, but they could not be seen from the great road—no enemy infantry formations in any direction could be seen.

It was only the act of rear-guard defenders, his aides suggested. The Lopritians had heavy guns to spare, thanks to the bungling tra'Dicovys, but only limited numbers of horses. Perhaps they had decided to expend some of their artillery in a way that might delay the Swordtroop.

They'd managed, he commented dryly.

It was provoking, the aides admitted, but not an important check. A day tenth of marching would bring most of his men safely past the guns with endurable losses; cut off from the north, the enemy gunners would abandon their guns and Mlart would recapture what the tra'Dicovys had lost.

Perhaps. The Warder of the Realm would have traded all their guesses for one Teep's certainty, and he privately cursed the obstinacy that made his countrymen prefer ignorance to the insecure loyalty of a mind reader. He growled at his aides, then issued his orders.

Three sections of the Algheran guns, half his own artillery, were laboriously unharnessed from their transportation and turned about on the road to reply to the Lopritian cannon. A regiment from the Cuhyon Division, battalion-size after its losses on the bloody ridge south of West Bend, was sent to demonstrate against the Lopritians. A cavalry squad was sent southwest, either to find a ford, or to pretend that one had been found. The rest of his cavalry was sent up the road, with instructions to enter the town and swing to the right to envelop the guns.

Then Mlart waited atop the road, not mounted but on foot, so his soldiers could see him walking. The Crovsol Division, this was—in name—with Crovsol and I'suboc Housetroops banded together in one regiment, and three regiments full of the unSepted, with foreign Blankshields to give stiffening to inexperienced soldiers. A good unit on paper, though only combat would show how much iron had formed in the berry; he was sadly aware that his conscripts were far from equal to the professional Housetroops, no matter how loudly their expensively paid mercenary officers shouted orders at them.

The Crovsol Division was also a fat unit, almost at full paper strength with six thousand men barely touched in his victory in the south. Too big a unit to waste on garrison duty, he reminded himself, though it was really with him so the Crovsol Sept could have the names of some cheap victories to stitch to their battle flags; that should keep their loyalty in the Muster.

Lord and Lady, what a way to run an army! Loprit's aristocrats might claim rank made them generals, too, but they had the sense to back out of the way when fighting began and left things to competent soldiers. A full-time national army, professionally officered, loyal to the government, with men at all ranks selected for ability—Loprit had those things, for all its failings, and his poor Alghera only had its troublesome Septs who never lost sight of advantage in their squalid little spats and that Cimon-taken Muster of inbred imbeciles which only gabbled like geese when someone suggested a modern world needed more than superstition and the obnoxious habits of their out-of-wedlock-born ancestors.

Not that the troops needed to hear his opinions. By asking, Mlart found six men among the unSepted who shared the name of his infant son. The Warder of the Algheran Realm laughed for his men to hear and said it was an omen sent by Lord Cimon; those six must be the bravest of the brave in the days ahead, for they were sure to survive him.

Farther up the road, brave men and cowards died alike.

As the cavalry cantered up to the bridge, ports swung up on both sides of the rickety fence that masked the far side. Gun muzzles, uncovered, spewed fire and thunder. Sleeted by shrapnel and musket rain, men and horses, like paper windows in a hurricane, fell in tatters.

On the Algheran side of the bridge, latecomers hauled in reins and swept right and left along the riverbank. Additional musket fire lashed at them, more guns. Horses screamed and fell over the banks. Men shouted.

Then the survivors were free and in retreat. The noise continued. The men who had fallen over the banks did not emerge.

He still saw no Lopritians. Only Algheran dead remained visible on the cropped grass beside the banks. Only Algheran wounded writhed and screamed for aid. On the hillside and behind Mlart on the road, cannons boomed.

Another trip, Mlart diagnosed, and quite as bad as the one old Cherrid ris Clendannan had set four days before. For that battle, the Lopritian general had hidden his smaller numbers behind a ridge. Now he had used the edge of the riverbank, but the principle was the same.

He should be pleased, Mlart thought. This time, only cavalry had died finding where the enemy was hidden. Men volunteered to be cavalrymen and expendable. He could afford such losses.

They had found something of where the enemy was hidden; ris Clendannan had a great deal of river to conceal his soldiers in. Mlart stared at it, as well as he could from his vantage point on the road, and made decisions.

The Cuhyon Division was to remain in place until it received further orders. The cavalry on the right was to continue its search for a ford, and the survivors of the abortive attack on the bridge were to pass to the left, between the burning farmsteads and the river, and to continue northward until a practical passing point for large numbers of infantrymen was found. The Crovsol Division was sent in the same direction; it would provide the men.

If Cherrid ris Clendannan thought Mlart was dumb enough to sacrifice the Swordtroop on his riverbank altar, the old man was due for a surprise. Mlart had decided to pull at the ends of the Lopritian line, instead, until it was as stretched as string could be and no more strong.

"Go as far north as necessary," ran his instructions to the tra'Crovsol. "Cross the river at a point or points where minimal force is required and return to the south along the paved road until significant enemy resistance is noted. Keep me informed of your progress. Leave detachments across the river to discourage enemy escape attempts."

By nightfall, the town had been invested.

Timmial lan Haarper was the last man to enter the inn. He came into the barroom with boards under his arms to support him. They were planks with holes drilled in the middle for him to rest his hands in. They reached from his armpits to the floor, and he moved by swinging them before him and alternating his weight between the boards and one foot. He held his wounded leg before him at an angle; Rallt could see the edges of the slats which kept it immobile standing out under the cloth of his dark trousers.

It was an awkward, half-stumbling progression, and his face showed pain as he moved. His knuckles were as white as his supporting planks, and from the landing outside ris Clendannan's room, Rallt stared down at him, feeling pity.

No one rose to meet him, though the tables near the bar were surrounded by men. Lords, Wandisha had said. Lords and high-ranking officers and their staffs from the regiments and battalions: all the commanders of the brigade.

Lords. He was conscious of ris Clendannan behind him, listening through his open door as he lay on his bed. If Lord Clendannan had been stronger, Rallt knew he would have been one of the men downstairs waiting to judge Ironwearer lan Haarper.

To condemn Ironwearer lan Haarper. Rallt stared down at the narrow eyes of the lords as they stared at lan Haarper and waited for him to approach them. To Rallt, who had never known nobility, they seemed patrons' eyes, angry and money-conscious, and Ian Haarper—who was not a noble, he had been told— seemed simple and peasantlike in comparison. The boy wondered what fears the man held as he stumped across the floor.

"Mlart's a pretty good general, gentlemen," the red-haired man said. "Faster on the uptake than I had hoped he would be." It sounded like a remark about crops.

It was the Ironwearer's only excuse. He coughed once, gruffly, and pivoted slowly on his boards. "Run along, Quillyn."

Rallt heard the door close. He watched as the Ironwearer looked around the room again, his eyes moving from table to table and then upward to the frightened refugees looking timidly through their bedroom doors.

"Figured you'd all want to have the trial before the condemned man put up an argument. I've been running around— in a manner of speaking—talking to the troops. They're in a pretty good mood."

He paused. Behind Rallt, ris Clendannan sighed.

Wandisha tugged Rallt's sleeve, then relented when he stood fixed to his place. "They won't really shoot him," she hissed, and Rallt flushed with embarrassment when the old man called the Hand of the Queen looked up at him.

Lan Haarper stood on his boards with his head tilted slightly, a wary expression on his face, watching a young blond man in a green and black uniform who sat alone at a table near the fireplace. It was the one man in the room he did not recognize, Rallt sensed.

Near to him was a handsome man in expensive clothing who stood as if to make introductions. "This is Mlart's envoy. He's here for—you know." He nodded abruptly and sat down again.

The Ironwearer grimaced. "Okay, Gertynne. So he's here for you know what. Have you people signed anything yet?"

No one said anything, until the Algheran spoke. "It is customary for the defeated party to propose his terms first. We were waiting for you, Ironwearer." He sat with a palm resting on a flat leather case and he rubbed his fingers along its edge when he spoke, as if to draw attention to it.

The Algheran spoke Lopritian with a high-pitched voice. Rallt could not tell if it was accented, but he had noticed that though the native Lopritians glanced at him when he was silent, none looked at him when he talked.

"Very civilized. I won't ask why I'm so essential to this cel-ebration." The Ironwearer smiled bleakly and stumped to an unoccupied table, then rested his boards over a vacant stool. He braced himself on the table and slowly sank onto another stool. Rallt noticed he was looking at the Hand, though his words were for the Algheran.

"Frankly, I don't feel defeated," he said. "You folks maneu-vered well today. You didn't fight us. We're still in the town, and you're still outside, and we still have the bridge under con-trol. You're the ones stuck in a foreign country with no fast way out, not us."

The Algheran was unconcerned. "Circumstances speak for themselves. Your condition is hopeless, Ironwearer, and I sug-gest it is time that you respond to those realities."

Lan Haarper smiled. "I'll need something to write on."

"You can use mine." The well-dressed man—Gertynne—brought a writing block to the table and left it without touching lan Haarper's hand. Rallt, watching the redhead from the railing overhead, thought he seemed amused.

"You folks all have a nice little chat waiting on me?" he asked.

A pleasantry. It was an alien remark for lan Haarper's deep voice, Rallt felt. It was a voice for giving orders. He swallowed, remembering that barely a day had passed since he first met the man, and that the Ironwearer had been given orders then.

How could so much change in one day?

Behind him, Cherrid ris Clendannan rested with his head on Wandisha's shoulder, his hand in her fingers. He could hear Wandisha whispering in the old man's ear but not what was said.

A woman, a Teep, and older than he was. The Ironwearer was "Timmial" to her. She knew him from events in the past, she had said. Rallt wondered what image of lan Haarper was in Wandisha's memories.

"We had an adequate discussion," the Algheran said. No one else spoke.

"Hmm. How pleasant." Lan Haarper pulled paper from the top of the writing block, then inserted darker sheets taken from its bottom. "I assume you all realize I'm going to propose le-nient terms."

"You can ask." The Algheran envoy rubbed his leather case

and looked at the other men in the room, smiling at their impassive faces.

Lan Haarper had not noticed. His stylus moved as he spoke. "The most important need is an end to the war. I'm suggesting that the two sides return immediately to their prewar borders and that the conflict end without change of boundaries, without payment of restitution, and without ransom."

"Quite impossible," the Algheran said. "Look where our armies stand."

"I'm thinking about just that." Lan Haarper stared at the Algheran until the envoy's eyes dropped. "When did you people last hear from the tra'Ruijac? Recently?"

"Recently," the Algheran agreed. "His condition is most satisfactory."

Wandisha moved restlessly. "Lying," Rallt mumbled, wondering if lan Haarper could hear him and if she wanted lan Haarper to know that, and the Hand stared at him again.

"Recently," lan Haarper said tonelessly. "It's been a few days since we got a dispatch from Lord Mockstyn, but he was fixing for a battle and his last message to us seemed fairly confident. The Northern Armies are not small, and I'm sure your boss knows that, even if you don't."

"That's not an issue," the envoy mumbled.

"I think it is. You people grabbed the Torn Coast from Loprit in the last war and you've held it. You had Nicole's cloak over you then but you can't guarantee you'll always be so blessed. How are you going to feel if you wind up this campaign with a couple fingers on the Shield Valley while ris Mockstyn puts F'a Alghera in his pocket?"

"That's not possible."

"It certainly is. Your boss had a reason for not tackling Loprit in the north. I'll leave this clause as is." Lan Haarper turned away, and for moments Rallt heard no sound but his stylus scratching over the sheets of paper.

"Prisoners on both sides returned—immediately, subject to needs for medical treatment—travel facilitated by authorities— no cost—without ransom for soldiers of any rank—without punishment for any action legally ordered by superior officers. Soldiers to retain—to the extent possible—personal possessions. Armies to retain wagons and horses—necessary for transportation of men and wounded—but—surrender of other—equipment in-

cluding—all weapons and ammunition. Negotiations to begin at
once for restoration of lasting and mutually beneficial peace—"

He glanced upward. His eyes met Rallt's.

"Representatives to be advised and supervised by—
commissioners, let's say—from Innings and other neutral states.
Truce to be supervised by same. This compact shall be preserved by the thoughts and actions of both human races and
witnessed by the spirit of the tiMantha lu Duois."

He put the stylus down and separated the papers carefully.
"Space at the bottom for signatures and witnesses. I've left the
date off, we can insert that later. Grahan?"

"Yes, sir?" Ris Clendannan's orderly drew near. Rallt could
not make out his expression.

The Ironwearer held out his paper. "Copy to the Hand. Copy
to the Algheran. Copy to Gertynne."

"This is totally impossible," the Algheran shouted.

Lan Haarper ignored him. "Anyone here from Leiman and
Scee?"

There was. A burly graying man stood, and the Ironwearer
beckoned toward him. "Good to see you've made it, Nallis.
Lopritian war aims. It's a scoop for you."

"What do I do?" the man asked. He looked about nervously,
lan Haarper's paper tight in his fist.

"Publish, publish," the Ironwearer said reassuringly. "People will be interested, even if nothing comes of it. Remind me,
lan Alpbak, one of these days, to tell you about something called
the First Amendment and the national question asker."

The Algheran had stood. "This is outrageous!"

"The hell you say," lan Haarper muttered, then reverted to
Lopritian as he turned away from the news gatherer. "What's
the sticking point, you? Killing your ambassadors? The fact that
Loprit tried to buy time that way and that afterward some idiots
mutilated the bodies to pretend the killing was done by bandits?

"Loprit did wrong there, I admit it, and so will every man
in this room. But the Teeps have got the truth out. It didn't take
your army. History's not going to hide our sins.

"And Loprit's paid pretty well for its sins, haven't we? You've
invaded us. You've sacked some of our cities. You've won battles
against us. You've killed our people—enough of our people. Do
you think you're making things any better by killing more of us?
You know you're not. Alghera's made its point, man. You can

end the war and history will praise you for it. You can praise yourself for it. Don't go beyond honor, though, or neither history nor your children will praise you.''

The Algheran stared incredulously at him, then at the paper Grahan had handed to him. His hand dropped. He shook the paper limply at his side.

"You can't offer these terms," he growled. "This isn't a surrender agreement. It isn't even a peace pact. This is nothing but a Cimon-taken Ironwearer's verdict!"

"More or less," the Ironwearer agreed. "It's only my suggestion, of course, since I was told to make suggestions. But I just work here. The queen speaks for Loprit. Still, her uncle is here, and if he and your boss sign this thing, I'd give high odds we can make a reasonable peace."

"You aren't behaving as if you understand the situation," the Algheran said. He took a long look at the Hand, whose misery was obvious even to Rallt, then raised the paper before him. He tore it in half, then fitted the pieces together and tore them again, and let them flutter onto the floor. "Is there any chance we can behave like sober men?"

Lan Haarper ignored the insult. "Good thing Leiman and Scee has spare copies," he commented. He tapped his writing block for a moment. "All right, I'll give you something smaller, suitable for your—uh—sober mind."

He looked upward again, grinning, and pointed a finger at Rallt, while slowly bringing down his thumb. "Must be past your bedtime, kid."

Rallt stepped backward, embarrassed to be noticed again, and lan Haarper, invisible below the landing, chuckled.

"Terms of surrender," the Ironwearer mumbled. "Hmmm-hmmm. Hmm-mmm. Soldiers to be exchanged—hmm huh—weapons to be surrendered—possessions—already covered—uh huh!"

His stylus scratched awhile longer, then he asked for Grahan to distribute the sheets again, and Rallt watched as the old soldier moved about the room, each step followed by the eyes of men who seemed about to cry.

Lan Alpbak, at the table nearest lan Haarper, was busily sketching ideograms onto his own writing block even before Grahan was done. The burly man seemed excited and very proud of himself; Rallt wondered if he already saw himself hailed as a national question asker.

"A little better," the Algheran envoy growled when he had his copy. "What's this nonsense about accepting the overall peace terms?"

"An idea," Ian Haarper said calmly. "It's up to your boss, isn't it?"

"Yes." The Algheran folded the paper and moved it toward his leather case, then opened it again for a final look. "Uhhh . . . One more thing, Ironwearer. You worded this with grammar— I guess you aren't very fluent in Lopritian—it looks like Mlart is surrendering to you Lopheads."

"That's exactly right, buster. Nothing wrong with my grammar."

Somewhere, out of his sight, Rallt heard a chair scrape. A foot, encased in one of Ian Haarper's boots, rose and settled on the table. Rallt watched eyes turn to it.

"Good terms, too," he heard the Ironwearer say. "Mlart's going to appreciate them, if not today then eventually. Be sure to tell him you Algies can't expect any better offer from us, uh, Lopheads. And be sure and tell him Leiman and Scee is going to print those terms for all the world to read."

"I'm not going to tell him—"

"Oh, yes you are." The boot came down, and Rallt watched as the Ironwearer laboriously rose to his feet and stepped stiffly toward the other men. "Mlart tra'Nornst is the Warder of Alghera, not you. You're an errand boy, sonny, that's all, and taking back these terms is your errand, not running off your big mouth. Now I advise you to turn around and take a good look—"

The Ironwearer turned himself at that point, his hand out, making the gesture he had made earlier at Rallt. "You see anyone here who's eager to surrender to you now?"

"I'm not surrendering," the man called Gertynne said harshly. He seemed surprised by himself, Rallt thought, but he stood despite that and glared at the envoy. "You haven't beat us yet."

"I'm not, either." A hatchet-faced man rose to stand beside Gertynne. "You Algies never have gotten through the Steadfast-to-Victory. Why should I think you will now?"

"I'm not." Another man stood. "I know what the queen

expects of me. Eh? Am I supposed to go back and tell her how I gave away her Guards?"

"And I'm too old to quit." Another man stood.

"I've still got ammunition to shoot, and I can fire off rocks when I run out, Timmial. You ask me and I'll keep going."

"And me."

"I'm not ready to surrender."

"Not me, either."

The room was filled with standing men suddenly, all looking at the envoy, then back to the table where one man remained seated—the Hand of the Queen. He held his copies of lan Haarper's papers in one hand. He came to his feet slowly, and Rallt held his breath, understanding from the way he was watched that the mood of all the others could be changed by one of his words.

"Loprit proposes a peace on Ironwearer lan Haarper's terms," he said carefully, and throughout the room men breathed again.

The envoy made a spitting sound. "You haven't earned it."

Rallt knew suddenly that the young Algheran was foolish but very brave, and he wondered if that was recognized by any of the others in the room.

Then the Hand snapped his fingers softly. "We have nothing to lose by trying. You've made that clear."

Lan Haarper turned to the envoy. "You've heard what we had to say. Now get the hell out of here, boy. You take Mlart those terms and you just pray we'll be willing to give them when he's willing to see reason."

He nodded slowly. "Grahan, see that our guest gets home safely. Get him out of earshot. The rest of us have got a battle to plan."

CHAPTER FOURTEEN

*M*lart had his men placed to the north, west, and south of the town. The east, consisting of forested hills and rolling plains, was still open but no roads went through it. Refugees could escape on foot to the wilderness, but armies could not move there. For military purposes, Midpassage was surrounded.

The Algheran general had seen no need for unnecessary fighting. Demonstrations against their artillery had amused the Lopritians, keeping them in place while the entrapment proceeded, and on both sides casualties during the day had been light.

Troop counts told Harper he still had 1,800 soldiers in good condition, another 300 who continued to fight in some fashion— he was counted in that category himself—and perhaps another thousand, consisting of the town's normal residents, refugees from West Bend, and camp followers, to worry about. Privately, he did worry.

A handful of civilians had managed to leave before the Algherans placed a regiment from the Crovsol Division across the road to the north, but most had chosen to stay. Despite Pitar lan

178

Styllin's urgings, few parents had been willing to evacuate their children; about twenty remained in Midpassage.

Lan Haarper's initial orders, therefore, were directed to lan Styllin and Ironwearer Wolf-Twin: tents were to be taken from brigade stocks and erected on the far side of the hills; children and their mothers were to be taken there and supplied with food; women willing to bear arms should be given weapons and left in charge; saws and axes and other tools needed for building should be stockpiled at the site.

"You expect women and children to build houses?" lan Styllin had demanded. He had had to admit that his own child had not been sent to safety; his attitude still showed the resentment born of deserved embarrassment.

The tools are for rebuilding Midpassage. That was the reason for the order, but lan Styllin had too little imagination to guess the answer, too much imagination to be told. "It might snow," Harper replied, purposefully vague, and turned to other matters.

"Kill the brave ones," Harper had said that morning, growling the words, angered at himself and at the weakness that made him limit his remarks so temperately to a handful of officers rather than shout them at all his troops before battle began. "If some Algie can be shot, shoot him. I don't want them to be brave. If your men don't like the idea, tell them brave soldiers set bad examples, on both sides." He said that again now, in response to Dalsyn lan Plenytk, and realized from the reaction of other listeners that the remark must be amplified.

"Shoot them whenever you see them," he said loudly. "If they're brewing breakfast stew, and you can hit them, hit them. If they're sitting on a latrine within range, kill them. If they're just trying to look at the river, kill them. Don't waste ammunition but don't ever stop. Shoot them in the back if you can. Set up ambushes. Shoot them from the tops of buildings. Hide under places where they can't see you and shoot them. Don't be sorry about it. Just do whatever works."

This is war, Dalsyn. War is hell. He couldn't say that, either.

And he was sorry there were still civilians in the inn to hear him.

Lerlt had waited and waited but the Algherans did not cross the river. Guns sounded and muskets rattled at intervals but whatever action was conveyed on that noise was out of his sight;

on the plain that stretched in front of Lerlt, he saw but a few thin lines of soldiers. They marched pointlessly to and fro. In late afternoon, they stopped even that semblance of courage and vanished from view. They had attacked nothing; it did not seem to him that they had even fired their muskets.

Herrilmin did not return.

Wherever he looked, there were only Lopritians pretending to victory. At nightfall, when scattered campfires which must belong to Algherans appeared across the river, he stared at them forlornly, wishing the men who crowded around them could behold him or knew of him. He had never felt more desolate than when he saw this evidence of the countrymen who had forgotten him.

Herrilmin could not come back in the middle of a battle, he realized. His time machine could not be risked. It was necessary for the Lopritians to be beaten first, for Mlart to trounce the defenders, to take their wealth away and destroy their possessions. Then, when the other Algherans had moved on, leaving a town as completely defenseless and vulnerable as the woman in Ian Haarper's house, the time travelers could all be safe.

Until then, he must be alone.

Even Lopritian soldiers had companions, but he had no one to share his solitude but Gherst, and Gherst refused to talk to him anymore.

He sniffed awhile, then picked up the musket and walked across the loft. Slowly, in case Gherst should call him back, he climbed down the ladder and left the barn. He walked across the back of the hill and hid himself in the woods, where Gherst would not hear him cry.

Mlart's south-ranging cavalry had found a ford below the artillery. In the morning, his infantry could cross there. Harper had no wish for a battle at the end of an extended line, so he had decided to pull back the troops stationed in the southern fields. As part of the contraction of the perimeter, orders were sent to bring back the guns in the pasture and station them near the main buildings of Merryn ris Vandeign's farm. The guns were cumbersome so the movement was to begin immediately.

The order reached its destination midway through fourth watch. Most of the gun crews were asleep then. A few were still drinking.

The four-man crew of one large cannon was in this category. They had liberated a keg of distilled spirits of indifferent quality from an otherwise ignoble basement in West Bend. Unlike the pack-carrying soldiers who had littered the road to Midpassage with souvenirs found more weighty than worthy, they had each maintained the collector's enthusiasm so necessary for keeping even such minor military memorabilia. A caisson with space for personal possessions had helped, of course, but in retrospect, it had only assisted what soldierly perseverance could have accomplished alone.

The plunder did not qualify as a "keepsake" in any strict sense. In fact, it had suffered calamitous loss for three nights running, but it was still far from empty. So was the gun crew.

They were not in good spirits. They were in rotgut, but it was close enough.

Because they were awake and because they were close to the exit from the pasture, their gun was the first to be sent north. It was to be placed in front of ris Vandeign's barn, and aimed to cover the bridge.

The night was cold and horses did the heavy pulling. The gun was already loaded and the finer adjustments of pointing required daylight. The gun crew had no reason to lapse into sobriety, and sought none, but the hour was late and morning would eventually come. They did what was possible and settled in their blankets around the gun carriage.

Wandisha wanted to take ris Clendannan to a safer place as soon as lan Haarper's meeting was over, but it took time to find the ambulance and the driver had vanished. Cherrid insisted on waiting to hear the questions, and when that came to a finish, he and lan Haarper were the only officers left in the inn.

They were not the only soldiers in the inn. A platoon from the Defiance-to-Insurrection had come and was already going from door to door evicting the refugees. Riflemen moved into the vacated rooms.

"Let's go in my wagon," lan Haarper suggested, and in the end that was what was done, with the two Ironwearers stretched side by side in the carriage and Wandisha and Grahan jammed beside lan Haarper's Quillyn on the front seat. Rallt would have walked but lan Haarper insisted there was space for him; he wound up squatting on the back corner of the overloaded wagon, feeling sorry for the horses.

Quillyn wanted to drive, Rallt noticed, but Wandisha took the reins first and handed them to Grahan. Though the little man pouted, the ride was smooth enough, if rather slow. The passengers were jostled only a little at the point where they turned from the great road onto a dirt lane. "Guns have made a mess," Grahan explained over his shoulder, and Ian Haarper mumbled something about tar. Rallt, looking backward as they started up the hillside, strained to see curl-topped ruts in the dirt; the paved road was almost invisible in the night.

"Well, Timmial," ris Clendannan said at last. There had been little conversation in the wagon, and Rallt sensed Grahan and Wandisha had forced themselves to be silent, waiting for this moment.

"Well, Cherrid," Ian Haarper said. "What do you think?"

"Interesting," the old Ironwearer said.

"Unpleasant."

"Sounds it. Where did—"

"Out west." Lan Haarper moved a hand vaguely, as if expecting the other man to read a direction from it. "It's been done."

"Not by you." The old man coughed and Wandisha turned awkwardly to hold him up by the shoulders as he spat over the side of the wagon.

"Not by Mlart, either." Lan Haarper had waited for ris Clendannan to lie down again. "At least I've read of such things."

"Hmm." A moment passed. Rallt, his hands braced against the wagon sides, sleepily listened to the hooves on the road. "Wonder if Mlart reads his Chronicles?"

"Wandisha?"

"Not very often, Lord Clendannan," Wandisha said.

"Not religiously, huh?" Lan Haarper chuckled minutely. "If I were an Algheran politician, I wouldn't want Teeps around either, Wandisha." His voice carried a note which told Rallt it took effort for him to speak evenly; the boy wondered how he would talk himself with a serious wound.

"No," Wandisha said in a small voice. "Will it be that bad?"

Lan Haarper shifted his position so he was looking at Rallt. "Case you're curious, there's a part in the Plates which describes how Kh'taal Minzaer—the capital of the Teeps during the First Eternal War—was destroyed in battle. We're talking about that. Very grim. If you haven't read it, I won't say more."

He shifted again. "It won't be like that, Wandisha. It can get bad enough, but if worse comes to worst, you should be safe back in the woods. I remember once, I talked to a Teep who told me both Normals and telepaths were more peaceful innately than they were during the Second Era. He said the wars had tamed people. The wild men are all gone."

"One hasn't," Grahan said quietly.

Lan Haarper moved his head suddenly. "What? Oh, the killer you're looking for. He's— I wouldn't worry too much about him, if I were you. I don't think you're going to find him."

"Is this the place?" Wandisha asked. Rallt, looking where she looked, saw a narrow house ahead with lighted windows and open shutters. The road bent here; he realized that traveling another two hundred man-heights would have brought them to lan Haarper's house.

The red-haired Ironwearer sat up to see. "Yeah. Teacher woman had it—you remember her, Wandisha?—had everything set up on the ground floor so she didn't have to go up steps. I thought you'd be comfortable there. Lan Styllin put his family upstairs, so you'll have some extra hands if you need them." He settled down again.

"Where is she?" Wandisha asked.

"She stayed, strangely enough." Lan Haarper stretched and rose back on one elbow. "Thought she'd go back to F'a Loprit and settle in for meals with her friend—big big woman, we're talking Fat City here, named Molminda, who was constantly talking about the queen—Pitar tried to get her to leave, but she wouldn't go as long as any kids were left in town. So she's next door, probably sleeping on a couch. You can close your eyes, if she comes to visit, Cherrid, and just imagine you're back in court, hearing all the royal gossip."

He paused. "Anyhow! I misjudged her. I shouldn't make fun."

Ris Clendannan grunted something. The wagon wheels churned though gravel, and then the wagon halted. Grahan went to open the door.

"Will you stay?" Wandisha offered. "We can find a place for you and your man to sleep."

"I'd like to. But I really have to run around some more and

tell lies to the troops.'' Ironwearer Ian Haarper sounded very
old and very tired.

Wind found chinks in the gun crew's armor of bedding. In
the background, vandals of the nighttime quiet were snoring. It
was impossible to avoid looking at what must be a nice warm
barn.

"Forget it," the sergeant-in-charge growled when Private
Thyllich rolled onto his elbow for the third time and pushed his
blanket back for the first. "It's a lord's property. We've been
told to stay out."

Thyllich was not an old soldier and trained to obedience. He
was a Midpassage man, in fact, a farm worker who had enlisted
with the hope of escaping the drudgery of farm work—or any
work—at war's end.

He hadn't realized the sergeant was still awake. "Thought I'd
get some straw," he lied. "Wasn't going to do anything else."

"Off limits. You know that!" Sergeant Wicherty rapped the
ground beside his bedroll to emphasize the point and skinned
his knuckle on hardpan.

Not quietly enough, he cursed.

Thyllich pressed what might be an advantage. "Awful hard
ground, isn't it? I could get enough for us all, Sergeant. A couple
of armloads and—"

It was dark but Wicherty recognized the face of sin and he
found it alluring. "How do you know there's straw in there?"

"Helped put it there, Sergeant. Wasn't much more than a
year tenth ago, and all the animals are gone, it's just up there in
the loft, lying wasted. It's like my straw, in a way. I just want to
borrow some of it back."

Reconnoiter the objective, Wicherty learned as a young soldier, and he still remembered the phrase, even if it came out
now as "You sure there's enough for us all without anyone noticing?"

There was, Thyllich assured him.

It took genius to recognize genius, and Wicherty had no
shortage of the proper stuff. "Get clean straw. Nothing with
bird droppings, Thyllich."

"Yes, sir!" Thyllich already had his shoes on.

A light went on behind him. Illumination came suddenly from
the barn door and sprang with illicit affection upon Wicherty

and the gun carriage. The imbecilic Thyllich had just made him the best target in town.

Wicherty was on his feet as fast as he could balance on them. Barefoot, he stumbled the few man-heights to the barn door and stepped inside. Overhead a line of arc-lights hissed like snakes. He looked for, but did not find, a light switch.

What he saw instead was Thyllich's boots and Thyllich's butt at the right of the barn. They were swaying at the top end of a ladder leading to the loft. The barn, other of his senses told him, had a terrible smell. Some of it, he was sure, was Thyllich's fault.

"Lord, ugh-h!" the private shouted.

"What?" The sergeant looked about frantically for the light switch.

"Sergeant? This is awful. Come up, please. There's a dead man." Thyllich sounded completely sober.

"What? So?" Wicherty had seen dead men before.

"Please, Sergeant. I think it's a soldier."

It was the note of desperation that carried Wicherty forward. Thyllich was one of his privates, and the private's voice said he needed his sergeant. When Wicherty ran, he was obeying habits more ingrained than instinctual.

But his instincts almost made him fall out of the loft when he reached the top. He stepped backward in shock, and only Thyllich's gasp made him realize his danger.

An intact human body holds about half a bucket of blood. It looked here as if someone had spilled such a bucket. Shrapnel fired at close range killed without doing such damage. Wicherty had never seen a body with as many cuts.

He had not seen all of it. "What's the head like?" he asked hoarsely.

"No head." Thyllich swallowed. "It isn't under straw. It isn't here."

Wicherty swallowed as well, but not before he got a solid taste of the liquor he had already drunk. He wanted to lie down somewhere and be very sick.

"Go back and wake the others," he ordered. "Get them in here."

"All right."

The sergeant closed his eyes, queasily, feeling the earth and his stomach whirling in opposite directions. What was the other thing that he had to deal with? Oh, yes. "Thyllich? Close the Cimon-taken door after you?"

He had time to throw up. He did it, intentionally, standing by a ventilation window, holding the bars to keep himself from falling into what he had vomited. In the brief period of privacy, he admitted the necessity and cursed it at the same time, for what would make him sober eventually always seemed to magnify the symptoms of drunkenness first.

The door scraped shut. He heard voices. Wicherty breathed out slowly, conscious of how foul his breath had become, and staggered to the open side of the loft. "Find me a head," he mumbled. He said it again, louder, and explained, "There's a body up here without a head. An Algheran. Stabbed."

"Right there, Sarge," Detzer said, pointing at the back wall. "I don't know how you missed it."

"I was drunk," Wicherty mumbled, not loudly. It must have been true. There were arrow marks made from dirt or some dark fluid along the back wall. They were on both sides of the door. They pointed down at something round and varicolored.

A head. That was hair on one side, brown and matted. That was—something else on the other. A neck. A cut-off neck.

The head looked very small from the loft.

"Pick it up," he mumbled. He gestured to make the order clear.

No one budged. Waiting on the sergeant, he told himself. Slowly, he came down from the loft and moved to the head in small steps. Just as slowly, he bent and picked it up by the hair.

It still looked too small to sit atop a body.

"Anyone recognize it?" he asked.

Silence followed. He hadn't expected anyone would.

It didn't even look human, he thought sickly.

"Thyllich, is there water around here?" he asked.

"Back room." The private pointed nervously, then led the way to a pump. Detzer, like an idiot, tried to help with the washing.

Water had come up without priming, Wicherty noticed. More evidence that the man had been living in the barn.

Why? For how long?

"What do we do now, Sergeant?" Thyllich asked.

"Let's have a drink." Detzer, as could be anticipated from a man of his rank and experience, had an answer. Wicherty had none better.

"What do we do with it?" someone asked eventually. The sergeant wasn't sure who had asked that. He wasn't sure of a lot. It took a deal of squinting at that point to make two images of the head back into one.

"It's Algheran," Private Bhisson said solemnly. "We ought to give it back to the Algherans." Bhisson had always been a stickler for obeying regulations, Wicherty remembered.

"Going to walk over with it?" Thyllich wondered. He touched the head with a foot. "Bet those Algies'd thank you for it."

"Wasn't thinking of that." Bhisson got to his feet on a third attempt, then picked the head up and staggered to the mouth of the gun. "Ought to fit."

He had to reach. He dropped the head. "Should have fit," he complained.

"Let me try." Detzer crawled over and braced himself on the gun carriage. Wicherty, with one eye closed to clarify the image, nodded approvingly as the corporal raised himself up and posed with one arm draped over the thick barrel of the cannon. "Gimme."

Bhisson gave him.

"Do it this way," Detzer said carefully as he lifted the head over the muzzle. He fitted it in place and patted the crown affectionately. "Just takes some maneuvering, you see."

He pushed a little harder and the head disappeared from sight.

Wicherty was pleased enough to sit up and clap, an action echoed by Thyllich, and Bhisson raised a length of match in salute. Detzer beamed at them all, then stepped backward to enjoy the applause. Being out of gun carriage, he did a pratfall.

There were reasons, the sergeant remembered, why Detzer consistently failed to earn promotion.

Bo-OOM!

Private Bhisson had fired the gun.

Lights were on in the barn when Lerlt returned to it. It leaked from cracks beneath the doors and the windows.

Herrilmin, he thought at first, then realized it was not. Herrilmin would come to him. Those were strangers in the barn. Lopritian soldiers—he could see that the space in front of the barn had been invaded by them.

He stood without moving, uncertain what to do.

Gherst led him then. "Come on," Lerlt heard him say. "We can find another place to wait for Herrilmin."

He hesitated, then followed into the dark, bent close to the ground, stealthily, invisible—just as Gherst was.

"One of these buildings. This one." Gherst slipped through a narrow opening, then waited inside, while Lerlt pushed the door far enough to make his own entrance. The door was heavy, but he did not help with it.

The building was dark inside and Lerlt's hand, groping along the stuccoed wall, did not find a light switch. It also smelled. It had a nose-cleaning acrid taint which Lerlt could not recognize, and he wanted to leave.

"It's a good place," Gherst commented. His Septling was hidden but Lerlt thought he could see his hand, gleaming in some errant ray of light. "No one will come in here."

That was a virtue, Lerlt admitted. He tried to look around the building, to see what its gloom contained.

"Maybe there's food," Gherst suggested. "Enough for you, anyhow."

Lerlt nodded absently. His hand touched something tall and cold, wall-like except that it did not reach to the ceiling. He traced it with his fingers as he walked toward Gherst's voice.

"A set of stairs here."

Lerlt had already seen it. He stepped onto it, then halted almost immediately, unsure what waited before him. "I need the gun," he mumbled.

"Go get it. It's just by the door." Gherst satisfied himself by moving out of Lerlt's way as the smaller man retraced his steps.

Lerlt hesitated when the musket was in his hands again, and peeked through the door back at the barn. In the space before the building, soldiers were prancing about among the cannons. As he watched, one gun exploded; a column of yellow flame lanced toward the sky, then billows of smoke darker than the night sky. The sound almost deafened his ears; he sensed rather than heard the noise echo from nearby buildings.

A man, roused from his blankets, moved toward the gun. Lerlt guessed from his attitude that he was an officer and swearing.

Stealthily, not wishing to be noticed, he slipped the musket over his shoulder and used both hands to move the door shut.

"You might have helped me," he grumbled when the building's interior was totally hidden from outside view, and Gherst kept quiet from shame. Lerlt had seen enough to move without light; he slipped across the floor carefully until he reached the stairs, then went up them with the gun in his hands.

At the top of the steps he came to a narrow landing with a slippery surface. Lerlt moved along it slowly, probing the darkness with his gun, until he come to another wall. "No one's here," he called out, and Gherst made a grunting noise, like a foot scraping the floor. Lerlt reached to touch the walls before him. His foot touched an obstacle and he bent to examine what it had found.

Cloth. Blankets! He glanced quickly toward the place in the darkness where Gherst waited. "Nothing is up here," he said, trying to control his voice. "I'm going to sleep on the floor, without any covering."

"I'll wait down here," Gherst answered. "I don't need any sleep, Lerlt. I'll guard the door for you."

Lerlt was already fitting himself between the blankets. He marveled how warm they were, almost hot in places as he snuggled into them.

He was asleep almost at once.

The second amputation left Fesch weaker than the first. Long days passed before he was fit for more than sleep and the meals Kylene fed to him leisurely. She put no demands on him, not even for conversation, and he knew he had her sympathy.

In his weakness and isolation, that was enough. Despite the panicked chill-and-fever notions of his convalescence, when she was with him he wanted nothing more than her eyes on his face, her smile when she came to him and left, her soft voice apologizing for mishaps as she sponged his head and truncated limbs.

He loved her fervently and she was aware of it.

Yet, in some peculiar fashion, her own sentiments—her willingness to accept his love and return it—danced about his in a pattern he could never grasp. She was patient one day as he stammered out his love, cynical on another. Sometimes she demanded elaborate compliments and praise for actions unknown to him; when his words were inadequate, she created phrases for him to parrot. Sometimes she simply laughed at all he said. Sometimes she sat beside him, her thoughts turned inward, lost in sadness she would not explain, and he watched the shifting moods as they rested on her face, trying to read them, trying to find words which would restore her spirits. He needed her to be happy, he knew. As she needed him.

When the healing from the amputation was far advanced, Fesch found a source of private pleasure. With the ropes over his torso loosened, he was just able to touch his genitals with his left stump. He could stimulate himself to erection again.

Turned over, ankles crossed and knees spread wide, he could thrust himself into the leaves under his body. Strength was left in his hips and belly. He could still force himself to ejaculate.

Kylene laughed at first when she saw what had stuck to him and the valleys his motion had dug in the leaves, but she refilled the cavities for him. When he had the courage to ask, she moved pieces of bark so they would not be in his way. She lined the hollows with soft brown grass and kissed him when he told her of his discoveries.

Requested one day—she promised a second meal as reward, though it was not necessary—he demonstrated his technique for her. In his fantasies, the rustling underneath him was the sound of Kylene's skin upon sheets as she fitted thighs about him, he kissed brittle sharp-edged leaves that were Kylene's dry lips and licked dew from her mossy eyelids.

When he was done, and his stumps met under the leaf-and-bark body he embraced, and he knew his nose smelled only dust and mustiness, he opened his eye and stared blankly at the dark sky and the circle that encompassed his existence. Sweat had matted leaves against his chest. His loins were sticky, his hip muscles and back fatigued.

"Turn over," she ordered. Huskily. He sensed she was crying.

He was not willing. He was suddenly ashamed of what he had done. There was no meaning in it. It had been a performance.

An amusement. All for her. Nothing for him. He could be no more shamed if he had bathed in the semen he had ejaculated and covered himself in it in public.

"I wish you had," she snapped at him.

It was the last she spoke that day.

She twisted at his head with strong hands till he had turned over and he saw that she was already naked. She squatted over

his face without ceremony and said nothing else. Her eyes were
tightly closed, her face tense and lined with stress. Her thighs
squeezed his ears painfully.

She squealed and grunted like a farm animal as he did what
she wanted. When he tired, she ground her hips and shook him
painfully to keep him busy.

When she was tired she left without a word.

She did not give him the second meal she had promised.

Days passed in which he was afraid to indulge himself, fearful
that she would demand that he repeat his performance.

Herrilmin ha'Hujsuon traveled at night, though he did not
enjoy it. He rode a horse. His legs needed a rest, and the relief
was welcome, but he realized that the horse would soon need
rest as well. It would have to be concealed in some spot at
daylight and left to graze. It would need time to sleep, just as
he did.

Riding almost seemed more trouble than it was worth, but
having acted as he had to obtain it, he was stuck with the animal.
The original rider of the horse was some thousands of man-
heights to the north, and only the moon would ever smile at his
face again.

A dispatch rider, Herrilmin had guessed. Someone dressed
as a soldier.

"Hoy, my captain," Herrilmin had shouted, using words almost identical in either Algheran speech or the Lopritian dialect,
and the rider drawing abreast of him on the empty road had
stopped to proclaim his haste and importance. Lan Haarper's
greatcoat, bulging with grass, carefully arranged behind shrubbery at the base of the embankment, had not been convincingly
manlike, but a second of attention had been all Herrilmin
needed.

Heedless of what the man on the horse was saying, he had
grabbed the man by leg and elbow as he craned to locate the
"body" and dashed him onto the pavement. It happened quickly
enough that Herrilmin was able to grab the reins before the horse
ran off, and he was able to keep the horse beside him with one
hand while he kicked its late master's throat and scrambled brains
with his boots.

The horse met his needs well enough after that. There was
something very satisfying and natural about animal loyalty, he

mused to himself during the course of the night. Obedience and lack of self-service did not make a horse less of a horse, or harm its dignity.

He thought sadly of his companions and regretted the comparisons he was forced to make between their conduct and the horse's.

Toward dawn, he rode through a soldier's camp. Dying fires glowed in beds placed against the banks of the road. A sentry called out a sleepy challenge which was lost in hoofbeats.

Reinforcements for Mlart, he assumed. He was out of eye range of the tiny obstacle in minutes.

As the nighttime winds blew outside, Wandisha waited for the house to fall asleep. Grahan and Rallt had gone to rooms in the third story; the boy had sought to stay on the ground floor in case he was needed, but Grahan had maneuvered him upstairs. Grahan was talking to him now. Quietly.

The boy was listening. To man things, she noticed. What-I-did-with-my-life, study-hard-and-always-tell-the-truth, people-mean-well-even-when-they-make-mistakes things. Father-son things. Grahan had a strange form of patience, which impressed her. In a world in which men became fathers infrequently and at great intervals, it seemed to her that Grahan, who had never married, would be a good father.

The walls of the unfamiliar building creaked. New sounds to become acquainted with, new steps to take to new destinations, new patterns to everyday deeds. She hesitated and leaned against the wall, daunted by the constant need to adapt to circumstances which changed so quickly.

It was a private moment of weakness. When she had admitted it, as ever, she found the strength to go on and be again the Wandisha others saw. Gently, she closed the stairway door and oriented herself against it. Rallt had left blankets for her on the couch along the opposite wall. She crossed to it and arranged the blankets as if for sleeping. She smiled ironically, grateful for the intended kindness, but amused by the small deceit which the boy's peasant sensibilities required.

She stepped from her shoes next, then shed her garments quickly, letting them fall to the floor. *Like a snake slithering from old skin,* she told herself, pleased with the image. A supple, sinuous snake, made new and fresh by the removal of a

false misleading husk of a body . . . The real Wandisha, when
she thought of herself that way, was nude, a creature more animal than human in its essence, unbound by the habits and names
and prejudices that limited other women to being slaves and
shop workers and nobles' wives. Nude, watched in her nudity,
released from everything that tightened or compressed or distorted, she was free and desired simultaneously.

She loved those sensations. She loved to feel men's eyes on
her body, to feel their lust build within them as she uncovered
herself, to toy with their desires. She was always the first to
undress with her customers, and nude, she posed for their en-
joyment as they undressed. Sometimes, before windows with
the sunlight gleaming from her sinewy, glistening body, she
stretched herself languidly before them or danced with mincing,
untrained steps, to show her freedom and her pleasure. At others, with fingers or cords about her limbs, she mimed her capture and her bondage and prayed for an owner's mastery. The
play was often more satisfying than the lovemaking, she had
found; it earned her bonuses.

Outside, the wind continued to blow. The floor was cold. She
traced her way along the wall with her fingers, and tiptoed to
the next room.

It should have been a room for dining or a family living room.
Instead, it held a mirror, a solidly framed bed, and wardrobes
for clothing. The fat schoolteacher's bedroom, Wandisha told
herself. Her fingers led her to a small table with one chair which
suited the room for other functions. Closed doors separated her
from the kitchen and a lavatory; she would learn which was
which when need came.

Cherrid lay on the bed. He was awake, though he was breathing evenly. He had wrapped himself in a cocoon of blankets and
was babyishly happy with their warmth. He was near a window
which was cracked or badly set in its frame, she thought. She
could sense a hairline of cold across her thighs as she brushed
her feet off and was grateful to climb into the bed and share the
blankets with him.

Cold, Cherrid's mind complained as her flesh and his touched.
It wasn't a serious grumble. She let him fit his arms around her.
"Warm you up," she murmured. "Warm me up."

"Not tonight." He seemed embarrassed, then accepting.

"Just hold me. That's all I want tonight," she assured him,

then realized it was not true. She had an emptiness inside her. She wanted more than holding.

"Will he win?" she asked to mask her confusion. "Can Ian Haarper beat the Algherans?"

"It is a matter of time," he told her, staring into a blackness even vision would not dispel, trying to keep his voice from being gruff. "He has to get reinforcements. Without them— No, my dear. He cannot win."

CHAPTER FIFTEEN

*T*hough they had Midpassage in a rapist's embrace, the Algherans could be said to have penetrated the town only to the north. Even that must be qualified: during the night there was a space of about a hundred man-heights between the forces. The Algherans occupied ground along the river on one side of the great road and the flank of a woods-covered hill on the other. The Lopritians had a similar position, but glimpses of houses and other buildings higher up could be had on their hill.

Not as visible, but also present, were artillery units. Lopritian guns were stationed in several of those overhead yards. They were trained on the road, and firing paths had been cleared by shooting down intervening trees and brush. Cannons were not enough to hold the Swordtroop in place had their commanders been willing to accept losses, but they had only discovered their exposure at evening time; night and the uncertainties felt by the tra'Crovsol had halted the Algherans.

Just beyond shouting range of the Algherans waited Lopritians—the rightward end of ris Salynnt's Guards Regiment along the river, and ris Maanhaldur's Midpassage company on the hillside. Bullets could cover the distance before the forces but neither contemporary muskets nor marksmen were accurate at such ranges. For most soldiers, when aiming was wasted effort, so was shooting. Their officers concurred. During the night, then, the troops endured an awkward unforced armistice.

The Algherans had managed to put one regiment across the river on the preceding day but the men had carried only their muskets—they were without artillery, without tents, without cooking gear or any equipment for establishing a camp. At nightfall, two of the regiment's three battalions waded back across the river to relative comfort and safety. The third stayed to block the road. Without food and without sleep, the Algherans waited for morning.

Fog formed during the night. When it began to lift, the Algherans looking down the road saw bulkier forms than men in the mist. The Lopritians had brought up a battery of small guns. The four guns straddled the road. Men were ministering to them.

The Algheran officers had received no orders for two watches. Many of them had fallen asleep. Time was wasted while they were awakened and while messengers ran to the tra'Crovsol. The guns opened fire on them abruptly, before they had time to pull the men into line.

Men fell. In the confusion, others ran, increasing the confusion. Sergeants bullied their units into position to resist Lopritian infantry.

The gunfire continued for minutes, but the Lopritians did not advance, because Perrid ris Salynnt, who commanded that wing of the brigade, did not feel he had sufficient men to make an attack.

In addition, the Guardsmen who could had slept during the night. When the cannons were brought up, they were still groggy. They had not yet had breakfast. Perrid, knowing it might be their only meal that day, had delayed the firing until they were fed.

Dighton ris Maanhaldur had considered moving his Midpassage men forward to occupy the hill on the Algheran flank, but the Guards commander had not issued orders to do so; Dighton was too diffident to make the suggestion. The movement would have left a gap between his company and ris Salynnt's force; the position and strength of the Algherans on the hill was unknown; and so his men had also been allowed to rest that night. They had piled up rocks and tree limbs to defend themselves. Dighton was not sure they would have obeyed orders to leave their position.

The consequence was that no Lopritians were within musket range of the Algherans. Paradoxically, the battalion was too close to the Lopritian guns for the most effective results, and by deploying in closely spaced lines the Algherans had further protected themselves. Shrapnel should explode from above. Here, fired at point-blank range, when the heavy metal canisters struck targets they hit like so many blunted shells; the men they hit were killed without time to scream, but bodies did not stop the canisters. When the charges within them exploded, they dispensed balls in narrow cones which struck only the men immediately before them.

The Algherans took losses steadily, but were not destroyed. While the Lopritian commanders waited for guns to tear them down like wash-day laundry, the lines stayed in place. Behind them, beyond range of the shrapnel, men from the regiment's remaining battalions were splashing across the river to their relief. Reinforcements raced along the opposite bank of the river. In the distance, the battalions were forming for assault.

The Lopritian attempt to clear the road had failed.

The guns had woken Cherrid, though he remembered his circumstances in time to avoid springing to his feet and calling for his staff.

Small-bore guns. He counted seconds. Three of them—four if not well served. Not enough for a major action. He lay under the woman-scented bedclothes, listening, motionless, until a hand touched his shoulder.

"Grahan," he said then and heard a chuckle.

"What makes you think it isn't Wandisha?" It was Grahan.

It felt like old times. He sat up and pushed himself back in the bed, wishing he could see his friend's smile.

"Not the same touch," he said. Not the same place, he meant. Wandisha gripped lower on an arm when she wished attention, and her hands were harder than Grahan's, both firmer and more callused.

It didn't merit conversation. "Wandisha isn't trained to wake people," he said lightly. "Her inclination seems to be to leave them sleeping and crawl back into her own bed. I think she disapproves of waking up too early. She is not a very soldierly person, Grahan.''

"I'll have to give her some training." The old soldier seemed amused.

"Well." The comment opened up vistas Cherrid was reluctant to inspect. It was unlikely he would need a nurse much longer. "We will see. Is she up?"

"Everybody is, since before dawn, everybody but you; you were like a baby. We couldn't sleep through the racket."

It was not dawn now, he deduced. "Have those popguns been firing long?"

"That just started." Grahan was scornful. "Those are our popguns, by the way. Other side of town. Wandisha says Mlart *is* low on ammunition."

"That's good!"

"While it lasts," Grahan said cynically. "The racket I meant was lan Styllin's daughter wanting her pants changed. I don't know how people survive parenthood, to be frank." He brushed a hand over Cherrid's hair, patting it into place. "You're a mess, you know. Wandisha ought to take better care of your looks."

He smiled. "Maybe she likes me as I am."

"You're a noble of Loprit." Grahan was still patting at him.

Was there warning in that? He moved his head. "I can fend for myself."

Grahan stepped back. "With your noble looks, you need all the help you can get, Cherrid. So, how much of your uniform do you want today?"

"All of it," he said firmly. "Shoes, too. It is time I returned to the living." He wanted to cough, but he held it back, to demonstrate his good health, and perhaps Grahan was taken in by it.

"Do you want some breakfast? Toast and stew?"

He hesitated. Wandisha and Rallt, together in a kitchen, experience had taught, did not add up to one chef. "Who fixed it?"

"Lan Styllin's wife. Very edible." Grahan leaned close and whispered, "Tastes like army chow. She's in the kitchen. Still want some?"

He did, even with the warning. He was ravenous, he realized suddenly.

Perhaps he was finally mending. In most ways.

He rubbed his eyes gently, producing none of the kaleidoscopic starbursts and colored fields he had once taken for granted.

Mending. In some ways.

He felt helpless.

"You want to stay in bed?" Grahan asked sharply.

"Just rubbing sleep from my eyes," he lied. "Lead me to breakfast."

So he had his breakfast at a proper table for the first time in five days. A window was open, admitting a crisp breeze and the smell of wet grass, and he was certain without asking that the sky was blue and cloudless.

An inviting day. He longed to be outside.

Inside, he was surrounded by people, it seemed. The schoolteacher's house was not a large one, and sound and other senses gave him the impression that the kitchen was particularly small. It seemed overfilled holding just himself, Zitta lin Styllin, and her baby, but Wandisha, Rallt, and Grahan all found excuses for being in the kitchen as well.

That was the result of putting two households into one dwelling, he realized. With the need to find accommodation for the refugees from West Bend and the houses destroyed across the river, most of Midpassage must be just as crowded and uncomfortable.

It only seemed as if his friends were unwilling to trust him with lan Styllin's wife. He smiled to himself and tried to make friends with the baby. It had been decades since Cherrid made conversation with an infant, but he told himself proudly and incorrectly that he still retained his skills.

"Hi there," he mumbled. He poked a finger toward the source of a gurgling monologue and tried to murmur in tune with the little girl.

Lan Styllin's daughter responded by seizing his hand with her own pudgy hands. Babbling happily, she dipped his finger into warm liquid, then sucked on it. "Mama see me!" she demanded, and Mama, having seen, lifted her up and carried her away while Cherrid discreetly wiped his finger on his pants leg. He hoped it had gone into stew and not something else that needed changing.

As he ate, the guns still boomed. They were a thousand man-heights distant, he estimated. Perhaps less—hills did strange things to sounds.

It seemed impossible that he should be sitting in a kitchen in the morning, like a small boy surrounded by family, eating his breakfast while guns went off so closely.

Like a dream. He felt that if only he could open his eyes wide enough, the noise and the kitchen and all he remembered from the past several days would go away, leaving him back on his couch in the command wagon, or in his bed a century ago at his estate when his wife still lived.

Behind his bandages, his eyes blinked but they did not open wide enough.

He was full suddenly. He pushed his bowl away and jerked himself backward in his chair and let Wandisha dab a cloth over his lips.

"What do we do today?" he demanded.

"We rest," Grahan said firmly. "You're still wheezing, Cherrid."

"Some rest," he said, "but I want to move around some. I want to ride. I am tired of doing nothing, Grahan."

"We could go along the hill," Wandisha suggested. "I can describe—you can see all the town if you go to the right places."

She could describe the battle to him, Cherrid interpreted. He noted her reluctance. Not a soldierly person, he had said to Grahan, and he had the proof of that again. But there was no reason for a camp follower to enjoy battles, not even if that was supposed to please him.

"We can let that go, Wandisha," he said, and listened to a hiss of surprise escape Grahan's lips. "This is not my battle. This is Ironwearer Ian Haarper's battle. I am not—uhh—involved with it."

"Wait a short while," Grahan suggested. "You'll be involved in it."

Musket fire was now mixed with the slow booming of the cannons, and Cherrid could guess from Grahan's voice that his hand was pointing in that direction. So Grahan, too, had not yet adjusted to his loss of vision. It was a comforting thought in some fashion.

"Knew we should have left this town," Grahan muttered.

"You know what I meant," Cherrid told him. "Wandisha did."

Not interested, he had started to say, and he had been only faintly surprised to find that was true. It would not be an interesting battle, because lan Haarper had elected to fight in a way which used neither strategy nor tactics. It might be seen as important someday, but there would be nothing note-worthy for a soldier to observe, nothing to appreciate. Men would kill each other till they stopped, just as they had in all those undistinguishable soldier-and-bandit brawls of his youth, and that would be it.

Without artistry, it all seemed pointless.

He was reluctant to say that aloud, afraid it would bother Rallt or lan Styllin's wife. "This started without me," he said instead, making a better excuse. "I have not been part of it, so I do not think even your descriptions, Wandisha, would really make me understand it as I should."

When he had said that, he realized the same reason would keep him out of every battle for the rest of the war, if it was true.

So be it. He sighed, feeling the heaviness in his lungs finally as an old man's affliction rather than simple illness. *I am old.*

Had he fought his last battle? He thought now that he had.

"I'd like to be home," he admitted, to himself as much as to Grahan or Wandisha or Rallt. "I'd like to sit on my porch with nothing to do but smell the flowers and listen to the wind and talk to my friends and be with—"

—my wife, his thoughts ran. *Brindylla.* Was that still true? He had been widowed many, many years. Was it true affection which brought her into his memories now, or only habit? How would the old man he had become react if the woman of his youth were restored to him? Would he still love her? Would she love him? Or would it be necessary to rebuild the time-destroyed relationship with the careful attention of a curator treating any other crumbling relic of the ancient past?

"—all my friends," he said, knowing his words sounded limp. "All of you." He put out a hand and Wandisha grasped it, then moved into his arm. Rallt came closer when he beckoned with the other hand and submitted to having his shoulder patted.

A good youngster, Cherrid thought fondly, pleased by the solid muscle on the still growing body. He'd have to do some-thing for the boy. Rallt had earned more than a peasant's life.

"Not the baby, I hope," Grahan said.

"The baby, too." Recovering from melancholy, Cherrid could be generous. "What's a house like without a child or two, Grahan?"

"Livable," the old man growled, and Wandisha laughed nervously.

"There still be the—you know," Rallt said awkwardly.

"Rallt," Grahan said.

For a few seconds there was silence. Then Rallt moved away from Cherrid's embrace. "What has happened?" asked the Ironwearer.

"Nothing important," Wandisha said. She tried to relax her stiffness.

He recognized the lie. "You might as well tell me."

"Nothing," Wandisha said. "Rallt just imagined—"

"Another body," Grahan said. "A soldier, maybe an Algheran. Headless. It's in ris Vandeign's barn."

So the killer had not left the town.

Above him, he heard chairs scraping as Ian Styllin's wife moved from room to room. Her baby chortled.

Life went on. As it should—with activity, instead of retirement. He stood quickly, feeling relieved in a way, and remembered that in the long-ago distance of his bed, he had been searching for an occupation to fill the day.

"We will go look."

Mlart's attack on the other end of town was spearheaded by his cavalry. Morning showed the tra'Nornst that the Lopritians had removed their artillery from the southern fields; it did not make clear that infantry had been pulled out as well. Some cavalry was already across the Bloodrill; their dawn reconnaissance found that the enemy had made a partial retreat along the riverbed, making it possible for Swordtroop infantry to cross as well.

The Algheran general knew he faced only one shrunken Lopritian brigade, and the actions of the enemy had shown they were incapable of taking the offense. An assault upon the center of the defenders was apt to be expensive in lives; for the moment, attacks against both ends of the Lopritian line seemed the best course.

In the north, the Crovsol Division was strong enough to continue its battle without reinforcements; he could use all the Cuhyon Division in the south. Two regiments from that force were sufficient to protect his own center, he judged. That left his cavalry and the division's other two regiments available for offensive uses or as a reserve; upon reflection, he decided to use them all and strike the Lopritian left with maximum strength.

Attack disclosed that the fields still harbored Lopritian infantry in small numbers. Pressed, the defenders fired volleys and retreated slowly, from fence to fence. They did not inflict great losses, but the Algheran commanders were not eager to incur casualties. Swordtroop infantry was allowed to lag behind, out of range of enemy muskets; cavalry was used to turn the Lopritian lines and pry the defenders from their positions.

Horsemen are not trained to occupy ground; they have other functions which make use of their mobility. Their function today was to die, and by dying, disclose the limits to which the infantry could safely advance.

By midmorning, several dozen dead or dying men and their horses spotted the fields and the lanes between them. Their lives had brought land that would never be Algheran territory, but they had forced the Lopritians to the back of the fields.

By Mlart's reckoning, the cost had been cheap.

"Well, let us see what we have here—examine what we have here," Cherrid ris Clendannan said cheerfully. The old Ironwearer turned about on the floor of the barn, moving his head just as if he could see. Rallt realized he was enjoying himself.

Rallt was not. It was cold inside the barn. The cold and moisture in the air should have masked any smells but they did not hide the stale odor of old manure nor the newer sticky-sweet taint that seemed to come from everywhere. It was an unpleasant smell, a puslike stench which he thought would be distressing even to someone who did not guess where it originated.

It was also noisy. Cannon had been spread over the hillside, from the side of the barn down to the orchard. The guns pointed from right to left; within an eye-burning mist of smoke, they boomed incessantly at the enemy. The sound must have carried as far as their shells.

God's coughing, he had told himself that morning, and wondered if the sounds pounding his ears would combine to shake the house down. Outside the noise had been louder, though the Ironwearer and Grahan, mounted on their horses, had seemed able to carry on a conversation. Wandisha had put her palms

over her ears for a while, then resigned herself to it and walked
beside Rallt with her face showing distaste. Rallt had wanted to
cover his ears also, but his hands had been full of reins, pulling
ris Clendannan's fourth-best mare and ris Clendannan up the
hill.

When the guns actually came into view at the top of the clover
field, it had troubled him that he could not see the targets most
of them were shooting at. He had wondered if the shouting men
who had gathered around the guns understood what they were
doing, and was only slightly reassured by the sight of Ironwearer
Ian Haarper in his wagon at the foot of the orchard. But both
Grahan and ris Clendannan had accepted the scene with the
insouciance of a patron watching field hands bring in the harvest.

"I'd like—" The old Ironwearer spun on a heel. "Sergeant—
Wicherty, you said? Can you persuade one of your men to climb
back to that loft and look that body over for us? We will be able
to tell him what interests us."

"Certainly," the sergeant said. He stepped backward a few
paces until he was in the doorway. "*Bhisson!* Bring your butt in
here!"

Ironwearer ris Clendannan turned directly to the noncom
when he spoke, Rallt noticed, as if sergeants were supposed to
stand in fixed positions when they came near generals. Rallt had
not even seen the soldier enter.

The boy turned to Wandisha and shook his head with amaze-
ment and she smiled back. Grahan seemed to take it in stride,
but Rallt wondered if the old Ironwearer left her surprised as
often as he was.

Bhisson, when he appeared, was a young man not much older
than Rallt, and heavyset, with an insignia-less uniform which
he had been told identified soldiers of the lowest rank. He was
unaccustomed to exercise, the boy guessed, inspecting the private's pearlike build; he huffed and puffed while climbing the
ladder and Rallt had to wonder why the sergeant had selected
him for the task.

"The body," Bhisson called down. He had a high-pitched,
nervous voice, and Rallt wondered if it troubled him to be observed by a general, even a blind general. "The body. The
body."

"Just summarize," Grahan ordered, after a quick look at

Wandisha. Rallt had thought Wandisha would speak for Lord Clendannan, but the Teep had been quiet since they entered the barn. She stood rigid as a statue, her eyes tightly shut, her lower lip trembling, and Rallt, uncertain what to do, moved beside her and put his hands around her fist. Her fingers slipped between his and tightened painfully as the soldier described what lay in the loft; he did not know if he helped her or not.

"No head?" ris Clendannan demanded of the sergeant.

"Go over the rest of the loft. Look in the straw," Grahan was ordering. "Look for—never mind." He took two steps to reach the ladder and scrambled up at twice Bhisson's pace. "Stay out of the way, Private."

"No head, sir," Sergeant Wicherty reported, his hands stiff at his side, his eyes fixed on some point just beyond the Ironwearer's shoulder. "It wasn't on the body, sir."

A gun boomed. Ris Clendannan waited for its sound to pass. "Where is the head, Sergeant?"

"Must be gone away, sir," Wicherty said with what seemed embarrassment to Rallt. "I wouldn't like to guess where, sir." He hesitated. "Would you like me to have the men look some more, sir?"

"If it turns up," the Ironwearer said. He clenched his fist several times, then raised his head toward the loft. "What do we have, Grahan?"

"Crap," the old soldier's voice responded. Rallt heard his steps on the straw and wood; then the man was at the edge of the platform, looking down. The sergeant had turned on the barn lights, but Grahan's face was shaded. He seemed annoyed to Rallt. "Just that, Cherrid. The dead person was shitting his pants—it's all mixed up, don't ask me how often—and someone else was going in the corner. Got that smell . . . I'd guess our man was doing some drinking."

"When?"

"How should I know, Cherrid? Find the man and ask him! If you want to know what he was drinking, ask him that, too."

"All right, Grahan." The Ironwearer held up a hand and shook it in a way that Rallt supposed was to mollify his friend. "What else did you find?"

"The smell of crap! What did you expect? Give me some time, Cherrid! I just got up here!"

"Sorry, Grahan." Ris Clendannan made his hand-waving

motion again. "Why not have the private look for more excrement—"

"He's doing that already, Cherrid."

"—so we can see if there were other—" The Ironwearer turned back to the sergeant. "I can be certain it was not your men who—"

"Absolutely not, sir," the sergeant said quickly. "Especially smelling of boo—uh-h, alcohol, sir."

The Ironwearer said nothing. Rallt could not see his face.

"We only came here late last night, sir," the sergeant assured him. "We were told not to—well, we just wouldn't, sir."

"All right." The Ironwearer glanced toward Wandisha, then turned away again. "I want to know what those men did to pass time, Grahan. How did they amuse themselves?"

Grahan stepped backward until he was out of sight. "Killing people, Cherrid," the boy heard. Then the old soldier giggled at his own remark.

Wandisha's fingers tightened on Rallt's. "I want to go out," she said.

Rallt led her to the doorway. In open air, she seemed to regain calm. She leaned against the side of the barn and breathed heavily. Rallt, noticing that soldiers were looking their way, stepped to guard her from their attention. She smiled at him wanly.

"It was awful in there," she explained, and he agreed quickly, though he was used to barns.

Her mouth moved upward again, then fell. She raised her head and her arm. Rallt noticed her forehead had a rough-looking reddish splotch and wondered if he could soothe it and if the brand mark just above her nose ever caused pain.

"I lived here," she told him. "Just up there, in the room over Lord Vandeign's office."

"I see." He felt disappointed and forced himself to realize she was older than he was.

In the distance, beyond ris Vandeign's house, he could see men spread in a thin line across an unplowed field. One by one, they turned and ran a short distance to a rail fence and turned about when they had climbed over. Farther away, a pair of men on horses watched them and Rallt pretended to watch back.

"Silly Rallt!" She pulled him closer with a hand behind his head and kissed his cheek. "You mustn't be jealous. There was never anything to be jealous of. He let me have it because it was a storage room. It wasn't used. He wanted to be kind. Merryn can be kind, Rallt. I know''—her head moved—''they make fun of him and I understand why, but he means well.''

This meant nothing to Rallt. He shook his head with confusion.

''I'd lie in my room and think of what would happen the next day and watch the minds of people sleeping in the town and sometimes I'd try to see what the cows and horses in the fields were dreaming about . . .''

Wandisha was talking to herself. ''. . . and it was quiet and peaceful and I was . . . I was satisfied with what I had and then the war started and I didn't have any choice . . .''

He patted her arm, grateful and relieved by an opportunity to help. ''Did thee leave anything in thy room? I can go get it, so thee will have—''

''No.'' She nodded her head minutely. ''There's nothing to get.''

Her possessions were to wait for her, he understood suddenly. Everything would be where she had left it when she came back to it. When she resumed her life after the war. He thought of Ironwearer ris Clendannan, living in his big house amid all the luxury Grahan had described.

When ris Clendannan was enjoying the comforts of his estate, Wandisha would be in a barn's storage room, living from day to day, with cattle to furnish her entertainment.

''I'm sorry,'' he whispered. His own life promised greater rewards.

''It's not all bad.'' She kissed his forehead. ''I don't have to come back to Midpassage. It isn't my home. I can go back to Northfaring or even to F'a Loprit and I'll make out. This isn't all my life, Rallt. Don't make it seem so big.''

In the doorway, someone coughed, and Rallt turned. Grahan was standing there. He had a hand out to guide ris Clendannan's steps.

At the north of town, Lerryn lan Halkmayne's small artillery guns continued to blast the leading Algheran battalion. Perrid ris Salynnt, watching the behavior of the men under fire, had recognized experienced soldiers; he had decided to inflict the maximum possible casualties upon them.

The tra'Crovsol was willing to cooperate. He had watched

the bloody repulses of the Cuhyon Division days before at ris
Clendannan's position. He was determined that his division
would make a better showing, and he was willing to pay in blood
for time to make preparations. During the next quarter of a
watch, he brought a second regiment across the river and put it
behind his Housetroops; a third regiment spread itself along the
bank to the north to keep ris Salynnt's defenders in place. His
fourth regiment waited in reserve.

He anticipated no difficulties.

"There are just too many of them," the man beside him said,
and Dighton ris Maanhaldur tried to remember how often he
had made that complaint. Once for each Algheran soldier, it
seemed, though that was scarcely possible.

He put a hand on the log in front of him and tried to rock it
from its position on the one beneath, but it was much too heavy
to move forward and inclined stakes kept it from falling backward. A good log, thick, and still oozing resin from the stumps
where limbs had been chopped from it. It had taken eight men
to lift it into place late last night, and they had all half expected
the Algherans to shoot at them while they did it. He wondered
if it would stay so solidly fixed when bullets struck it.

He was with the Midpassage men. They waited in small
groups like this behind their own log ramparts, scattered across
the lower portion of the hill. The positions were on the crest that
overlooked the road.

There had been a long straight drop once, Dighton thought,
from where he waited to the roadbed, but time had taken it away.
Farther south, the road passed through mountains; where the
ground should be higher than the road, its surface remained flat
and level but rock walls rose perpendicularly at its edges. The
builders of the Fourth Era must have sliced through this hillside
with equal brutality when they laid down their road, but with
time the sharp outlines they had left had been softened. Earth
had slumped over the edge of the cut and rested long enough
for grass and trees to take root; the ground above had wasted
away. Now his company was spread over gently sloping ground;
only a steeper section of the hillside lay between them and the
Algherans who would be on the road below them.

Farther up the hillside, behind his men, was a trail. An old
trail, owing more to animals than to men, the most recent of the

dozens of trails which must have developed and faded from existence in this place since the Fourth Era builders reshaped it. A narrow trail, overrun with brush and not cleared so it would be hard for the Algherans to see from the road.

At the end of the trail, across a hump of hillside, he told himself for reassurance, were more barricades, more waiting soldiers—Dalsyn lan Plenytk and the surviving militiamen from the North Valley laboriously marched from one side of Midpassage to the other under cover of night.

An escape route. He tried not to think of the trail.

Up the hillside patches of snow remained. On level ground, the snow had all melted away by now, but shade from the trees and hills had kept the temperature below freezing in the valley, so it was impossible to forget that winter had arrived. It was the season for all but peasants to stay indoors whenever possible and for exploring the dusty never-visited garrets and basement recesses of Molminda's palace in F'a Loprit, the season for log fires which burned all night in deep fireplaces and for drinking until dawn with old friends and for boisterous parties in crowded high-ceilinged halls.

He wondered what it would be like to die alone and in the snow.

"There are just too many of them," the nervous man said again.

Shut up, he wanted to tell the man, but when he looked to his right beyond him, the other soldiers in the position seemed unaffected by the words. They were holding their muskets confidently and waiting patiently for the Algherans to appear, while keeping their heads below the top of the logs as they had been told. Some had crouched to look to the front through chinks between the logs; others were sitting on piles of leaves or bark. They seemed preoccupied rather than frightened.

They were all very dirty, he realized. He was very dirty, too, dirtier than he had ever been as a small boy at the times when the woman who pretended not to be his mother had taken his ear and dragged him to a bath. He had always known she was pretending and that he was not the orphan she said he was and that she knew what he knew and did not really mind his knowing; he had almost always known the tall fair-haired man who came each tenth day to visit his mother was his father even when he pretended not to.

They had loved him, he knew, even if it was not possible for them to show it. He had loved them—still loved them. He had tried so hard to be good for them. He had tried to earn their respect.

He needed his soldiers' respect as well, he knew. Not for himself now, as he wished from his father, but for their sake— the people deserved aristocrats who ran the country capably; soldiers deserved officers who they knew would not waste their lives. He decided it would be better to show no reaction than too much as long as the men were not disturbed. He wondered if the nervous man would be quiet if he agreed with him.

On the road, at the foot of the hillside, one of the guns boomed again. Earlier, the guns had fired without stopping, it had seemed. Now there was more time between the gunshots. He wondered if he was simply more observant or if the gun crews were tiring—the ammunition handlers bent further when they reached into their caissons, he had noticed; the men who swabbed out the guns pushed their long-handled brushes more slowly down the sizzling barrels; the individual gun commanders spent more time in conference with the grizzled Ian Halk-mayne.

Dighton stood and looked to see if Algherans were still crossing the river. They were.

Thousands of Algherans, he thought. He had tried to estimate how many and lost count of the estimate. They were making themselves into short fat columns along the road, but in the distance men's heads merged with the feet of the men following them; he could not count the columns accurately.

The Algherans crossed at a ford they had found. Some of them tripped jumping from place to place in the water but most of them got wet only to their knees. The places where Lopritians waited along the river were all deeper, he was sure. The Algheran ford was five hundred man-heights away, he thought, and wondered how accurate his guess was and if it mattered.

Since he was standing, he knew his men could see him. "Give them a couple of good volleys," he called out, and wondered how many of them listened to him and how many would obey.

A couple of volleys. He hoped Ironwearer Ian Haarper would not be disappointed with what he did. He hoped his father would understand.

He wanted to do more than that. He wanted to hurt the Algherans and stop them at the foot of the hillside. But it would not be possible, he knew.

Abruptly, the tableau spread before him changed. The Lopritian gunners on the roadbed became more active. Farther ahead, Algheran officers who had been huddled in conference separated and ran to places at the sides of their columns. Dighton thought he could hear his own men breathing more loudly.

His ears caught a scrap of a command. Then each Algheran soldier lifted his musket from his shoulder. Each put the butt of his weapon on the ground beside his left foot and raised a ramrod from beneath the barrel with his right hand.

Each slipped a hand into a belt-held cartridge patch and brought out a paper-wrapped cylinder. Each soldier brought the cartridge to his lips, and with identical motions each tore the paper with his teeth and a jerk of the head; each turned the cartridge of the mouth of his weapon to pour in powder, pushed the wadded paper down the barrel with his ramrod, spat in a bullet and pushed it down as well and returned the ramrod to its holding place.

At a command unheard by the Lopritians or with the habit of training, the Algherans brought their weapons up and held them at chest level with both hands. Dighton, watching frozenly, caught his mind trying to compute how many man-weights of metal all those bullets comprised. At the corner of his eye, he noticed all the men in his group were standing now.

A soldier from the barricade behind ris Maanhaldur had wandered from his place; he was at Dighton's left, staring at the Algherans. "Just looking, Captain," he said shyly, when Dighton's arm waving caught his attention. "I didn't mean no harm."

"Get back to your place and mean some harm," Dighton muttered, but the soldier did not hear him. Then thunderclaps sounded around him; he grabbed the soldier's arm and tried to thrust him backward.

Then Algheran dead were visible before him. The nearest of the enemy formations was scattered and men were lying on the ground. All too obviously, they were bleeding. Dighton saw a spreading puddle of red.

Another thunder crack—another swarm, behind the first, of fallen men.

Shrapnel, Dighton realized. The cannon up the hillside were in action. He stood with his mouth open, the wandering soldier forgotten, as men in green uniforms pulled themselves erect before him or crawled on hands and knees to the side of the road.

Then the Algheran column was in position again. He did not have time to decide if it had become smaller before it was in motion, marching—no, running—he could see the blurred legs of the soldiers shimmering as they came along the road, he could see their arms and muskets moving up and down as they ran.

"A couple of good volleys, men!" He stepped onto the log at the bottom of the rampart to shout that, hoping his men would obey, then down, feeling self-conscious and simultaneously aware of what the soundless moving lips of the man beside him were saying.

Too many Algherans. He had two hundred men to use against all those Algherans. It seemed folly suddenly.

Fire good volleys. He wondered if it was the right order to give. He wondered if he could change his mind and tell his men to retreat now to Dalsyn lan Plenytk's position, or to abandon their barricades and run up the hill to the sheltering cannon, to anonymity between the abandoned houses, to the wooded hillsides where the women and children waited, to the forests beyond the hills, to—

He stopped himself and swallowed to end his panic. The soldiers besides him were not showing fear, they did not show they had seen his.

"Let's give them a warm welcome, men," he called down his little line, trying to make his voice steady. Ironwearer lan Haarper's words, at his meeting last night, as reported by Dalsyn lan Plenytk—Dighton hoped they were new to these men who had served so long with lan Haarper.

A man turned and nodded, his hair tousled, his cheek grimy and torn by a long scratch which ran toward a missing earlobe. A ruffian, Dighton's court-reared sensitivities told him. Then he recognized the grime was mostly bruise and the scratch was a bullet wound. It was blood which had crusted on the bottom of the ear and not dirt.

"Hot as home cookin', sir," the man called back, and Dighton felt calmer and pleased to hear reassurance from a soldier with so much luck. He smiled, then turned away and rested his own musket on the top of the barricade.

The Algherans were within musket range now, almost at aiming distance. Yellow flame blossomed suddenly before him, from the middle of the first formation. The Swordtroop soldiers stumbled in unison, then staggered on. Thunder clapped again, the sound from behind almost simultaneous with the booming before him, and the splat of shrapnel hitting the road.

Behind that formation, left lying on the black pavement, were green and red shapes, like leaves. As he watched, one of the fallen men rose on his knees and lifted his hands to the side of his face as if he wished to surrender. The men in the next formation broke ranks to run about him.

The small artillery guns below Dighton fired as one. He watched them bounce upon their wheels. A partial row of men at the back of the Algheran formation suddenly vanished from sight; the gap showed like a break in a picket fence; it reached back to cut into another row in the following formation. The artillerymen turned and ran away. They left the guns but Dighton noticed that in their haste some of them still carried their swabs and other tools. Despite his own worries, he smiled wanly.

In moments, the Algherans stood where the gunners had been and shot at the fleeing men with their muskets. Dighton aimed his own weapon at a soldier in the front ranks of the Algherans and pulled his trigger. At his ear, the musket exploded; he felt a fan of hot spray hit along his jawbone and knew a dark line of powder had marked his skin.

Without thinking, he broke his musket open and blew down the barrel, heedless of the hot metal that pressed against his lips. As he reached for another cartridge, he was conscious of soldiers firing on either side, some silently, others shouting with exultation as their targets went down.

At the side, overlooking the road directly, was the soldier he had earlier pushed back to his place, out of place again, his musket cradled in his arms and stepping with the care of a squirrel hunter. As Dighton watched, he came to the edge of the slope, bent to one knee, then fell forward, facedown. Dighton could not tell if he had ever fired his musket.

Then Algheran heads were visible at the crest. Algheran torsos.

The lead battalion had reached the hillside, he understood. The Algherans had come to attack his force.

He froze, his head above the rampart, staring almost without comprehension as more of the enemy soldiers appeared at the crest, as their waists appeared in clear view. Their hands and guns.

A splinter flew from the log before him, tearing at his finger.

He pushed his musket out to his side awkwardly and pulled the trigger without aiming, not certain if it was aimed at the enemy, not certain if he hit anything.

"Get back!" he called out. "Get away, you men!"

And behind him, other voices, crying "Get back!" and "Retreat" and "Pull out." His men. He cast up a wordless prayer for them.

Then Algherans were all along the crest and some were over it and he could see their legs and their feet and space beneath their feet as they ran—he wondered if they had stepped over the man who fell over the side of the hill or if they had kicked him as an enemy as they came up and he went down—and they were lifting their guns and pointing them—

—pointing them at him, he realized suddenly, and noticed that his men were gone, he was the last man behind this barricade except for one man sitting at the end, holding his leg with both hands, incredulously staring at the dark fluid that pumped from his pant leg, and that the sun had gone behind clouds and that men were shouting as—

—he turned and ran, toward the trail, holding his heavy musket by the barrel in one hand, seeing he was the last man to leave the barricades and that the green-dressed Algherans were behind him, running to the trail where he could see his men making their escape across the green- and snow-dressed hillside and he shouted to speed them on and tripped as a fist hit his back and he was falling, onto his hands and face, falling and his side was hurt where it hit his musket, falling and he tried to get back onto his feet and move forward, falling and pushing with his disobedient feet, reaching with a hand to grasp the edge of the trail as if he could pull himself up to it and safety, falling and the face of a man, falling, the man who been nervous, his face bright in the gathering darkness before him, then his mother, radiant, smiling, falling and feet beside him, strange voices loud above him, falling, a leaf beside his eye, falling.

CHAPTER SIXTEEN

G*uns continued to boom as Grahan brought up the horses* and helped ris Clendannan to a seat. To Rallt, it was evidence that lunch was near. He began planning his steps back to the house.

"I would like to examine those other buildings for bodies." The old Ironwearer waved a hand toward the apple orchard, but it was obvious he meant the foundry buildings at their side. Rallt was about to say he and Sugally had already searched them, but stopped when he remembered days had passed.

Grahan nodded at him. "Boy, go ask that sergeant for—"

"They will not be available." Ris Clendannan sat comfortably, but his head was turned so he could concentrate on sounds from the north, and Rallt noticed his mare had lifted an ear as well.

"Perhaps we can put it off then." Grahan had not refused, but he was looking toward the house. Rallt wondered if he was hungry, too.

"We can do it ourselves." Ris Clendannan made a puffing sound with his lips which Rallt first thought was impatience then realized after a moment was supposed to be laughter. "We may not have many more opportunities, Grahan."

Grahan sighed. "How should we do it then?"

"We split up." The Ironwearer pulled himself erect. "You will have to check half the buildings, Grahan. The others, Wandisha and I will inspect, using this gentleman's fine young eyes."

It was a compliment, Rallt understood, but he suspected it was intended to butter over the use of his fine young legs. He glared at Wandisha, knowing his expression would be wasted on ris Clendannan.

By midday, the Swordtroop had forced back the Strength-through-Loyalty Brigade on the south to the immediate vicinity of a large house and other farm buildings. As the Lopritians retreated, additional men came from the river to join them; the resistance the Algherans faced increased with time.

Mlart had anticipated that; during the morning, he had moved his artillery closer to the town; he would use his limited stock of ammunition now to support his troops. Pragmatically, he had accepted the losses he would suffer by moving nearer the defenders. Lopritian shelling had already disabled many of his guns, but more damage had been done to the gun carriages than the thick-walled cannons. It took metal to cut metal; only direct hits from Lopritian shells would harm his guns beyond repair.

Shrapnel annihilated living things, though. A lucky shot before a carriage killed three of the horses drawing one gun; the fourth had to be destroyed. Soon after that, a single round of canister struck down most of two gun crews.

Realizing they could not hide, the gunners piled dirt around themselves on the roadbed. The heaped earth was thick with pebbles which Mlart suspected would inflict as much damage when exploded as glass and metal pellets. The sham of protection eased his men's fears, however, and it had taken little time to move the guns up; victory was the best defense, but Mlart did not begrudge their effort to construct shielding.

He could accept that the Lopritians killed his men. What seemed unfair was that the shells which made their bodies into haggled meat left the road completely untouched.

His guns had the range but target spotting was difficult. By inference, where his own troops were visible on the hillsides, Lopritians were before them, but they could not be seen. Messages arrived eventually from his leading commanders to tell him the Lopritians were defending their front with guns; the troops were not in musket range of each other. Mlart cursed and ordered his cannon to shift their aim.

Another report told him the defenders were inside and around a large white house. The house could not be seen from the road; the message was not definite enough to locate it. With sufficient ammunition, Mlart would have fired until the entire backside of the hill was devastated and been sure of eliminating the improvised fort; as it was, he was forced to send a staff officer with engineering experience to make measurements.

It all took time.

Rallt's guess came true with almost Teeplike prescience. Ris Clendannan and Wandisha loitered at the edge of the orchard, talking about varieties of apples as far as Rallt could determine, while he and Grahan did the work.

"Evens and odds," Grahan had said when asked for instructions. "I'll go evens." Seeing Rallt's expression, he pointed with a finger and added, "You take that one and that one and that one and so on. Don't be a hero—we're only looking for bodies. If you find anything alive that's bigger than a mouse, come tell me."

"Why bodies and why here?" he wondered.

Grahan spat, expertly besmirching the only patch of clean snow within spitting distance. "Cherrid's bright idea for the day. Except for the innkeeper, all the killings have been on this side of town. Since you and I never looked at these buildings, we get to do it now. Thank you, Cherrid." He spat again.

More bodies. His face twisted into a scowl.

Grahan misread his expression. "Anything else, you come running back. Not that that's likely," he said complacently.

Neither Grahan nor ris Clendannan believed Wandisha's account of a killer with a hidden mind, Rallt saw suddenly.

He felt annoyance. What was Wandisha's point in spending so much time with the old man who refused to credit her beliefs?

"I'll take the evens," Grahan repeated. "You'll be odd."

Northward, the tra'Crovsol was also making progress, though not at the pace he had hoped for. The Lopritians clung to the hillside rather than facing his men frontally. Their numbers were small but they could not be left to harass his troops, and inevitably the attempts to chase them from their positions disrupted his own advance.

The men had been trained to fight in formation. Only his Housetroops were adept at irregular warfare, and while climbing, they were at a disadvantage. Even ignoring the carnage caused by enemy artillery, he suffered more casualties than he inflicted.

As in the south, defenders came out of the riverbed positions as he reached them. They fell back at a satisfactory rate, pulling their guns with them, but he was uneasily aware that they were not yet beaten. He had Lopritian dead and captured wounded in sufficient numbers to allow a victory claim in his midday message to Mlart, but the engagement he had sought had not yet taken place. It was not success to take pride in.

Irritably, he gave orders for his reserve regiment to cross the river. The one that was left was to continue to threaten the remaining defenders.

The first building Rallt checked had been a storage shed for lumber when he and Sugally examined it. It was empty now; he guessed the wood had gone to build the platforms that underlay some of the guns, or to fuel cooking fires.

The contents of the next building were unburnable: bulky machines constructed from metal. Lathes, joiners, band saws—he gave names to the equipment he recognized when he lifted the heavy canvas that covered them, but most of the machinery he was unable to identify. He was tempted to stay longer, but he remembered Grahan's comment that baby-making bore no resemblance to the final product; whatever mysterious functions the metal tools had would not be disclosed in a cursory inspection.

The third building was the one ris Ellich had called an epuratory, and the heavy sliding door had become no easier to move in the past several days. Grahan was lost from sight as he struggled with it, but Wandisha and ris Clendannan came to help. Rallt was surprised to see how much strength remained in the sick man's arms.

The smell was also just as bad and the door had been opened just enough to make the interior gloomy. "I found nothing in the other sheds,'' he said to them, but ris Clendannan's expression made it clear he was to search this building again.

"There is a light at the top of the stairs,'' Wandisha told him. "It's on your left when you come to the landing.'' She smiled reassuringly and gripped ris Clendannan's arm with both hands, and Rallt could only hold back his annoyance and be sorry that whoever's mind she had plumbed for that information was not here to do her bidding.

As he passed it in the dim light, he hit the big tank with a fist, and made sure his thoughts blamed Wandisha for his wasted time and sore knuckles.

Lerlt did not know how long he had been awake when he heard the doorway creaking. He waited nervously while the sound went on and on, then remembered that Gherst was below to defend him.

Gherst had been too stupid to ask for the musket. That was still beside him, its muzzle cool against his arm. Gherst would be helpless against intruders. If it was Lopritians who came into the building they would find Gherst and take him away. They would be satisfied with Gherst and they would not find him.

Cautiously he huddled closer to the corner of the walkway and draped himself in the blankets so he could not be seen. He was invisible now and the Lopritians could take Gherst away and not find him and when Harrilmin arrived he and Herrilmin would go away together without Gherst and without Fesch and he and Herrilmin would be famous, he wasn't sure for what but it would come to him soon, he and Herrilmin and especially he had done great things for Alghera and for the Project and for Hujsuon and everyone would be happy and no one would blame him for—why should anyone blame him for anything? He had only done what he had to do and everything would work out fine and everyone knew that, it wasn't as if anyone really liked Gherst, was it?

Gherst. Something about Gherst. Gherst had done something bad, he recalled, and he tried to reason with Gherst about it but Gherst had not listened but Gherst deserved to be punished for it and Gherst knew that when he and Herrilmin went back to the Project everyone was going to agree that Lerlt was right and Gherst was wrong so that was why Gherst was trying to please him now and why Gherst did not want to return to the Project

and why the Lopritians were going to capture Gherst. Gherst
the coward was going to let the Lopritians find him and they
were stupid they wouldn't guess someone clever as Lerlt was in
the same building as the stupid Gherst and they would find Gherst
and stop looking for Lerlt.

He smiled secretly as he heard the door scrape against the
ground and as the frightened Lopritians mumbled their pagan
prayers outside.

Almost to his surprise, the Lopritians had enough courage to
enter the building. One stumbled in the opening; Lerlt heard his
head strike the tank and hoped he had hurt himself.

Gherst unexpectedly managed to keep himself concealed.
Lerlt waited for the Lopritians to find the man below but they
failed.

Almost immediately, there were footsteps on the stairs to the
upper landing. Lopritians—one of them, then another. The steps
came closer, then stopped. He knew they could not see him but
Lerlt held his breath anyway and touched the gun beside him
for extra reassurance.

"Something," a voice said nearby. "I need more light."
Lerlt felt sick, listening to the hatred he heard in those few
words.

A boot kicked at him. It moved his bedclothes, then, unsa-
tisfied, smashed at his shin. With difficulty, he held back a gasp.

"A body!" The Lopritian feigned surprise. "There's another
body here, Wandisha, under some rags."

A body, yes, a body. A dead body. Think that. Go away.

He held his breath and remained motionless, astonished at
his will and cleverness, which would convince the Lopritians to
think him dead and leave him alone.

Two Lopritians, small when he looked at them through
squinted eyes. They would think he was dead and go away or he
would overpower them, surely they knew he would overpower
them, he would strike to his right and to his left and overpower
them and they would be left for dead, killed by—

"Cherrid!" one of the Lopritians called out, fearing him.
"There's—Rallt! Get back. That's not—"

That was Lerlt rising to his feet, he told himself proudly.
Mighty Lerlt, afraid of no one. They could not stop him. He
had concealed himself to save the Lopritians from danger. He
had given them the unimportant Gherst to satisfy them, but they

had been too dumb to settle for that, and now they had blundered into waking the wrath of Lerlt.

It was proper to punish them for their folly, and he reached out to cast them down in succession, and they cowered before him. As supplicants, they knelt before him and begged for his pity.

A woman. He recognized a voice. The one at his feet was a woman.

There was some special treatment to bestow on women, but surprise had driven it from his mind. He looked down at the woman uncertainly, waiting for the memory. As she crawled from him, bumping herself along the walkway, he turned to watch her. He prodded her with the musket and wondered what he should do next.

"The killer!" Rallt called out, and Cherrid heard the sound of fighting. "He's got a gun! Get Grahan, Lord Clendannan! Get soldiers!"

Someone fell on the walkway.

The killer. Wandisha was exposed to the killer, and it was his fault, his stupidity which had caused her danger. Cherrid cursed himself for his folly.

His blind folly. Bitter, he drove himself into the darkness, racing forward, following his memory of Wandisha's steps. He tripped over obstacles he could not see, bumped against things that could not be seen, crashed awkwardly against a wall and caught himself before he fell. His hand clutched at a railing. He pulled himself upright and forward, stumbling up steps as Rallt called to him and the sound of struggle continued.

Wandisha! He wanted to weep. He made himself go faster.

He turned on the landing. He ran forward screaming. He hit against something. Someone. A body was in his arms. He fell against it, felt it falling with him, heard Rallt screaming as he fell across another body, heard the body in his hands gibbering at him, felt it squirming.

Ka-BLAM!

He felt himself lifted by the explosion, felt his ribs break, felt his ears bursting from the sound. A gun, Rallt had called out, and urged him to watch for it. He remembered, now that it was too late.

A musket. He recognized the pain in his side and felt his

blood flowing from it. He had been hit by a bullet and he had little time to react.

A fall, he told himself. He must fall, and not alone. Falling from the walkway would disable the killer long enough for Wandisha and Rallt to escape, long enough for Grahan to rescue them, and he still had his hands on the man's clothing. Clutching the killer to himself, he threw himself sideways. He twisted and rolled and pulled with all his might as he came to the edge of the walkway and tossed himself backward.

He felt himself falling and waited for greater pain to strike.

He tumbled, hit the floor, and splashed.

Not the floor! Liquid.

Liquid which burned his side and face like flame. It tore into his nostrils and seared his throat as it went down.

Somehow, he kept himself from screaming, kept himself from struggling with the liquid, made himself remember his purpose. He felt himself sinking through the flame-filled liquid, felt it boil and bubble about him, felt the impact as the other man fell beside him, and scrabbled with fingers which already seemed afire to tighten his grip and pull the man down through the liquid beside him.

Fists and feet hit at him as the killer panicked, but they had little effect. He guessed that the other man had swallowed some of the liquid. He struggled to strike the man in the belly. He flailed about until his arms were around the man and tried to wrap his legs around him, to hold him down.

His limbs were already weakening, he sensed. He was desperate for breath but he could not breathe, he could not stop struggling. He felt the fire lancing through his bullet-torn side, felt it pushing through his eardrums and at the surface of his brain, felt his skin dissolving.

More horribly, he felt darkness spreading through his awareness which took away all sensation and knew it could not be overcome.

Life was not long enough, he wanted to protest. He wanted anything else to happen, but he had no choice and when he was certain his arms could not be pulled from the killer's neck, he opened his mouth deliberately and pulled burning liquid deep into his lungs.

The pain was far worse than he could have imagined. It filled every bit of his body until it seemed there was nothing left of him but burning flesh. He screamed soundlessly until there was nothing left of him but sensation which only intuition realized was his body thrashing about in the liquid. He tried to weep blazing tears from his sizzling eyes. He tried to ignore the pain but could not. He tried to remember the time he had faced death without fear, and the times he had imagined his death and the times he had caused other men's deaths, and when those attempts failed he tried to be brave knowing what was happening to him.

He tried to be without regret. He tried to be pleased he had committed himself beyond recall and he tried to reassure himself Rallt and Wandisha would be helped by what he had done, that Grahan would understand.

He wished he could say good-bye to Grahan.

Finally, he could not feel the man below him moving.

Finally, all other sensation died.

Finally, he died.

CHAPTER SEVENTEEN

*B*y evening time, the Crovsol Division had reached the north-ernmost buildings along the great road. The bridge was less than one thousand man-heights distant. The tra'Crovsol's leading troops could exchange arm waves with men from the Cuhyon Division, though written messages had to take the longer route, across the river.

Other buildings of the town overhung the Algherans from along the hillsides. They were occupied by Lopritians; small artillery guns had been hauled into place between them to pre-vent an assault. Other guns had been stationed across the road to discourage a further advance. At nightfall, they began firing in a desultory fashion, as if to remind the Algherans of what they had failed to accomplish.

Twelve hundred of his men were dead or wounded by now, and the Lopritians had not stopped fighting. The tra'Crovsol was not beginning to feel discouraged, but he was in a grim mood. Before he rode to a meeting with Mlart, he gave orders to transfer his last regiment of unSepted from across the river to exchange places with his Housetroops. He would use the poorly trained recruits in future assaults and save his expensive professionals for finishing the battle.

He didn't want to miss a Lopritian when it came time for mopping up.

Mlart's day had been less successful than the tra'Crovsol's. After a promising beginning, the Cuhyon Division had gone no farther than the white farmhouse. The building had been ringed by Lopritian guns, firing from what seemed inexhaustible stocks of ammunition. His troops had not taken great casualties, but they had also not been able—or willing—to advance.

What hurt was that he did not know whether to blame them. He should have gone to watch, he knew. He should have taken over direction. Instead, he had waited all day for the breakthrough he expected, and all day the breakthrough had seemed only moments away and had never happened.

His guns had destroyed the farmhouse. There had been soldiers in the farmhouse, according to reports; his men had seen uniformed men leaning out windows shouting instructions to the gunners below them. Spotters—he hoped that was what the enemy soldiers had been, and not wounded men pleading to be spared. But it was too late now to change what had happened. Sound or wounded, some Lopritians had been killed, and his men had not gone beyond the splintered wreckage of the farmhouse.

In return, the Lopritians had killed his men and punished his guns. Mlart had brought almost fifty artillery guns to Midpassage. After two days of battle, he had only thirty-one which could still be used, and his gun crews had taken proportional losses. "Mad at us, they must be mad at us so we're doing something right," his chief gunner had quipped that morning, and Mlart had gone away smiling, thinking of the remark off and on during the day. In the afternoon, a splinter knocked from a gun carriage had torn a finger-wide hole through the chief gunner's throat and severed his jugular vein, and no—Mlart was not going to repeat his old friend's witticism to his widow.

Thirty-one guns. The only artillery he had taken back from the Lopritians were the small guns overrun that morning by the tra'Crovsol's men. Three guns, and one had fired its last charge into a plug of mud; it would never be used again.

Thirty-three usable guns. And he would bet the Lopritians

had more than that, for all the smallness of their force. They had the guns from the Dicovys Division with them, after all. He thought he minded that loss more than all the disabled men the Lopritians had left to him.

It had been a bad day, he concluded, communing privately with his thoughts as evening thickened. There had been times when he wished he had machines to scoop up his men and throw them into the midst of the Lopritians. The defenders were outnumbered, he had stressed in every conversation with his subordinates; press our advantage, attack and walk through them. And every time the objections came back: the Lopritians don't stand to meet us, we're always attacking from the bottom of a hill, we're always attacking against guns, they don't fight like they're supposed to, General, they aren't shooting as if they're outnumbered, sir, that's the Guards Regiment, Warder.

That's the Guard's Regiment, Warder. As if that were sufficient excuse for any failure. This is the Swordtroop, he had wanted to scream back. *My* Swordtroop, which I have spent fifteen years building and what have you done with it, my Alghera, tearing apart my finely woven mixture of professionals and recruits to re-create this quilt of Housetroop and UnSepted regiments I tried so hard to destroy? Why did the Muster permit this abomination?

He knew the answer to that. The fault was his own. He had retired from politics and for ten years the Septs had had their own way in the Muster. In the Muster, and in the Realm. Reform was his goal, not the Septs, and he had chosen retirement until the Muster could agree the Realm needed him again.

The Realm did need him, and the end of the war would not change that, but the Muster would be eager to retire him. There were implications to such realities, paths before him which led to uncertain destinations. Mlart was not ready yet to examine those paths but events were pushing him toward them. He wondered how many choices he would have at the end of the war and whether any of the paths he chose would be good for his nation.

Ironwearer Ian Haarper came into the room on his improvised crutches, making large sweeping gestures with the planks as he turned about, and Rallt suddenly realized the bottom floor of the house was crowded. At the same time, he wondered if anyone but he had seen the Ironwearer enter.

Wandisha was in the kitchen. She was not weeping now but her face was still frozen in the expression of crying. She sat on a stool beside the back door, hunched forward with her arms wrapped about her as if for warmth, with her feet one rung too high for comfort, and three quarters of the small room was filled with her grief. In the part that was left, by the door to the room Cherrid ris Clendannan had slept in, Pitar lan Styllin's wife bustled back and forth pretending business, unwilling to leave Wandisha and unable to go into her section of the room.

Lan Styllin himself was in ris Clendannan's room, looking lost. He was there to support his wife, Rallt guessed, while his wife supported Wandisha. It was a form of duty for him; he was not present as a friend of anyone else; he did not enter any conversations.

Grahan was in the front room, where Rallt was. He sat on the couch, with a slightly dazed look, but he spoke to people. A drink was in his hand. Whenever he set it down, someone took it away, someone replaced it with another drink. At intervals, he stood and walked into the kitchen and back. Rallt did not know what he said to Wandisha, or even if he spoke to Wandisha. His expression was as blank when he sat down as it had been when he stood.

The rest of the space was filled with people. Talking people, drinking people. Too many people in a space too small, speaking in voices too loud or too soft and always too quickly. They were not the townsfolk but soldiers and officers from the brigade, including the Hand of the Queen and two young women who stayed very close to him. Friends of Ironwearer ris Clendannan, they had said when entering, but it seemed to Rallt they spoke of themselves in their conversations rather than the dead man, and when they mentioned him it was in anecdotes from the distant past.

"Young Rallt," the Hand had exclaimed when he entered, and slapped him on the shoulder. "I've heard about you. Very brave thing you did there. Good to have you here, son!" And then one of his young women had held out a drink to him; the Hand had taken it and wandered toward the back of the house. When he returned, he had nothing more to say to Rallt, but the boy had noticed the Hand glancing his way from time to time.

His face had its own blank look, much like Grahan's, though he did not share Grahan's quiet, distracted tone of voice. An important man, ris Clendannan's friend had once said of the Hand, and Rallt could believe it now, seeing all the people who crept up to ris Andervyll and spoke with the tiny voices of favor beggars.

Rallt felt guilty. He had done nothing brave.

In the background, the big guns boomed, casting shells in all directions. From time to time, Rallt heard nearby explosions; red and yellow flares lit the sky; the tints flickered on the walls inside the house despite the bright interior lights. Once, before the Hand arrived, the earth under the house had lurched, and he had helped lan Styllin's wife pick up the small objects which had dropped from shelves.

"Mlart is pissed," lan Haarper said. "I hope he's pleased with himself."

Rallt was not sure who the remark was intended for, but the Ironwearer was looking at him. He nodded to show he was listening.

The red-haired man nodded back. His uniform was grimy and Rallt saw again how big the man was. Even the tallest men in the room would barely reach the Ironwearer's chin, and he wondered how it would feel to spend his life surrounded by people with the stature of children. Did lan Haarper notice the size of other people?

He fidgeted, seeing the Ironwearer's gray eyes aimed at him.

"You look like you could do with a drink yourself, Rallt. Being sober is no virtue at a wake."

"No." He nodded quickly. He did not want a drink, even from a glass of beer tonight. He had his own feelings and did not want to replace them with emotions poured from a bottle.

"All right." Lan Haarper jerked his shoulders up and down, then turned to look across the room. "Where's Wandisha? We need to talk to her."

We? For the first time, Rallt noticed that lan Haarper had brought a companion. The sharp-faced man from the North Valley had been waiting beside the doorway, his body lost behind the Ironwearer's bulk.

"The kitchen. She—" He gestured.

"We'll be gentle. Thank you." The Ironwearer did not signal, but the North Valley man followed as if instructed. The two men detoured to speak to the Hand, and Rallt noticed that Ian Haarper reached with both hands to grip ris Andervyll's arms. "Very brave," he heard the big man mutter. "Posthumous. Should have been a battalion. Dalsyn." The second man shook his head in agreement.

Another shell exploded nearby and people outside the house called out. Rallt's attention was diverted, and when he turned back, the Ironwearer and his companion were not visible.

"Come on, Rallt. Let's go outside, have a talk."

He hadn't heard Ian Haarper approach, hadn't noticed as the big man's hand dropped to touch his shoulder. To his surprise, no one else seemed to have noticed Ian Haarper's voice, though the man from the North Valley nodded at both of them as he left.

Rallt did not want to talk, but he had no reason to stay inside. He followed the Ironwearer through the door.

Ian Haarper had a horse outside. He unhitched it and led it and Rallt into the backyard.

A quarter moon was overhead so there was light to see shapes but not features. Made into a silhouette, Ian Haarper's body took on additional bulk. He leaned on his horse's saddle with an arm and stared skyward before he spoke. "Feels like snow, doesn't it? Wandisha says it doesn't mean anything, but it's definitely getting nippy."

It was not cold to Rallt. He hesitated, then realized Ian Haarper was waiting for him to speak.

"Was it weather thee asked Wandisha about?" He wasn't really curious.

"Basically." Ian Haarper hesitated. "So much for Wandisha. She says you're feeling guilty about Cherrid."

He swallowed.

"Don't be. Do you know what happens in a war, son?"

"People kill." He said it doubtfully, sure it was not the answer to Ian Haarper's question.

"Some people are killed. Some people are not killed. Look at it that way. And nine times out of ten, it's chance that decides which—where Nicole's cloak happens to lie, if you want to call it that. And chance depends on little things, but life is very important, so ever afterward the little things all take on great significance.

"If my knapsack had ridden a handbreadth higher on my back, the bullet would have hit it instead of Boris and Boris would still be alive. If I had tied my shoelace by that puddle, I'd be dead now. If I hadn't looked when I came to that fence . . . That's the sort of thing soldiers think. And all of a sudden sensible people start to worry about where they carry their packs and how often they can tie their shoelaces.

"And it means absolutely nothing. Good things happen to you in life and bad things happen and you can't predict them. It's like crops, Rallt—you plant seeds and things grow up and you water them and weed them and sow them and you don't spend your time brooding about the seeds that don't sprout. That make sense?"

"In a way." His father would not have liked lan Haarper's simplified notion of farming, he sensed.

Perhaps lan Haarper agreed. He hurried on.

"Well, it doesn't matter. The point is, unless you do something shameful or stupid, you must not blame yourself when bad things happen to you or to your friends, even very bad things."

The words brought back memories Rallt did not want to recall. He made gagging sounds when he tried to speak.

Lan Haarper had seen ris Clendannan's corpse when it was carried to a resting place in the hills behind the barn. Acid had worn unevenly into the soft tissues of the body. In places, the skin had been left red and roughened, as if sandpapered. In others, flesh had been torn down to the bone—not cleanly, as by an animal bite, but in the craggy mottled patterns of decay. Unlike Rallt, he had not stood in the gloom of the epuratory staring down at dark shapes twisting sinuously like fish in the depths of the acid bath; he had not seen the dark bubbles rising to the top, nor watched the scum thicken on the liquid and know its source.

He had not rushed to push at the tank to overturn it. He had not twisted the the thick handle that caused the tank to drain or stood by while acid bit into his shoes and clothing. He had not run for soldiers, not patted Wandisha uselessly as she choked and shook in Grahan's arms.

He had not seen two bodies bound so tightly together by saponified fat that soldiers needed knives to separate them. He had not seen wounds caked with black flecks of dead skin; he had not seen smoke rising from the bodies when the acid was drained from the epuratory tank. He only imagined he knew what caused Rallt's reaction.

"Wandisha tells me you ran at that gunman and got mixed up in the fight. That was brave. As for Cherrid and that man falling into the tub . . . call it accident. It wasn't your fault and if you hadn't acted, Cherrid probably would have taken a bullet through the gut and be just as dead."

"Wandisha says that." He clenched his jaw.

"And you ought to believe her. Anyway, you can't change what happened. Sooner you admit that, you can get on with your life. Be better, you had a good cry—like Wandisha—and get it out of your system."

"Little boys cry," he said stiffly.

Lan Haarper coughed. "Didn't say I was telling you to." He nodded at Rallt, then turned to his horse. He propped his boards against the animal's side and grunted as he hauled himself into the saddle. "Cherrid died to keep you and Wandisha alive, Rallt. It can be the last good thing he did for anyone or his last mistake. And it's your choice now how people remember it, not his and not mine."

"I know."

Lan Haarper nodded. "End of the sermon. You've got a gun." It was not a question.

He and Grahan both had rifles now. Rallt shook his head soberly.

"*The American Express card.* Don't leave home without it." Lan Haarper reached backward to pull a musket from a holster fastened to his saddle. He fastened a leather strap at the top and bottom of the gun, then fitted his arm through the sling and pulled it onto his shoulder. "And I do mean that. You're going to look after Wandisha, aren't you? Don't go running off to see what the soldiers are doing, and keep low when bullets are flying."

"Yes, sir—well, me and Grahan."

"Then maybe we'll live through this. I'd like that." Lan Haarper leaned forward to pick up his boards. He propped them over his knee and the knob at the front of his saddle. "*Damn*, it feels like snow."

Before Rallt could answer, he rode away.

* * *

Herrilmin's horse floundered late at night. It had been plodding all day and slow to obey the reins since afternoon so it came as no surprise.

Hunger and weakness had affected it, he supposed. No doubt a horse, like a man, grew hungry when it had nothing to eat. And thirsty, when it was not watered.

The animal had been for his convenience. He had neither fed it nor watered it.

It staggered, giving him warning. He dismounted quickly and waited for it to sink onto its side. He grimaced as it raised its head on its long neck and looked at him. He wondered if in daylight its face would have shown an expression he could read.

The animal's big teeth looked dangerous, so he moved around it cautiously, staying clear of the hooves. When he was behind the neck, he knelt and pulled his knife. It took four tries before he was sure he had cut the jugular vein.

Meat, he told himself while blood was spilling from the animal's neck. He had been about to walk away. He chided himself for the oversight and wondered if exhaustion had affected him as well.

It had, he thought dully, but so had relying on the horse. Walking would restore his wits. Perhaps in the morning, he would see landmarks he recognized and know the journey was over. He hoped so.

End this journey. Find his time machine. Rescue Gherst. Rescue Lerlt. Find Fesch. Find Timt ha'Dicovys. Kill Timt ha'Dicovys.

It was astonishing how simple his desires had become.

Eat and sleep. Those were needs. He kicked at the dead horse.

The animal had fouled its hindquarters as it died, so he settled for a foreleg. Inexpertly, he sliced through the thick skin to bare the flesh and hacked at tendons and muscles until the shoulder girdle could be seen. The full leg would be too heavy to carry, so he settled for the meat that could be cut easily from the bone.

He left the rest for the animals that had been following him. They were wolves, he was sure. Or bobcats, badgers, raccoons—whatever animal it was that traveled in packs and called out *Yip-yip-yip!* in chorus.

He was in their territory. Wild animals had to be placated.

* * *

There was a day when Kylene lay across him, letting Fesch caress her with his stumps of arms, her knees around his genitals moving minutely and lazily as she stimulated his captive erection.

His gentle arousal was a counterpart of her pleasure, he realized, the echo of her post-orgasmic glow. It was all she would allow to him today. He could not build to release.

"Why was it wrong for us to use time travel?" he asked. He was remembering what she had told him recently.

"Not wrong," she said after thought. "It was wrong for you Algherans to use it without understanding it."

"We had to use it," he said. "We had a need and it was given to us."

"By Tim." She was quick to insist on that.

"By Tim." He was less sure of that, but the point was not important. "We didn't have time to do experiments."

She snorted, a single ladylike forced exhalation. "How can people with time travel claim they have no time to study?"

He hesitated, looking with success for an answer. "All right, we didn't think we needed to experiment, so we just went ahead. I suppose the entire Project is an experiment, really. We've wasted enough time to please anyone, and nothing has come of it."

"What if something did?" she asked. She moved closer to him, her body tense. "What if you made a big change someday—if your City changed, so it wasn't your City, no matter how much it looked the same?"

"If I could still recognize it, it would be the same, wouldn't it?" He wanted to be reasonable. He wanted her to be reasonable. And he wanted—

He urged her closer and upward, then sucked delicately on a nipple until it was hard and oozing fluid. "Let's do this instead of talking."

For a time, she let herself be distracted. She held his body closely to her own and moved so she could be kissed. Then she fell away from him as he tried to manuever his legs between hers.

"You can't surprise a Teep, Fesch." She was breathing deeply, her body lean and straight beside his, nowhere touching. "If you want, we can—"

"No," he admitted. He was also breathing deeply, but his rejected erection was already drooping. She smiled for an instant, looking down at it, and he saw her nipples were also subsiding.

"Not the day for it, dear," she said. He sighed, telling himself falsely that he heard regret.

"You never answered my question," she told him next, and he guessed that was less complaint than a device to ease his disappointment. "Suppose your precious City had all the same buildings, and the same language, but a totally different history?"

That was the Project's purpose, wasn't it? To make a different history for what would be the same Alghera? He stared at her, puzzled, wondering what was wrong with that obvious answer.

"Very different." She turned her hand over, inspecting its back. "As different as Mlart being dead or alive. In every respect."

He still did not understand.

"Dear stupid Fesch." She stroked his side, taking sting from words which had not been harshly said. He smiled comfortably.

"Different Septs in charge," she explained. "Maybe no Hujsuon Sept. Maybe no Institute. No Teep Septs—almost no Teeps. Different sciences, nothing like the ones in the Plates, so you could do different things. Live like a fish underwater, go to the moon—"

He laughed at the absurdities.

"Don't laugh!" She tore hairs out of his side to punish him. "Your precious time travel isn't in the Plates. Can't you imagine *anything*?"

"Herrilmin's bombs!" He still wanted to laugh.

"Bombs?" Her attitude changed. "Tell me."

"Just an idea of Herrilmin's," he explained, wondering why she was so curious. "I heard about it from Gherst."

"How big are they?" she asked. "You didn't see them, but can you guess?"

"Sounds more like something Lerlt would have thought up." He smiled to tone down her stiffness. "He was surprised as me when—"

"Fesch, does he have—"

She stopped suddenly. "In his time machine. And with Tim's . . . Fesch, this in't funny. Don't you know what Tim's time shuttle is?"

"It's big." He grinned at her.

"*It's a warplane, Fesch!* A Fourth Era warplane! It was built to fight in battles during the Second Eternal War. It's got guns, Fesch, all kinds of guns, and things Tim added to it, like little birds to throw at other planes and blow them up. Snakes. Things to let you see at night, and things that make it impossible for other planes or levcraft to escape from you—all sorts of things I don't even know how to describe! I mean—it's Tim's. He showed me how to fly it, but he doesn't want anyone else to know about—"

"Timt." Without fingers to snap, Fesch could only copy Kylene's odd shoulder movement.

"Tim told me once that with six planes like his, the Algherans could have beaten the Chelmmysians."

"Maybe you're right, Kylene." It was hyperbole as certainly as Herrilmin's city-destroying bombs, he was sure.

"You don't believe me!"

He sighed. "I don't believe Timt or any other ha'Dicovys. If his time machine is so wonderful, why didn't he just give us six of them, so this war wouldn't be necessary?"

More than this war. His sweeping arm was intended to draw her attention to herself, to the mutilations she had inflicted on him, even to the war Mlart and the Algherans of this year were fighting against the Lopritians. Timt ha'Dicovys's creations, if not imaginary, were nothing to be praised.

"How could he give you weapons like that without giving away time travel?" she asked. "You couldn't destroy Chelm-force and keep every Teep in the world from finding out how. You couldn't pretend those planes didn't exist. You don't know how much of Nicole's cloak was over you to keep time travel from being found out by the Chelmmysians!"

Stalemate. She had an unassailable answer, at least in her mind, he recognized. Nothing he said would penetrate today. He sighed, wishing he could do more to show his feelings than waving his stumps in the air.

Timt's super time-shuttle versus Herrilmin's superbombs. The absurdity of it all came back to him and he had to smile, no matter how hard Kylene glared at him.

"We'll have to let them fight it out!" He chuckled openly, knowing the notion could not be hidden.

She slapped him and rolled to her feet, then shouted something brief and totally incomprehensible at him.

Days passed before she returned and he became very hungry. He learned not to argue with her.

Eventually, Fesch lost track of time. He reckoned days by the appearance of Kylene; a night for him was the periods between her visits. Her changing moods became his seasons.

She watched him for long periods without speaking. She talked to him. She sang songs to amuse him and she taught him nonsense rhymes and prose in never-used languages which he was to repeat for her over and over at demand.

He practiced when he was alone, wishing to please her, wondering what truths and stories the alien sentences conveyed, but she never told him. And when his memorization was done and he could recite his lessons in letter-perfect form, she asked to hear them no more.

Alone after that, waiting on her return, staring at the always misty sky, he sometimes whispered scraps of those stories and verse to himself, thinking their meaning must come with repetition. He was half-convinced Kylene wished him to find an understanding of them, an understanding which would enrich his understanding and love of her.

When he knew enough, everything would be explained to him, he was sure. Everything would be set right.

She spoke no more of Timt ha'Dicovys, nor of herself. She did not bother to wear clothing anymore. She was there for Fesch alone and he for her and nothing came between them. Everything in his life before he met her seemed as distant and indistinct as yesterday's dreams, and from words she let fall he realized she felt the same.

Nothing she did or said surprised him now, and his mood of acceptance did not change when she took away his lower right leg.

Then his lower left leg.

Then his upper right leg, to the hip.

Then his right arm, up to the shoulder.

Then his upper left leg—the two of them joked about that, during the Kylene-daytime, before she removed it from him, and Fesch pushed down the bandages wrapped about his belly with his stub of a left arm to trace the knob that was his hip for her and distinguish it from his side, though she assured him it was not necessary. He chuckled to show his good cheer, and told her not to miscalculate when she removed it.

Knowing his thought, she smiled and fondled his scrotum. She would be very careful, she told him. She knew how he valued his body.

Before she left, knowing he would be too weak to please her when she returned, he insisted that she squat over his face for a long spell of lovemaking and kept her with him until his face was slathered with her secretions and his tongue was too raw to continue.

"I'll keep you with me forever and ever," she promised before she left, and he remembered that happily in the Kylene-empty night, then slipped into dreams in which he did not run or throw.

When he woke, he had nothing left of either leg or either arm.

"My egg man," she called him when he revived and her voice was harsh. "You don't mind it a bit, do you?"

He didn't. He moved his head to agree and she stepped over him.

Her eyes were red, he saw, when he focused on her. Lines had been drawn from her nose to her lips and along her forehead. Her face was gaunt and her hair was bedraggled. She seemed to be aging before his eyes and he knew it was from her concern for him. He felt unworthy of her attention.

Something like hatred showed on her face. "I made you this way, egg man. You're happy because of what I did to you—something a Teep did to you. Does that bother you?"

No. He moved his head again.

"Watch me!" Fluid splashed onto his chest, then all along his body as she rocked her hips backward and forward. It was hot. It scalded him as it fell upon him. It glittered brightly and beautifully as she expelled it from her body but the drops that splattered onto his lips were bitter when he licked them up. "Do you like this, too?"

He nodded weakly. Eagerly. *If it makes you happy.*

"It doesn't." She stared down at him without speaking for a long moment, and he noticed the beads of liquid that dotted the dark hair on her groin. Slowly, lethargically, the golden drops slipped down, giving her thighs and legs delicate caresses which he yearned to echo with his own breath and saliva.

Suddenly she stepped away from him and ran to hide in her time machine.

"Teeps used to rule the world!" she shrieked at him. *"Don't you see what you've made of us?"*

Come back, his mind urged. *Let me make you happy, Kylene. Be my little girl, Kylene. Let me be Daddy for you again!*

Uselessly. In his all-alone night, he wept for his little girl.

Long before first watch, Ironwearer Ian Haarper was walking through the remnant of the Steadfast-to-Victory Regiment, in the street below the one on which his house lay, waking the men with kicks and proddings from his crutches. "Get up, lazy-bones," he growled at them. "Stay awake. Wake up the others."

Corporals and sergeants and officers were greeted with scowls and sent to a vacant house where Dalsyn Ian Plenytk awaited them. A lamp was burning on the mantel of a brick fireplace. A bowl on a small table showed that the regimental commander had already prepared and eaten breakfast; none was offered to them.

Lan Plenytk shoved the bowl onto the floor with a fist and ordered the men to gather around him. Unlike Ian Haarper, he had never bothered to select an orderly; it was an officer who held the lamp above him as Ian Plenytk drew a knife from his pocket and scratched lines across the tabletop.

"You all see this? Our street, the next street, then the next, then the great road. Gully here. And these four houses—Algies got up to that street last night. Took those houses." He hesitated for a moment. "We let them. They've got officers in those houses, sleeping."

"In my bed," someone from Midpassage muttered.

"In your wife," someone else called.

"Listen up, assholes!" Dalsyn snapped. "We want to wake up those gentlemen and get those houses back."

"Wake 'em fatally?" the man with the bed suggested.

"That's the best way," Dalsyn agreed.

"How we supposed to do it?" a noncom asked.

"Very politely," an officer said, and chuckles rose around the table. References to politeness always drew laughter in this regiment; Dalsyn could see puzzled faces on the men who had just come into the room.

"I meant knife or gun," the noncom said when he could be heard.

"Knife preferably," lan Plenytk said, then noticed lan Haarper shaking his head beside the door. Familiarity had taught him the gesture's meaning. "Guns will do. I guess it's close enough to daytime, it won't matter much."

Lan Haarper shook his head again. His mouth moved silently. One word.

"Sentries," Dalsyn said, remembering. "There will be sentries in the street, just a couple. It'd be wonderful if you could take them out quietly, but it isn't likely, so you'll just have to shoot them and rush the houses before those Algies inside are awake enough to react."

"Lovely," someone mumbled. "Why not let them sleep late?"

Dalsyn grimaced. "Take those houses back, men, and keep them, and get the two houses next to them also. One platoon to each house. Move out as soon as you can. Show the Guards how it's done, because tomorrow it's their turn."

Men looked about, seeing the Guards officers who had joined them, and Dalsyn was intrigued to see some nods of recognition. He stood and pointed at these officers. "You—house one. House two. House three. Four. Five. And six. Any questions?"

A lieutenant put up a hand. "Food. The men got to eat."

"We'll get support from the Guards," Dalsyn said, hoping it was true. "Get those buildings and someone will bring a meal up to you. Okay, gentlemen, the sooner you're inside, the sooner you have breakfast."

He watched lan Haarper approach as men left the room.

"Went well enough," the Ironwearer commented. He pulled a couch closer to the table and dropped his weight upon it, then used both hands to lift his wounded leg and rest it on his plank crutches. "I hate to give briefings. Maybe I should dump this Cimon-taken job onto you."

So that was why lan Haarper had let him give the orders? Dalsyn had trouble believing that. "How's the leg? Getting better?"

"Not yet." Lan Haarper sighed. "Give it a year tenth."

"Too bad, Timmial. We win this thing, I wanted to see you dancing at the victory celebration."

"We win this thing, Dalsyn, and I'll give you the first slow waltz."

"One *woots*," Dalsyn agreed, trying to force the word into his memory.

"How many men do you have left?"

"Maybe three hundred fifty." Dalsyn paused, then snapped his fingers. "Total. It's hard to tell how many are sick and wounded."

Lan Haarper grunted, and copied the number onto a scrap of paper. "Just under two thousand men, and about a quarter are out of it. Shit!"

More mattered than numbers, Dalsyn thought. Dighton ris Maanhaldur dead, Lerryn lan Halkmayne missing . . . They had counted for more than their bodies.

"Can I have lan Styllin back?" he asked.

"No. I want him kept safe. He's to replace you." Lan Haarper had not looked up from his paper.

Dalsyn sighed. "How about Mlart? What shape is he in?"

"Call it nine thousand men. He must be terrified right now."

"Sure he is," Dalsyn agreed. It was not what he wanted to say.

Have they found your wife? Is this attack going to work? "Does your staff know where to find you?"

"They'd better, or they're fired. I'll stick 'em into cannons and fire 'em off myself."

"Good." Lan Plenytk bent to pick up the bowl that had fallen on the floor and moved it to the fireplace mantel, then settled companionably on the couch by lan Haarper.

Together they waited for the gunfire to begin.

CHAPTER EIGHTEEN

*T*he early morning gunfire came as a surprise to the tra'Crovsol. He and his senior officers had spent the night in their normal quarters, close to Mlart. It took time for news of the trouble to reach them, more time to return to the northern force and reestablish control.

No one had expected the troops to reach the houses they had captured and no orders had been given which concerned them. The men had thought that Lopritians would surrender after their successes during the day; the officers who had taken over the houses had done so anticipating a victory celebration rather than additional battle. They were young men, supernumeraries and battalion commanders and below, who normally slept two to a tent. The prospect of individual beds softened their judgment; it was luxury after the living conditions of campaigning.

Eleven of the two dozen men died to pay for their comfort. Six wounded men were carried back under flag of truce to the Algherans. Two officers escaped with nothing but scrapes as they went through second-story windows.

Lan Haarper had decreed that to conserve food prisoners were not to be taken, but five officers surrendered. Four were paroled to the custody of the brigade's surgeons; Ian Plenytk had given them the choice of assisting the medical men or having their legs broken. A fifth man, a Blankshield originally from Loprit, offered to change sides and was released with the requirement that he leave the town and Algheran service.

The tra'Crovsol had begun the battle with sixty company and battalion commanders; the loss was not fatal but it was disruptive. The toehold his division had established in the town had been lost; halfhearted attempts by troops without officers to recapture the houses were easily beaten back.

A day tenth was wasted determining who had died in the houses and appointing successors; that process was not completed before Lopritian artillery began to fire upon the division. Unprepared for battle, the Algherans were forced to fall back beyond the guns' range. Most regrouped farther up the road, near the positions captured from the Lopritians the day before. Additional time was spent reintegrating the men who had first scattered into the riverbed and crept back one by one to the main force.

Mlart was furious when the tra'Crovsol reported his difficulties. He called the unexpected retreat a "disaster," although the division leader had correctly reported that he had suffered only a few hundred killed and wounded. He ordered an immediate attack to reclaim the lost ground.

The tra'Crovsol promised to obey, but inevitably the occasion for the "immediate" attack slipped into midmorning.

Mlart had issued orders for his own attack the night before. Two regiments of the shrunken Cuhyon Division were to feint toward the farm buildings on the hill while artillery shook up the defenders. One regiment and the cavalry were to form behind the elevated roadbed and wait for orders to assault the bridge. One battalion of the last regiment was to enter the riverbed and expel the Lopritians who occupied it. This would open a gap in the Strength-through-Loyalty Brigade's perimeter which would allow two more battalions to attack the flank of the farm's defenders; pushed far enough, it would leave the bridge and the apple orchard beyond exposed to attack.

To an extent, this worked. The Lopritians began to draw back their guns in early morning. That had not been anticipated in Mlart's orders, but a regimental commander had the wit to convert his demonstration into an attack, and hit surprisingly light resistance near the destroyed farmhouse. His troops met only an enemy skirmish line; the Lopritians fell back quickly to buildings beside the orchard, leaving the barn and several sheds to the Swordtroop. This was the impact area for Mlart's planned artillery barrage, but displaying unusual brilliance, the regiment leader communicated his intentions before acting, so the Algheran general had time to cancel the orders to his gunners.

In the riverbed, however, the Lopritians continued the struggle. At the westward bend of the river, they had built earth-and-rock barricades along the banks. The Algherans had not expected obstacles; surprised by Lopritian marksmen when they came around the bend, they fell back leaving half a dozen casualties, then rushed forward again. Men died on both sides of the barricades, but it was the Lopritians who broke. As the Swordtroop battalion moved along the river, Mlart had the satisfaction of seeing his enemies pried from their position; their tiny forms suddenly appeared on the edge of the riverbank and retreated to the orchard.

The bridge was free of defenders before he could order it taken.

Occupying the road without the buildings which overlooked it was useless, the tra'Crovsol decided. Which meant the houses the Lopritians had taken back that morning. Recapturing them promised to cost unacceptable losses, but he did not expect to find Lopritians in every house; occupying the buildings around the enemy-held houses should neutralize the defenders.

Necessarily, his advance was slow, because its pace was set by the troops moving up the back of the hill. But by midday, his men were in place.

"Run from cover to cover," he had told his nervous subordinates. "Don't give the Lopheads time to aim at you. Walk into the houses. Chase out anyone inside them, and put your men beside the windows. Shoot anyone who comes close who shouldn't be there. Forget formations and organization. Act like

you're in some pissant town—which is where you are—trying to
keep the bandits out—which is what you're up to. You can do
that, can't you?''

They could, they promised, and he told himself he believed
them, but the present generation of Algherans did not have his
experience. They had grown up in cities and peaceful farming
settlements; they had never had to defend a town from a barbarian onslaught, nor had they been barbarians.

But they did not disappoint him. Soon after the attack started,
messengers came back to report his men had taken the first
houses on the streets behind the defenders. They even came up
with an unexpected bonus: a prisoner, an officer found sleeping
on a couch in a house at the end of the street.

The prisoner had no useful information for the tra'Crovsol.
Questioned, he revealed only that his name was Ian Plenytk and
that his title was Force Leader, an ambiguous Lopritian rank
used for commanders of ad hoc forces of all sizes. Unguarded
remarks he made to the soldiers who escorted him to the rear
disclosed that he had much less than a battalion of troops, so he
was not an important captive.

The tra'Crovsol felt no need to collect prisoners, particularly
foulmouthed prisoners who assured their captors Loprit would
eventually win the war. He was tempted to shoot the Lopritian
out of hand, but his attack had not yet yielded more glittering
prizes. Nothing glittered on Ian Plenytk but the spittle on his
teeth, but the Sept Master sent the man off under guard to Mlart
tra'Nornst.

It would show that progress was being made.

Rallt arrived, out of breath from running, at the edge of the
clover field. In the distance, someone was beating on a metal
pan. ''Ironwearer Ian Haarper?'' he called out, and a soldier
tugging the collar of a horse attached to one of the cannon looked
at him incuriously and gestured with his head.

Better directions were unnecessary. Half the clover field was
filled with soldiers and guns and straining horses, but with the
hint, it was easy to find the Ironwearer. He was in the back of
his wagon, in the shadow of a foundry building. He was hidden
behind men on horseback, but Rallt could see his orderly's head
above the driver's seat.

The big man's voice could be deep. It carried well.

"Yes, the big guns first," he was shouting, "but you've got horses standing around, you can shift a small gun àlso! Or a caisson! I want to save them all, *dammit*! Isn't that clear?"

A gun went off and Rallt turned and saw it rolling backward until ruts in the field stopped it. Smoke billowed from its base and muzzle. Soldiers ran to it and began attaching ropes.

Lan Haarper's voice sounded again. "Do I have to do all the thinking around here?" Rallt was sure it was a scream but it seemed small and distant. The Ironwearer's arm was suddenly visible to him, outstretched beyond the chest of a horse. After a moment the rider moved off. Rallt saw an opening and ran toward it, but another horseman filled the gap.

"I'll get to it when I can!" the Ironwearer shouted behind his screen of attendants. "Tell that boy to go home!"

Rallt started, then realized lan Haarper had referred to him. "Wandisha sent me!" he called back, and wondered if the buzzing in his ears that affected his hearing had changed his voice.

A horse turned. He was able to see the Ironwearer behind a man's leg.

"Wait someplace safe," lan Haarper snapped, sitting up straighter in the wagon bed. He pointed with a massive hand, and behind gaps between the buildings Rallt noticed soldiers in the middle distance, moving through the space around ris Vandeign's big barn and orchard.

Soldiers in dark green uniforms, with guns pointing in his direction.

Algherans. He swallowed instinctively.

"Get in the shadows," lan Haarper shouted. "*Goddammit* boy! Someone get him out of here!"

For an instant, he stared at lan Haarper's orderly, wondering why he stayed so fixed and motionless. Then he collected himself and noticed that the path to lan Haarper was still open. He went closer to the wagon and repeated, "Wandisha sent me."

"Well, fuck Wan—duck down, *fercryssick*! Those are real bullets, boy." Lan Haarper's face was red; his lips were chapped, and the knuckles on one hand were raw.

Rallt smiled tightly, sure the enemy soldiers were safely distant. Then something *zing*ed overhead. Then another. He saw muskets aimed at him.

He realized suddenly there were no men in brown or blue uniforms on the other side of the wagon. Just as suddenly, he understood from the white tips of his ears that Quillyn was terrified and realized that the metal hammering sounds came from bullets striking objects in the foundry buildings.

The red spot under the nearest wagon wheel was not a flower.

"Lan Plenytk's captured!" It seemed better to blurt out the news. He breathed hard and resisted the need to hide behind Quillyn.

Lan Haarper muttered something. It seemed to refer to ancestors.

Rallt's eyes moved past him, to a man on horseback giving orders to the soldiers in the orchard. Were the Algherans moving closer, he wondered with part of his mind, or were they satisfied with their orchard and barn? He wondered if they had found the body in the loft.

He was shilly-shallying, he sensed. His father would have smacked him.

He started over. "Wandisha sent me to tell—"

"I heard," the Ironwearer said quietly. "Is he dead or wounded?"

"No. He just— Wandisha didn't say. He were sleeping and—"

"Yeah." Lan Haarper brought his head up quickly. "Gertynne! Orders to Pitar lan Styllin. He's to take over the Steadfast-to-Victory at once."

He looked back at Rallt. "What else?"

"The Algherans—" He looked at Quillyn, noticing again how rigid and uncomfortable the ugly little man had become. Were his own ears so white? Then he told as much as he could recall of Wandisha's account.

It didn't take long. "I don't know what happened after that," he said.

"Nothing good." Lan Haarper's head tilted, as if he looked for rain. "Okay, I heard you. You go back and—is Pitar near the house, by the way?"

He nodded quickly. "He be at the back hill place. Wandisha sent Grahan for bringing him."

"Doing my job, huh?" Lan Haarper smiled quickly. "All

right. You go back and if Pitar's there, tell him we'll get the men out tonight. Go that? We'll get the men out *tonight*. I think they're safe as long as they stay put. Tell him we'll use a couple Guard companies if we have to, and ditto for the guns near the scene. Can you remember that?''

He turned away immediately and bellowed, ''Get me Iron-wearer Wolf-Twin! On the double!''

Rallt looked at the Algherans again, and realized his memory could not be trusted, but that he was unimportant.

''Wandisha been listening,'' he told the Ironwearer and himself when he had the big man's attention again. ''It's not a mattering thing if—''

If a bullet killed him now, he meant. He understood suddenly how quickly death could come on a battlefield.

''Stay low and run.'' Ironwearer Ian Haarper had read his mind.

The tra'Crovsol's position was not as advantageous as he hoped. There was not space in Midpassage's narrow streets for four thousand men, and inevitably many of his men were left waiting on the hillsides. They were safe from artillery in that position. They had not had breakfast. After the experiences of the morning, it was hard to persuade them to move. It was the news that the leading troops had met no resistance and the prospect of loot which motivated them, rather than the orders of their officers. Finally, they were poorly led, by officers who could not see beyond fighting the enemy.

The troops which entered the town were moving through a vacuum. They were not advancing along the great road, nor facing the gauntlet of fire from ris Salynnt's riverside batteries; their casualties were negligible.

But they had not pressed the Guards Regiment. Ris Salynnt was able to extricate his men from the riverbank and place them in the buildings along the great road. He was able to move troops of his own onto the hill and to shift his guns into the streets. It was his artillery which commanded the intersections.

It took time for Mlart to move up his laggard troops, time to reorganize would-be looters, time to check that the abandoned foundry buildings were free of defenders, time to permit hungry soldiers a midday meal, and more time to move his own guns forward to the bridge where they commanded the orchard and the nearest buildings.

On paper, his gain seemed considerable. He had his troops across the river. The tra'Crovsol had seized a substantial portion of the town. The defenders had lost almost half of the territory they had controlled at daybreak, and even the incessant pounding of Lopritian artillery which had cost him so many casualties had slackened.

But the foundry buildings and apple trees were useless. He had not destroyed his enemy. The fighting in the riverbed had been intense for the numbers engaged, but only small forces had been involved; most of the Lopritians had escaped to the orchard, and then into the town.

He had taken only a few prisoners, and most of those were too wounded to survive for long. In any event, he did not have supplies to waste on injured Lopritians and his surgeons were overburdened with his own casualties. Mlart had no eagerness for shooting captives, but he could be practical. He sent orders to his officers that no more Lopritians were to be taken as prisoners and looked the other way while his troops implemented their own solution to the problem.

It was afternoon before the Cuhyon Division was ready to move again, and it marched into a buzz saw.

Between the foundry buildings and the town itself was a large field bordered on the west by the orchard and on the north by a line of trees and brush and the town's main street. East lay additional woods and the start of the valley that ran behind the town. The field rested on the shoulders of two hills; it was about two hundred man-heights wide. To reach the town, the Algherans had to descend a gentle slope and start up another. It should have taken only a few minutes.

They sent in a battalion at first, a triple line of infantry which was supposed to occupy the wooded strip between the field and the road which ascended the hill. It got to the middle of the field without difficulty, started up the slope and was met by musket fire.

Clear instructions had not been given to the battalion's officers, and its losses were heavy. In places, lieutenants led their platoons forward at a run, hoping to reach the Lopritian line before the defenders could reload. Elsewhere, with or without orders, the troops retreated to the foundry buildings. From that refuge, the men who had returned could see Lopritians emerging from the brush to shoot at the men who had fallen on the slopes.

The Strength-through-Loyalty Brigade was also not taking prisoners.

The enemy line had been found. The Algherans reformed quickly. Cavalry was sent along the great road to take the position from behind. Two regiments attacked across the field.

The assault was met by the big guns. Behind their trees, the Lopritians had stationed much of their artillery. It could not be seen until the Algheran regiments had reached the upward slope, and this time the troops had been ordered not to stop. Hit from front and side by shrapnel and solid shells, the Swordtroop suffered horrendously.

The men did their job. They crossed the field. They hit the Lopritian line and broke it. They reached the enemy guns and captured many of them.

But they could not hold.

When they emerged from the trees, the Algherans were met by musket fire from Lopritians waiting in houses across the street. At their rear, guns continued to fire at them from the western end of the field. The guns fired in salvos, methodically, raking the flanks of the Algheran columns, sending shells though the formations to kill men as far away as the great road.

The field was covered with bodies from the shelling. Enough, the survivors claimed, to let men march from one side to the other without touching earth, though Mlart was sure that was an exaggeration. The guns did not stop when the Algherans reached the Lopritian line. To their horror, the cannonfire went on and on. To hold their position, the Lopritians were shooting at their own guns—their own men.

The Algherans could not stay where they were. They could not go on. They could not fall back, but one by one, they did. They slipped into the orchard. They ran back across the field. And as each man left, there were fewer men to hold the strip at the edge of the field, fewer men to resist the Lopritians returning to the position, and more cause for them to run.

The Lopritians had been hurt. Badly hurt, Mlart was sure, but they had not given up yet.

He had muscles left to turn onto his side, but not to keep him there. Fesch turned his head and stared for watch after watch at the huge time machine beside the river. What did Kylene do as she waited to return to him?

He tried to ask her that when she was with him next, after she had received pleasure from him and had fed him. "Are you lonely, dear?"

"I have you. How could I be lonely?" Her face was frozen.

"I mean—in your time machine, by yourself. I think of you when I'm alone, all alone yourself, sitting in it, with nothing to do. Do you miss me when you're not here?"

"I'm not always there in the time machine." He thought she had considered that answer carefully.

His one eye blinked. "The time machine is always there."

"I have another time machine. A part, cut from one of your other Agent's vehicles. I can come and go when I choose."

Two time machines. He remembered how he and Herrilmin and the others had scurried about trying to find one. Long ago.

In the world outside only a few days had passed. He tried to rise, with limbs which did not exist. He gagged. His heart pounded.

Kylene pushed him down. "It's over. Be calm."

He was, finally. "It seems unfair. Your—" He could not find a word.

"Power." Her shoulders moved up and down. "Actually I have three time machines now. There's also the one my sister left. That's—somewhere else."

She still did not trust him, he noticed. "Where?"

"Somewhere else."

He stilled his thoughts. "I don't understand how you can have identical time machines."

"Time travel." She settled herself over his face. "If you don't know how time travel can work, it was a mistake for you to use it."

"It brought me you, dearest." His lips rested on her thigh. She stroked his hair gently while he fitted his mouth to her and began licking.

"This will end someday." Her voice was distant. It didn't matter at that moment.

My darling little girl. He was happy, he realized.

CHAPTER NINETEEN

Snow began to fall in the late afternoon. The air was filled with fat wet flakes which settled slowly and had no inclination to melt. It did not stop, and as the sky—and the world—turned from white to evening gray, the fighting tapered off.

Lan Haarper gathered his officers in the living room that night. Not all his officers, Rallt had inferred from remarks made by Grahan, but the few important ones or the ones he wished to argue with. The boy was not sure if they were the same or different men.

In the living room with nothing better to do, he stared out the window, seeing nothing of the world but the falling snow. Unstoppable snow, not to be held back with human palms.

Lan Haarper was like that, an intruding force which it seemed impossible to keep from ris Clendannan's household. It was unfair and indecent.

The Ironwearer had come to ask questions of Wandisha, he knew, more questions than even Cherrid ris Clendannan had asked, and to Rallt's knowledge he never thanked her for her help. In fact, he ignored her when other people were around, unless that was blatantly rude, then fastened onto her like a courting male when only he or Grahan was present to see his behavior. And afterward, when the Ironwearer was gone, Wandisha would be troubled and unhappy about what she had told him, and Grahan would complain about lan Haarper's bullying until she asked him to stop. And in a watch, the big Ironwearer would come back to ask more questions.

It had started immediately after ris Clendannan's death, with no respect for the Teep's grief, and Rallt had kept quiet about it because he did not want to upset Wandisha, but he wanted to shoot lan Haarper.

"The important thing is to get those men out," the Ironwearer was saying, and Pitar lan Styllin was shaking his head in agreement. Rallt remembered it was a discussion about the militia soldiers from Midpassage who had been trapped by the Algherans.

"It's not that important," a second man said. Rallt had forgotten his name, but he was young and slim and wore the brightest uniform in the room.

"They've got Algies on three sides," the man said, "but they could just walk out the front and go down the hill to the great road."

"What are the Algies doing while this happens?" lan Styllin asked.

"Depends," the young man said. "Nothing if it happens at the right time, like right now. But I'd like to leave them there. The Algies aren't attacking them, after all, and they are in a position to shoot at the road, and they're keeping the Algies off one of the streets. They are doing something there."

Lan Haarper sighed. "I see your point, but the idea was, those troops were supposed to make a hard crust the Algherans couldn't get through. But the Algherans did get through, and they're in the pie, and that hard crust is on the outside, where it may be doing something, as you say, but it isn't doing what I wanted. So I think we should pull them back."

"Suppose we wait," the brightly uniformed man urged.

Rallt, leaning against the wall, noticed Wandisha beckoning to him from the kitchen doorway, and slipped away from the boring conversation.

He was back within a minute, to whisper in lan Haarper's ear the words Wandisha had rehearsed with him.

"We have another problem," the Ironwearer announced be-

fore Rallt could step away. "Mlart is about to move to the intersection with the great road and up the hill." He said something
else in a language Rallt did not recognize. "Bastard's just decided it. He's going to do it tonight. Soon?"

The question was for him, Rallt understood. He nodded.

"Soon," Ian Haarper said. "With two regiments. We need
to stop him."

"What's he after?" Ian Styllin wondered and the young officer said "Housing" very quickly.

"Our guns," a man with much lace on his uniform and shiny
boots said. "He's trying to take them from behind."

"Doesn't matter," Ian Haarper said. "He can get both. We've
got ris Daimgewln's regiment. What else do we have to stop him
with?"

"The Midpassagers." That was Ian Styllin's contribution.
Rallt wondered if he was thinking about anything else.

"All right. Go get them," the big Ironwearer said. "Bring
'em out the front . . . You're sure that's safe?" The last question
was to the young man in the bright uniform.

"Yes," the young man said. He held a hand in the air to
model the hillside and traced lines with his other hand. "Algies
here, road here, our men *here*. Bring them down this way, Pitar,
and the Algies will never notice."

Lan Styllin grunted at that, then left.

"What about your troops, Perrid?" Ian Haarper asked, and
the young man looked chagrined.

"They're holding the intersections in the center of town, and
I think that's enough for them. I grant you, if the Algies on our
north don't move, then the Guards might as well be somewhere
else. But if they do try to move, you'll be grateful to have all of
them right where they are."

"You're probably right." Lan Haarper made a hissing sound
behind his closed teeth. Rallt noticed him looking his way, and
prepared himself for carrying a request to Wandisha.

The Ian Haarper shook his head. "No way of telling what
they might do. Yeah. Stay where you are."

"There are the men in the inn," the man with the lace-covered
uniform said. "They're within range of the intersection. If they
know to pay attention to it." He seemed uncertain.

"They were told to look for trouble from the north. I don't

know what they're going to see through the snow." Lan Haarper seemed equally uncertain.

He turned to Rallt. "How much time do we have?"

Not much time, the boy knew, though Wandisha had not been specific. He snapped his fingers and enjoyed lan Haarper's grimace.

"I can go tell them to stay alert." The lace-decorated man stood, and lan Haarper hesitated, and then shook his head.

"Go ahead, Gertynne."

Rallt could see no reason for staying in the room. He retreated to the kitchen, then put on a jacket. He went out the back door and ran around the side of the house to catch up to Gertynne.

"You're coming along?" Gertynne did not seem surprised to see him.

"I want to see the inn again." That was his motivation, he decided. The time he had spent in the inn made him wonder how it had changed. "I were living—lived—in it for a long time."

"Doubt it's gotten any prettier." Gertynne did not explain his remark.

It was cold. Snow was already as deep as his shoe-tops and Rallt could already feel its weight on his head. His hands were bare and he put them in his pants pockets. Gertynne had gloves and tall boots which vanished inside his pant legs, but his uniform did not look thick. Except for the boots, Rallt did not envy him.

He turned his head when they reached a pine tree with a bent top. Snow kept him from seeing across the street but he knew an intersection was here. "Better if thee would go that way," he suggested.

"The Algies are that close?" But Gertynne veered to his right without waiting for an answer, and Rallt sighed faintly.

"Close," Wandisha had said, but not how close. He wondered at times at the vagueness of her language. She did not have his excuse of not being born to the use of Lopritian. Perhaps a Teep, finding spoken language always less definite than the truths his or her mind knew, instinctively resorted to imprecise words to fit what must be said imprecisely. He could ask Grahan about that, he thought. It was the sort of thing Grahan would know, or have an opinion about.

He followed for a while, then took the man's elbow. "New intersection."

"Yes?"

"Just ahead. Algherans on the other side." He gestured. "Thee would surprise them. They would surprise thee back."

Gertynne considered his tone. "You want me to follow you."

It had taken long enough for the older man to understand that. Rallt crossed the street immediately and found a path that had already been beaten into the snow. "Good trail," he commented, and mimed to match his words. "Runs close to houses. No branches to hit at thy face."

"You grew up in this town?" Gertynne was soon short of breath from the rapid descent but he was curious.

Rallt almost snorted but politeness kept it from his speech. "Innings. Farm working. I been with my father, we move around."

Wandisha had told him of the trail. It seemed pointless to say so.

"Ah! I like to know what goes on here, you see. My family is very much associated with this town."

"Yes." Rallt wondered what the man was speaking about. With his elbow, the boy pointed to a group of a people gathered around a leaf fire in a vacant lot. "We need look like that. Should look like that. Crossing the road, thee must be bent over, look old and lost."

"Look like refugees and the Algherans may ignore us? All right." Gertynne seemed amused.

Look like refugees and run when seen was the actual idea. A shot fired at what first seemed a slow target would miss, according to Grahan, and he had recommended the technique as the best possible for evading border guards. Rallt had crossed international boundaries on major highways all through his short life without ever meeting a border guard, but he was certainly willing to believe they deserved to be evaded and he had half-seriously contemplated looking for some to elude when he returned to Innings.

"Yes, sir," he said again, humoring the older man.

"Steep here. Be careful with thy feet, Lord." Gertynne had no title, he knew from remarks Wandisha had made, but the pretense was a courtesy, to pay the Lopritian for his compliance. They had crossed the lowest street on the hill and arrived at a shortcut pounded out by generations of Midpassage residents. The great road was just ahead, though snow and nighttime hid it from sight.

But the path leading to it was clearly visible. It was a trough of snow. Left to himself, Rallt would have run down the hillside without mishap, but he went slowly in case Gertynne needed assistance and so he slipped and traveled the last few man-heights on his pants seat. Gertynne, to his annoyance, descended without difficulty and asked if he was hurt.

"No." He was sure Grahan would have produced a better answer.

"We go that way." He was following Wandisha's instructions again. Dutifully, he listened for gunshots in either direction before he crossed the road, but he heard none. He suspected the snowfall would muffle the sound. "Stay low and run, Lord."

"This is terrible," Gertynne muttered, and at first Rallt thought he meant the running, but he added to his remark. "We shouldn't be alive now! There are troops here. They should have stopped us before we got to the door."

It seemed a strange thing to complain about. The boy looked around the big bar and dining room. No lights were on, but his eyes had acclimated to the outside darkness and the inn seemed much the same. Perhaps there were more dirty plates on the tables. Soldiers, he had learned from observing Grahan, left dishes to be washed by civilians.

"Well, go bang on their doors," the older man growled. "And if the Cimon-taken fools are all sleeping, don't tell me about it. Tell them to watch for Algies on the right and tell them to watch their own security."

What will you do? Rallt wondered.

"Did you bring a musket?" Gertynne demanded.

He flushed. For a few days, ris Ellich's gift had been a constant companion. Since then, it had only been an encumbrance.

He had a rifle and he had forgotten it, he confessed.

"And I'm staff. I don't carry—" Gertynne made a growling sound. "Tell someone to drop me a gun," he snapped. "And have some of them come down here. There ought to be soldiers all the time to watch the door. Tell them to leave their doors open also."

So Gertynne would wait and leave the labor to him. Rallt

sighed, but not loud enough to be noticed, and went to obey. Being here was his idea, he remembered. His father would have told him he could not rightfully complain.

Most of the doors he knocked on were answered quickly, and most of the soldiers listened politely to what he said. One, which stayed closed, he pushed open and found a sleeping man and empty bottles on the floor; he said nothing about it to Gertynne, but it was the musket and ammunition he found in that room which he dropped to the older man. The soldiers had been ordered to leave their lights off and in comparison with the outdoors their rooms were warm; it was not surprising that some had fallen asleep.

He had finished the third level and was about to take the stairs to the fourth when he heard a gunshot.

"Algies! Algies!" Gertynne was shouting shrilly. "Get up, everyone!"

Rallt heard running steps. He leaned over the rail and stared into the gloom. Gertynne—the silhouette he interpreted as Gertynne—was crouched behind the bar now. The officer's movements told Rallt he was trying to reload his borrowed musket. There was a dark shape on the floor near the spot where the innkeeper had died. The little light that came in the open doorway was flickering.

There were more gunshots. More silhouettes on the floor below.

Doors slammed open below him.

"Get out, Rallt!" Gertynne called, and he thought he saw the white blot that was Gertynne's face. There were moving shapes in the darkness which he knew were other soldiers.

Then the older man came out from behind the bar. He was swinging his musket like a club, and he was yelling. Somehow, Rallt understood he had not had time to reload. He hit someone with his musket—the sound was unmistakable, and a foreign voice screamed—and then someone hit him. Gertynne fell down. His body was lost behind shouting Algherans.

Rallt had nothing to defend himself with. He sprinted up the stairs and up the ladder to the rooftop and cursed the time it took to push aside the cover over the ladder. As he went though the opening, he looked down, and saw a darkness filled with muzzle flashes.

Algherans were inside the inn, firing into the rooms the soldiers occupied, and the braver soldiers were firing back from the balcony.

Rallt swallowed and pushed the cover back over the opening, hoping the Algherans would not follow him through it, or notice him and think to send a bullet in his direction.

Gertynne was probably dead. Rallt made himself accept that. And Algherans were in the inn. He could still hear gunshots from below.

It was still snowing and wind was blowing ice-gritty snow in his face. He turned from it and brushed snow from the cover over the roof opening and sat with his back to the wind. He would have to wait for the Algherans to leave. He wondered how long that would take.

He was looking toward the river, but it could not be seen behind the curtain of snow. The riverbank was close to the inn, he remembered, but there would be nothing to see even without the snow, for the river was dark and featureless at night—peaceful in its fashion. Incongruously peaceful.

Distantly, like a contemplation of harvest at sowing time, he realized men were killing each other beneath his feet and that he could not leave the roof safely until the killing was over. The Algherans would kill the Lopritians, he was sure. He was sorry now that he had come with Gertynne.

And Gertynne was dead. Like ris Ellich. Like ris Clendannan. Like the faceless bodies he and his father had carried in ambulances. *Stay low and run.* It was so easy to die in a battle. *Stay low and run.* And he was on a rooftop, with no place to run.

When would the Algherans leave?

Nervously, fearing a slip more than exposure, he crept on hands and knees across the roof. Muzzle flashes showed as he came close to the edge, and he realized that men inside the building were still shooting at men outside. Had the Algherans been repulsed?

There was light from more than musket fire. Across the road, a building was burning. Flames leaped into the air and the snow that fell about it was tinted pink. It was a house a short distance up the hillside, Rallt decided. Was the fire an accident or had it been intentionally set? He could not see men fighting the blaze.

Men were nearby, though. The light from the fire showed

many men at the intersection of the great road and the hillside street. They were in lines moving up the street, Rallt saw.

Mlart's attackers. Two regiments, Wandisha had said. Two of Mlart's eight regiments, and in those two regiments Mlart had more men than Ironwearer lan Haarper had in three. Two regiments. The men shooting from inside the inn seemed to have no effect.

He swallowed. *Two regiments.* It was only a short distance up the street to the house where Wandisha and Grahan waited. Lan Haarper would try to protect them from the Algherans if he were there, Rallt was sure, but the big Ironwearer could not be there all the time.

He had to get back to them himself, he knew. Who else would protect Grahan and Wandisha?

The inn lurched suddenly. Rallt felt it tremble and saw light flash from the vicinity of the marching men. He heard a sound like thunder.

Then the building shook again and he knew it was being hit by shells. He heard something smash beneath him. The thunder repeated over and over. Men were shouting. The musket fire from the windows below had stopped.

A shell hit the building with an even stronger shock. It threw him sideways, and Rallt fell onto his side and felt little pieces of pitch and snow tossed into his face and tried to stop himself from rolling. Anther shell exploded nearby and for an instant the roof was bright and yellow-painted and warm, acid-smelling air flew over him and slapped his reaching hand.

He was blinded. It was the afterimage of the roof that he saw. *I have to get out of here,* he told himself. He forced himself away from the edge and pushed himself up with both hands and walked jerkily toward the opening and felt the building stagger beneath him.

Men were screaming but it seemed to have nothing to do with him.

All at once there were three large shocks, greater than any he had felt before, and he felt the slope of the roof change beneath his feet and stop, with the roof tilting down toward the river. There were crashing and screeching sounds beneath him and he felt himself twisting.

The building was falling.

Grahan had described what Algheran cannons had done to

Merryn ris Vandeign's house. They had knocked it into splinters, he had said, and Rallt suddenly realized they were doing the same to the inn.

There was no way to survive this. He had no time to escape. No time to go back into the building and down the stairs.

Blindly, without hope, but without choice, he ran to the edge of the roof and threw himself toward the river.

He coughed. In the darkness, he could not be sure if the sound was from his own cough, but Rallt felt his lungs and throat produce the cough.

His mouth tasted vile. His gut ached. Someone was squatting over him, he realized suddenly, and rhythmically raising and lowering his belly and squeezing his stomach. He hurt all over.

He coughed again, gagged, then vomited up water, a weak stream.

He was weak. The water flowed out of his mouth and against his chin and he could not summon the strength to raise his face.

"Coming around," the man punishing him said, and somewhere else another man said something about a fish.

Fish. Water. The river. His leap—

He had drowned.

Almost drowned. He needed air! His heart raced. His hands twitched with the effort he made but he was not getting air.

Then he felt his belly rising again. Fists pulled into his stomach and he felt air flowing over his tongue, out of his mouth.

Cooperate with it, he told himself. He made himself swallow when his body was lowered, then relax when it was raised, and all the while his mind focused on the fact that it might not work, that dying was very easy and that living was very hard and chancy.

He found the pattern finally. He was able to breathe with the help and finally he was able to breathe without help when the man who had saved him stopped and sat beside him and breathed heavily himself.

Breathing. Life. It was marvelous.

He listened to the hollow rasping of his breath and the hammer-beat pounding of his heart and the gurgling in his stomach and he was enchanted by each sound and decided he would never take them for granted again.

"My thanks to thee," he said when he thought he could spare

breath for talking, and it was not his own voice anymore. It was a deeper, more reflective voice, and to his ears and mind, a less childish voice—the voice of a man who had survived death.

"Where be this?" *Who saved me?* that meant, but as breath continued to flow through him, he decided it was unlikely that he had been rescued by Algherans. By Lopritians, then, and safety lay with the Lopritians. That was as reassuring as several deep breaths.

He noticed suddenly that he was nude and lying on pebble-strewn ground. There was a blanket over him. How long had he been here?

He heard water lapping. It was dark, so it was still night. And snow was still falling, he guessed from the touch of a passing breeze, though the blanket or some other cover kept it from falling on his body. In the distance, he heard cannon booming, and shrieks which might have been wind or human voices.

Darkness was overhead. He turned onto his back and saw square edges which held back the sky. Yes, it was still snowing. It was like looking out from behind a waterfall, wherever he was. He sat up slowly. The darkness overhead was above his outstretched hand.

Water sounds and smells. Pebbles, and more mud than soil beneath when his fingers probed. He was beside the river, he understood.

In the background, a man was feeding twigs to a tiny fire in a hollow in the riverbank. Somehow a small light made the night seem even darker.

The light showed a blue uniform. A Lopritian. It only confirmed his belief, but Rallt felt relief.

"Just scoot yourself back to the fire," the man beside him said. "Keep your voice down. We don't want them to notice us."

Explaining "them" took no words. "Did anyone else get out of the inn?" he asked. He began looking for his clothes. He did not see them, so he sat himself on the edge of the blanket and began drying himself.

As he became drier, he became colder. He started to shiver and leaned toward the fire. But the fire was small, more a comfort to the eye than a source of heat. Obviously it was something else Algherans were not supposed to notice, and he brushed the blanket over himself more vigorously, to create heat from his body's motion.

"Out the front maybe," the man said. "But I doubt it."

"Gertynne been wounded," he said, then added "He were an officer" when neither man said anything.

"He's dead then. The Algies aren't taking prisoners." That was the second man. His voice was sour.

"Where be this?" Rallt asked again. He had already been certain of Gertynne's death.

"You're under the pier," the man beside him said. "The Lady must love you, you didn't hit it on the way down, though you landed close. You want to thank someone, though, you thank Balthin over there. He's the one who waded out to get you."

Waded? He remembered his leap, then nothing more, though his hands and feet were scratched and bruised-feeling. And he was wet all over, inside as well as out. He had goose bumps. Surely he had been drowning.

"Must have hit your head," the man said gruffly, as if understanding his confusion. "The water's not deep there but you did a belly flop and didn't come up, so Balthin went to get you."

"Thought you might have something in your pockets," the second man said sourly. "You didn't though." He was a short, squat man with a deep scowl which seemed permanently carved on his face, even when Rallt thanked him politely. "Would have threw you back but Ettlich was softhearted."

He wasn't sure whether he should believe that, but it didn't matter.

"I need to go. Can I have my clothes?"

"Go where?" Ettlich asked. "The town is lousy with Algies. Best thing you can do is wait the bastards out."

"I've got friends. I have to get back to them."

"I'm telling you it can't be done. Give it a day or two, youngster, and the fighting ought to be over."

He couldn't wait, he knew. He began to feel desperate.

"I'll get through somehow," he vowed. "I got to. I been't supposed to be out, you see. So if I can have my clothes—"

"Let him try it," Balthin said suddenly, and Ettlich acquiesced.

"Well, believe me, you don't want those clothes," he said.

"Not in this weather. Why don't you take Giels's there? They're dry."

Giels? His eyes followed a pointing finger to a third man, lying on the ground behind Balthin. Giels appeared small and dark-haired. He was sleeping without a blanket, and Rallt began to feel guilty.

Then he saw the hole in Giels's temple.

"Friend of ours," Ettlich commented. "We'll have to bury him when it thaws, but he won't be choosy about he wears, why should we be?"

He hesitated, but Balthin was already unlacing the dead man's pants.

"Sure."

There was a wooden ladder on the side of the pier, its rungs cold and topped by snow. Rallt climbed to the top, then made his way to the riverbank and around several small boats brought to land for the winter. He collapsed against the back side of an old building.

Death was fatiguing, he had discovered. Every one of his ribs had a separate ache, and he had additional pains in his limbs and back and head. He needed to get his breath back before he went farther, and since he had insisted on leaving them, he did not want Balthin and Ettlich to see how worn out he was.

He missed his jacket. Giels's uniform shirt was not thick and when he crossed his arms and slapped at his shoulders, it did little to make him warm.

Fortunately, the snow was slowing. He could see much farther now, where there was something to see. He could make out the end of the pier and the edges of this building. He could see scuffed-up snow where he had walked.

About six fingers of snow had fallen, he estimated, and hoped it would not get much deeper, because the dead Giels's boots were loose on his heels. They were also heavier than he had expected, and he thought they might slip off if he had to run or came to much deeper snow.

He could not see the buildings beside this one. This was the warehouse, he remembered. The inn had been next, and the lumberyard buildings had come after that, and now he could not see them.

Not as buildings, anyhow. He coughed again, weakly, and

felt his insides jostling as he coughed and wondered how much water he still carried in his lungs and stomach. Death. The memento of his death. The closeness of death. People drowned in peacetime, too, he remembered, and now it seemed terribly unfair.

The innkeeper had died at the right moment, he thought. It would be a long time before Midpassage needed an innkeeper again.

The fire he had seen earlier was still going. It did not cast much light but there was enough for Rallt to see that the inn was gone. A jumble of boards and plaster slabs had been dumped in its place. For an instant, as he stared at it, it seemed the raw material for building another but much smaller inn. Then he remembered the heap contained the bodies and pieces of bodies of men. Dead men—the inn was so smashed up, he was sure no one inside could be any different.

And at the center and bottom of the heap was a body in a uniform with fancy lace on the sleeves and across the chest and shiny boots on its feet. Rallt thought about that body wistfully, understanding all the while it would probably be the last one recovered from the wreckage. Gertynne had worn what he was sure was the most expensive set of boots he had ever seen, and they were much of a size; he was positive Gertynne's boots would have fitted him better than Giels's. He sighed.

Gunfire recalled him from regret. He had had enough of a rest. He got back up on his feet, bracing himself against the stuccoed wall of the warehouse, and went around the side of the building.

Aside from the fire, which was fading down, now that he could see it, Midpassage did not seem to have changed much in the period while he died and was reborn in another man's clothes. Not at first. Then light flared in the center of the hillside, bright yellow in the middle of gray and black. A *BOOM* and a crashing sound came to him almost simultaneously.

A cannon, he realized. One of Perrid ris Salynnt's guns from its position—he marveled at his own understanding.

Another gun boomed, higher up on the hillside, to the right, and he realized it must be one of the guns under Ironwearer lan Haarper's control and that Wandisha would only be a short distance from where it fired.

Then another gun, from the base of the hill. One of Mlart's.

It seemed worth noting that the flame that lanced from Mlart's cannons when they fired was just the same as from Ian Styllin's and Ian Haarper's guns.

Another gun. One of ris Salynnt's. Two of ris Salynnt's—he heard a double crash of impact and wondered what targets the guns had found.

He could not see the lines of Algheran soldiers that had been on the road up the hill. But the guns were still firing, so they must still be there, somewhere in the town.

"Lousy with Algies." Ettlich's phrase. But Ettlich had not been speaking with current knowledge of the town, he was sure. Ettlich had been beneath the pier, and perhaps not for a very short time. A prophecy then, which might or might not have become true.

There had to be a path back to Wandisha and Grahan which did not involve danger, would not lead him into a nest of Algherans. Streets, trails, the passages beside houses . . . One of ris Salynnt's guns went off again and he tried to place exactly where it must lie, on which of the narrow streets night and distance and snow concealed from him, near which invisible houses. Somehow the existence of the guns proved to him that he could find a route back to Wandisha and Grahan.

After returning to life, anything else was achievable.

His sense of mastery lasted about six seconds.

Moving around the warehouse had exposed him to a company of soldiers marching south along the great road. He stepped backward toward shadows but he had been observed. A gesture he did not see sent two soldiers after him; they grabbed his arms and pulled toward the company.

Another soldier came to meet him. "What unit are you with?" he demanded. He had an officer's attitude; a sudden gout of light from a cannon showed Rallt his uniform jacket was green.

"None. I be supposed to be with Wandisha and—"

"You can tell me better'n that." The officer hit him in the chest and Rallt struggled but his arms were not released. The rear of the column of troops had stopped moving and he saw men staring at him.

Algherans. Most of the uniforms were green. None were blue.

"Let me go!" he shouted, "I be'n't Lopritian! I be'n't a soldier!"

The officer ignored him. "Where's his weapon, Railstenn?"

"Didn't have one, Sergeant," one of his captors said.

"These been't my clothes!" Rallt shouted.

The officer slapped him. "Shut up till I'm talking to you."

"Deserter," the man on the other arm said. "You want, we shoot him?"

"Ought to," the sergeant grumbled. He poked Rallt in the chest and leaned close. "Hoy! Listen you. You're getting one more chance. You join up with us and when this is over we'll get you back to your outfit and nothing will be said. You fuck up or you tell me one more lie— You understand?"

His Lopritian was flawless. Rallt understood.

They wanted him to kill Lopritians. He swallowed.

"Give this man a musket," the sergeant ordered.

"Not loaded." A man handed Rallt a musket with a strangely courteous gesture and looked at him carefully. "He's going to need cartridges, boss."

The officer swore. "Worry about that later. We're wasting time. You—you drop this musket, soldier, and I'll personally kick your asshole through the top of your head. Understand?"

He shook his head, but not quickly enough for the officer, who jabbed his sternum with a finger, then turned away before Rallt could say a word.

"Fall in, ladies, and jiggle those butts! Men are waiting on you!"

That included him, Rallt discovered. The soldiers holding him pushed him into the middle of the short column and did not let go until the line was moving again.

It was more of a shuffle than a real march. He was able to keep up though his breathing became loud and labored again. He was not the only tired man, it seemed. The column was filled with Algherans who sounded as if they should have been in hospitals alongside ris Clendannan.

For the first time, he began to think that Grahan might be wrong and that Ironwearer Ian Haarper might win his battle.

A hand gripped his elbow and pushed. "Keep going, keep going. This isn't hard yet." He recognized the voice as coming from the captor who thought he was a deserter and wanted him shot.

It was hard for him. He tried to explain. "I were in the river."

"One of ris Daimgewln's, huh? You've had it soft till now. C'mon, soldier, there's Algies waiting."

"Algies?" It wasn't an Algheran expression, he was sure.

"The enemy, remember? The bastards whomping on our town."

"It's not my—" Light dawned. "You're Lopritian!"

"Midpassager." The man tugged at him again. They had fallen behind the others, Rallt noticed, but it was not important now.

This was the Midpassage company! He could leave and no one would blame him for deserting! Everything could be explained immediately and be would be back with Grahan and Wandisha almost at once! "I know Pitar lan Styllin!"

"I know Pitar Styllin too. Big deal—he's my cousin, used to beat the crap out of him regular. C'mon, fellow, get up the hill. You do your part or I'm going to shoot you."

This time there was no escaping the man's pull or the message in his harsh voice. Rallt swallowed and followed him up the hillside.

Their path ended on a flat shoulder of ground. A house was just ahead and beyond it Rallt could see flames curling from the bottom edge of the roof of the burning building. He could also see part of the lane that climbed the hill and part of the intersection of the lane and the great road. Despite his exhaustion, he could see that the Midpassagers had not come far up the hill. Grahan and Wandisha were still far distant.

Explosions and flares of light showed that shells from the artillery were striking uncomfortably close. Cannons were simpler machines than wagons, Rallt had told himself. Surely with less to go wrong, less would, but he was unwilling to ask any of the soldiers for confirmation of his theory.

"Eight volunteers," the sergeant said. "You you you you." He slapped men on their shoulders and Rallt was not surprised to find he had been picked. "You ladies run through that house and don't stop to wet your wicks. Get going, ladies." The sergeant gestured with his musket, and Rallt found himself running before he could ask what he was supposed to do.

Was there a light in the upstairs part of the house? Were there Algherans waiting inside? The bottom of the house was dark but something seemed to shine overhead, and he wondered suddenly if it came from a lamp or was a reflection from the burning building. Did light in a house mean safety?

Suddenly he was beside the house and men were moving back from the door, to let one of them—Nellim?—rush at it and kick and lead the way through. The man was bent over to a child's height and he was running, Rallt noticed.

Stay low and run. It was an echo from another world.

The house was empty, which was fortunate for Rallt, since he was the first to enter several rooms. Only when he was downstairs again, surrounded by the other soldiers and waiting for the sergeant's return, did he remember his weapon was not loaded.

"Take this one," Ian Styllin's cousin beside him said, then watched carefully as Rallt inserted the cartridge into his musket. "You move like an old lady, boy. No wonder the Algherans did what they wanted to you people."

I been't a boy. Life had taught him it was useless to make that particular protest. "My name be Rallt," he said sourly. "From Innings, not Loprit."

"Yeah." The man turned away. "Hoy! Everybody give this boy one of your cartridges. This Rallt here. He don't have none."

Hands reached toward him. It felt like coming home.

But everything turned very bad at the next house.

When Rallt and his companions ran forward, flames lanced out suddenly from windows in the first and third stories. The man at Rallt's side stopped and fell down. Then another man, and a third, and Rallt tripped over his hand and fell down himself.

There was more fire from the windows, and suddenly it had meaning for him. Algherans were in the house, and they were shooting at him. Should he move forward or crawl backward? He did neither. He lay where he had fallen and waited for more understanding.

Snow spurted before him and splashed over his hands.

People were shouting at him—over him—he sensed. None of the voices had anything that resembled words in them. It was only noise, from people who knew no more than he what to do. He was all alone, despite the sound.

But Lopritians had to get into the house, he was sure, and the Algherans had to leave. He focused on that certainty.

Slowly, keeping his head close to the ground, he looked about him. He wished he could see some of the people shouting at him, but was not surprised that he did not. Then the hand that had tripped him wriggled, and he realized the soldier behind was still alive, still conscious, and perhaps still as unwounded as he was. The fight for the house had not ended.

He felt very small and very fragile at that moment, and his mouth tasted of vomit though he could not remember throwing up. He was hollow, a shell of Rallt-ness waiting for a stone or a sharp word to burst and dissolve and melt into the waiting ground. It would come very soon, he knew, and the bubble that was Rallt wanted to cry but something like his father's voice but without sound told him he could not do that, could not spend time thinking of that, would never do that.

Slowly, surely, steadily, the hollow, lonely thing that Rallt had become moved its musket forward and placed the weapon against its hollow shoulder and hollow face. For just a second, he ceased to be an automaton, and wondered if he would be blamed for breaking a window. And then the hollow thing aimed its musket at a place where it had seen a flash of light.

This Rallt here, he remembered suddenly. He was not alone. He pulled the trigger with a human's finger.

CHAPTER TWENTY

*M*lart's nighttime attack had rapidly become a disaster. Like many disasters, it seemed inevitable when it began and preventable after the fact, and thoroughly unpleasant as it unfolded.

He had expected that the Lopritians would remove their heavy guns from the main road leading up the hill. He had not anticipated a second row of enemy cannons in the center of town, nor that guns mounted in the cross streets would dominate the intersections on the main road. As a result, the first five minutes of artillery fire cost him five hundred casualties among his fifteen hundred attackers.

The loss rate had not improved after that. It was unfair to say that the troops had broken. They had not run helter-skelter from the field. But they had sought refuge from the artillery barrage in the houses across the road, thinking the Lopritians would not shell their own homes, and they had been wrong. The troops had also not expected to find those houses filled with armed Lopritians, and that mistake had killed many of them.

In the disorganized struggle for the houses, the Algherans had suffered the greatest losses of the night. The troops would not disengage—they could not have disengaged safely at such

close range, he admitted—and the outcome of that type of fighting depended more on strength and luck than on skill. Mlart's
lieutenants and sergeants had fought as privates and died as
privates; both as a general and as Warder of the Realm, he knew
Alghera could not afford those deaths.

A concerted attack by the tra'Crovsol might have redeemed
the situation by overrunning the midtown artillery parks, but it
had not been arranged. Mlart let his staff claim the blame for
that, but he did not really hold it against them. Night attacks
were so difficult to coordinate that excuses for them came about
once a century. It was most unreasonable that old ris Clendannan—capable of stretching tradition, in Mlart's estimation, but
not of breaking it—had fought his first battle of the campaign at
night, and then had been prepared for this one. The Ironwearer
was so ancient that he ought to be senile, after all; it was not
good news for the Realm if the old fox was getting better with
age.

Reluctantly, since the fighting could not be stopped, Mlart let
the struggle for the houses continue. The Lopritians were paying
for this battle, too. In the morning, he would replace his shattered regiments with the two which had slept during the night,
and renew the attack. He did not think the defenders would
prevail.

Just to be sure, he sent a high-ranking aide to wake the
tra'Crovsol and demanded an all-out attack from the north on
the following day. The Lopritian acorn was about to meet the
jaws of an Algheran vise.

The tra'Crovsol, though unhappy about being pulled from
bed at such an hour—there was enough of a racket to keep any
man with full use of his faculties from sleeping—was willing to
play his part in Mlart's plan.

In fact, he was amused to find he had been ordered to continue the attacks on Lopritian houses that he had begun under
his own initiative the day before, though he was careful not to
say as much to the aide.

He might have served his country's interests better if he had
made that remark, for he and Mlart tra'Nornst had very different
ideas, despite the use of similar words. Mlart wanted frontal
attacks against enemy-held positions. Time was critical to him

and he was confident that in open battle his superior numbers would soon destroy the Lopritians.

The tra'Crovsol was leery of such tactics. Every direct assault he had witnessed in this war had been beaten back or proved not worth the cost of success. Maneuver had been the key to each of Mlart's victories, and he had heard the tra'Nornst himself stress the fact in conversations. When scouts sent out in the early morning returned to tell him that the Lopritians he had isolated in the buildings near the great road had abandoned their positions, he interpreted that as success for the same policy. The Lopritians could be defeated by taking their town from them. In the coming day, he intended to do just that.

It was not an absurd decision, but it did not fit Mlart's strategy. In effect, one jaw of the Algheran iron vise would be rubber-cushioned.

Dawn was terrible.

Rallt came awake from a boot in his ribs and when he was conscious enough to make sense of what surrounded him, he knew the day would only get worse. Probably in a hurry.

"Get up, get up! Show me you're awake!" A sergeant's voice. His father had never spoken so harshly. Rallt sensed the return of a boot and forced himself to stir. It hit anyway and he forced his eyes to open.

He didn't have much bedding to leave.

Not much house to leave, either, if it came to that.

He had slept on couch cushions and covered himself with torn curtains. He was sore all over. And cold. He had acquired a hatred for drafts which he intended to nourish for the rest of his life.

He was in a shell of a building, which had been gutted by Lopritian artillery. It did not have a roof now. It did not have four intact walls, and the ceiling above Rallt was not complete— he had spent his few moments of "sleep" huddled in a corner, with every expectation of seeing much less of the ceiling in the daytime. He did not think there were any unbroken windows.

There had been Algherans in the building when the Lopritians entered it. Live ones, perhaps. Rallt had shot one propped up in a corner. Afterward, he had thought that artillery had killed the man first and his bullet had only knocked him down, then decided it had not mattered. Just to be sure, corpses had to be shot, after all.

The bodies had been pushed beyond the kitchen door, and he was sure he would not recognize which was "his." It was something which had been out of his control. He didn't feel pride or shame or reluctance to do it again.

What would Grahan say when he told him he had killed a man?

He should go look at the bodies, he reminded himself. He still needed a better pair of boots.

"Get up, get up!" The sergeant's voice had weakened, and Rallt decided he had gone into another room. How many men were there to awaken? Three, counting him, in this torn-apart living room. Two in the next room, visible through a hole in the wall. One man sitting on the bottom of the hallway stairs. He didn't think anyone had risked the upstairs of the building.

Midpassage soldiers, he told himself. In daylight, it was obvious they were not Algherans. They had been given brown uniforms originally, but most of them only retained a shirt or a pair of pants of that color. The Algheran clothing many of them wore was badly fitting. More than one man wore his peacetime clothing with a green or brown military shirt on top laced just enough to keep it on his body.

Of course. They're home. These men had all had time to go to their houses and change clothes before coming back to their war. He wondered what they felt as they looked around now at their homes.

"Get up, get up!" the sergeant shrieked. "I swear, Force Leader Ian Styllin will give you ladies to the Algies if you can't get out of the sack! What do you think you're here for!"

Similar exhortations were audible from elsewhere, where soldiers slept in other houses. Some were in Algheran Speech.

Rallt wondered if the Algherans would really take any of the men they were being offered. None of them had bathed since the beginning of the war, and combat had not improved their habits or manners. No reputable patron would have used them to bring in an overdue harvest.

"Buddy, buddy, buddy!" the sergeant shouted when he returned. "Find your buddies." It was Lehmell, Rallt noticed, a self-important strutting man who gave orders to Sergeant Ian Gunnally as well as privates. In the nighttime, Lehmell had been an unpleasant but faceless voice shouting Ian Styllin's desires at the men. It was probably worth noting that Lehmell could be unpleasant in person.

He wasn't willing to see the Algherans conquer all of Loprit, Rallt told himself, but he was willing to let them conquer Sergeant Lehmell.

He staggered to his feet, and when he was up a man slapped him on his arm and shouted. Other soldiers were doing the same, he noticed. What was this about? The man who had touched him was one of his captors from the night before—not Ian Styllin's cousin, but the other man.

Railstenn, he remembered. He had never heard the name of Ian Styllin's cousin. That man was still facedown in the snow, two houses behind.

"What been 'boody'? Is 'boody'?" he asked cautiously. Military life had far more complications than exposure to Grahan and ris Clendannan had led him to believe, and most of them were not worthy of civilian emulation.

"Pals. Friends," the soldier said. He wore a brown shirt over green pants. The shirtsleeves were torn at the elbows, and Rallt saw pink fabric below them. "We do things together, we fight together, we stay together, we look after each other all the time. You guard me and I guard you. Sounds silly, doesn't it, but it works."

He nodded thoughtfully. Grahan and ris Clendannan had been "buddies" in a sense. Ironwearer Ian Haarper and his ugly little driver were probably "buddies." Sarlso and his father were close that way. It did make sense.

"Sure," he said, and the soldier slapped his arm again.

"Ought to be food around here. Buddy, you look good at scavenging. Why don't you find us something for breakfast?"

"One other thing," Harper commented. "Grahan's been after me. He's lost a boy. That sidekick of his from Innings—remember him?"

"Seen him once or twice," Pitar Ian Styllin said. "What about him?"

"He went out of the house last night, got picked up as a straggler by one of your platoons. Wandisha wants him back." Harper leaned carefully to the side of the wagon and spat on the ground. He was feeling well enough to sit beside Quillyn at the

front of the wagon, but incautious movement still hurt his leg.
He did not want to grunt in pain with soldiers looking on.

The sun was in his eyes and it was troubling to think that the
defenders along the main street would also have sun in their eyes
this morning. *If Mlart stays still and the tra'Crovsol does the
attacking . . . Asking for the moon, chum.*

"Wandisha, huh?" Lan Styllin looked down the dirt lane to
the houses where his troops were stationed. "She sure it was an
accident? They were giving all the chores to that kid, as I recall.
Wouldn't be surprised if—"

"Pitar, I promised."

Lan Styllin sighed. "If I see him, I'll let him go."

"Fair enough." Harper had not expected the Midpassage
man to start a search for the boy. One boy in Ian Styllin's 270
men, in the 1,460 that remained in the brigade—Rallt had taken
as much of his and Pitar's time as he rated. "How you doing on
supplies?"

"Fair. We got a bunch of men using Algheran muskets already, so . . . maybe Mlart will keep us supplied with ammunition. Must love us, he comes so hard at us with so many
gifts." The Midpassage man grinned.

"No doubt." Harper was due to meet Perrid ris Salynnt next;
he was already planning that conversation.

"Interesting," Mlart said mildly, and the news was interesting but no more than that. He waved a hand in dismissal, and
the obviously disappointed aide withdrew and let Mlart return
to his breakfast.

The news—all aspects of army life have a hierarchical structure, so that what was "gossip" when told by ordinary soldiers
became "rumor" among sergeants and "intelligence" when
related by lieutenants and was surely "news" when it had to be
brought *on the run* to a general by a colonel, though it would
be "gossip" again when Mlart wrote his daily undeliverable
letter to his wife, which amused him since the letter writing was
at her order—was that Ironwearer Cherrid ris Clendannan was
not commanding the Lopritians. He had been wounded himself
at the battle where he had caused so many Algherans to be killed
and wounded.

The story—he liked that word better—had come from the
Lopritians themselves. From two Lopritians, soldiers at oppo-

site ends of the hillside road, calling out chitchat at breakfast time to Algheran soldiers who had doubtlessly shouted back vital military secrets themselves. Ris Clendannan was still in Midpassage and alive, one soldier had said, without giving an account of his injuries. The other claimed the Ironwearer had died the previous day in an accident, after being blinded and wounded in the chest.

Fifty-fifty, Mlart told himself, evaluating the stories. If ris Clendannan were still alive, he might be blinded and incapacitated. He might also be directing the battle, using another man as a figurehead. He wished he had a Teep to tell the truth.

And if ris Clendannan were still alive and in the town, he wished he had a reliable account which would tell him precisely which house the Ironwearer had occupied. He wasn't sure whether he would tell his gunners to avoid that target if he could point to it—he had met old Cherrid during the peace negotiations after the last Lopritian war and bore no grudges—or if he'd have them let go at the spot with everything they had—the old buzzard hadn't become a close personal friend, after all, and business was business—but he would like to know where it was, in case he did make up his mind.

Of course, the story of ris Clendannan's death might be true. An Ironwearer Haarver or something similar was supposed to be in charge over there now, and Mlart had a way to check that. He still had his copies of that bizarre surrender proposal the Lopritians had made, in which they agreed to give up the Strength-through-Loyalty Brigade if he let them win the war—at the time it came to him, he'd simply assumed ris Clendannan was far gone in drink or senility when he dictated those terms, or following the orders of a Hand of the Queen in one of those states. They were in an envelope in his camp desk, in one of the letters in that small mountain of letters addressed to his wife, and he could dig them out if it became necessary and look at the signatures. Not that it would prove anything—on documents that Mlart signed for posterity other men resorted to illegibility.

And it didn't matter. Outnumbered, old Cherrid had fought a good tenacious defensive battle on his little ridge until he slunk away in the darkness, and the current Lopritian general—whoever he was—was fighting another good tenacious defensive battle.

A defensive battle, with no hope of victory. Mlart did not begrudge the poor devil his unreadable signature.

Happer or Haagart or something like that, with an almost Algheran ring. The Warder of the Realm smiled.

Fesch woke to find that Kylene lay nuzzled against him. Her head was on what was left of his shoulder, her body bent around him so he could see all of her and remember what it had been like to stroke her side with his arm and watch as her body moved against his and wait for the moment when her body positioned itself above him and she slid down upon his thick pole of erection and merged with him, body to body, joy to joy, mind to mind . . .

A young man's hopes. A young man's dreams. Nothing like it had ever happened, and Fesch realized now they never would. He was not a young man.

"You're twenty-three," Kylene said sharply, with a voice he was sure was intended to hurt. She sat up and looked down upon him.

It was only a number. "Twenty-three," he agreed with his old man's mildness, and she saw he was beyond her hurt.

Overhead the sky was dark. Gray. Feather-textured. Dome-like.

Snow, he realized at last. It would melt long before it reached him.

"I've never needed anything you could give me, like this." She put a hand on his limp penis and shook it idly for a moment. It did not stiffen.

"This little rod that seems so important to you—it was never much, you know, and you let it run your life. I never wanted any part of it."

Distant words. He closed his eye and let her play with him, enjoying the recognition her touch entailed, even if he knew it would never go so far as an erection again.

An old man. A sexless, erectionless man. He needed very little from life now. A meal, a few words of attention from time to time. He needed Kylene less now than Kylene needed him, he was sure. And Kylene, for all her scornful words, had needed him.

I am caring. I am loving. I am giving.

He thought of the long day tenths he had given to Kylene and how she had squealed and grunted and quivered with rapture as he ministered to her.

I am skillful, a perfect tool, expert at what I do.

He was only sorry that Kylene had kept him for her own pleasure. He wished that others could have used him in his youth and strength.

She snorted, then got to her feet and went to the river. He heard her splashing in the water.

Finally she returned. "You're hungry?" She stood behind him, so he could not see her.

He was. He was always hungry, he thought, but it had become part of existence. "I'll eat when you feed me, dear."

He wriggled his tongue, thinking more of how he would please her today than of food, and writhed so she would see his body was waiting.

He was hungry. Very hungry. He forced the knowledge away.

"No more of that. I'm out of food." Her voice was cold.

"I'll make you happy, and then . . ." He wasn't listening. He was already anticipating her actions as she moved above his eager mouth.

"I'm going. I'm not coming back."

Not today? He started to feel disappointment.

"I'm going away for good. I'm leaving you. Like you left my sister."

He tried to understand her. Her sister? Her sister.

It was an old memory, too tenuous to have meaning. He wondered why Kylene brought it up.

"It's another pleasure you're giving me." She came near and stared down at him, her head inverted. "Good-bye, Fesch. I suppose I should tell you I'm sorry, but I'm not. I wish you'd lasted longer."

He blinked his single eye, not believing she meant her words. *Another of her games,* he told himself. She would be back. She had to come back.

"Leave me some food." He pretended to play her game.

"No food." She balanced above him on one foot and stretched the other in an arc so her toes patted softly at his genitals. He salivated, looking at her crotch, and waited for her to squat over him again.

"That's all that's left." Her voice was distant. "I told you I wouldn't ever take them away from you."

His mouth was dry. His body was cold.

"You know what you ate."

He hadn't, he told himself. He hadn't. He hadn't.

He didn't.

Suspicion didn't count.

"You could have asked. I would have told you."

No more food, and Kylene was leaving. He was too scared to think about anything else she had said.

He would be all alone. Unneeded. Alone.

"Don't leave me, please." He shivered and felt himself quivering on the ground. Tears streamed from his one eye. "Please!" he begged. "Don't leave me. It doesn't matter about the food, Kylene! It's all right about the food! I don't mind it, really. I don't even have to eat anymore, you know that. But don't leave me. Please don't go!"

"Be a man!" she snarled, and the tone of her voice startled him. He stopped crying, stopped writhing among the leaves and dirt.

Be a man. Was he a man anymore? He was lonely. He was—he was—

"I'm hungry, Kylene," he said simply. He swallowed, afraid of her response, knowing what he had to ask to keep her with him, knowing she was waiting for his words. "Please, if you have to leave, don't leave me hungry."

"Say it." Her voice was expressionless.

He swallowed. "Stay with me, Kylene. Please. Cut off my balls, my prick, anything else you ask. *But don't leave me!*"

"Try asking my sister." Kylene's words were faint. Her footsteps were already distant.

CHAPTER TWENTY-ONE

The night before, Rallt had seen a house taken away from the Algherans by Lopritian attack. Men with muskets in the front of the building had monopolized the attention of the defenders while an assault party formed at the rear. A pair of artillery rounds through the windows had left the Algherans inside in disarray, and the Lopritians had stormed the building. Rallt's contribution, frightening enough at the time as he lay on the ground, had been to shoot into the house several times, then fire at a fleeing Algheran.

It had been brutal and quick and deadly effective.

It had not prepared him for Algheran tactics.

He had thought he would see Algheran artillery. He did not, though he heard it; Mlart was using his guns on other targets today. A runner had been sent to the Lopritian guns up the street, he had been told, but they had been silent so far also.

As time went on, it seemed to him nothing would happen without the guns and that the guns were waiting for a signal which would never come. Railstenn's fright seemed less and less sensible.

Of course, Algherans had massed across the street. First had

come the group Rallt had seen from inside the doomed house—
a platoon, he had been told, as if that should define it for him,
though to Rallt a platoon was simply a formation smaller in
some fashion than the regiments and divisions of which Grahan
spoke so confidently. Then another platoon, also across the
street, also diminished by its preliminary dropping of green
bodies onto reddish dirt and dingy snow. It waited behind yet
another house; from time to time Rallt got sight of a head or
arm and wondered if he should shoot at it, but between the
thought and aiming the target always moved away.

He did not shoot. The sergeant here lingered in the main
room instead of wandering through the house. Rallt was always
close to him and had learned he was quick to reprove unnecessary shooting.

"Make 'em count," he muttered as he strolled through the
room and leaned over the men at the windows. "Make 'em
count, or don't make 'em at all." Now and then he put his hands
on a man's shoulder and moved him to a position that pleased
him more or adjusted a leg.

Rallt, watching from the corner of his eye, tried to copy the
other hunched-over soldiers. It was an awkward way to sit, he
found. Uncomfortable.

There was no comfortable way to hold and aim a musket.

The sergeant was Ian Gunnally, and Rallt was reluctant to
draw his attention, expecting the sergeant to remember he had
been picked up as a deserter, but the sergeant had only nodded
once at him in recognition and accepted his presence after that.

In a moment of introspection, Rallt reflected that armies were
run by officers who dominated sergeants who dominated lower-
ranking soldiers and that no alternatives were possible in Grahan's accounts, but that he had seen very little of that structure.
Officers were scarce beings—roosters among hens was the analogy that came to him—and it seemed ordinary soldiers were left
to fend for themselves more often than Grahan had imagined.
And so they had freedom despite the condition of their lives
because no one above them could imagine them capable of making their own decisions.

There were non-soldiers in the house as well. Old men and
women of varying ages, mostly shabbily dressed and worn-
looking. Residents of the town, he had thought at first, until he
had seen them ordered about by the soldiers, or—more remark-

ably—doing things in anticipation of the soldiers' orders. Fixing food in the kitchen, moving furniture, drying soldiers' clothes over the stove in the wall between the kitchen and the main room—the sort of unending chores Grahan and the others had expected of him. He wondered if the civilians felt the same indignation and why, since they were adults, they put up with it.

They did not keep the house clean. It was as cold and dusty as the place where he had awakened.

At the back of the room, a soldier with a knife stabbed it over and over again into a chair. Sand and cotton trickled from the slashes. The knife thunked hollowly against wood. Rallt stared and wondered why he did it and why no one but he noticed.

Then he heard the sound of musket fire increase and turned his attention back to his window. The Algherans were shooting steadily now at the next house. They were in the buildings across the street now. He could not see the soldiers but flickers of light danced behind the open windows as they fired. And they were beside the buildings, nerving themselves for the rush.

Herrilmin ha'Hujsuon's time machine was in a grove far enough from the great road that travelers would not see it. He reached the spot shortly after noon and approached only when he was sure he was alone.

Finding the machine was embarrassingly easy—though it was invisible except at close distances like Timt ha'Dicovys's machine, it rested at the center of a circle of dead grass which would have attracted the attention of any but the most stupid passersby. He could not understand what had caused that and he cursed volubly.

Inside the circle and inside the machine, however, everything seemed all right. The freight he had brought from six hundred years in the future was still in place beside the cargo hatch, and the seals on the lead-shrouded crates had not been tampered with. The air was still fresh. He sighed with relief and climbed a short ladder that brought him to the upper compartment, then sat at the pilot's seat to check his controls.

His time machine was compact. For a man as tall as Herrilmin, it was cramped—a bubble two man-heights in diameter sectioned to provide a hemisphere of storage space and a half hemisphere for motors and batteries. The portion left for him held a pilot's seat, a vision screen, a control console, a small table, and a couch not quite long enough for comfortable sleeping. He had truthfully told Lerlt he did not have room for two passengers.

Battery readings were his primary concern. Separate banks of batteries powered both the levcraft motor and the equipment that carried the machine through time; both had been used heavily since their last recharge. He had left the time-changing project clandestinely, without the maintenance his machine required, but gauges told him he had more than enough power left to collect Gherst and to return the three thousand years to the Station.

He shook his head with approval and started his motors, then lifted up.

Men were running suddenly, a crowd of them from across the street, dark-faced with effort, without order, bent over in their haste, and Rallt wondered if they could see the destination they hurried toward. He shot and a man stumbled at the side of the crowd and fell forward, trying to break his fall with hands encumbered by his musket.

Other men were shooting. Muskets rattled from across the road, and more loudly, with harsher barks, from around him in this room, and with coughing sounds from upstairs and the house that was being attacked.

Shrapnel exploded in the air over the running men, one burst, then another. Algherans fell, but he could not tell if it was from that or from musket fire. It did not stop them, and after the second burst, no more shells were fired.

Powder smoke was filling the upper part of the room. It was not dark but it stung his eyes and he crouched to avoid it as he reloaded.

He could see into the house being attacked. Not well, or far, but a shell hole had torn open a view of a yellow-painted interior wall. Earlier, he had seen a head moving past the hole. A man's head, dark hair long and tangled, carried past quickly over a torso Rallt had not paid attention to, leaving the suggestion of a beaklike nose which might only have been Rallt's imagination. He had not recognized the man and he had not been seen; he had turned his eyes away, feeling guilty and strangely embarrassed by the sight. Now, as he reloaded, he looked again toward the shell hole and wondered if he would see the same man or any other soldier inside the building.

He fired his musket a second time, and this time he thought he missed. The Algherans were thick around the damaged house, including the sides he did not see. They clamored and waved their arms with excitement, and Rallt wondered if they were so eager to enter as they appeared, though he was sure some had.

When he reloaded again, he noticed that the volume of firing had gone down. The Algherans across the street were shooting at the upper stories of the building they were attacking—at windows where he knew no soldier stood because none remained—and the defenders were not shooting at their attackers outside the building as often.

Waiting for the Algherans, he thought, dry-mouthed, and imagined himself with one bullet left in his musket, inside the house, knowing he was outnumbered and would have no time to reload when that bullet was fired.

He noticed suddenly that the civilians had vanished and that the soldier hacking at the furniture had gone away as well. Bullets were striking the walls on this building—he remembered now that one had struck a window and splayed glass through the room—a splinter had cut a shallow line across the back of his index finger.

They'll attack this house next.

It was true, but after his flash of imagination, not important. He aimed and shot at an Algheran waiting behind the house and sensed as the soldier fell that everything which happened to him was proper and inevitable.

Kylene missed Herrilmin at first. Tim Harper had commented that it was possible to track an individual with a time machine without being seen; he had not stressed the difficulties and most of the instruction he had given her had been simply aimed at flying his giant levcraft.

Pursuing a walking man was not an easy task. Tim's levcraft had been designed for speed. It might be capable, as he had claimed, of traveling eight times around the world in one day's time, but air and the machine's own velocity helped keep it aloft. Drifting, its batteries were drained; the elaborate machinery Tim had installed to recharge them did not work.

Similarly, the machine was intended to travel through time

rapidly. "A million times faster than time," Tim would say
enthusiastically one moment, then complain in the next that was
"too slow." A day traversed in less time than it took to blink
an eye, a man's life from birth to death passed over in less than
one watch—at that pace, Herrilmin's long journey to the south
was over in a single heartbeat; he could not be seen.

People were too slow and they moved with blinding speed.

She had wondered why Tim would not use his time machine
to assassinate Mlart tra'Nornst and he had answered her with
metaphysics. She learned now there were simpler reasons.

There were adjustments that could be made. Tim had mentioned them, but she had not sought the details. Fesch
ha'Hujsuon, characteristically, had known none of them. She
taught herself by trial and error. She reasoned out techniques
that let her achieve her goals.

"Herrilmin is by *that* tree," she would tell herself. "He will
be near *that* ridge in one day tenth." Then she would move to
the ridge and a day tenth later and Herrilmin would be there, or
he would not be there and she would go back to her starting
point and try a shorter interval. It was tedious but it sufficed.

Tim Harper must have used the same methods long ago when
he traced her path to Kh'taal Minzaer, she realized. It gave her
an odd sense of companionship, as if she were sharing his pursuit of the naive barbarian child that only with effort could she
remember being.

Long ago. It came as a shock to realize how much had happened since then. Three years had gone by in her memory. Tim,
with his duties for the Algherans and his other absences on this
mission, had aged more than a decade.

She had never noticed. He had been little older than a boy,
she realized suddenly. The huge implacable bear-man monster
she remembered had been only a young man, uncertain of himself, but politely and resolutely determined to do what conscience and honor compelled.

As vividly as if he sat beside her now, she saw in his mind
the hunter's passion and skills he had used to follow her across
half a continent. And for the first time she was able to understand the sense of obligation and compassion that had dictated
his actions. *She* would not have spared the life of Kylene Waterfall.

All along, she admitted to herself, she had thought he had

forced her into captivity to serve a kidnapper's lust and she had been wrong. He had not committed the sin for which she had pardoned him.

Long ago. She wished she could beg his forgiveness, but the same exalted awareness which made him seem present beside her made her perceive that it was not necessary.

He had sensed her feelings. He had accepted them. It was a greater gift than forgiveness, greater even than a Teep's understanding.

All along, he had loved her and the knowledge supported her during the tedious days of tracing Herrilmin to his time machine.

"Well, don't expect me to do your thinking for you," Ian Haarper had said. "*Gawdawmighty*, Pitar, I've got enough to do doing ris Daimgewln's thinking and holding the Hand's hand, I'm not going to do more than tell you what I want and that's to hold the street if you can and I don't give a flying fuck if you put one soldier into each house or the whole company into one house, but try and hold the street. Make Mlart pay for what he takes, that's the main thing, so if you do lose the street and it costs him enough, it's not the end of the world, but I would like to keep the street, too. Or win it back. Is that clear?"

Pitar heard tiredness in the deep voice. Tiredness and the querulous tone of an old man befuddled by new experiences.

It dawned on him, at last, the truth Dalsyn Ian Plenytk had told him, that Ian Haarper had no secret plans for winning the battle, had no more experience of fighting in towns than the lowest men in the ranks, and had elected to fight Mlart tra'Nornst in this way only because he was sure Mlart was as ignorant as he.

Dalsyn's jealousy, he had told himself at first, hearing the unkind remarks from the other man as they walked back to the regiment after the conference in the inn that first night. And later, Dalsyn's annoyance, as he sought for kinder words to categorize what was really only a tone of voice, then Dalsyn's jealousy again, when he admitted it was natural for an older man with accomplishments like Ian Plenytk to resent someone untried like Ian Haarper who had mounted to prominence by what appeared flukes.

With Ian Plenytk captured and himself in Ian Plenytk's place, it must be inevitable that he should think Ian Plenytk's thoughts.

But without Ian Plenytk's customary cynicism, he hoped.

"We will lose a fight on the plains," the big Ironwearer had told him, walking beside Pitar in the falling snow on the night of the retreat to West Bend, in his only comments about his strategy that Pitar could recall. "We have to fight in other conditions to have a chance to win."

Like in snow, he had suggested, and Ian Haarper had snorted and said, "Under water, too, if I could figure out a way."

Everything that had happened since had shown Ian Haarper looking for those "other conditions." Pitar had no blame for him and no unkind remarks.

Dalsyn had gotten himself captured. He supposed that was the North Valley man's final comment on the issue.

It would be different, Pitar thought, if he had cared for Midpassage as strongly as Ian Plenytk cared about this town. But he did not. He cared for his family strongly, though some days it seemed as if he did so not because of his own inclination, but because it was simply part of the definition of Pitar Ian Styllin, which he could not prove wrong because being true to the definition of himself was part of that definition. And he cared for the men under his command, not as strongly as his family, of course, but more truthfully because that was emotion called out by more than habit. And he cared about—

He cared about Pitar Styllin, now Pitar Ian Styllin.

Nothing else, he had learned. Not his past job, not his employer Merryn ris Vandeign, not the town of Midpassage, not the people within it.

Shot away, he told himself, feeling as if sentiment and affection had all along been only some strange but nonvital appendage of himself which had been struck off his body in some mishap of battle, leaving behind only the selfish core of Pitar Ian Styllin, and the memory of emotions he had once known which could still affect him but really meant no more than the itching other severely wounded men experienced from the ends of their amputated limbs.

He was severely wounded, he was sure, though his wounds did not show to the world, and he could not remember the point at which he recognized the wound. But it was there. His soul felt the injury.

Like Timmial Ian Haarper, he thought, or dead Ironwearer ris Clendannan. There was something about them which made him recognize the same affliction—half despair, half duty—had struck all of them.

Hold the street.

He had two guns and two hundred men, and the task did not seem possible.

He stared down the street. A pink house . . . A yellow house . . . A bend in the road and part of a gray house . . . If the Algherans could be held beyond the bend . . .

He sensed the gunners watching him, waiting for orders.

He held up a hand to attract a runner. "Take a message up for me, to Sergeant Lehmell or Ian Gunnally."

Then enemy soldiers *swirled* and ran about the house and into it, disappearing, it seemed to Rallt, disappearing like soap scum on water pouring through a drain, and when he had created that image to his own satisfaction and fired his musket once more, the good targets were all gone and dying men were stretched out before him.

The Algherans were inside the building they had attacked.

The firing died down, from the Algheran side of the street because Algherans were in the building at last, and from the Lopritians around him because no one saw a target worth shooting at. Rallt wondered if the cannon would fire again.

Muskets sounded in the captured building. He heard screams—they would be shouts, if he had to recount this moment, but to his ears and knowledge they were screams. More musket firing.

"We have to get out." It was Ian Gunnally's voice. The sergeant's. Low and hoarse. Rallt stared at the bodies on the ground and tried to understand why the Algherans had not used artillery as Lopritians did.

"We've got orders! Let's go!" Lan Gunnally's voice again, with an intonation of begging. Rallt stared at him and saw that his eyes were tightly closed. He did not believe Ian Gunnally and he could see that no one else did.

Someone groaned from a corner. The man who had stabbed the furniture. Blood soaked the side of his shirt and another soldier was leaning over him.

"We're moving to the next house," Ian Gunnally said, his voice calmer. "Railstenn, Valthiel, you help Lorrens."

Lorrens was the wounded man, Rallt sensed. Railstenn was

the man leaning over him. And Ian Gunnally would lead them
from this building.

Away from the Algherans. He felt relief.

There was barely time, it seemed, but the Algherans gave
them time.

Rallt had thought the soldiers would run, one by one, from
this house to the next, but Ian Gunnally simply went out of the
room into the kitchen and out the kitchen door. After a moment,
a man followed him. Then Rallt. Then another man, and another.

The sun had moved past the clouds and it was very bright
outside. The snow on the hillsides gleamed.

"There." Lan Gunnally stood at the base of the porch step
and pointed not to the next house, but the one beyond. Rallt
noticed other Lopritian soldiers in the distance, moving toward
the same building. He sensed Railstenn behind him, at the top
of the step, with his arm around the wounded man.

Lorrens, he remembered. The wounded man was standing
on one foot.

We do things together. He waited for the other soldiers to
move past and stepped backward. The wounded man stared at
him dully, and Rallt slipped under his arm to assist Railstenn.

The wounded man said something he didn't hear at the foot
of the step. He was heavy, and Rallt did not reply to save his
breath. Lorrens's body smelled and there was something hard
and angular which made holding him up painful. Rallt finally
noticed the man's musket was slung over his shoulder; its sights
had dug into the fleshly part of his forearm.

That was less important than a real wound and he was sure
the Algherans were close behind. He stumbled along with Railstenn, supporting the man, making the best time he could.

A cannon boomed, bringing his head up, and at the foot of
the hill he made out figures standing on the edge of the great
road. They were looking up toward him and Railstenn and the
other soldiers. They seemed to be waiting. The civilians who
had been in the house, he thought.

Waiting to see what happens to us. Curious. Spectators.

Curious. Uninvolved, standing in safety to watch soldiers dying. He felt anger, and at the same time he wished it were

possible to drop his musket and the man he carried and run down the hillside to join with them.

He should be with them, he knew. If his father returned this minute, it would be with the spectators that he would expect to find him.

But he could not watch the soldiers with them.

Thee's to die. He remembered saying that to a soldier, the officer he and his father had carried into the inn a few days before. He had spoken coldly, he remembered now, unemotionally, half wondering how the maimed man would react and half knowing it did not matter what was said to one so close to death.

Thee's to die. He would never say that again, he vowed, never use that tone of voice to a soldier or any other person.

Herrilmin's first intimation of trouble came immediately. Something went *zinggg!* in the compartment behind him, and there were other noises. He dropped back to the ground immediately and moved into normal time, then went to investigate.

He found cause to curse again. A hole had been chopped through the outside wall of his levcraft, and the projectile which had done it had also knocked through a battery and smashed against an inside partition. The partition had held but it had a dent big enough to rest a fist in. The battery, which was heavy, had been pushed out of the rack which held it, and had fallen onto the floor. Dark fluid had poured out of the torn casing onto the floor; not much was left but a trickle when Herrilmin picked it up and when he held it before his eyes he saw that the row of thin metal plates inside the battery had become twisted and warped.

The battery was useless now. Somberly, he put it aside and reset connections to complete circuits without it, and looked for a rag to mop up the spilled acid.

It was while he was cleaning up that he found what had done the damage: a lump of metal with the conical shape of a musket bullet, but as long as his thumb and much wider. Solid metal, he was willing to bet—the bullet weighed almost as much as the empty battery casing, and it was still hot to the touch, so he had to juggle it from hand to hand before he could transfer it to a table and get a clear look at it.

Metal. Hard and gleaming. It was not informative, but— Metal. Machined metal, and thus doubly expensive. There were lines etched along it to record its violent passage but they were only lines, not deeply scored.

Almost a cannonball's weight of metal, but more finely made. It seemed almost magical, until he remembered the shell had been fired at him and had damaged his vehicle. He was suddenly very serious.

Herrilmin was here, *now*, and there, then, and in between, he must be in between. So Kylene reasoned and she stationed herself between here and there at halfway between *now* and *then* and turned the big time machine slowly while she sprayed the countryside from beyond *here* to past *there* with forty-millimeter-diameter shells.

She sat in Harper's seat. The controls for flying were the same in the consoles before her seat and his, but the cannon mount and triggers could be directed only from his panels. She felt awkward, more because it was Tim's seat than because of what she was doing.

Of course she did not know what she was doing. "Guns" was all Harper had ever said to her. "Antiaircraft guns, but they ought to make powdered eggs out of anything softer than a Sherman tank." Only the word "guns" had stuck in her memory and she was sure that was all he had intended—Harper conveyed praise with the sound of his voice rather than sensible words.

"Guns" meant muskets in Kylene's mind, or maybe the silent stunning hand weapons the Algherans called neuroshockers. She was unprepared for the whine of gear-driven turrets and the ratchety fence-strumming rattle that penetrated the cabin when she pulled the trigger. It felt to her at first as if Tim's time machine had been struck by bullets, but no warning lights came on and she was still in the air. She persevered, but her aiming was off. She fired high.

Still, the gentlemen from the very discreet and cash-minded Swedish firm which had done a little export business with Tim Harper in the distant First Era year of 1976 had been justly proud of their product's reputation. After more than nine hundred centuries without even a test firing, their slaved pairs of twin-mounted cannons had functioned flawlessly.

But it did not seem that way to Kylene.

Blood should be on the grass. She was *owed*.

* * *

All the men in one house, or one man in each house, Ian Haarper had said to Pitar Ian Styllin, and neither idea, as he had known, would work. Putting ten men in each house as a compromise had not worked, either, because the Algherans had not attacked in equal numbers.

Very well, Pitar thought coolly. He would try something else. He called his runners and gave the orders.

CHAPTER TWENTY-TWO

The house was crowded with soldiers, and Rallt found himself wondering what the watchers at the foot of the hill had thought as they saw men gathering in it. Upstairs and downstairs, and he wondered if the entire Midpassage regiment had been brought here.

"Over there," Ian Gunnally said, seeing them from across the room despite the men in between. The sergeant pointed with his head, and Rallt and Railstenn interpreted that as meaning Lorrens should be left in a corner.

The wounded man was either not conscious or too weak to seem conscious. He did not speak when they laid him down, though Rallt was sure it must hurt him to be moved and saw sweat on his forehead. The blood on his shirt had stopped spreading. He was still breathing. Rallt hoped that was a good sign.

There was really nothing useful to be done for Lorrens, he realized, but he tried to make the man's extended legs parallel to the wall. Maybe he would not be stepped on by other soldiers.

Railstenn checked that his musket was loaded and tried to put the wounded man's hands on it, but they slipped off, so he left it beside him in the corner. He shook his head, looking down, and beckoned to Rallt, then led him to the stairs.

"Up," he said curtly, but like Rallt, he needed to catch his breath before he could challenge the steps.

Standing close to his partner, Rallt could see heavy muscles under his uniform shirt and he guessed that in bygone times Railstenn had worked at hard labor all day long without rest, as he had in the fields, with a steady economy of movement. It was another way war tore men apart, he sensed, a way of hollowing them out while leaving them intact only in appearance.

He listened to the soldiers settling into the house and realized that to them, when they noticed him, he was a soldier also.

"Up," Railstenn said, clinging to the banister and nodding at him. "Top floor. We'll have the best chance there."

Herrilmin backslipped in time. He did not see an opponent, but that was no surprise. He did not need to. He knew his enemy.

Timt ha'Dicovys was not stupid but he would not be subtle and he was a gambler. From his duel with him in the Station, Herrilmin remembered the Ironwearer as a brutal opponent, who relied on his great strength.

Greater strength than Herrilmin's. It was an unusual admission.

For himself, he had superior cunning. Herrilmin cataloged the rest of his assets. Strength of his own—moral strength, primarily, but physical strength for any man-to-man combat. More intelligence. Resolution—willpower was another name for that— proven in countless duels in the City fighting arenas. Self-confidence. And ruthlessness, also proven in combat.

Timt ha'Dicovys had no stomach for killing disabled men. He had shown that when he fought Herrilmin as convincingly as the native-born Algheran had ever shown the opposite, and Herrilmin had heard the same remark from men who had served with him in the field.

Herrilmin owed his own life to that weakness; it was a piece of irony he enjoyed. An enemy's flaws were Cimon's gift to the strong.

But he lacked weapons. Useful weapons. He had nothing like the shells Timt ha'Dicovys had fired at him. He had no guns of any sort but a primitive musket and a neuroshocker under his seat. They were short-range weapons, valueless against a hidden opponent.

Batteries. A levcraft. A flying vehicle . . . But Timt ha'Dicovys had that as well. A larger vehicle, in fact, with capabilities Herrilmin could not guess. He could not find a point of attack there.

Time travel. Timt ha'Dicovys's time machine had been vacant when he first saw it, he was sure. That had been the time when the man was unprotected. To exploit that vulnerability, he had to return to Midpassage.

It was as simple as that.

An opponent's feint had touched him, but not caused serious hurt. The real fight had not yet begun.

The tra'Crovsol's plan to circumvent the Lopritians worked without flaw as long as there were no Lopritians to circumvent. Perrid ris Salynnt had too few troops to place men in each building in his sector; after consultation with Ian Haarper, he pulled his Guards Regiment back to the uppermost and northernmost roads on the hill and stationed his soldiers in those houses. To reach him, the Algherans had to cross the open streets, and guns had been arranged at the ends of the streets and the intersections to prevent that.

Released in the morning to "flood" the town, the Crovsol Division did just that, until it dissipated its force in spreading.

The primary trouble came from the unSepted troops, which lacked discipline. All too often, units which reached houses with well-stocked pantries took root; they prepared "proper" meals for the first time in twenty days and refused to move on until their orgiastic repasts were completed. They had been told to search the houses and avoid serious combat with the defenders; the tra'Crovsol's complaints about lack of progress were met with bland declarations that they thought they were following orders.

Some such difficulties the tra'Crovsol had anticipated, but he had trusted their officers to keep command of the ordinary soldiers. He had overlooked that most of the unSepted battalions and smaller formations were led by Blankshields. As mercenaries, forecasting long unemployment after this war ended, the Blankshields were as eager to loot as the ordinary soldiers were to eat. The gargantuan meals gave them opportunity to search in private for the householders' hidden valuables. On the whole, as Midpassage's residents of longer duration would have predicted, their effort was wasted.

It was the tra'Crovsol's regiment of Housetroops which first met the Lopritian line, at the western end of town, shortly after midday, and they were too few to cross the guarded streets—and even fewer after half a dozen canisters of shrapnel pushed them reeling down the hillside back into their corner of the town, with forty men left dead and dying in snow-covered dirt. Not long after that, they hit the southern flank of ris Salynnt's bent line, with similar results. They took root themselves, in houses facing the road, and called for help.

In a sense, the tra'Crovsol was facing an already-solved problem. The Mongols, of Tim Harper's distant First Era world, had broken through fortified lines by mixing their troops with prisoners and captive women and children. Defenders are usually reluctant to fire on their own families, Harper could have explained; their living shields brought the Mongols unscathed into close-combat range and against sickened opponents that was more than enough advantage. Part of Harper's thinking when he ordered the town's noncombatants into refuge beyond the hills had been his fear that the Algherans would find a way to use such hostages against him.

But the tra'Crovsol was not a Mongol. Though he pleased himself now with recollections from his barbarian youth, that time was three centuries past, and he remembered what had pleased him then—flamboyant boasts, duels, and combats between champions—not the battle tactics forced on desperate men by poverty and scarcity of numbers.

Truthfully, the barbarian conquest of the tiny settlement that grew to be F'a Alghera had not been that violent. The original residents had been farmers and more than reconciled to paying tribute in grain to the nomads who occasionally invaded their land. There had been no great resistance until the nomads chose to settle and become year-round overlords, and much of the fighting fondly described as "the conquest" had been feuds over the spoils among rival groups of nomads.

The tribes which became the Septs of Alghera had understood implicitly some economic maxims; a warrior of another Sept was always a better choice for murder than a productive and tribute-paying peasant. Peasants flourished under this dispensation; which is to say, they survived. The novel circumstances

attracted migrants, until barely one Algheran in three belonged
to a Sept. Seeing great numbers of commoners about them in
the present day, Algheran aristocrats born after the conquest
presumed similar numbers had existed in the past and praised
the martial talents of their ancestors. A taste for slaughter was
evidence of good breeding in their estimation—the passage of
centuries and the growth of organized government did not change
vocabularies particularly, but commercial rivalries between the
Septs had become more common than actual bloodshed.

Furthermore, the tra'Crovsol was not a product of a fecund
human society. He lived in a world of barely twenty million
people, in which centuries could pass between a woman's first
and second—and probably, last—pregnancy. He was emotionally incapable of conceiving a Mongolian-style attack, and even
more incapable of ordering one.

He fell back on his original plan, therefore. He sent troops
around the hill, through the woods, to find other undefended
entryways into the town. He sent orders to his stationary units
to consolidate near the roads, and then he waited on events.

And he sent a message to Mlart tra'Nornst, to say that he had
captured a full third of Midpassage by the end of the second
watch, and that combat with the enemy was "continuing." To
him, it was an accurate account.

"The whole regiment," Railstenn repeated, and Rallt thought
from his voice he might have stared at the boy if he were not
preoccupied. "No. We were only a battalion."

The soldier peered out the attic window. He was on one side
of it, already in his sitting position with his musket in his lap
because the attic was shallow and even along the center ridge
there was not height enough for the shorter Rallt to stand erect.

Rallt was on the other side, also on his seat. When he touched
the floorboards, grit adhered to his fingers. There were cobwebs
between the boxes in storage here. The window was gray-tinted
with age and dust and only as wide as his arm was long. It let
in very little light, and he wondered if he and Railstenn would
both be able to use it at the same time.

There were no other men in the attic and no other windows.
The corners were all dark, but at its center light shone through
the entrance from the empty room beneath. The top of a ladder

protruded from it. Rallt tried to remember if he had heard soldiers entering the room.

"Here. Use these." He pushed something like a leather sack across the floor to Rallt. It was a cartridge pouch, Rallt found when he picked it up, like the one on Railstenn's belt. It was heavy; when he opened it he saw it was filled with neatly stacked rolls of brown cartridges.

Lorrens's, he guessed. The wounded man must have fired a few shots at the enemy which had almost killed him.

A musket went off downstairs. He heard Ian Gunnally's voice in response, but not the words. It seemed annoyed.

"Put it between us," Railstenn said. "We can both use it." And then, as if no subject had intervened, added, "There's about a platoon here, maybe it's called a company these days. I guess there's a platoon in the house across the street and the house behind us, too." He paused, and they could hear muskets in the background. "Sounds like ris Daimgewln's regiment."

Rallt had not been able to place the direction of the firing. A cannon shot made the window rattle. He waited for the impact, then touched the window to silence it. He stared past the dirty glass but the house where Wandisha and Grahan waited for him was upslope and trees were in the way. He could not see it, though he looked in its direction until he was sure Railstenn would notice his preoccupation.

More cannons sounded, at intervals. He thought he saw smoke rising and guessed their location.

Cannon side by side. He had seen cannon side by side the day ris Clendannan died. Was that only two days ago?

"Stand aside." Railstenn smashed out the window with his musket butt.

Rallt blinked. The gloomy attic became no brighter but a welcome current of air moved into the attic. The musket fire could be heard more clearly from before him, and almost like an echo, from somewhere in the rear.

"The Guards," Rallt commented, unnecessarily. "That's a good outfit."

Rallt shook his head politely, remembering that Railstenn and the other Midpassage men thought he came from the Defiance-to-Insurrection Regiment. He wished he knew enough about ris Daimgewln's force to defend it, but he could not recall anything favorable. He could not even remember ris Daimgewln's face,

though he was sure the man must have attended some of the
meetings he had observed.

"Coming up." Railstenn duckwalked closer to the window
and brushed fragments of glass into crevices with movements
of his boot. His musket slapped into place. Rallt saw him scowl
as he aimed and fired.

Mlart was pleased with the tra'Crovsol's progress, not so de-
lighted by his own progress. He had gained very little ground
in the day's fighting—Lopritian ground at that, and thus worthless to anyone but Lopritians. His men had captured the houses
next to the main road up the hill, and the houses next behind
those, but otherwise he was in almost the same position he had
reached four watches before, when he made his entry into the
town.

The ground taken today had cost him four hundred men. In
twenty days, the Cuhyon Division had been worn down from
six thousand healthy soldiers to twenty-three hundred almost
starving wretches, and victories had accounted for all those
losses.

"Victories." He almost snorted when he heard the word.
There should be a better name for such "victories."

The tra'Crovsol claimed that nearly three quarters of his original force was still fighting. It seemed unlikely, but an aide sent
to the hospital tents had reported that the count might be accurate. Most of the men taken to the surgeons in the last four days
had been from Sept Cuhyon.

That would have consequences after the war, he recognized.
Cuhyon had provided a full division of prime Housetroops, and
as Master of a Sept himself, he knew the cost of that. The casualties could be replaced in peacetime *and he was sure they
would be*—soldiering was a traditional route into a Sept for commoners without dowry money—but it would take time to make
recruits into genuine Housetroops, and political power rested
on calculations of real military might.

This war might destroy Cuhyon's importance in the Realm.
He was sure it would enhance Dicovys's strength. It was laughable
for an entire division to surrender to one under-strength Lopritian brigade. Dicovys would have to face that embarrassment
for centuries. But most of its soldiers would survive the war,
perhaps more than in any other Swordtroop division. Raw feet

did not kill. The men he had captured back from ris Clendannan were only fit for garrison duty now, but they would recover and fight again for Dicovys.

My supporters. Mlart did not trust Dicovys.

He did not trust Ruijac, either, and he needed them both to command the Muster. Nornst was too small to be significant. It was what made him acceptable to the larger Septs as Warder of the Realm, and he had not found a way to break the power of the large Septs.

Not all of them, anyhow. Ruijac and Dicovys had cooperated with him to reduce Minursil, and that was a start, but it had been done with their own gain in mind. Someday he would have to play Ruijac and Dicovys against each other to keep their strength in bounds—he had waking nightmares about that, foreseeing futures in which one giant Sept survived to dominate the Realm as irrevocably as a royal dynasty in Loprit.

Even more irrevocably. Loprit had had a coup less than half a century ago and replaced its rulers with very little violence. He feared Alghera would not be so lucky.

The Realm needed weaker Septs to preserve its own strength and the independence of the Septs which were already small, he had decided long ago. It could be done by granting the unSepted representatives in the Muster—in carefully chosen company, Mlart argued that the UnSepted *deserved* representation, regardless of what it might do to the power of the Septs—and more Septs should be formed to preserve the balance of numbers between commoners and aristocrats.

But every effort he made to push the Realm in that direction failed.

Cuhyon was a strong, second-tier Sept, and now its military force was being impaled on this stick of a Lopritian town. Cuhyon had been one of the Septs which sought war and bore responsibility for this gut spilling. Those were new factors in Mlart's long conflict with the Septs; he would have to find a use for them.

"Keep the attacks going," he told his subordinates when they appeared to plead for assistance. "I can't give you reinforcements but the Lopritians hurt more than we do, and I have every confidence in the Cuhyon Division. Do you want me to keep it from the victory it deserves?"

* * *

Where had Herrilmin gone to? Kylene asked herself. The illegitimate spawn of a consanguineous cross-clan mating—it was a short word in her native language, reminiscent in sound of an improper body function, and she used it several times, with complete satisfaction, but it did not find Herrilmin for her.

She did not think he was dead. He had all of time to hide in, and all of space. She had made a mistake, she realized. She should have killed Herrilmin cleanly before he reached his time machine. It was too late now. The world was a complicated place which punished meddlers—her own experiences demonstrated that.

She had wanted to destroy Herrilmin's time machine.

No. That was a lie. She had wanted to kill Herrilmin and for Herrilmin to know he was being killed, and that had let the Algheran escape.

For the moment. She knew Herrilmin's destinations, she reminded herself. Midpassage and the Project Station. Whichever he went to first, he would return to Midpassage. Men from his Sept were there, and Fesch's memories had shown how intense the bonds between clanmates were. Fesch and Lerlt and Gherst— he had to go back to rescue them, just as she had always had to return to Tim Harper. Herrilmin could not escape her indefinitely.

Herrilmin had a flying vehicle. If he returned to Midpassage, it would be in the air, and Tim had outfitted his vehicle with instruments that detected flying vehicles. Her understanding of their principles was small—Tim, ironically, usually so eager to show off marvels from his First Era world, had mentioned *radar* only in passing, because he had expected her to see no flying machines except those which were flown by his fellow Agents— but it did not take great knowledge to switch the machinery on, nor to realize that the blips which showed on the glass plate had some relationship to a target's distance and bearing.

She practiced on *Scent O'Claws* itself, tracing her passage from point to point above the barren landscape, until she was satisfied with her new skill, and then turned back to Midpassage.

The first attack on the house was beaten off, then the second. After that, Rallt lost track.

The ground outside was covered with bodies. The snow was

pitted with hand-size craters where blood had pooled, and still the Algherans came on.

In the attic the smell of smoke could not be escaped, no matter how hard he tried to fan it away. Railstenn seemed unaffected.

It smelled nothing like burning grass, no matter how often Rallt told himself to pretend. Eventually his nose noticed it no longer, but that was only a slight improvement.

The reason for peace is to avoid gunsmoke. He would tell Grahan that.

More smoke drifted up from downstairs. Rallt coughed till his throat was sore, then forced himself to keep his mouth shut, even when it was so thick he was sure the building was on fire and only the voices below kept him from thinking he and Railstenn had been left to burn to death.

Once the Algherans managed to break in. There was a mass charge and as he reloaded he could hear them enter. Windows smashed and objects landed on the floor and he heard shouts. The ground floor of the house rang with screams and gunshots and the sounds of smashing furniture, even as additional Algherans rushed from the next house to this one.

It seemed to last for full watches. When he heard men rushing down the stairs to join the fighting, he was about to join them when Railstenn grabbed his wrist to stop him and pointed at the Algheran bodies lying still outside.

There were enough defenders to expel the Algherans from the house already, the Midpassage man told him. If there were not, one more fighter would not help. He was in the attic to defend it from there.

"Besides, it's a brawl," the soldier added critically. "You're too puny. Or have you ever been in a fight where a tavern got smashed up?"

No, he signaled, which saved him from admitting that until leaving Innings, his father had never permitted him to enter a tavern at all.

"Then you ain't going to be good at it. Leave it to them fellows who like to make a nuisance of themselves when you're trying to have a quiet drink, Rallt. If you aren't like that in peacetime, you aren't going to be like that just because you're in a war."

Rallt did not accept that reasoning but the hand on his wrist prevailed. He had not wanted to struggle and lose to Railstenn's greater strength. And after a while, the commotion inside died down and he saw men rushing away. He shot at one, hitting him in the leg. When he had reloaded, he heard only Lopritian voices below and knew the Algherans had been beaten again.

But there were fewer footsteps of men coming up the steps, and none of them went up to the top story.

Then he noticed men in green uniforms lining up behind the corner of the next house for another charge, and the argument became pointless.

It stopped finally. The Algherans ran away—or limped away, or tried to crawl away and failed. Time passed in which they did not come back and Rallt had the leisure to realize he was hungry and thirsty.

He wanted a toilet also.

Railstenn, more practical than he, stood up as the Algherans made calls for retreat and moved to the back of the attic, where the floorboards ended. Rallt heard liquid splashing on a wall. A touch of the odor reached him, and he was grateful to be near an open window.

"You want to go?" Railstenn returned, still lacing his pants.

"No. I can hold." Not that it would be true much longer, he knew, but neither Grahan nor his father would have approved urinating in an improper place. When he broke the taboo, he wanted to justify it with necessity.

Railstenn murmured to himself and sank onto his haunches.

Lan Gunnally's voice could be heard distantly. Then the steps creaked, and they heard the sergeant's voice again. "Volunteers! For across the street! They're getting hit hard, too. Any volunteers?"

He waited to hear volunteers respond, but Railstenn grabbed his sleeve and pulled him close. "Stay shut!" the soldier hissed. "Don't make a sound. Don't move."

Lan Gunnally reached the fourth floor and called out his offer again, and Rallt held his breath as the sergeant walked through the rooms below.

Feet crossing wood flooring. Steps on carpet. Doors creaking. Glass splinters crushing under a man's weight. Eerily, hearing the sounds between distant cannon booms, he could picture lan Gunnally's progress through the house below him without seeing the man or being familiar with its rooms.

"Railstenn?" the ghostly voice called. "You here, Railstenn?"

Rallt felt Railstenn's fingers digging painfully into his arm. He kept quiet and the other man finally released him.

The footsteps went on. At last they entered the room below and Rallt knew the sergeant must see the ladder that led to the attic. He tried to decide what to say when lan Gunnally came up and saw him.

"Anyone left here?" the sergeant asked, and from some note in his voice, Rallt wanted to descend the ladder and reassure him, even if it meant he must volunteer for the danger the sergeant had in mind, but before he could react, the footsteps had gone away and soon he heard them going down the stairs.

Unattended.

"We could have answered. Lan Gunnally just wanted to know who were alive," he explained. His voice was strained, and he realized he had breathing to catch up on.

Was the light outside starting to fade?

"Maybe he had a quota," Railstenn hissed back, grumbling. "Besides, maybe I don't want him to know I'm alive, did you think of that? It isn't like the volunteers he picks always volunteer, you know."

Rallt blinked and thought again of Grahan and Wandisha. The benefit of being known to be alive seemed almost as important as being alive. One of two main consolations of his soldier's existence was that he was sure they both knew he was alive and well.

The other, of course, was that he was still alive and well.

And Railstenn was a third. He was sure it was better to have a partner, even a grumpy one, than none at all. He wondered if he would still be alive and well without Railstenn.

And the light outside was fading, he told himself. Evening was coming.

"What's going on out there?" Railstenn asked, and he lifted himself onto his knees and examined what he could see.

Bodies. Houses. Snow. Trees. It all looked the same.

It all sounded the same, too, except for the cessation of the Algheran attack. There was close musket fire and shouting somewhere near, but he could not see the source. *The house across the street,* he guessed to himself. *The one Ian Gunnally wanted volunteers for.*

He swallowed, and admitted that someday he would have to decide if he should have resisted Railstenn's words and volunteered to go there.

"Nothing be happening." He had to say something to his partner.

It meant only that Algherans were not preparing another attack against this house, and Railstenn interpreted it correctly.

"Don't understand why their cannon hasn't hit us," he said. It sounded like a complaint, and Rallt guessed he saw himself as a general whose expertise was being neglected by the men in charge of this battle.

"Mlart be low on cannon ammunition," the boy explained. "Wandisha says he'd been expecting more but it hasn't come yet. She can't reach far enough to tell why."

"Tomorrow then," Railstenn grumbled. Then more of the message penetrated. "This Wandisha—that the whore? The Teep? Huh? Why'd she tell you that sort of thing?"

He blinked. It wasn't news that Wandisha had been a prostitute—she had mentioned it to him in passing, several days before Grahan brought the subject up and told him not to mention it. But Railstenn's indignant tone of voice was new, and he was not sure how to respond.

"She didn't tell me. She told—" He stopped himself and let certain recollections pass through his brain before he spoke again. "I heard from someone else—another soldier—I forget who—that she told him that—about Mlart. Why?"

It was the last word that mattered. He was remembering Ian Haarper's reluctance to acknowledge his conversations with Wandisha. He had even seemed unwilling to admit his acquaintanceship with her. Suddenly the leaden memory of the big Ironwearer's rudeness rang again in his memory, like the reverberations of a huge bell after the first loud clapper-forced note had passed overhead, and the peals sang of danger.

Danger to Wandisha. He could not excuse himself.

Fortunately, Railstenn was easily satisfied. "Show-off," he muttered, and Rallt guessed he had decided to blame his nonexistent informant. "Wouldn't count." The rest of what he said was lost in mumbles and Rallt felt relief, sensing danger to Wandisha had been averted.

CHAPTER TWENTY-THREE

*H*errilmin *came in low over Midpassage, emerging in nor-*mal time near dusk. Nearly invisible in his transparent levcraft, he drifted below the clouds, surveying the scene below. It was not the town he remembered, and he had to check his instruments to verify that no time had passed since he entered his levcraft and that he had come to the right place.

Buildings which had been landmarks had been removed and others had been destroyed. Fire had erased all signs of occupation on the western bank of the river. Fallen trees blocked many of the streets.

At first, he thought the town was unoccupied. Few houses were lit, and at his altitude human beings were small. It took awhile to realize the dots moving across the ground were people, and somewhat longer to understand their apparent aimless wandering had purpose, that he was watching a battle.

Toward evening, the Algherans used cannon to destroy the house across the street. Rallt did not see them, but he felt the impact as heavy shells struck down and exploded. He heard the noise and felt the earth shake. Then the volume of musket fire increased. From below, he heard scraps of voices as the soldiers on the first floor picked targets.

"Across the street." Railstenn. "Thought Mlart was out of shells."

"I were told he were low on shells. Maybe he captured some of ours." He was tense, too. It took an effort to speak reasonably.

Something whined overhead, *thack*ed against a ceiling beam, and fell on the floor. Rallt, blinking, suddenly noticed a thumb-wide hole in the window just over his head. It was perfectly round and surrounded by a narrow ring of cracked glass. It had not been there before.

Someone had shot at him. He blinked again and brought his head down.

Railstenn seemed not to have noticed. "Someone shot," he said stiffly.

The other man said nothing. He brought his own head up slowly and put it at the edge of the window and turned it, bit by bit. "Could be from anywhere," he said carefully.

I know that. Rallt did not raise his head to confirm the statement. The Algherans could have put sharpshooters in all the houses across the street for all he knew. It was not easy to see a target behind a window.

Something hammered on the wall before him, then below, many times.

"That one missed." Railstenn pulled his head back.

This is what we did to them last night. He couldn't complain about a lack of fairness.

The hammers struck the wall again. He saw dust from the plaster fall past the window. Another miss, but still evidence that someone was shooting at the window.

Why did it take the Algherans so long to learn to storm a house?

Railstenn grunted when he asked that. "You're the big regular, supposed to know all about fighting. You never do this before?"

"No." He had given up explaining he was not a soldier.

"Neither'd they. Neither'd I." Railstenn spat at the wall.

Someone must have done this before. He looked for a way to express his reasoning concisely.

"Haarper told us what to do. *Lan* Haarper." Railstenn seemed disgusted.

"The Ironwearer? The red-haired one?" It seemed improbable.

"He told us what to do. Told the officers and they told us, anyhow. We all got talked to, before the Algies showed up, how to capture a building, how to hold one. Just in case we had to, they said. Just in case!"

Railstenn spat again.

That was the day lan Haarper was shot, Rallt remembered, and surely he had been too busy and too unhappy to invent tactics.

"I must have missed it, sleeping," he said, temporizing.

"They wouldn't tell the likes of you," Railstenn said sourly. "It was just for us Midpassagers. We get the shit jobs, the Ironwearer makes sure of it, and he makes sure we're told how to do it. All sorts of shit—you wouldn't believe it. I had a noble as company commander for a while and he said he'd never heard of anything like it. He asked me how much time we spent learning regular drill, marching, shooting in ranks. And you know what I had to tell him? I had to tell him nothing, we didn't spend more than one morning on that when we were training, and that was just to make us look good for the old Ironwearer when he came to inspect. I mean, we didn't know any better, we were getting trained, we thought we were getting trained proper, but, no—"

Drill and marching sounded very tedious, Rallt could not help feeling. Why did Railstenn miss them?

"You wouldn't believe it," the soldier insisted. "What we got taught was how to crawl on the ground. How to shoot lying down. How to move from cover to cover. How to walk quietly in a woods, for Cimon's sake. How to cut someone's throat and stab a belly. Even where to dig latrines."

Rallt laughed.

"I'm not joking! Even shitting is a military matter to lan Haarper! You want to know where to dig a latrine? Downside of a river, in hollows, preferably in clay or lined with clay, and when we was marching, if he didn't like where we'd dug, he'd make us fill it up and dig where he showed us. Said it was to keep us from getting sick!"

Railstenn shook his head. "We didn't get marching sickness anything as bad as the other regiments, you know."

Rallt smiled politely. He had too much sense to believe any of this.

Musket fire put an end to the conversation. Another found the window. In the interval while the shooter reloaded—Rallt kept telling himself the window was a minor target that no more than one Algheran would select—he sat up and looked down, then subsided quickly.

Railstenn read his expression, even in the twilight. He put his weight onto his knees, hesitated for a moment, leaning on his musket, then leaned forward quickly with the gun in his hands and shot, then jerked himself back.

Rallt did the same. It wasn't necessary to spend much time aiming.

The space below was filled with soldiers. This time, Rallt noticed, they were not rushing directly at the house, but were running about it, apparently in circles. *To make aiming at them from a low window hard,* he thought as he reloaded. Like most clever ideas, it was childishly simple to understand when put into practice.

"They must have got both houses across the street. So they can come at us from three sides." Railstenn was wasting his time on thinking.

Fragments of glass tore at Rallt's nose. He jerked backward, still hearing the bullet that had missed. The breeze from its passage had touched his face. He put his musket down and touched his nose to assure himself it was intact, then his cheek, and cautiously licked at dots of blood on his fingertips.

I can tell Grahan I've been wounded. He felt strangely distant from what was happening to him.

"Your turn." The other man prodded his knee. "What's wrong with you?"

I'm almost dead.

"You're fine. Not even a scratch." His buddy had already performed his diagnosis.

Splintering sounds rose up from below. Shattering glass. Crashes.

Gunshots. Shouts.

The Algherans were inside the house.

The space outside was suddenly drained of running men.

Rallt looked out quickly, but the threat of the unseen musketman shooting at the window kept him from deciding how many more were on the ground.

"Shoot them when they run off." Railstenn's voice was not as confident as the words.

"No. We're done here." Rallt shook the cartridge pouch to make his point. Only a few cartridges were left to rattle inside it. He stood and reloaded carefully, then bent to put the last cartridges in his pocket.

"You're going down?" Railstenn stared at the exit from the attic.

"Or else, they come up." He swallowed, surprised to find moisture in his mouth.

"We don't have to. Pull up the ladder, fasten the cover, they wouldn't notice. They aren't going to waste time here." Railstenn spoke quickly.

"You want to be surrounded by Algies?" It would be intolerable to be cut off again from Grahan and Wandisha, he realized. He had to go down.

Down. In his mind, Cherrid ris Clendannan's voice repeated it. *Down.*

He was beyond arguing. He walked the few paces to the exit. It took forever and he remembered none of it.

"You don't know what to do."

He didn't. He shook his head and stepped on the ladder.

"Wait!" A convulsion brought Railstenn to his feet. "Buddy! Wait! I'll go with you."

Mlart against the Lopritians. Herrilmin felt no emotional involvement in the battle, and even if he had, the sides could not be distinguished from the air. The little dots inching from building to building were lacking in every sign of humanity. He had the feelings he would have had watching a war between ants and was sorry that he did not have a straw to intervene in their minuscule conflict.

Intellectually, he realized that the fighting below him, which he supposed would seem so important to other Algherans, was unimportant. This whole squalid malodorous world, fragile as the memory of a dream, was unimportant. It was the real world, in the time after the Present, which mattered to living men, and the war for the world was to be waged at the Present, with the

weapons of the Present. The rulers of the world would not be
men who carried swords and muskets but those who commanded nuclear weapons, plagues, pests, and killing mists.

He could be among those rulers.

It was a concept which had grown slowly in him, imperceptibly during the last tenth of a year, as the poverty of this age
and the real inferiorities of his companions had impressed themselves on him, and he had kept his developing ideas to himself
so that even to his Septlings he had seemed no more than the
loyal Hujsuon Septling he had ever been. But the idea had grown
irresistibly, and he, the source and the concealer of the notion,
had had to become larger than himself to contain it, or be destroyed.

"Look for extra cartridges—on dead men." That was Railstenn's first instruction, at the foot of the ladder.

There were only a few other rooms to search, but the time
seemed enormous, while men fought below. There were no dead
men, no cartridges.

Bedrooms. One for a child, two for guests, he guessed. Nothing of interest was in them, but he felt he would remember their
undistinguished furnishings for the rest of his life.

Normality was memorable, now.

Railstenn waited at the steps. He swallowed as Rallt approached.

"Lean over the banister. If you see someone aiming at me,
shoot him. I'll go down first and cover while you come down."
His directions were quick.

To go down stairs, you walk down. Rallt blinked, then realized the man was in earnest, and frightened. "Sure."

Awkwardly, he leaned over the rail. There was nothing to see
from that position but walls and the stairs, and he found himself
wondering half-seriously if stair climbing was another of the
military skills Ironwearer Ian Haarper had imparted to his grown-
up students.

Railstenn went down the steps crouched, slowly and quietly
until his waist was level with the floor where Rallt stood, then
at a rush. He threw himself in a corner at the bottom and looked
around quickly with his musket held before him. It was an echo
of the performance Rallt had seen when he had accompanied
Midpassage soldiers into other houses.

"C'mon," Railstenn hissed. He sidled along a wall till he was next to a closed door and waited, with his hand on the latch.

Rallt went down the steps as he had, feeling like a grown man forced to play toddler's games with children as strangers watched. He felt no less ridiculous jumping from door to door as Railstenn jabbed a finger at them.

More bedrooms, all of them empty of people. He found himself wondering why Lopritians built houses with so much wasted space. Lord Clendannan's house had more than forty rooms counting servants' quarters, Grahan had told him, and it had seemed inconceivable when the old man seemed content with one, but Grahan had assured him of the number and that it held marvels. He was sorry he would never see that house.

"Over there, after me." Railstenn gestured till Rallt was in place beside the closed door, then opened it suddenly and tossed himself after it. He lit on his shoulder and rolled over and came up, holding his musket all the while. Rallt, standing in the doorway, admired the feat and noticed that the room smelled of diarrhea.

Then he saw the dead man on the bed.

He was stretched out like a sleeping man with his musket in his hands. The tip of one finger still touched the trigger. The others on the hand dangled over his thigh. His face was undisturbed even by dreams. It was a face that asked for nothing. It was the back and top of the head that was missing. His sphincters had failed as he died. His bowels and bladder had drained. Rallt wondered if he had had time to feel them or if it had happened before he died.

He kept that thought silent, and unfastened the man's belt and pulled free the cartridge pouch. It was not empty. He wiped the damp corner of the leather pouch on the bed covers and put it on his belt.

Railstenn was staring at the body. Rallt left the room quietly.

It was not quiet elsewhere. Muskets were firing continuously and other sounds of fighting continued below him.

A dead man lay on the next set of stairs. He had been shot in the back. The hand at his side had been mangled; it was missing one finger and another was held on only by skin. The other hand stretched before him, the fingers loosely wrapped about a banister rail. His face was down. A smudged trail of blood ran behind him on the stairs and on the landing below.

He was not carrying a musket and Rallt did not want to lift him to reach his ammunition pouch. He stepped past quickly.

On the landing he could see the fighting. A Lopritian body lay in the entrance to the main room. Two men swayed back and forth, standing over the body's leg: a heavyset blond Lopritian in a white upper garment had wrapped one arm around a smaller and darker Algheran and was trying to push a knife into his throat with the other; the Algheran was pushing away the knife and clawing at the larger man's eyes.

Bodies lay in piles in the doorway to outside. Through the windows, he saw parallel lines of flames lance out as a musket volley was fired.

A man lay faceup over the edge of a couch; his throat had been cut open but it was curiously free of blood; blood from his wrists and palms dripped onto the floor. Behind that, a Lopritian lay on the floor kicking as an Algheran sitting astride his belly stabbed at his chest; another Algheran clubbed his head with a musket butt. In a corner, three Lopritians huddled together with their arms above their heads; bodies of their comrades lay at their feet, and in front of them, Algheran soldiers were hurriedly reloading muskets. A pair of men rolled across the floor, slashing at each other with knives. In another corner, a man, bent over, was vomiting. A man leaning against a wall was slowly falling down. Another man . . .

The room was filled with other men, other bodies.

The sound was tremendous.

It made no sense to catalog what he saw, Rallt sensed. There were more Algherans in the building now than Lopritians, and there would be no escape.

Almost, he wished he were back in the attic with Railstenn.

He brought his musket up and aimed at the man sitting on the Lopritian. He fired and shot the man in the back, then retreated to the landing where he could not be seen and reloaded.

When he returned to the steps, the man he had shot lay across the Lopritian he had stabbed like a lover. The man clubbing the same victim was now swinging his musket at the Lopritians in the corner. Only two of the three were still standing; one was on the floor with his arms still raised to the ceiling. Rallt shot the musket-wielding man at the junction of his right arm and shoulder and had the satisfaction of seeing blood jumping from the wound. As he turned away, he saw one of the captives reaching to wrest the musket away from the man he had shot. The heavyset blond Lopritian was kicking the dark Algheran at his feet; the Algheran was still bleeding from wounds in his neck, and one side of the Lopritian's face was gory.

A bullet tore through the landing by his toes as he reloaded. Splinters cut his fingers as he poured powder down the musket barrel. The bullet did no other damage but he spilled powder and the bullet in his mouth dropped out when he opened it in surprise.

He had to reload from the start, he realized, and just below, another man, who had probably heard the sound of his musket butt striking the floor, was doing the same thing.

Rallt was inspired. He screamed suddenly, a loud groaning moan that tapered off as he stamped his foot on the floor. Simultaneously, he reached in his pouch for another cartridge.

There was not time to reload properly. He dropped the entire cartridge into the mouth of his musket and pushed it down with his rammer, hoping it would stay in place, and spilled what was left of the powder from the original cartridge into the priming pan. Under him, he sensed almost as Wandisha would have another man reloading with the same feverish pace.

He had barely time to kneel beside the steps when the Algheran came into view, a large man, dark-haired, with a beefy face and ham-size hands, who took the steps two at a time. The musket in his hands seemed no larger than a child's broom.

Rallt aimed and squeezed his trigger.

Nothing happened.

But the Algheran saw him. He started to run up the stairs.

Misfire misfire misfire! Rallt's mind yammered at him. He pulled the trigger again, without success, and scrambled to his feet, and ran to the back of the landing as the Algheran reached the top, and then up the next flight of steps as the Algheran raced toward him.

He tripped over the body on the stairs. He fell facedown and bit his lip and one knee slammed painfully into the edge of a wooden step and the other hit on the back of the dead man and slid so it seemed his groin was being pulled apart. One arm was numb.

He could hear the Algheran after him, even through his own breath and pounding heart, even through all the noise from the first floor.

He gasped and rolled over and tried to pull himself higher on
the steps. And he could not. A band had fastened in one ankle,
something unyielding and tight and pulling irresistibly. He felt
himself starting to slide downward.

The Algheran—his face, broad, heavily fleshed, nostrils flar-
ing, red with effort, wide-mouthed, eyes squinting—seemed to
fill the space before him. Rallt, despairing, trying to defend
himself, brought up a hand to fend the Algheran off. It was the
hand which held his musket and his fingers were still around the
trigger guard. He had no chance to aim but—

Thunder sounded. A bolt of lightning above him blinded him
as he pulled his trigger—

He heard thunder again. Sudden force threw his arm back
against a riser. He squinted against the pain, and realized when
he continued to feel the hurt that he was alive. His gun had
finally gone off.

There were other sounds in the darkness. Footsteps.
Scratches. A mewing sound—kittenlike. A cat?

He opened his eyes. The Algheran was still standing close to
him, moving backward slowly. His musket had fallen from his
hands, and he was trying to hold himself upright with a hand
on the banister. The other hand was at his throat. Blood was
draining from a shoulder onto the front part of his green uniform. Under his fingers, his throat was blackened and more
blood was welling out.

The Algheran was trying to cover a hole in his neck, Rallt
realized. The mewing sound came from his mouth. His eyes—
surprised and hurt—pleaded for him.

His last words. The Algheran wanted to say something before
he died.

Rallt felt, rather than saw, Railstenn standing beside his head.
He glanced upward and saw the older man was waiting expectantly.

Two wounds. The Algheran counted for nothing now. Rallt
could see with what effort he was straining to stay erect and
preserve his dignity as the blood spilled from his body. Deliberately, he sat up and braced himself against the railing, then
took up his musket with both hands and swung with all his might
to hit the Algheran in the groin with the muzzle.

The jolt hurt every muscle in his back. But the big Algheran

folded up and lost his hold on the banister. The enemy soldier
fell backward and collapsed at the bottom of the steps.

The body continued to make sounds, but it was not moving.
Rallt concentrated on sitting up, and when that was done he
shook his musket out.

Railstenn went past him, down to the fallen man, and hesitated for a moment, then knelt. When he rose, there was red on
the knife in his hands; the Algheran was silent.

Rallt stood. He was shaky. For a moment, at least, his only
ambition was to lean on the railing and stay on his feet.

Suddenly there was a man in a blue uniform on the landing
below. He noticed Rallt and Railstenn and seemed surprised,
then recovered and gestured with a thumb.

Downstairs, the gesture read. Then Rallt realized he had heard
the word as well. The Guards soldier was shouting.

"Downstairs! Anyone else up . . . Out . . . the house!"

He was too tired to think what it meant. Wearily, Rallt went
down the steps to Railstenn, trailing his musket behind him.

He had become a great man, Herrilmin realized humbly.
Conqueror of the world. Greater than Vrect tra'Hujsuon, who
had helped create him. Greater than Mlart tra'Nornst the Uni-
fier, who had been Alghera's greatest soldier. Greater even than
Jablin Hemmendur, who had steered Chelmmys on its path to
domination. Greater perhaps than the shadowy historical form
that in legend had become the majestic Lord Cimon, God and
ruler of the world and judge of all men's souls.

He felt his greatness swelling within him, filling every portion
of him, and threatening to burst through his skin and every
aperture of his body. Soon it would be revealed to lesser humanity. Then every facet of his personality would mirror what
he had become to peoples of the world, and it would be known
that every one of the experiences he had known had shaped him.

No. He alone knew that the experiences were unimportant.
It was what was inside his mind and soul that mattered. He had
created himself.

At first, secretly freed from Dicovys captivity and the con-
fines of the Station by Vrect tra'Hujsuon, his goal had been the
reward promised by the acting Sept Master—that he should meet
Timt ha'Dicovys again in combat and kill the man who had
humbled him. Later, from remarks he had made, Gherst

ha'Hujsuon had thought he was motivated only by unreasonable jealous hatred of Timt ha'Dicovys, and when he had understood that, it had amused Herrilmin to pretend that was so.

But it was not the case. He disliked the man, but the Ironwearer had no conception of what mattered in the world; Timt ha'Dicovys was a powerless toy to be manipulated and enraged, not a person to fear or hate. And as a toy, the Ironwearer could not escape his manipulator, as Herrilmin now realized he had escaped from Vrect tra'Hujsuon.

It was at the Present that his escape—and his Awakening to larger issues—had begun. Steal some of the weapons of the reborn Present, Vrect had asked of him, learn their secrets so they can be re-created.

Re-created for Alghera, he had said, to hold as threats against the Alliance when history is put back on its proper track. The former track, a listener scurrying back to the tra'Dicovys or the tra'Ruijac would have reported. But like Herrilmin, Vrect had scorn for the begging, powerless state that Alghera had become in the years after Mlart tra'Nornst. A better track, Vrect had meant, and Herrilmin had understood what could not be said aloud in a Teep-infested environment: a better track to a better world, where the other nations of mankind responded in fear and trembling to the wishes of the Algheran Realm.

Not a reborn Realm. Vrect was old and impatient—and outdated. The acting Sept Master had already been full-grown in the troubled years after the fall of the Magnates, during the struggle for influence that brought Hujsuon from being an Association into a full-fledged Sept. Emotionally, he had not developed beyond that time, it had seemed to Herrilmin and the other Agents with whom he shared confidences. Vrect spoke openly of a stronger Alghera, and in private of his desires for a more powerful Hujsuon Sept within the Realm, but nothing he had said or done indicated more inspiring dreams. Perhaps, as Gherst had often suggested, his secret ambition was no more than that an election would give him by right what he held now by chance, and that his services to Alghera would cause Hujsuon to make him the real Master of the Sept. If so, he was mistaken, Herrilmin was sure.

And pathetic. Sept Master! It was an old man's ambition, a weak man's idea of power, which a modern man could barely comprehend. A Sept Master was nothing more than a leader of a handful of swordsmen in a nation ruled by the Warder of the Realm, a relic of the barbaric past.

Herrilmin was young. He had the patience to wait as the world was reshaped, and the willingness to take an active role.

At the Present, on a frozen plain far north of F'a Alghera, he had seen a demonstration of the weapons which dwarfed imagination. Watching a tiny speck of light explode almost instantly into a horizon-filling tower of flame, he had glimpsed the future.

His future. The lightning-girded pillar of the bomb cloud had demonstrated how rapidly and how high a man's aspirations could reach. The spreading orange and white blossom atop the stem of the explosion showed how resolution and courage over-reached the normal limitations of humanity. The irresistible force of the invisible shock wave was a metaphor for determination. The great trees tumbling about his levcraft in the wake of the bomb burst had been snapped away from their ground-fastened roots no more than he.

CHAPTER TWENTY-FOUR

*I*ronwearer *Ian Haarper was at the foot of the stairs. He was* leaning over his crutches as Rallt had leaned over the railing, and he looked every bit as old as ever Cherrid ris Clendannan had.

Behind him, Guardsmen and other soldiers filled the room. They were separating Algheran and Lopritian bodies and carrying them outside. An officer Rallt did not recognize was on his knees, with his ear on one man's bare chest. As Rallt watched, he sat back on his heels and shook his head, then pointed to a pair of Guardsmen, who came and took the body away.

It was Sergeant Ian Gunnally's body, Rallt finally recognized. Skin and muscle hung free along the body's rib cage, and there was a bruise about a red line on his right side. Blood dripped from the body's fingers.

Rallt stopped beside Ian Haarper as Railstenn went past. He hesitated, wondering if he should speak. His eyes were downcast, and he saw that the base of one of the Ironwearer's planks was red. The stained wood was splintered and cracked.

"Hello, Rallt." The Ironwearer had noticed him.

"Is the sergeant dead?" Rallt asked.

"Not yet. How are you? All right?"

"I think so. I—" He stopped. What had almost happened to him was not important. "Yes, all right."

"Good." Lan Haarper seemed not to have noticed his hesitation. "You ready to leave here? People are looking for you."

"Where are the soldiers here going?"

"The Midpassagers? Center of town, where they're out of the fighting. We're going to let them rest tonight. God knows they deserve it."

"Shouldn't I go with them?" He made himself look up into the Ironwearer's face. Lan Haarper's gray eyes were bloodshot and his cheeks were hollow. His face was grimy; there were crow's-feet around his eyes.

"No." The Ironwearer smiled wearily, and in a thickly accented voice said to Rallt, "For you, soldier, the war is over."

He was surprised to hear that. He shook his head unhappily.

Lan Haarper leaned so his hand fell on Rallt's shoulder. "Come on, boy. You did your part. Now Wandisha and Grahan want you back. Believe me, they've been shouting about it all day long."

"I'm needed here." He tried to move away.

"You're needed other places as well. Come on, Rallt. If you're going to be a soldier, you have to learn to follow orders."

"This the boy? You want us to carry him?" It was the Guard soldier he had seen on the stairs. The Ironwearer held up a hand to silence him, and after a moment the soldier went away.

Rallt looked around at the shambles that had been made of the room, listening to the moans of dying men and staring at the body he had shot in the back. Almost none of the men left alive were people he recognized, but those who were not in Guard uniforms wore the ragtag clothes he had learned to associate with the Midpassagers.

The militia battalion was still alive.

"I'd be all right with them, Ironwearer. Really. They're friends."

"My friends, too," the Ironwearer said mildly, "but they'll stand things without you tonight."

He still hesitated.

"Go with him, Rallt." Railstenn had returned. Rallt did not know how much of the conversation he had heard, but he felt embarrassed by it. He shook his head angrily, wishing the soldier would go away. Lan Haarper made his gesture of dismissal again, and Railstenn did not leave, but was silent.

"Rallt, what am I supposed to tell your father when he gets back?" the big Ironwearer asked. "That being disobedient got you killed? That what you want to have me say?"

It was mention of his father that convinced him. "All right," he said unhappily. His eyes were down and he was afraid to look at Railstenn as he left with the Ironwearer, though his partner only patted him on the back.

Timt ha'Dicovys's time machine was down there, somewhere. Its presence was registered on instruments in Herrilmin's cockpit, though he did not have the training to match his machine's path through time to it.

He drifted aimlessly across the village above the clouds and considered what he might do.

Gherst and the others needed to be rescued, of course, but there was no haste. Timt ha'Dicovys's threat could be dealt with first.

The time machine was there after dusk on this day, not before, unless he went back to the day when Lerlt cut up the Ironwearer's woman. His maneuvers showed him that, but not how to reach it. It seemed to be on the hillside where he and Gherst had found it originally, but he was not prepared to go near it without protection from its guns. He berated himself for not bringing the equipment to destroy it.

And then he smiled. He had the best possible equipment for destroying anything that other men had built.

"No!"

Herrilmin's time machine was suddenly visible again, hovering above the center of Midpassage for the few seconds it took to dump a metal box from its bottom. The box tumbled and sparkles from the last rays of the setting sun flashed from its corners. Then it entered the first wisps of cloud tops and was lost from sight. Kylene's scream coincided with its disappearance.

Instinctively, from her watching place in the sky, she guessed what Herrilmin had done. Tim Harper had described weapons which tore cities to shreds, and Fesch had joked that Herrilmin claimed to have some of them. It was all too conceivable that the blond Algheran had chosen to destroy Midpassage to reach his enemies.

But could she stop him?

Yes. She had a time machine. She made herself be calm.

"This the boy?" Pitar lan Styllin asked as Rallt climbed into the rear of lan Haarper's wagon, then looked carefully and said, "Hello, Rallt." He was in the driver's position. He shifted the reins to one hand and put out the other to assist the Ironwearer, but lan Haarper ignored it.

The big man half hopped, half pulled himself on his side of the seat, and handed his crutches to Rallt. "Don't lose them."

To Pitar, he said, "This is the boy. Doesn't want to come, if you can believe it." His voice suggested he was amused. Rallt, remembering him as he had been minutes before, was surprised by the difference in him.

Lan Styllin clucked at the horses, and slapped them lightly with the reins. Rallt noticed he was trying to stay in paths already cut into the snow. Soil showed under the wagon wheels, and he guessed that the snow was melting but would become firm again during the night.

Night was very close. The sky was dark, under a dark gray cloud. Only a narrow ribbon of blue remained on the horizon, but no house lights were lit.

Before him, a file of soldiers—Guards and Midpassage men, though in the twilight gloom, uniform distinctions were hard to see—was crossing the street. The head of the line was lost between a fir tree and a house. As they made way for the wagon, Rallt noticed that each of the men was carrying more than one musket.

Beside the fir tree was a small group of women. As he watched, some of them went to men in the line. A few took muskets for themselves.

"Are all the Algies dead?" he wondered aloud.

"Be a shame for him to miss ris Andervyll's party," Pitar said at the same time, and chuckled, so Rallt's question was lost.

"Wouldn't it though," lan Haarper agreed; and turned to Rallt.

"Say again, son?"

"Are all the Algies back there dead now?"

"A lot of them," the Ironwearer said. "Those that didn't have the sense to surrender."

In that instant, as he hung above the unsuspecting town, Herrilmin held to the doorframe of his levcraft, and watched admiringly as the bright box that held his gift to Timt ha'Dicovys dropped through the sky.

Over the dark clouds, the sunset rested in pink and purple layers. It was another marvel the little beings beneath would never see.

At the foot of the ladder, before he climbed, he paused to catch his breath. The bomb had been very heavy and his arrangements for shifting cargo very primitive. He had labored hard, for longer than he wished, and he had not fully recovered from the wound Timt ha'Dicovys had given him. Nor had he eaten properly for what seemed seasons.

It seemed a marvel that the people of this age had survived long enough to be parents to the people of his.

Some of them would not, of course. He had just made sure of that. He wished he could find a safe place to watch the flash of the bomb wipe Midpassage from existence.

He giggled. He had just remembered that Mlart tra'Nornst would be vaporized along with Timt ha'Dicovys. How trivial it was to modify history.

Then, abruptly, through the open hatchway, a translucent shape appeared. It was fishlike in silhouette, rounded as it turned, and very large. He could see the clouds behind and through it, and for one insane moment he felt he was actually watching a levcraft as it traveled through time.

Timt ha'Dicovys's levcraft. Flames blossomed from rounded humps on the bottom of the fuselage, and Herrilmin felt his machine shaking about him.

Frantically, he pulled himself up the ladder to the controls.

She had not considered that shells fired from her cannons would lose velocity as they departed the field of the time machine, and Kylene was disappointed again in what she did to Herrilmin's levcraft.

It vanished from sight abruptly and she cursed, realizing the man had escaped once more. Then, practically, she began the weary job of resetting her controls to return to the same period of time. She would make another pass, and another, as long as her ammunition held out.

But before she was done, Herrilmin's levcraft was before her again, so close she could see the man inside at his controls. Flame was darting from the hatchway at the bottom of the vehicle, and she saw smoke in the tiny compartment behind the pilot's quarters.

It was an image which lasted only a fraction of a second, and then was gone. She had only the fading blip on her radar screen to tell her it had been real and not hallucination.

She had hit Herrilmin's machine. She remembered now that shells became hot when they were fired, from the explosion which propelled them and from friction with the air. Somehow, one of her shells had found tinder in Herrilmin's machine and started a fire.

Herrilmin would roast before he reached the ground.

It would be a lovely ending.

But, no, he would not roast, she remembered. Herrilmin would stop the fire somehow, but the damage would keep him from reaching the Project. Herrilmin would shriek "This is all your fault" and leap into the air and die on the ground, beside a river twenty centuries in the past. His head would sink below the surface of the water as his lifeblood drained from his throat, and it would be one of her throwing knives which killed him.

Had killed him. Herrilmin had died long before he came to Midpassage.

She smiled.   •

"Do we take prisoners?" Railstenn had told Rallt neither side tried to capture men from the other.

"No. We took their muskets, and let them go, those that could walk. We'll let Mlart feed them."

"We ought to shoot them!" He was thinking of Ian Gunnally.

"We should persuade them not to fight." Lan Haarper's voice told Rallt not to argue. He changed the topic.

"Been people mad at me?" The question was supposed to be an apology, if it were needed, but he did not feel he had done anything seriously wrong.

"No." Pitar turned to answer that. "We worried some and it wasn't necessary. You could have gotten away at any time, you know, if you had explained things to Sergeant Ian Gunnally.''

He had not thought to try, and he had had good reason for not drawing the sergeant's attention to him. ''I suppose,'' he said carefully, and was grateful when Ian Styllin turned his attention back to the road and steered the horses through a sharp turn.

The sky brightened. The blue along the horizon was suddenly orange and gleaming red, and Rallt realized the sun had broken through a layer of clouds.

The glittering box fell.

There were controls attached to it to set the time of explosion, but Herrilmin had not set them. The cryptic words stenciled on the cover which might have guided him were the product of a culture which had diverged technically from his own for almost six hundred centuries; he had understood them no better than writing in any other foreign language. In default, the bomb was set to explode at sea level or at impact. After it dropped from Herrilmin's levcraft, Kylene had all of forty seconds to catch it.

Harper's levcraft did not have grapples to snare falling objects, but it took great force to expel material from within a time field. Atmospheric pressures outside the field looked immensely higher—almost like solid matter—to objects within, he had told her once, and although that was probably a guess because he had not seemed satisfied with his analysis, the phenomena still existed. So she was sure she could approach the falling bomb in Stoptime, then switch to faster-than-time travel, and carry the weapon away, for disposal in the ocean.

She had not reckoned on what this would do to the bomb.

The metal box, falling within a bubble of air, suddenly struck the walls of the moving field at high speed, bounced, tumbled down the side, and finally hit at the bottom of the shell.

The bomb detonated.

It was not a full-scale explosion. Nuclear weapons can be designed to handle considerable punishment, but Herrilmin could not fit full-size missiles in his time machine. He had sought weapons which could be studied easily, and those were primarily test weapons, designed for placement by humans using levcraft. They were not devices intended for unevenly placed hammer blows.

Inside the metal box, safety devices functioned suddenly. Barriers rose in the evacuated tube which housed two fist-size hemispheres of uranium. Conventional explosions thrust the pieces of metal toward each other, but the barriers retarded them. The fissionable halves did not slam together with the speed needed to start a critical reaction. Instead, at a much slower pace—still faster than a human eye could see—the lumps melted and flowed together in the bottom of the tube. The explosion which resulted was comparatively small; it failed by orders of magnitude to provide the heat and pressure required to ignite fusion in the jacket of deuterium and tritium which wrapped the atomic bomb.

And so Kylene did not die immediately.

They passed artillery guns. Rallt noticed they were quiet and that their crews were gathered around small fires. The men were eating, he saw, and he was suddenly envious of their pleasure. It would be good to have back the mug of grain and water Railstenn had kicked from his hand that morning.

There were other fires, on both sides of him, roughly forming two sides of a triangle, and he realized finally those marked the places where soldiers were placed. The narrow lines marked the boundaries of the land that remained Lopritian—the limits of lan Haarper's kingdom.

"Pitar was looking for you," lan Haarper said. "And Wandisha came and started shouting, so he had to borrow a Guards platoon to get to you—good thing I was there, to authorize it—and I suggest you say thanks very politely to ris Salynnt when you see him or any other of the Guards."

Rallt, pulled from consideration of his hunger, translated that and realized people were mad at him.

"I be sorry," he said. "You didn't have to do that. I weren't trying to cause trouble." But he wasn't sorry, he realized. He was angry and part of his anger was pointed at Wandisha and Grahan.

And at being hungry.

"I been't a little boy now," he snapped. "Don't treat me like one."

"No, you're not," lan Haarper agreed, surprising him. "But

you've got powerful friends now, so it's easy to make trouble for people, even when you're not trying.''

"But it been't my fault!"

"Didn't say it was," Ian Haarper said. "Fact remains, we busted up a platoon of Guards to get to you. Now if we hadn't, you'd be dead, and probably all your friends would be dead— and just between us chickens, the Guards can stand to lose some men a lot better than the militia can right now, so I'm not going to weep about it—although God help you if you tell ris Salynnt I said that. But people died to keep you alive, young man, and I sincerely hope you remember that the rest of your long life and—"

"Which ought to run about two watches," Ian Styllin interjected.

"Go to Wolf-Twin's Hell, Pitar!" Ian Haarper growled. "Now, young man, you got something more to say, you spill it and then I'll finish saying my piece. That okay? Say what you're going to say."

"I were . . ." Rallt sighed and looked for more of an explanation, sure now he would have to repeat it again and again. "I did what were needed."

"Sure. You were being a good soldier," Ian Haarper agreed, and Rallt listened for sarcasm but did not hear it. "No quarrel with that. Now, I'll say my piece. Which is that all those soldiers but you had training and experience. No one in their right minds puts someone raw as fresh cauliflower right into a battle, Rallt, and that's what you were. Maybe you're a mite more cooked now."

He didn't understand the analogy. "I did all right."

"So you did. You did your part, and from what I hear, as well or better than some men who are now dead. I thank you for it. Loprit thanks you. You've done something good for more people than you will ever know, but you were one very lucky person. Don't ever expect that kind of luck again."

He sighed. Would he be expected to say thanks to everyone in sight every day for the rest of his life?

"Who was your buddy?" asked the Ironwearer.

"Railstenn." That could be safely answered.

He doesn't like you. He was sure Ian Haarper wouldn't care.

"Okay. How long would you have stayed alive without Railstenn?"

"I don't know," he admitted, and they rode in silence for a minute.

"Not very long," he said at last.

"I rest my case," Ian Haarper said. "Railstenn's a survivor. Bit of a *goldbrick*, as well, but a survivor. You were lucky."

The ride finished in silence, and when it was done the sunset had gone and the sky was black.

"Small" is a relative term. Shock from an explosion or any other disturbance travels eleven hundred feet per second at sea level, faster in a denser atmosphere. Kylene's levcraft was in a bubble with a fifty-foot radius; the shock waves crossed through in under a tenth of a second, struck the opposite side of the bubble, and bounced back with almost the same force.

The only barrier to the waves of air, which could finally baffle them, was the levcraft itself. It shook like a struck bell, at a frequency which rips apart the human body's supports for internal organs.

The explosion gave off heat, which increased the pressure felt within the bubble. The combination of heat and vibration was more than the bonding material which held the skin of the vehicle to its frame could withstand. The mirror-bright panels which cloaked *Scent O'Claws* shook, then warped, then were thrown free of the vehicle, exposing bare girders, machinery, and the inner walls of the vehicle. Deformation of the vehicle's internal supports only made the situation worse.

With the streamlining destroyed, the vessel had the aerodynamics of a one-winged pigeon. It was no longer capable of high-speed flight.

As her levcraft shook to pieces about her, Kylene was simultaneously bombarded with radiation. The explosion had released many moles of deuterium and tritium—natural neutron emitters, which were brought into her body with each breath and would be only slowly eliminated. The explosion had also strewn her environment with gobs of neutron-emitting uranium isotopes; within a fraction of a second this source had drenched the cells of her body with ionizing radiation. Finally, the explosion produced gamma rays, at fatal intensity, within the same fraction of a second. Most were blocked by the giant levcraft's armor but some pierced that shielding, and some secondary radiation was thrown out.

There was more than enough radiation to kill an unprotected First Era human being, and more than enough to ruin most of the electronic devices within the vessel.

Scent O'Claws became uncontrollable. It tumbled and fell.

"Here's your bonny boy," Ian Haarper said, as he escorted Rallt into the house. "A little worn, but not much worse for the experience."

Wandisha was there. She hugged him maternally, and Ian Haarper said something over his head about the Guards Regiment. Behind Wandisha, Pitar Ian Styllin kissed his wife and child.

Rallt, embarrassed, noticed other people staring at him and stepped away quickly when she released him. He wanted to recite his adventures for Wandisha but the house was crowded.

Very crowded, he realized quickly. Besides the Ian Styllins, he saw that the man called the Hand of the Queen was there, and some of his officers, and a man with pure white hair sitting in a chair who might be Pitar's grandfather, whom he had never met. Along the wall was yet another elderly man, someone thin and gray who looked a bit like Gertynne, although Gertynne's features were fading in Rallt's memories. Had they all come to welcome him back?

"One more push," a blue-uniformed man said in the background. "No room to retreat any more, and then—" He drew a finger across his throat.

"Lesson about artillery," another soldier said. "Bodies out there . . . Strewn around . . . Looked like a Cimon-taken flower garden. After this, we station guns close up to—"

"Hard on artillery crews," a third soldier said, breaking in. "If they had a choice, you know they'd—"

"Use punishment squads." "Volunteers. Special pay." "Early release." "One way or the other." He lost track of the voices in the laughter.

"Where's Grahan?" He had noticed one vacancy.

"He's coming," someone said, and he heard the note of semi-embarrassment which meant Grahan was out back, at the privy. Wandisha smiled at him.

"He won't be much longer," she said, looking at the Hand. "Sir, perhaps we could start—" Her hand moved toward the place where Ian Styllin's wife stood, cuddling her daughter in her arms as Pitar toyed with its pudgy hands. "The baby is sleepy."

Rallt heard Ian Haarper moving behind him. To express skepticism, he thought. The room had a sour smell of unbathed people and overcooked food, and he was sure the baby was contributing to the odor from both ends.

"Yes." The Hand seemed pleased to have a decision made for him. Rallt looked but could not see either of the women who had attended him when he had last been in this house.

"Pitar Ian Styllin, come and kneel before me." The Hand spoke again, his voice suddenly more confident. It was not loud, or deep, but Rallt thought it would carry past the walls to the artillerymen in the street outside, and for a moment he worried that it would attract shells from the Algheran guns.

Lan Styllin approached the Hand and went to his knees slowly. He swallowed and moved nervously. As his dark shirt billowed around his waist, Rallt noticed it had been darned along one side.

"Put your hands on the floor," the Hand said, obviously coaching the younger man. "We don't have— Ah! We do."

Another man came in with a pan and placed this before the Hand's feet. Rallt, half surprised to find Ian Haarper's hand on his shoulder, felt himself pushed forward into the front row of observers, so he could see it was filled with dirt. Lan Styllin, still on his knees, leaned forward to put his hands into it; Rallt glanced at his wife, but the dirt did not seem to bother her as it had when it was her child playing outside.

"This is the soil of Loprit," the Hand said solemnly, and Rallt wanted to giggle, but Wandisha reached out and pinched the fat part of his palm. "It symbolizes the common earth from which we have come and which our bodies return to, because we remain mortal beings."

"We remain mortal beings," Ian Styllin said hesitantly, and Rallt noticed that the man who had brought in the dirt was whispering in his ear.

"Because the soil is Lopritian, it symbolizes that we are ourselves Lopritians and exist to serve the people of Loprit."

"We are ourselves Lopritian," Ian Styllin echoed. "We exist to serve the people of Loprit."

"Do you accept this?" the Hand asked, and when Pitar had agreed, said, "Stand."

Lan Styllin stood, stiffly it seemed to Rallt, awkwardly though he had done nothing difficult. He seemed frightened.

"Shake my hand," the Hand said. "It shows that we work together."

"We work together," lan Styllin repeated, and as he grasped the older man's hand the Hand struck his head with his other hand made into a fist, not viciously, but with enough force to make the younger man's head rock. Rallt noticed that lan Styllin's wife moved suddenly to hide that sight from his grandfather and bent to let the baby pull at the old man's silver hair.

The Hand was deadpan. "This symbolizes that the nobility is subservient to the Crown."

"The nobility is subservient to the Crown." Lan Styllin seemed more surprised than hurt, and Rallt realized the man whispering to him had not warned him of the blow. He was sorry that Wandisha had not been given the task so it would be done properly.

"Now kiss me." The Hand spread his arms and lan Styllin stepped into them and somewhat gingerly bussed the older man's cheek with his lips. *Like a little boy meeting a relative*, Rallt told himself, amused by the thought.

He missed some words. "Vested in yourself and the heirs of your body for as long as the rivers run and the land endures," the Hand said, and Pitar echoed the words softly. Then he stepped back and the Hand held his arm out stiffly and said, very quietly, "People of Loprit, I present to you the Domine Pitar ris Styllin."

People began applauding and pressed toward Pitar. Rallt, trying to get out of the way, suddenly noticed that Grahan had returned and was in the door to the kitchen. He was speaking to the Hand, and beside him, nervously looking through the crowd, was a burly man in worn clothes who—

"Father!" Rallt shouted and rushed toward the man.

Kylene fell.

"West Bend," Pitar lan Styllin—ris Styllin now—said, when the first wave of congratulations had passed over and he and Harper could speak in a corner. "I'm looking forward to it. Not like the army, of course."

Harper raised his eyebrows. "I thought you wanted a commission."

"I did, but—the Hand told me this was available. He wanted someone local to take charge there and the more I thought about it, the more I thought I'm local." Pitar laughed self-consciously. "Zitta's pleased, and that's a consideration. Higher rank and it's out of the army and she won't have to move to Northfaring."

"That place was an independent town," Ian Haarper said woodenly. "Those people weren't serfs to anyone."

"It was," Pitar agreed. "I'm going to preserve things for them, Timmial, as much as I can, as soon as we're through rebuilding. You know I will. But the Hand wants an armory there. A small garrison, some warehouses. You know the sort of thing."

"Competition for Merryn. That sort of thing."

Pitar paused for a moment. "I don't think it's that, Timmial. There's too much open space between Midpassage and Port Junction. You know ris Clendannan was always grousing we should have stores in the south. Well, he was right. Besides, if we're going to build up the kingdom, it makes sense to plan where the population grows."

"Yeah," Ian Haarper agreed. "That's all true. But while you and the Hand are building up the kingdom, what about Merryn? He's going to have to rebuild this town after the war and he won't have two shoestrings to rub together to do it with."

"I'm going to be poor also, Timmial." Pitar tried to smile.

"You're going to get loans from the Crown, Pitar," the Iron-wearer said harshly, and the young noble's face froze. "That's how the game is played and the Hand would have told it to you. Don't tell me you don't know it."

"Well— Say something else, Timmial. I'd like to hear you're pleased."

"Yeah, you would. Congratulations, Pitar, if that's what you want to hear. You're a fine asset for the nobility."

Kylene fell. Miles away. Centuries away.

The huge time machine tumbled down, falling through the air, and Kylene fell with it, shaken from side to side in the giant's-fist grip of her cockpit seat as air currents buffeted the falling vessel or erratic surges of power passed into the levmotors.

Glass from broken instruments gashed her arms and face.

Nausea seized her as the giant craft spun from side to side. She vomited and the vehicle rocked and through her tears she saw the straw-colored wastes from her stomach spew across the control panels and roll back as if a tide propelled them.

She hammered on the controls. Uselessly. Endlessly.

She did not know how much longer she would fall, but she prayed for each additional second and knew her death was near.

Dying, she did not see her life flash before her eyes. Instead, over and over, her memory showed her two women standing before the entryway in Tim Harper's house. Identical-looking women, arguing as a doorbell rang, until one of them went to answer it and the other scurried into another room, and only memory could tell her which woman she had been.

Over and over, she asked unanswerable questions.

What if I had answered the door?

What if I had not hidden in the study?

What if I had saved her sooner from the Algherans?

What if I had not saved her?

And then the vehicle shook once more and blood spilled from her mouth and she felt her consciousness falling into darkness for what she knew would be the last time and as she fell, her mind shrieked with protest and affirmation, *It was me he loved! Me, not her the interloper, but me, the Kylene who was always with him and did not leave him, me!*

And in the moment as she passed into final darkness, *Scent O'Claws* struck against a hillside and broke into uncountable pieces and as the time field died, Kylene was catapulted from the restraints of her seat and thrown out into the air, to fall and fall.

Her last sensation was—

Falling . . .

CHAPTER TWENTY-FIVE

*H*arper left quietly as soon as he could be missed and went into the backyard. For him, the festivities were tainted with the aura of the *Führerbunker*. Outside, watched only by the dark clouds which hid the stars, it was easier to control his expression.

He was sorry for the trace of anger that had touched his conversation with Pitar, sorrier still for the references to Merryn's finances while Lord Vandeign was virtually within earshot. It was unsettling to discover he still had a bad temper and that it could not be ruled.

Lord Vandeign, Lord Styllin. And a war. The world had gone crazy, he told himself, unable to make sense of everything, and it was no surprise if he had gone a little mad himself. He had reason for his actions, if not excuse.

He smiled grimly to himself and hobbled, on his crutches, to his wagon and began inspecting the traces. In a metal-poor world, the fastenings which could have been made with buckles were done with knots, and it was necessary to check the horse's harnesses at frequent intervals.

This was Quillyn's job, normally, since Quillyn fancied himself as a driver, but Harper had sent his orderly back to his former position in the Midpassage battalion. Quillyn would be safer there. Harper wondered if he would ever see the ugly little man again, or if they would have time to speak.

It was unlikely, he admitted, and thought bleakly of the coming morning. It seemed impossible for a day to begin without Quillyn's cheerful voice.

Someone coughed at his elbow and he started, then stood up. An artilleryman was before him. A sergeant from his sleeve insignia. A trace of light from one of the house windows made the face recognizable, but Harper could not immediately pin a name to it.

"Lady to see you, sir," the sergeant said stiffly, and Harper wasted a second wondering if his formal tone came from addressing an officer or from the presence of a "lady."

Not a camp follower, he told himself, though "lady" could be a very elastic term in Loprit. A resident of the town, most likely. Some housewife seeking the return of her house, or reporting abuse from a soldier.

Shoot them or let them go free. No more prisoners. He remembered Cherrid's dictum. Shoot or free, and someone would be upset, no matter what he decided. He swallowed unhappily, waiting for the woman and her complaint.

Steps sounded on the gravel, muffled by the snow, and he looked up, seeing a slim form moving toward him in the dark. It was cloaked. Below the cloak he saw a dress cut in a pattern he had never seen locally.

"That'll do, Wicherty." He waved a dismissal.

"Tayem." He heard a soprano voice, tense with strain.

Harper swallowed, resenting the uncertain footing and the irresolution which kept him from moving toward her. Gunfire had left him partially deaf; he did not trust his hearing.

"Tayem," she said again, and as he moved away from the horses, "I didn't know you were hurt."

"Kylene?" His voice quavered. He watched her approach and tried to get its tone under control. "It's not important. Where have you been?"

"Away." She came close to him, then stopped, and it seemed to him she was as nervous as he. He wondered if the crutches bothered her.

"Well, you're back." He was sorry for the banality. He spread his arms so the crutches fell away into the snow and let her move into them, and hugged her awkwardly, with embarrassment.

"I'm glad you came back." That was true and easily said. He rubbed his head against her hair, enjoying her fragrance, and hoped she would not expect many words from him. He tried to keep his weight from pressing on her.

"It was hard." Her voice seemed distant, and her body was stiff. It struck him suddenly that she did not want the embrace, and put up with it only to please him. His hands let her go and she stepped away.

He knelt to pick up the crutches and got back to his feet in silence.

"I'm sorry." Her silhouette was turned so he could not see her face, and he thought that she deliberately did not look at him. "This is harder than I thought it would be."

"You were away a long time," he said. There was an aura of reserve about her which was new to him. And disturbing.

Maturity. She's grown up now. The idea was troubling.

"Outgrew your little-girl crush, huh?" He tried to laugh, but the effort failed. "It's about time. That why you went away this time?"

"I was in a hospital, Tayem. I almost died." Her voice was small, and he realized that the tone he had thought was adulthood was a lack of joy. "I'm not pretty anymore. I don't like being touched by a man."

A long moment went by.

"Do you want to tell me about it?" His voice was almost a whisper.

"No. I don't want to remember it."

He closed his eyes. "I'll need to know who was involved." *To punish them,* he meant. His voice grated on his ears, and he was suddenly reminded of the unknowing, uncaring people within the house.

Shadows—only he and Kylene had reality, only he and Kylene suffered.

"They were taken care of. I had a friend . . ."

That made him feel worse.

Kylene evidently sensed his feeling despite the distance between them. She came and laid a hand on his forearm. "My gallant defender." Somehow, she kept it from sounding like sarcasm.

She swayed to one side and back. "My—my sister, Tayem. The version of me from another history. She took me to a hospital near the Present, and then . . . she avenged me."

Avenged. Even said softly, it spoke of cruelty returned with cruelty.

As he hesitated, she turned away from him. "I'm not a good person, Tayem. I'm not kind, like you."

"I—" He stopped. He was not kind, either, he knew. He could not be kind and fight the war as he fought it, but that was not the response she wanted from him. "I would have hurt the people who hurt you, Kylene."

"You'd hate yourself for it," she said, and he knew she was correct.

Do you? He tried to banish the thought.

She was close enough to touch, and he wished he could seize her and turn her about and hold her in his arms and make everything all right by saying it was all right, but he was afraid to touch her.

"I still need you." Her voice was thick and he could tell she was near tears. "I want to be with you, Tayem. I want to be your little girl again. I want you to tell me what to do and make me good and punish me when I'm bad and—someone has to mind for me, Tayem."

"It's too late." Unbidden, his mind remembered the words said in Eden. *Of the tree of the knowledge of good and evil you are not to eat, for on the day you eat of it you shall most surely die.*

He tried to soften his voice. "You're not a little girl now, Kylene. Not for me or anyone. We all have to turn into adults— somehow—and adults have to run their own lives."

"Do you want me?" she asked and he heard desperation. "You aren't getting younger, Tayem, and if you want someone to stay with you, this is your chance. I'm not a virgin now, you know. I learned how to please men."

He felt sickened.

"If there was a button in the air right here that I could push that would make me love Kylene, I wouldn't do it. You understand? I wouldn't push it. Not for any reason at all." His vainglorious boast to Dieytl lan Callares. He felt he would gladly rip his tongue out if that would keep those words from having been

said, but at the same time he knew every word was still true. He was glad now he was not touching her.

"I'm sorry," he said as softly as possible. "I like you, Kylene, more than any other woman I know, but I think I'd better get old by myself."

She moved against him, nuzzling him, and toyed with his jacket lacings while he stood with his fists tight on the crutches. "You can give me a trial, can't you? One night and we'll do what you want and then decide, that would be fair." Her voice was kittenish, wheedling.

Impossible. He wanted to step away but he made himself be still.

"What I want is for you to go away, Kylene," he said carefully. "This is a very dangerous place. There's a battle going on and I don't want you hurt. I want you to go back to the time machine and go somewhere safe and I want you to get well and meet some nice man who will—mind you—and make you happy and not think about me anymore."

"What will happen to you?"

It was not necessary for her to ask, since she was touching him and could see his thoughts as if they were spoken aloud, but he answered anyhow.

"I have to be in the battle, Kylene. If it doesn't go well, someone has to tell the men they can run away with a clear conscience, and that'll be my job." He brought a crutch into the air and waved it slightly till she turned to see it.

"Good thing my conscience will keep me from running." He smiled. Making the joke silenced his imagination.

"You can't die, Tayem," she whispered against his chest.

"It's the best cure for getting old." He made himself grin down at her, then sobered. "I won't really mind it, if it's in a good cause, kid. I've done enough with my life. If some of it's good . . . Well, you can go away and think nice thoughts about me, if you want to remember me that way. I won't be able to stop you, will I?"

It was an exit line. He pulled himself erect and away from her and looked toward his wagon and horses. "I have to go make a round of the troops, Kylene. When I get back, I want you to be gone."

But when he had climbed into the wagon and taken up the reins, she was still standing in the same spot, looking small and

vulnerable. It hurt him, like a blow in the chest, to see her and
know this was his last glimpse of Kylene, and the last she would
see of him. He could not leave her without some final words.

"You're still beautiful, Kylene." He had not seen her face
clearly. He wondered now if she had deliberately averted it from
him.

"The other thing you said—about—about—learning to please
men—that's not going to bother any man who's worth anything.
Believe me."

And then the wagon was rolling and Kylene made a tiny gesture which might have been good-bye or an attempt to call him
back, and he had to turn his eyes to the front and watch his path
and could not see her.

He was desperately glad his last words had been true.

"We will work together," the Hand of the Queen said, and
Rallt echoed his words awkwardly, feeling the eyes pointed at
him like guns. Then he winced, remembering what came next,
afraid he would cry out and disgrace himself before his father.

But his father was not his father anymore, was he? He looked
sideways for reassurance, trying to find it in Wandisha's motionless face and Grahan's smile and then his father's anxious
looks. His father was as uncertain and confused as he was, he
realized, and the thought was troubling but it could not stop
what he was doing.

It was what his father had told him to do.

His hands were dirty. He grasped the Hand's hand mechanically, hoping the older man would not object, embarrassed because he had not thought to wipe his hands on his trousers.

The actual blow was slight. The Hand's hand barely moved
his head and that was due to surprise more than the force. He
missed the prompter's voice after the Hand's. The words had to
be repeated and he stumbled over the unfamiliar words, afraid
to misspeak them in his non-Lopritian voice. "The nob—
nobility is subver—subservient to the Crown."

We are ourselves Lopritian. Had saying that really made him
Lopritian? Grahan had said it would, but suddenly it seemed a
mistake, something which could not be despite what he had
been told, and which made everything happening to him false
and unreal.

Nervously, he rose on his toes and kissed the Hand's cheek,

remembering what he had thought watching Pitar lan Styllin perform the same action, but the old Lord was nothing like a relative and he could not imagine why he had thought it would be the same.

"Vested in myself and the heirs of my body," he whispered as the Hand said the final words and felt as if this were not happening to him, but to someone else standing in for him, who would walk away when the ritual was over and never recall anything which had happened, so only Rallt would be left to remember what he had said and felt at this moment.

"People of Loprit," the Hand said gently, over his head. "I present to you the adopted son and heir of Ironwearer Cherrid ris Clendannan, legatee of his lands and hereditary titles, the Domine Sunhold of Sparkling Lea Estates, Domine Morningrise of Golden Bend Highreach, Domine Sentryside of Falcon Guide Tor, Knight-member of the Companeers-of-Royalty, Knight-Commander of the Band of the Finger-of-Greatness, Speaker of the Rood Martial and Valorous, Wildgrand-Established of the Western Reach, Prevailant-Eternal of the North, Shield Uplifted of the Land, Lion of Loprit, Eye of the Queen, the Margrave Rallt ris Clendannan."

As the meaningless phrases passed beyond him, Rallt noticed Wandisha turning away from him. He had wanted to please her and was sorry to lose her attention, a feeling which intensified as first Grahan, and Pitar lan Styllin and his wife, and then even the Hand turned to the door behind him and said his final words in a monotone.

A woman stood there. She was slim and about his height, with dark hair and eyebrows. He could not tell her age. Her dress was tight-fitting and dark; it covered her arms down to her wrists, and her body from her neck to below her knees. Her face was irregularly shaped, with one cheekbone higher than the other. Her eyes seemed to be slanted; they were squinting against the light so he could not see their color, and her lips were tightly pressed. A scar ran from one side of her jaw down her neck to the collar of her dress; it was pink against the pallor of her face, like the exposed flesh below the split skin of an apple.

He wondered what had wounded her and suddenly, from the expression on Wandisha's face, knew this was Kylene lin Haarper.

The woman who had died was still alive.

* * *

"Wolf-Twin," Harper called out. "Wolf-Twin!"

For gawdsake, Wolf-Twin, come out and keep me from thinking!

Not that it would matter. After stopping to speak with officers at the three regimental headquarters, he was numbly aware he was only stumbling through his duty. Fortunately, Mlart was not taking advantage of his lethargy. He stared at broken shrubbery and snow and wondered why the night remained so quiet.

After eternity, a soldier with Requisitionary Corp insignia came from out of the house and helped him from the wagon. Assisted, he stumbled up the stairs and into the house.

The house smelled of mildew and woodsmoke and unwashed men. Rahmmend Wolf-Twin was in the kitchen. The squat Iron-wearer was on a stool at the table without his shirt on. His feet pointed toward a tiled stove with an open cover. He was drinking from a stained mug which he set down as Harper entered. He rose slowly.

"Ironwearer." Wolf-Twin spoke without enthusiasm.

From somewhere in the house, Harper heard laughter. A woman, and then a man laughing. He felt inexpressibly alone.

In the stove, twin horns of blue and orange stuck out from stacked logs. Harper felt no heat as he passed by it. Behind him, he heard men mumbling and dice bouncing from a slanted board. He pulled a stool from beneath the table and sat on it, then propped his crutches against his knee.

"Thanks for offering me a seat," he said.

"Have a seat, Ironwearer." Wolf-Twin sat himself again and brought his mug to his face, then tossed it toward a sink. It bounced and fell to the floor. The handle broke. Neither man looked toward it.

"Having it rough?" The stink of brandy was thick in Harper's nose.

"We manage. One more man wounded, no dead."

"Serious?"

Wolf-Twin snapped his fingers. "Crate of shells slipped while we were loading a wagon. Crushed a man's toes. Not fatal, but he's gone worthless for heavy labor."

He the one getting consoled upstairs? Harper limited himself to a nod.

"Well. Tomorrow's the last day, Rahm."

"Next stop, Cimon." Wolf-Twin's eyes moved to a cupboard, and Harper sensed from his expression that a bottle waited there for his disappearance.

"Not for many more, I hope," he said calmly. "We'll fight as long as it make sense—my idea of sense, Rahm, not yours— then we clear out, those that can. You can spend the morning smashing up wagons. When it gets time, kill your horses."

Wolf-Twin cursed in a monotone. The dark Ironwearer seemed smaller before his eyes now. His skin still glistened from unguents, but the odor of cinnamon that normally hovered over him had faded. Harper waited for him to run down and thought to himself:

> *"The time you won your town the race*
> *We chaired you through the market-place;*
> *Man and boy stood cheering by,*
> *And home we brought you shoulder-high."*

Harper swallowed, cutting short his memory of the verses. Houseman, of all things, and Kylene, several months before, has asked why he no longer quoted poetry to her.

We are not the men we used to be. We have worked to make ourselves lesser beings, and in our cups, we call ourselves satisfied.

He had an answer for her now that he had sent her away.

"We don't have a way to get wagons onto the road or I'd try to evacuate some of the sick," he said unemotionally. "Since we can't, I want to keep the wagons and horses out of Mlart's hands. No point giving him any help."

He looked toward the ceiling for a moment, as if his eyes could penetrate the stucco and lath overhead. "It ought to snow soon enough. That'll cost Mlart a day or two, sure as fighting."

"Us, too." Wolf-Twin bent his head back. His lips began to move silently. His eyes were closed. "We can't get anything out."

"Just the people. I'm hoping you and the other officers can keep the men together. Look after the women and children."

"All the way to Cowards Landing?" Wolf-Twin opened his eyes.

"Northfaring. There'll be cannon and reinforcements there. It's too late to put anything into Cowards Landing."

"And what do we do there?" Wolf-Twin stared at him.

"The same thing all over," Harper said. He struggled to his feet and put his crutches under his arms. "You ought to stir up that fire, Rahm."

"I'll get around to it." Wolf-Twin did not move.

Harper stared down at him. "Get around to moving out that tramp upstairs. I know the men want to relax, but this is no place for a woman."

Wolf-Twin looked at him with an unreadable expression. "You march up the stairs and give that order yourself, Iron-wearer. That's a Midpassage man up there, not one of mine. This is his house, and that 'tramp' is his wife, and I'm not going to interfere."

He should be with his unit. Harper inhaled slowly and shifted his weight on his crutches. "Okay. Maybe I was out of line."

"You were," Wolf-Twin said flatly.

We used to be friends. Now it's over, Harper realized.

"I'm sorry, Rahm. Good luck tomorrow. Good-bye."

It is well that war is so terrible, else we would grow too fond of it.

Harper could not get the quotation to leave his mind as he turned onto the last street. Beautiful war—had it ever been true?

Cannon filled much of the upper lane, and he had to maneuver his wagon through the narrow spots between the gun carriages on his right and the hedges on the left. There were lights in nearby houses, and he guessed that artillerymen slept in them, where fires could be built without the risk of igniting powder. The guns were neatly arrayed, with banks of snow between them but no men to block his view, and he used the opportunity to stare at them.

They were not beautiful, he thought. In daylight, they were ugly things, stained and chipped; bulges along the metal barrels and crude gouges showed how primitive were the techniques which had built them. But at night, with their individual imperfections hidden by the darkness, it was possible to see them in an idealized way. Great masses of shaped metal waiting for battle . . . The silent guardians of armies. At night, mute and alone, the guns carried a certain dignity.

It was not the conclusion he had intended to reach. He grimaced and flicked the reins to drive the horses faster.

At ris Clendannan's house—the teacher's house, he corrected himself, wearily—he turned into a narrow drive, then stopped the horses and persuaded them to let the wagon slip backward at a different angle. The slope was not extreme; the wheels had slipped but the horses could probably pull the wagon without corrections. However, the drive was deep under snow and he wished to ease their task.

He wanted to use up time as well, he admitted to himself. He was exhausted but not in a mood for sleep.

The house was dark. He was reluctant to go in and look for a place to sleep, or a place to sit and wait up through the night.

Maybe I'll stay up the rest of my life. The thought failed to amuse.

As he released the brake and urged the horses forward again, a soldier came down the drive and saluted casually. He stood beside the front team of horses and tugged on the harness.

It was moral support that the horses had wanted. They stepped briskly and Harper heard the wheels whisper to the virgin snow as the wagon rolled.

The soldier stopped the horses at the stable behind the house, then opened the doors before Harper could descend from the wagon and sparked on a light within the building. Harper smelled manure.

"Help you with those, sir?" the soldier asked, returning to the wagon, and Harper noticed other men sitting around a small fire behind the stable. The light made the soldier's face visible as he bent over the harness.

Wicherty. "You're on sentry duty, Sergeant?" he asked. "I can unhitch these animals myself."

It was true, but he felt a reluctance to get down from the wagon and struggle with the bulky knots that was even stronger than his unwillingness to accept help. He half wished Sergeant Wicherty would vanish on patrol into the darkness and force him to tend to the horses himself, but practicality kept him from giving such an order.

Not as if sentries have to go far to find Algherans for us.

"You people eaten tonight?" he made himself ask. There should be leftovers from the Hand's reception earlier in the night. It was senseless to waste them on a handful of aristocrats and civilians in the morning, when soldiers were hungry and faced another day of battle.

"Very nicely, sir," Wicherty said, looking up from the traces. "Your lady wife brought us out something a little while ago. Very kind of her."

It was a mistake, Harper thought, when his heart was back in his chest. He hoped Wicherty had not seen his start.

An honest mistake. Wandisha or Pitar lan Styllin's wife had come out to feed the soldiers. Or Kylene had done it, but left afterward.

"Told us you'd understand about the fire, sir. Begging your pardon, but she told us you hated cold weather more'n a baby."

It *had* been Kylene. "Like a baby," he mumbled stupidly, but the sergeant, busy with knots, did not hear the words.

"Very nice to all of us, she was, sir. Asked about our families, what we did before the war, what we wanted after. Isn't often an officer's wife notices ordinary soldiers, sir. What I mean is, we all appreciated your lady wife's looking to us, sir, and if it's all right, we'd be pleased if you'd tell her so."

Harper swallowed. "I'll be sure to do that," he lied, knowing Kylene must be gone, and hoped Wicherty would not hear the false tone on his voice. "I appreciate my lady wife a whole lot myself."

"If there was a button in the air right here that I could push that would make me love Kylene, I wouldn't do it. You understand? I wouldn't push it. Not for any reason at all." Harper had visualized that button, speaking to lan Callares. It would be red and mounted on a silver plate, and a glass cap would protect the unwary from pushing it down.

He saw it again now as his eyes closed. The glass cap had been lifted up and the button pressed down.

He felt content at last. He even smiled as Wicherty stepped away from the horses and opened his mouth to ask for help.

"I'll get the doors if you can lead the horses into stalls," he said, and dismounted from the wagon.

"Not necessary, sir," the sergeant said quickly. "Your lady wife—she said she'd wait up for you, sir. You weren't to mind that it's dark. You just go on in and she'll look to you, sir."

She'll look to me. It dawned on Harper that the sergeant was being as tactful as possible to a superior who was unaccountably avoiding a wife. Slowly, he fitted his crutches under his arms and turned toward the house.

Then lights came on in the kitchen.

He saw Kylene's face behind a window.

Then Kylene was on the steps. He stumbled toward her.

Then she was in his arms and he kissed her face over and over while she cried. He dropped his crutches away and folded onto his knees in the snow before her and in the middle of what he said but never remembered he was horror-struck to see she had left the house barefoot. Before he could stumble, tongue-tied, to a conclusion, Kylene had tugged him up and wrapped her arms around him and Harper stood holding her in his arms above the snow while Sergeant Wicherty came scurrying to his side and held his crutches for him and tried to pretend he was not listening while Kylene hugged Harper and between kisses said yes-yes-yes-I-will-marry-you-yes!

And Harper had to threaten Sergeant Wicherty with being shot out of his own cannon to get rid of him.

CHAPTER TWENTY-SIX

Morning came, and Harper woke in a bed with sheets over his body and a woman's head on his shoulder.

Kylene. It was half surprising, half very natural, totally pleasant. She was still asleep, and he inclined his head to kiss her forehead.

He became aware at the same moment that another force was pressing on his other shoulder.

"Lord Haarper, Lord Haarper," a shrill voice was saying excitedly. "You have to get up!"

Getting up and out of bed was very low on Harper's list of desires. The highest one was—

He blinked. He and Kylene were in the bed on the ground floor of the schoolteacher's house, he remembered. In the room next to the kitchen. It was the room everyone in the house walked through.

Fuck fuck fuck. "Oh. Well."

His *second* highest desire was more sleep, with breakfast running third.

"There's a soldier who has to see you, Lord Haarper! Please get up!"

He recognized the voice, finally. He turned his head and blurrily found himself being viewed by a boy who was still dressed in a too-large soldier's uniform. For an instant, a Lopritian commoner very seriously contemplated spanking one of the land's highest-ranking nobles.

Then the message penetrated. He noticed that Rallt's father—his real father—was standing behind the boy, looking at him seriously.

A real problem. He sat up quickly. "Get him in here, Rallt."

Four hundred effectives in the Guards, he remembered as the boy went away. *Three hundred in the Defiance, one fifty left of the militia, two hundred sick and wounded, twenty with Wolf-Twin . . .*

Where was the threat coming from this morning?

He saw suddenly that Kylene's right breast was exposed to view, and covered it quickly with the blanket, feeling proprietary and exceptionally awkward at the same time. He was helpless without Quillyn to face the morning for him, he recognized, and for a moment he worried whether he and Kylene would survive married life without an orderly.

Simultaneously, he listened for guns but he could not hear firing from any direction. That seemed surprising. What time was it?

Rallt's father was still in the room, and he turned to the man, then away, determined to do some things for himself. He leaned over Kylene to lift the curtain over the window.

The windowpane was cold. Outside, it was snowing heavily. Behind the flakes, the sky was completely overcast. Its color was blue-gray, with a shade of darkness that suggested early first watch. The ground was gray-white from snow. Depressions that had been clear footprints the day before were only dints in the surface now.

It looked thoroughly miserable outside, and Harper loved the sight of it. No soldier in the world would be eager to attack in that kind of weather. He turned back to Rallt's father. "This been going on long?"

"Mayhap half for a watch, Thy Honor," the man said, in a heavily accented voice. "Not that I were up when it were started, but weren't long afore." Overriding the accent was a curious tone which Harper finally deciphered as nervousness.

Not used to being around nobility, he decided. *Last night must*

have been a real scream. Poor bastard. There wasn't much he
could do about that, but Harper suspected common sense would
eventually prevail. At some point, the Domine, Wildgrand,
Margrave, etc. etc. Rallt ris Clendannan was apt to discover his
titles would not let him escape parental discipline.. Meanly,
Harper wanted to be there to watch.

Practical at last, he swung his legs from beneath his blankets
and reached for clothes. The things he had worn yesterday were
mingled with Kylene's garments on a nearby table. He sorted
them out with one hand and started to put them on with the
other.

"Don't call me 'Your Honor,' " he ordered. "I'm just common folk myself. You can see that I put my pants on one leg at
a time."

"Honor? Thy pants?" the man asked, in his thick accent,
and Harper decided he was handicapped by a lack of humor.

For the first time, he felt some pity for Rallt. He suspected
there would be days when the youngster looked back enviously
at the simplicity of a soldier's life.

Just like I do. He reached for his shirt.

The boy himself returned shortly with a blue-uniformed soldier on his heels. The man was middle-aged, with blond hair
and a broad face. There was a dusting of snow in his hair which
he had not wiped off. He saluted sharply, and Harper acknowledged it, and kept his face straight while he acknowledged another salute from the new Lord Clendannan.

"Good morning, Ironwearer," the soldier said politely. "I
trust I haven't disturbed you."

"Not at all." Harper was awake enough to tell social lies
with the necessary grace.

This was one of ris Daimgewln's troops, he decided from the
color of the man's uniform. *Do we have an insurrection in the
Defiance-to-Insurrection?*

The man wore sergeant's insignia, but Harper did not recognize him. He was smiling and that was unexpected. *By God,
the mutinous bastards have mutinied,* he told himself half-
seriously. *We're surrounded by troops and they're here to kill
us all.*

Automatically, he looked down at Kylene. She was awake.
She smiled at him and he could see her legs stretching beneath

the blankets, but she only murmured and pulled the blanket back to her neck, then closed her eyes again.

It didn't seem a threatening omen, and he could still not hear guns.

A problem with rations, Harper diagnosed. Well, he could solve that, or he couldn't. *Alternative B. They let us officers get fully dressed before the necktie party.*

That's nice. I'd hate to dance on the yardarm with my tootsies showing.

Would my dearest darling loving thoughtful caring wife send me off to something like that without a warning?

Was I that clumsy last night?

"No," Kylene said clearly, without opening her eyes, and Harper noticed that no one in the room was looking at him. He felt obscurely slighted, even as he understood that she wanted the attention.

Minx! "I don't think we need to wake up my wife," he said cheerfully and mendaciously. He picked up his boots and tossed them to Rallt, then reached for his crutches. "Let's go into the kitchen, Sergeant, and you can tell me what the trouble is."

"No trouble, sir," the sergeant said, reaching into his uniform for a dispatch envelope which he tendered to Harper. "I'm to bring back a message if you have one, that's all. Three of us were sent; I guess I'm the first to get through to you."

Harper blinked and sat back on the bed with the unopened envelope in his lap. "My mistake," he mumbled. He had finally noticed unfamiliar insignia on the sleeves of the soldier's uniform. "What unit are you with, Sergeant?"

"Assurance-from-Dignity Regiment, sir, Domine Lorrens ris Fryddich commanding. Confident-of-Her-Majesty's-Grace Division. Southern Corps."

Harper swallowed. "Southern Corps? Ris Cornoval?"

He had to swallow again.

"Yes, sir. Confident-of-Grace Division—all of it—and Soldier's Glory-Is-Eternal, with five of the six regiments, and the other brigade of Foes-Shall-Tremble-and-Be-Trampled. We'll be in position to attack by the end of the watch, sir, unless you have other orders."

"I—I—" Harper could not speak.

The sergeant stared at him. "Didn't you know, Ironwearer? We sent out messengers before this. Didn't they get through?

Lord Cornoval recruited locally to build up strength after you pulled Mlart off, and the Algies down there—we don't know what you did to them, sir, but they weren't willing to fight. We had just a skirmish and gave them the slip. We've been on the road since then, day and night ten days now. We've got our guns, our rations, our ammunition, our transport, everything we need, sir. We're ready, sir, our cavalry already's fighting with theirs, that's what the message says.''

"Jesus Christ," Harper muttered, and not even he could say if that was a prayer or a curse. He opened the envelope and stared at its contents.

He read the letter inside three times and not a word of it changed.

Finally, Kylene stirred in the blankets beside him. It was the first sound in the room he had noticed, and he blinked his eyes, then shook his head to clear it.

"Rallt?" He looked up to see the boy staring owl-eyed at him. "Lord Clendannan, please, would your Lordship possibly be so kind as to go upstairs and wake Lord Andervyll—that's the Hand, Rallt—and bring His Lordship down here? He'll want to read this, too.''

He smiled. "And I guess everybody else in the house.''

"Is it over?" the boy asked seriously.

Harper sighed softly and nodded at him. "Yeah, it's over. I won't say we won, but we survived. Go get him.''

"It's over!" Rallt shouted, and ran for the stairs. "It's over! Wandisha! Hand! Grahan! Everybody! It's *over*! It's *over*!''

Harper felt Kylene's hand holding his and squeezed back. Saved from tears at this last moment by Rallt's behavior, he was able to look up at the boy's father and smile.

"I wouldn't do it now," the Ironwearer said carefully, "but I don't think he's too big to have outgrown a spanking.''

Slowly, the farmer shook his head in agreement.

CHAPTER TWENTY-SEVEN

It was not yet "over," of course.

Mlart tra'Nornst had lost his chances for victory, but he was far from defeat. He had only a slight disadvantage in numbers, and his troops were not as exhausted by marching as ris Cornoval's were. They were also still in control of the road and much of the town.

By remarkable circumstances, then, Mlart had been placed in almost the same situation his opponents had occupied five days before. In what remained of the day, he regrouped his artillery and organized the Swordtroop for defense, then waited for the Lopritians to attack.

The Lopritians did not make that mistake. Advised by Ironwearer Ian Haarper, under cover of the snowstorm, ris Cornoval advanced along the west bank of the Bloodrill and prepared to cross the river with three brigades on the following morning. One division was left to block the road to the south.

What was left of the Strength-through-Loyalty Brigade remained huddled around its artillery on the hillside. No one expected more of its infantry. The brigade's guns alone continued to fight, and now Ironwearer lan Haarper directed their fire at Mlart's wagons and horses as well as his artillery.

Mlart suffered from a steady trickle of casualties that day, which could only grow worse, and the Algherans had been cut off from reinforcements. They were about to lose their transportation and soon they would be encircled. The outcome of that was obvious. To stay longer would be disastrous.

In the night, Mlart withdrew to the north. Technically, this was not a retreat, since it continued the line of his original campaign, but movement to the south was barred by ris Cornoval's divisions; the difference was slight. Perhaps, even at this late date, the Algheran general still hoped to combine with the tra'Ruijac in northern Loprit and crush ris Mockstyn's Northern Army together, though by now he must have known the possibility was moot.

Osrild ris Mockstyn, after almost a year tenth of diligent marching and countermarching, had finally placed himself between the Swordtroop's northern corps and F'a Alghera. He had found a superb position for defense. During his campaign, he had preserved his manpower, hoarded his reinforcements—including Northfaring's Bulwark-of-Victory Regiment, for which the Hand of the Queen had uselessly begged—and mercilessly rejected any plea for assistance from other theaters. His wisdom was soon proven. At Gold-of-Father's-Inheritance River, after a day of maneuvering, he inflicted a crushing defeat upon the tra'Ruijac's right and center divisions. The shattered Algheran formations withdrew to the north. Ris Mockstyn began moving forward his reserves for an advance on their undefended capital.

Mlart was besieged in Cowards Landing by ris Cornoval's Southern Corps and several ad hoc militia battalions when the news reached him. The impact was apparently devastating. The Algheran general immediately proposed an armistice while he waited for confirmation of the disaster. This was not granted, though the Lopritians postponed offensive moves they had planned.

A second request for an armistice, two days later, was countered by a demand for surrender from the Lopritians.

Mlart's terms were submitted the following day.

The surrender was accepted for Loprit by Hand of the Queen Terrault ris Andervyll, Southern Corps commander Haylon ris

Cornoval, and Southern Corps strategist Ironwearer Timmithial lan Haarper.

Loprit's emissary was Strength-through-Loyalty Brigade commander Dalsyn lan Plenytk (later, Dalsyn ris Plenytk), himself a resident—and onetime mayor—of Cowards Landing. Voridon Mlaratin tra'Nornst, both as Warder and commanding general, signed for Alghera. The pact was witnessed by the tra'Crovsol and ris Cornoval's chief aides.

Ratification in F'a Loprit (by Queen's Beloved Counselors) and F'a Alghera (by the Muster) came almost immediately and was only a formality.

The war was over.

Controversy was not, however. In fact, postwar controversy began before the guns were silenced.

The most troubling allegation was that Ironwearer lan Haarper had accepted Mlart's surrender terms—and broadcast the news as fact to both armies, thus making continued operations impossible—before either Hand of the Queen Terrault ris Andervyll or Haylon ris Cornoval had received them. This charge has been examined in numerous scholarly forums and in Nallis lan Alpbak's well-intentioned but sensational biography *"Tim" lan Haarper: In the Service of Another's Country*, and has never been completely refuted, though subsequently, in their memoirs, both ris Andervyll and ris Cornoval stated that only a clerical oversight had kept their signatures off preliminary drafts of the terms. Teeps familiar with the issue have preserved their silence, on the grounds that statements on either side of the matter would constitute violations of the Second Compact. The matter remains unsettled to this day, but really concerns only specialists.

The terms of the surrender agreement were not controversial. They called for a return of prisoners on both sides and for a termination of the war without restitution or blame for unlawful actions committed by either side. They bear considerable resemblance, in fact, to surrender terms originally proposed by the Lopritians themselves at the celebrated "Council of War" so movingly but inaccurately depicted in lan Alpbak's work prior to the so-called Battle of Midpassage.

The consensus of reputable historians is that Mlart deliberately proposed similar terms because he felt the Lopritians could not comfortably reject what they had asked for when they felt themselves in danger. Some revisionists—we cannot bring our-selves to apply the term "scholars" here—have suggested that Ironwearer Ian Haarper himself secretly proposed the terms to Mlart with the promise that they would be accepted (careful chronologies leave several day tenths of the Ironwearer's time unaccounted for on the crucial date of the delivery of the sur-render demand). Needless to say, this conduct would be trea-sonable and totally incompatible with even a very minor Ironwearer's sense of honor. Teeps have refused to comment on this issue as well, again citing the Second Compact's ban on political interference, but it is not recorded that any Teep ever impugned Ironwearer Ian Haarper's title, and this can be re-garded as an authoritative rebuke to the slur.

Ironically, because the proposed surrender terms were so similar, in popular belief Mlart tra'Nornst has become the au-thor of both documents. Mlart is famous, and Ironwearer Ian Haarper—whether he conceived, as some claim, or simply wrote down the Lopritian document as it was dictated—is unre-nowned, so there is really no hope of changing this perception, and indeed it matters only to pedants at this point.

One ambitious but ill-advised attempt to draw the general public's attention to the Ironwearer's putative priority has been made in recent years, by the late Nallis Ian Alpbak (*op cit*), but it must be said that this so-called biography is a turgid mishmash of speculation, personal opinion, rumor, unlabeled guesswork, charitable interpretation, special pleading, and nonsensical meta-physics only sparingly touched by verifiable historical fact. It deserves to be struck from the hands of the credulous, but for-tunately—according to the few savants intrepid enough to peruse the volume to the end—it is exceptionally dull as well, and te-dium poses no threat to scholarship. Lan Alpbak's book sold 17,592 copies in its one and only printing and is unlikely ever to be reissued.

The "Great Defender from Midpassage," it can be safely said, is in need of a better defender. But with facts so hard to ascertain, it is unlikely that another account of Ironwearer Tim-mithial Ian Haarper or his lackluster battles will ever be prepared, and frankly, the public neither wants nor needs a full-length biography of this uncelebrated and no doubt deservedly obscure soldier of a bygone age.

Serious historians of the period, of course, find the campaign most noteworthy for the belated appearance of Perrid ris Salynnt. This young military genius, unfairly eclipsed by the fading sun of Ironwearer Cherrid ris Clendannan (incidentally, an up-to-date translation of Grahan Hemmendur's *Life and Campaigns* is sorely needed in all major collections), finally emerged from the penumbra of obscurity to which he had been inequitably relegated to gleam in the public's eye with his own bright light during the so-called Battle of Midpassage. His inspirational example, courage, and burning resolution have been noted here and in all recent biographies, and his leading role in rejecting Mlart tra'Nornst's surrender demands at the "Council of War" has already been recounted. Most authorities regard the choice of Midpassage as a battle site as his doing, and virtually all agree in crediting him with the tactical innovations which ultimately made victory in this arduous campaign achievable. Our improving knowledge of the facts steadily burnishes this fine soldier's already shining reputation.

Mlart tra'Nornst himself did not continue long in the public eye. Mob opinion in Alghera, always fickle in such peculiarly governed states, turned against him for his "failure" in Loprit (military historians, aware of the many difficulties he faced even before his campaign began, have been kinder). He was severely criticized in the Muster both by old enemies and by erstwhile allies, including the tra'Crovsol, who never forgave his misguided and impetuous attacks at Midpassage. His governing coalition collapsed the following spring (Algheran City Year 313), and he was forced from political office, though he continued to serve as Nornst Sept Master.

In early summer, the ex–Warder of the Realm was assassinated in his retirement by a political dissident (never traced, although popular sentiment put the blame onto the Cuhyon Sept). The Ruijac and Dicovys Septs attempted to continue his policies in the Muster for some years but without great success; even today they lay claim to the threadbare mantle of Mlart's reputation in their factional propaganda.

However, the political unrest, feuds and other factional violence which have disfigured Algheran society for so many centuries have done much to rehabilitate Mlart tra'Nornst and his reputation amongst his compatriots. Even outside Alghera, where his allure is understandable, the public's fascination with this flawed but enigmatic and potentially great statesman continues unabated to the present day.

The soldiers who came back to Midpassage were not aware of their roles in history, or even interested in them. They had families to return to and lives to resume. There was rebuilding ahead, and a winter to survive.

Alone, finally, with Kylene, Tim Harper stood in his yard one night soon after this. With her beside him, he stared at the lights and fires below and wondered how much time must pass before Midpassage showed no signs of damage.

He shifted his weight awkwardly. Algheran surgeons had inspected his damaged leg after the cease-fire. They had been scornful of the treatment he had received—even bossy in their manner toward him, as if they had won the campaign, which had amused him—but they had assured him the bone would not have to be broken again to set properly. They had been surprised by the pace of its healing, and he had not been able to explain it to them.

Sweln ha'Nyjuc, he remembered gratefully now. His medical treatment from years before was still working in his body. That had been Algheran medicine, too. He was sorry he could not tell the surgeons what heights their art would someday scale.

"There's a lot of junk in this house," he commented to Kylene. "The books and paintings and metal, I'd like to save. I may have to come back to get everything, but we'll see. And the other stuff can go to scavengers." It was time to be practical, though his body ached in advance at the thought.

"Your prospecting gear?"

He smiled. "Midpassage will have to find another prospector."

"Will you miss this place?" Kylene leaned against him.

"No." He tightened his arm around her, and let his cheek rest on her hair. "I used to think I would, but now I see it's going to change so much, it'll be another place entirely. It can go on well enough without us."

He chuckled softly. "Maybe the sooner we leave, the better. I wouldn't really feel comfortable, having people stare at us each day, remembering how much I had to do with the changing."

"Pitar's leaving tomorrow with some of the West Bend people. He's eager to start rebuilding. Dalsyn's promised to help with the surveying.''

"Good old Dalsyn. Lord Dalsyn." Harper smiled. "So Pitar's going to have the highest ranking surveyor in the country help with his buildings?"

"You're not mad at him now? He wanted to say good-bye before he left.''

"No." Harper picked his words. "I wasn't ever mad. Disappointed a bit, but I can't blame him for taking a peerage. That's the reward system here, and he earned a reward, so— sure, we'll go say good-bye.''

Domine Pitar ris Styllin of West Bend. He tried the name experimentally and found it sounded natural. And Domine *Dalsyn ris Plenytk* of Cowards Landing. That sounded natural, too, and he smiled as he recalled Dalsyn's willingness to take the title while not letting it change his life in other ways. That had left the Hand nonplussed.

Of course, Dalsyn had a perfectly satisfactory life before the war. He had no reason to seek changes and had the strength to resist them. Pitar, on the other hand, had ambitions which could never be formed, let alone satisfied, in Midpassage. So now Pitar would settle in West Bend and build his armories and warehouses for the Queen and a mansion for himself, which Harper expected would be a grandiose copy of Merryn ris Vandeign's house, and encourage his peasants to be fruitful and multiply and plant more and more fields and over time his little town would grow . . .

"I envy him in some ways," Harper admitted.

"It's a tribute to you, you know. Having your subordinates made nobles. Even if you won't—"

Harper chuckled. "They earned it on their own."

And they had, he told himself. It was hubris to think he had any part in making Pitar and Dalsyn aristocrats, unless one wished to argue that he had been lucky and luck sometimes rubbed off. No doubt, if he checked detailed histories—real histories, from worlds which never knew of Timmial lan Haarper— he would find they had become nobles in the course of time without his interference.

The course of time. He smiled and quoted softly,

> " 'Tis all a Checquer-board of Nights and Days
> Where Destiny, with Men for Pieces plays;
> Hither and thither moves, and mates, and slays,
> And one by one back in the closet lays."

Kylene heard him patiently, but it was not poetry she wanted to discuss.

"You could have had a title, too, and then I could have had a title," she reminded him, and he wondered if he heard a note of regret, but decided it was only make-believe.

"Maybe two titles," she insisted. "And you had to turn them down!"

He shrugged. "I didn't have to."

She attacked him with her fists. "I could have been a duchess or a countess or a margravine! And I won't be and it's all your fault!"

Surprised, he caught her wrists. "Or a dominatrix," he said, then laughed when she laughed. "Did you ever hear of those titles before you came here? Can you tell me what the differences are between them?"

"They're higher than a Domine's wife," Kylene said primly, and Harper had to laugh again.

"If you want to keep up with the Joneses, milady, we have to go someplace where there are Joneses to keep up with. Do you want to go pile our stones in the First Era, hearthsharer?"

"Did you have a title there?"

"Do I look like— What would I ever do with a title?" he asked finally, feeling homesick. "I'd never feel right using one. We had a great country once that deliberately avoided having an aristocracy, Kylene. It worked fine. There was enough pride for any of us, just in saying 'I am an American.' Maybe I ought to take you back just to show you."

"And are you still an American?" she asked. "Your country's gone."

"Yeah." He thought for a moment. "I still am. And to me, so are you and so are all these Algherans and Lopritians. It's the same land, so it's basically still the same people."

"And Cherrid and Grahan?" He wondered if she was smiling.

"Them, too. We would have had space for them, Kylene. It

was a country full of immigrants. It was one of our strengths, that we were made up of people who wanted to be there. By and large.''

"You do want to go back to it."

He had to think about that. "No," he admitted at last. "I've left it, and it was good but not perfect. I'd like to find a perfect country someday, or found my own. You want to start a country for your next home?''

She murmured and moved against him. "Grahan's going home, you know. To his country, across the ocean. He's taking Wandisha. They're going to marry.''

He blinked. It must be a mistake. "Grahan? The one we know? Marrying? Kylene, that's got to be the world's most stubborn bachelor.''

"She's pregnant." Kylene seemed not to have heard him.

"With Grahan's—" He almost choked.

"Cherrid's son. Grahan wants it to be legitimate."

He blinked again. So Grahan Junior would be Cherrid ris Clendannan's son, and Wandisha would be the mother.

"A noble's child, huh? Sounds like Wandisha is going up through the ranks as fast as little Rallt. Who'd ha thunk it?'' He shook his head, amazed by the way history worked out. *If I hadn't asked her to nurse Cherrid—*

"That's only part of it, Tim. He's from Chelmmys. Don't you know Grahan's name?'' Kylene had turned serious.

Grahan. That was all the name he had ever heard.

Grahan from Chelmmys. He shook his head cautiously.

"Grahan ris Hemmendur from Chelmmys," Kylene said carefully. "And Wandisha's child will be named Jablin Cherrid Hemmendur, after its father.''

Jablin Hemmendur? Why was that so familiar? He remembered and swallowed. "You aren't serious!''

"I am. The dates check out." Even Kylene seemed awed.

"Oops!" Harper tried to smile. "The Algherans will never forgive me if they find out.''

"Does it bother you?''

"No," he said slowly. "My Algheran loyalty's getting a bit thin, isn't it? My Fifth Era loyalty, too.''

She hugged him, and he sighed, then hugged her back.

CHAPTER TWENTY-EIGHT

*F*alling . . .

It is sensation rather than knowledge. She is not aware that she is falling, not aware that this is a sensation, not aware that in her life she has felt other sensations, or known anything other than—

Falling.

It stops.

It is her second piece of knowledge. Sudden pain in her palms comes first, then her left elbow, shoulder, head . . .

Pain. She does not localize it or identify it. It is a different sensation than falling and the cessation of one seems linked to the initiation of the other. She wishes the falling to resume, even as she forgets what she felt then and the new sensation fills her mind. In an instant, she remembers nothing but the pain.

She writhes mindlessly, the reflexes of her body trying to escape its sensations. The pain moves in response, though she does not realize it, but it does not stop.

Yet, blurrily, despite the pain, she sees shapes and colors, and knows they are not part of the pain. Things unknown, moving but somehow constant. As time passes, their purpose becomes no clearer to her but a dark aura of menace is removed.

Outside, she senses. There is an inside, which is her and hurts. There is an outside, which is not her and does not contain pains, does not share her sensations.

Inside. Outside. Inside-outside different.

Which is it better to be?

It is a third piece of knowledge. Other conditions are possible, other sensations. It accompanies the fourth: *Questions are possible.*

And a fifth: *I have choices. I am aware.*

She is aware of being aware. Stunned, she stops writhing, mesmerized by her knowledge, conscious suddenly of thoughts as entities, fearing they will escape her awareness, leaving her—

Alone. It is a definition. To be without thoughts is to be alone. Alone empty incomplete.

She gasps, suddenly filled with terror, for the new awareness has erased her memory of the old. She has forgotten and does not know what it is she has forgotten but the awareness of her deprivation is clear. Frantically she moves about, clutching without success for the missing knowledge, her mind filled with awareness of her ignorance.

The pain returns.

Sharpnesses and bluntnesses. She has enough awareness now to recognize different sorts of pains, not enough to realize it is her own motion which births new agonies.

As *outside* recedes, she does not understand that she writhes nude on the surface of a well-traveled roadway, that she bangs her head repeatedly on the hard dark pavement, that while her body jackknifes on the road she smashes already broken toes into the pavement and tears away the raw flesh of her side and elbow, leaving diamond-glistening patches of skin and sera, that the spreading slickness beneath her body is blood, that the sore tension in her throat is a breath-emptying moan. She is not aware that her heart races laboriously, that the black-rimmed pressure within her head is approaching unconsciousness.

She does not realize blood oozes from slashes between her breasts and along her sides.

She does not know she is dying.

* * *

At last, other sensations intrude, like but not-like the pain. She moves slightly, seeking to return to the comfortable and soothing darkness. Something waits for her there, something which has always waited, patient and expectant, no matter where she might be.

Where she might be. Has she been elsewhere then? Has she known conditions other than these, gently folded in the warm enshrouding darkness? Fitfully, as smoke rising from doused fire embers, images appear to her, kaleidoscope shapes and colors without significance which erase the darkness for brief moments. Uncomprehending, without curiosity, she watches, secure in the knowledge that the darkness will each time return triumphant, fitting itself around her, holding, filling, permeating her body.

She moans with contentment.

The intrusions persist. And now she senses other events, of a different nature, neither outside nor inside but somehow both. Sensation without pain, without shape or color. What?

She waits, expecting clarification. Darkness wraps her softly, patient yet insistent. Yet the inside-outside event continues despite her wishes, now plain and near, now far and undetectable, maddening in its lack of meaning.

Pattern.

There must be a pattern, she senses. Pain and blackness, shape and color and this intrusive inside-but-outside experience, perhaps even the pain-like but not-painful exterior sensations she feels . . . There is a pattern to be understood, to give meaning to all this.

The darkness presses. She senses a warning: she cannot have both darkness and the knowledge of the pattern.

But the darkness is familiar now. The glittering promise it holds is near but not at hand and she is impatient. The pattern—the mystery of the pattern—is closer, and thus more attractive.

She concentrates, not yet searching for connections, but girding for the effort. She has chosen, not knowing she has chosen, nor what she has chosen.

She does not realize concentration has brought a grimace to her face, nor that the same reflex has lifted her chest. It is unimportant to her that muscles powered by balancing reflexes pull the displaced rib cage downward in response, creating a pressure which is automatically countered by other muscles. The breath which moves now within her throat and lungs is unnoticed, inconsequential as the returned fluttering in her wrists and the arteries of her neck.

She concentrates, unconcerned as what waits in the darkness departs.

She is alive.

She Now.

Cheerful, curious, she looks about.

There is an outside, which is not her, and an inside, which is her. She is very conscious of being *her* now, without understanding how, just as she now realizes the passage of time.

One of her. One inside. Many many outsides.

Or is it one outside with many things? She frowns, pondering that. Her fingers move, examining outside.

A hard shiny thing is beneath her, pushing up on her bottom and thighs. Softer, pliable things lie about most of her. Hardnesses intrude into her body. Another hard thing, not shiny, is fastened on part of her, and does not move when she pushes at it. Things of different color and shape on all sides. All new, all worthy of investigation.

She pitches forward eagerly.

There is pain again, a stinging sensation in her upper arm, but small and not lasting. She frowns for an instant, till it is clear the pain will not return. She feels something similar when she breathes in, but it too fades as she notices it. That is all. The real pain does not come back.

Still, she cannot move easily. She squirms experimentally, feeling a pleasant coolness under her bottom as she slips along the hardness, and her legs kick at covering things and break free satisfyingly. Then constraints hold her around the shoulders and chest, then tug her back into their place.

Disappointed, she pouts. Tears run down her face.

When the constraints relax, she moves again.

They catch her again.

The inside-outside phenomena she had noticed earlier repeats. It is like but not-like it had been before, and though she tosses herself mechanically against the constraints, they have little of her true attention. How can a thing exist which is not pain and which cannot be seen?

More things present themselves: ovals, circles, bars. They

have different colors; their superimposed shapes seem to alter as she looks at them.

Face, a tiny inward voice tells her. *Face*. The here-now there-now constraints are *hands*.

Open mouthed, she stares. Face. This is a thing and it is also a face. Would it—

Yes! she realizes exultantly. This thing will be a *face* whenever she sees it. It will not become something else.

And if—yes! There must be other constants in the outside, other things which do not change.

What? Wild-eyed, she turns her head about, seeing additional *faces*. Can there be more than one?

Yes. It is not a word, but a conviction, emerging complete from somewhere within her.

Be patient. It is another conviction, welling upward from inside her, like water from an invisible spring.

An inside to her inside. A real inside.

Dismay comes with the realization. She sees herself as an outside thing. She is incomplete, an emptiness around a true inside, a reality which she will never be.

Stunned by her discoveries, she tosses herself backward. The hand-restraints hold, then move with her, and go away as she weeps for her lost integrity.

Then hands return, touching her, changing her position.

She gags, feeling vertigo, but the sensation passes.

Nothing at all seems important now. She lets her empty self be pulled upright and waits passively.

The inside-outside sensation comes again. Simultaneously, the watching face changes. Then it is still.

Speech. The word comes suddenly. The inside-outside feeling is *speech*. It is something people do to—

People. A face is part of people. She touches a finger to her forehead, pulling it down over nose and lips, then reaches to feel the nearby face in the same manner. Yes, it is similar.

She frowns, then returns her hands to her face. Chin, neck, chest, arms, legs . . . Whole things but parts . . . So complex!

A constraint-hand lifts her wrist, placing her palm down on another constraint-hand. Fingers wriggle, pushing her fingers. There is more speech.

Uncomprehending, she blinks. The constraining hands drop away, then touch her face, pushing her lips apart and manipulating her tongue while the other face moves close to her. Its mouth opens; its tongue moves. She hears speech again.

She blinks. Is there a connection between faces and speech?

One makes *sounds*. She knows that much, somehow. Sounds together are speech and speech is—

She doesn't know what use *speech* is.

There is speech again, then a light slap on her cheek.

Startled rather than hurt, she pulls herself back, staring unhappily at the face. After a moment, she slaps back at it.

The face recedes. She hears more speech, short and loud.

Then there is speech which is different in tone and volume, and all the faces but one recede and leave the room.

This is another face, more complex than the others. Lined, creased . . . *Older*, she senses. What does it mean to be *older*?

Man. That is another word. *He.*

When the man is alone with her, he comes near and perches on the edge on the hardness she lies upon, and looks at her patiently. Slowly, gently, he strokes her arms, but does nothing else until she relaxes.

"Harl." He makes only that much speech. Then again, "Harl." The man touches a finger to his lips. "Harl." He touches his chest. "Harl."

Her eyes widen, then—daringly—she points at him.

"Harl." He taps her mouth, then his chest again. "Harl."

"Oll," she grunts.

It is difficult to do that much. She feels restraint in some fashion; she senses she should not attempt this. "Oll."

The face looks at her gravely. "Harl. Harr-ull."

She tries again. "Ull, ull—"

Wrong! Speech does not need sounds. The knowledge squeezes like a giant's fist, bringing fear to erase the realization. Tiny, diminished, infinitesimal, insignificant . . . she stares, breathless, mindlessly frightened, sweat-drenched.

"Harl." A hand strokes her softly, then mops her forehead, taking away moisture. "Harl. Try again, child. Say it once."

She stares again, sensing danger recede with the passing moment, but still apprehensive.

"Harl. Harl. Harl. Harl . . ."

"Hhh." It is barely more than a whisper.

"Harl." Hands gesture before her. The face waits.

"Hhh." She licks her lips. "Hull. Hull. Hullel."

"Harl." The man—Harl?—strokes her arms again, then places her fingers on his throat. "Harl."

"Holl. Har. Hur." Despite the continuing discomfort, she experiments with sounds, holding her own throat, trying to produce a vibration that matches the one she had felt. At last, "Harrel."

"Harl." The face shakes approvingly. Then a finger points at her. She senses a question, half demand, half entreaty.

"Ah," she says. "Ah-hh aaah." But there is no harl-dom within for her to find, no sound to complete her initial gasps. "I . . . I . . . I—" Then, hurriedly, in a forced explosion of sound, "I 'ylinn! 'yleen 'aful!"

"Amilynn," the face echoes, showing appreciation. "Amilynn. So you're Amilynn. Good."

"Uh-uh," she stammers, frightened by nothing than can be understood.

"Amilynn," the face says again, gentle but terrifying. "Say your name, child. Amilynn. Amilynn."

"Ami—Amilynn," she whispers softly, despairingly, and something immaterial is torn within her, something insignificant dies, shrieking with pain which is instantly forgotten. "Amilynn."

She is Amilynn.

EPILOGUE— JUDGMENT DAY

The hillside stank.

Snow had eventually stopped the fires, but the timbers of the houses continued to smolder, and the charred possessions of the people who had lived in them were strewn over the seared land.

Animals and people, too, lay on the ground. The animals were horses and cows and household pets which never understood the catastrophe which slayed them. It is difficult to die in dignity with four legs. They lay as bullets and shells and the occasional knife thrust had left them, in grotesque shapes.

And they rotted. Cold preserved the shapes of the smaller dogs and cats and unlucky birds, but the larger animals were swollen by the gases of decomposition. Their legs and heads and tails seemed like twigs on their elephantine trunks. Here and there, a body had already ruptured from the pressure, releasing the sticky-sweet gases into the air—the smell was very bad at those places.

The lucky birds feasted on the bodies.

The people were soldiers and civilians. They were men and women, or had been when gender mattered to them. They were adults and—where passion or accident had tipped the scales of

369

fate—children. By now, without exception, all were dead. They rotted. They smelled.

The birds feasted on them.

And on the frozen plain and in the snow-carpeted forest, wolves and wild dogs which had governed their hunger by their fear of men sniffed the tainted air and grew bold. It was winter and they were so very hungry.

At the base of the hill, at the foot of a dirt road, a silver axe-head shape appeared. An opening appeared on its side.

A man stepped forth. He looked up and down the arrow-straight pavement under his feet, then moved to the dirt road. He wore a brown uniform. His hair was red-brown and he was very large. He carried a shovel on his shoulder and he walked very slowly.

As he walked he looked at the bodies. All the bodies, and frequently he had to use the shovel to turn them over to see their faces.

He vomited before he had gone very far. It did little to change the smell on the hillside. He had nothing left to vomit, but at intervals it was necessary to stop and try to vomit.

When it was dark, he went back to the vessel for a flashlight, and continued searching.

It was almost dawn when he found the bodies he had sought. There were two—a big man with Ironwearer's insignia on his collar, and a woman with dark hair and a freckled face. The man's body overlay the woman's and they had been killed by bullets, perhaps by the same bullet.

"Probabilities," the man with the shovel muttered. It was the first word he had spoken. He had a deep baritone voice.

He dug a grave beside the bodies. It was large enough for two people and it was afternoon before he finished.

Then he brought canvas from his vehicle and moved the two bodies onto the canvas with his hands despite their smell and lowered them into the grave. By dusk, he had refilled the grave and tamped the excess soil into a shallow mound on top.

The fading sun glinted on his shovel and on the small crossed swords on his collar. He stood at the foot of the grave, looking at it.

"We're going away," he said at last. "Not sure where. I don't know if you two would have approved, but we decided—

> *"Ah, Love! Could thou and I with Fate conspire*
> *To grasp this sorry Scheme of Things entire,*
> *Would not we shatter it to bits—and then*
> *Re-mould it nearer to the Heart's Desire!"*

"So that's where we're going. Off to conspire and shatter and maybe we'll end up just like you before we get to the re-molding part, but it's worth a try. You'd understand that."

He stood silently for a minute, then brought his hand to his collar and slowly unclipped the crossed swords on either side of his neck. He tossed them onto the grave and they were lost in the dusk. He grimaced.

"It is wrong to ask only a few to do their best."

That was the only epitaph he could give them. He turned and walked away, carrying his shovel over his shoulder.

When he reached the bottom of the hill and drew near his vehicle, his stride lengthened. He was whistling a long-forgotten tune once called "The Colonel Bogie March."

The End

READ THE OTHER EXCITING
NOVELS OF

THE DESTINY MAKERS

Available from Del Rey Books

With Fate Conspire

In which Tim Harper, Vietnam vet and MIT graduate student, is captured in a mysterious time field and walks 90,000 years into the future, arriving just in time for the destruction of the City of Alghera.

Morning of Creation

In which Tim Harper and the telepath Kylene Waterfall prepare for the secret mission that will determine the fate of Alghera.

Soldier of Another Fortune

In which the mission to assassinate Mlart is endangered by the arrival of an enemy telepath—and fellow time travler.

Death's Gray Land

In which Tim Harper gets a second chance to change history and finds instead that history is changing him.